HOME FOR CHRISTMAS

Lydia is in training to be a nurse when she first meets Robert and, despite the difference in their class and background, they fall head over heels for one another. Robert is the nephew of a Lord, and Lydia a mere doctor's daughter – and a German doctor at that. While her parentage is no hindrance to their relationship in peacetime, when war is declared Robert's family makes it clear they no longer approve of the match. With no means of contacting Robert on the Western Front, Lydia volunteers herself, joining the Red Cross. But her love affair with Robert has had more than one consequence...

HOME FOR CHRISTMAS

HOME FOR CHRISTMAS

by

Lizzie Lane

Magna Large Print Books
Long Preston, North Yorkshire,
BD23 4ND, England.

British Library Cataloguing in Publication Data.

Lane, Lizzie
    Home for Christmas.

    A catalogue record of this book is
    available from the British Library

    ISBN   978-0-7505-4125-1

First published in Great Britain in 2014 by Ebury Press
an imprint of Ebury Publishing
A Random House Group Company

Published in Large Print 2015 by arrangement with
Ebury Publishing
one of the publishers in the Random House Group Ltd.

Magna Large Print is an imprint of Library Magna Books Ltd.

Printed and bound in Great Britain by
T.J. (International) Ltd., Cornwall, PL28 8RW

This novel is a work of fiction. Names and characters are the product of the author's imagination and any resemblance to actual persons, living or dead, is entirely coincidental.

*To my husband Dennis, who sometimes wonders
if he's living alone. That's what it's like
being married to a teller of tales.*

Chapter One

Christmas, 1913

The main defect of the papier-mâché angel was that its nose had broken off. Lydia Miller, whose nose was perfect, eyes dark grey, and complexion as clear as northern light, decided that nobody would notice, seeing as the place for a Christmas angel was on the top of the tree.

'Now, where are the wooden animals?' she muttered to herself.

The wooden animals were brightly painted and, although not perfectly shaped, looked pretty in the light of the candles.

Determined they would take their usual places on the tree, she delved further into the large tin box in which they were kept, far deeper than she usually needed to go.

The tin box had her father's initials on the lid and the address in Dresden where he'd been born. Although a bit battered on the outside, the inside of the box was divided into neat layers from the top to the bottom.

She'd never removed the bottom panel before because everything she'd wanted had been on the top. Today she found herself struggling to dislodge the final division even though the wooden animals had never been there before.

There was no real need to struggle on, but once

11

Lydia had set her mind on doing something, she rarely gave in.

Gripping the tin layer with one hand, and forcing her fingers beneath the gap at the edge of the metal, finally produced a result.

The wooden animals, no more than three inches in size, had fallen through the gap. She picked them out one by one, placing them to one side with the angel and the other decorations.

Her attention strayed to the only other item at the bottom of the box. At first glance, it looked merely to be a piece of pale blue silk, shimmering slightly in the pale wintry light.

On reaching in and touching it, she realised the silk contained something firm.

Leaning back on her haunches, she placed the package on her lap. Once unwrapped, she found herself looking at a book – not a book to read, but a diary or journal. The cover was of burgundy leather. The initials *EJM* were engraved on the cover. Her mother's initials.

Fingers shaking, she opened the cover. The pages inside were crisp and clean, unwritten on except for the first page.

'This is the journal of Emily Jane Miller. Today the doctor confirmed I was expecting a child. My husband will be overjoyed. I myself am quite petrified.'

Lydia felt her throat tighten. It was as if she had known she would die in childbirth. Tears sprang to Lydia's eyes as she caressed the pages lovingly. Her mother's journal, but with nothing written in it except for those few cryptic – and rather prophetic – words. Her mother had died giving birth to her.

She lifted her head to look at where the chill light of a December day filtered through a round window. Finding the journal had put an end to her task of seeking out Christmas decorations. Finding this journal was much more important, a small link between the mother she had never known and herself.

She reflected on the words her mother had written, wondering whether she had felt any joy at her predicament, or purely fear. There was no way of knowing and no one to ask, certainly not her father. However, there was Aunt Iris.

She hugged the journal to her breast and vowed never to part with it. Up until this moment, the only memento of her mother was a small, grainy photograph in an oval frame, given to her by Aunt Iris.

'You're very much like her,' Aunt Iris had proclaimed. 'The same grey eyes, dark lashes and glossy dark hair. You can have it,' she'd said. 'Just don't let your father know that I've given it to you. You know how he is.'

'Yes. I know how he is.'

Her father had never got over the death of his wife. It was sometimes as though he denied she'd ever existed. Just mentioning her name would cause him pain. He kept no likenesses of her, no mementoes of their lives together.

'As though he's still in mourning,' Aunt Iris had sighed.

The small oval frame with its picture of a lovely woman who looked so like her own reflection, Lydia had hidden in her writing bureau.

She ran her fingers over the smooth leather,

tooled with her mother's monogram on the front, presuming her father had given it as a present to her mother. It struck Lydia instantly that he must never know she had it. Everything to do with her mother brought him too much sadness, even any celebration of Lydia's birthday, which just happened to fall on Christmas Eve.

Closing the attic door behind her, she made her way down the sweeping staircase. Halfway down she stopped and looked out of the huge window that filled the landing with light. The view was good enough; the rear garden with its mix of flower beds, vegetables and fruit trees.

Her father was a good man, a good doctor and a good father. There was nothing he wouldn't do for her or talk about – with the exception of her mother, and more specifically her mother's passing. Although she would like to, she must not mention the journal. The wound left by her mother's death was still raw.

She carried on down the staircase of the grand old house that she and her father called home.

Doctor Eric Miller's house in Kensington was spacious, and the furniture well cared for and imposing. Large armchairs sat like sentinels either side of the fireplace and the polished surface of the Sheraton dining table that could easily seat fourteen people reflected the sky outside the French doors that opened on to the parapet above the rear garden.

Spacious consulting rooms took up one side of the front of the house where certificates gained at universities in his native Germany lined the walls.

He had arrived in England in the early 1890s

following in the wake of Emily, the love of his life, whom he had met at a lakeside hotel in Austria.

Doris the parlour maid occupied one of the attic rooms at the very top of the house and Mrs Trinder the cook occupied the other. Discarded trunks, chests and furniture were stored in the attic space at the rear of the house, where the eaves swept low, diminishing the height of the attic ceiling.

The housekeeper Mrs Gander had a room on the first floor at the opposite end of the house to that occupied by Doctor Miller and Lydia. A locked door separated her realm from that of the family and was reached by the back stairs that went on up to the attic. It was obvious to all including Doctor Miller that Mrs Gander was in love with her employer. Locking the door that separated them had been his idea.

It was not a large staff, but the Millers were comfortably off and the doctor was ambitious. He lived and breathed the medical profession, and was pleased when his daughter decided to become a nurse. He would of course have preferred her to become a doctor, but Lydia had not attended a suitable university. Women did not become doctors unless they were exceptionally well educated.

With the journal tucked under her arm, Lydia hurried along to her room where the walls were duck egg blue, the curtains white and scattered with daisies. Soft muslin drapes rather than heavy lace gave her privacy from the outside world during daylight hours.

She sped quickly to her writing bureau, un-

15

locked it and hid the journal behind a secret panel that sprang open when she pressed an inlaid flower. The small cavity was just big enough to hold the journal as well as the picture in the oval frame. Her father would never know that she had it.

With something akin to reverence, she shut the bureau lid.

My mother's journal, she thought, laying her hands flat on the glossy walnut surface of the panel. I actually have my mother's journal.

The sudden decision to tell her father that she had found it flashed into her mind. He knew nothing about the photograph Aunt Iris had given her, but the journal was not a likeness; it was just a thing.

With that in mind, she breezed off down the stairs. At this time of the day he would be in his study completing medical notes of the patients he'd seen that morning.

Perhaps she might indeed have told him about what she had found if she hadn't heard excited voices coming from the front parlour.

'Will you look at the monstrous thing? Rumbling and spitting like a train without rails.'

Lydia stopped at the sound of Mrs Gander's voice and headed to the parlour instead, curious as to what could possibly be so monstrous.

The smell of frehly applied beeswax polish and lavender from the muslin bag hanging from Mrs Gander's waist greeted her.

The housekeeper was standing with her hands on her hips, her elbows forming sharp angles. Thin as a stick and as tall as a church spire, she wore a pinched look on her face that was made more squashed by the ties of an old-fashioned lace-trimmed cap fastened in a big bow beneath her chin.

Doris the parlour maid was with her, peering out of the window from behind the thick lace curtain. A feather duster poked out from beneath her arm and her large backside was stuck out behind her.

Mrs Gander was first to notice Lydia, jerking upright like a wooden doll. 'Oh, Miss Lydia. You startled me.'

Doris heard and let the curtain drop, pretending to dust the window ledge before moving aside.

Curious to see what all the fuss was about, Lydia took her place at the window and looked out. Her breath caught in her throat. 'Oh, my word!'

The car's burgundy bodywork gleamed almost as much as the brass headlights perched like birds of prey on either side of the windscreen.

'It's got a roof,' she murmured in a voice full of wonder. 'How splendid! Whose motor car is it?'

'It belongs to Sir Avis Ravening. It's been sent to fetch your father,' declared Doris. She said it imperiously whilst flicking at pretend dust and sweeping away a scuttling house spider.

Lydia took one more look at the car before heading for her father's study.

Her father was closing the study door behind him. Mrs Gander had gone ahead of Lydia, holding his hat, scarf and Gladstone bag as he shrugged himself into his coat.

'Is it true?' she asked, breathless with excite-

17

ment. 'Are you going to ride in the motor car?'

He looked into the striking face of his daughter, wincing because he could see so much of Emily in her. He coughed as though clearing his throat. The loss of his wife cut deeply at this time of year.

'The prime purpose of the motor car is to take me to the man who owns it. Sir Avis Ravening is getting on in years and not feeling too good. He's also very rich and very modern minded – a little eccentric some say – to the extent that he sold off his horses and carriages and bought one of the very first motor cars. I believe this one outside is his third.'

'It's a fine car. Does he live far away?' Lydia asked.

'Belgravia.'

'Will it take long to get there?'

He shook his head as he attempted to sidestep his daughter and reach for the door.

'I'm not sure. Not too long I think.'

'Quicker than by carriage?'

'So I am told, but noisier. A bit smellier too.'

When Mrs Gander opened the front door, Lydia took the opportunity to peer at the beast waiting outside.

'It smells dreadful,' she said wrinkling her nose. 'Not so nice as a horse. And it is noisy. Still, it looks like fun.'

'I don't like it,' said Mrs Gander. 'It's shaking the windows enough to make them fall out of their frames.' She shook her head as if she were as shaken as the windows.

Lydia's father laughed at his housekeeper's comment. 'If that happens I shall add a little extra to my bill to cover the cost of replacing them.'

Lydia dogged his footsteps all the way to the front door. 'Is Sir Avis very ill?'

'I won't know that until I get there.'

'Do you think it advisable for a trainee nurse to be in attendance?'

Eric couldn't help grinning. His daughter certainly had a way of getting round him.

'Do you by chance happen to know any?'

'She comes highly recommended,' said Lydia brightly. 'And she speaks German. Just like her father, the doctor.'

'Does she now?' said her father, still smiling while in the process of donning his hat.

'And she'd love a ride in a motor car. She's never been in one before.'

He looked down into the dark grey eyes. His face was serious, his voice a dark brown timbre.

'They frighten some people.'

'They don't frighten me,' she said with a confident jerk of her chin. 'I think they're going to replace horses, so we might as well get used to them. Don't you agree?'

'Wait and see.'

He was no prophet, but even he could see that the streets of London were changing. Electric trams running on rails had already replaced those pulled by horses and people who could were buying horseless carriages.

Lydia had inherited the creamy skin, dark grey eyes and brandy brown hair of her mother. She'd also inherited the same stubborn streak, the same laugh, the same liveliness. When she wanted

19

something, she persisted until she got it. At this moment, she was determined to have a ride in the motor car.

'I've never been in a motor car,' she repeated.

The words hung in the air, pleading without really asking. Those dark grey eyes looked up at him, willing him to say yes. Her voice was as pure as silver.

Eric felt something inside crack open. Suddenly he wanted to indulge her and the black mood that usually descended on him at this time of year receded. He couldn't control the twitching at the corners of his mouth.

Lydia was astute enough to sense he was weakening. Now, she decided, was the time to persist.

'I needn't accompany you into the house. I could sit outside and wait in the car; or on the pavement if I have to.'

'You would stay shivering in the cold outside?'

She tossed her head so that her hair fell exactly as her mother's in the picture Aunt Iris had given her. 'Well, only if you brush your hair back from your face,' he said with a frown. 'It looks untidy. Extremely untidy. Moreover, wear a hat. A big one that hides all that hair.'

He turned his back abruptly, busying himself with his gloves and seeing that all was in order in his Gladstone bag.

Lydia swiftly pulled her hair back, tucking the long strands behind her ears.

'I need a hat,' she yelled at Mrs Gander, excitedly. 'I'm going for a ride in a motor car.'

Chapter Two

On arriving at the elegant house in Beatrice Square, Belgravia, Lydia tilted her head back so she could see all the way up the front of the building. It looked very grand; the pillared portico twice the width of their own house. The broad front door, with eight panels of gleaming black paintwork, opened as they both alighted from the car.

The wind sent a flurry of crisp brown leaves dancing along the pavement. More leaves blew down from the trees standing behind green-painted railings in the middle of the square. The bare branches creaked and scraped against each other, the sound attracting Lydia's attention.

Beneath the trees, a flower seller sang out that she had ivy, mistletoe and snowdrops for sale.

'Can we buy some snowdrops?'

'No.'

'We have time. I can run over there and...'

'I said no. I meant no. I am here to be of service to a sick man and you are here as a nurse. Remember?'

Lydia recognised this as one of those times when her father was focusing entirely on his work. When he did that, nothing else mattered.

The door of the house opened. The man who appeared had clearly once been taller than he was now. Age had bent his back, and whitened his hair, a pair of bushy white eyebrows almost meeting over a prominent nose.

'Doctor Miller, I presume?' He bowed stiffly from the waist, his head lowered so that his firm jaw scraped the starched collar of his shirt. 'My name is Quartermaster and I am Sir Avis's butler. I've been asked to give you every assistance.'

His kindly gaze moved from the doctor to the girl at his side.

'My daughter, Lydia. She's training to be a nurse and sometimes assists me.'

'Really? How very nice to meet you, Miss. Perhaps you might like to wait and see if you are needed; I have strict instructions to admit only the doctor. Sir Avis is very protective of his privacy.'

Lydia was not looking forward to waiting outside.

Her father knew that. 'I would prefer if my daughter is allowed into the house – if possible. I hardly think it safe for a young girl to be left outside and unsupervised even if she were to wait in the car.'

The butler's response was courteous as well as generous.

'I quite understand, Doctor Miller. A young woman should not be left unchaperoned. Might I suggest that your daughter waits in the kitchen? I did hear that Cook has just made some coconut biscuits. Perhaps your daughter would like to try some. And if you should need her, then she could be fetched in a trice.'

Doctor Miller shot him a grateful smile.

'Your kind offer is accepted. I'm sure Lydia would love to sample some of those biscuits.'

'Then if you would like to come this way, Doctor? Miss Lydia, if you would care to make your way down the steps you will find the kitchen entrance at the bottom. Just open the door and enter.'

He indicated a set of steps leading down to the basement area.

Doctor Miller watched his daughter go down the steps thinking – not for the first time – how like her mother she was, how fortunate she had been to survive.

Turning away from her and his thoughts, he sighed and followed the butler into a splendid hall. A gilt-framed mirror dominated one wall above a white marble fireplace. The mirror reflected a chandelier hanging from a high cciling, the crystal alone catching the light. He noticed something else. The most modern type of lighting.

'Am I mistaken, or are those electric light bulbs?'

'Yes, Sir. Sir Avis is a very forward-thinking man.'

'He is indeed – electricity! The wonder of the twentieth century.'

'Excuse me, Doctor Miller, while I send a message to the kitchen. We have an internal phone you see. The kitchen maid will open the door to your daughter.'

'Amazing!'

The butler gave a wry smile. 'The master is very progressive.'

'He certainly is – and not just as the owner of a motor car. I must say I'm impressed.'

The butler rang down by turning a handle at the side of a wooden box, picking up an earpiece and talking into a matching mouthpiece – very much like the telephone the doctor had had installed only two weeks before.

'You have not purchased a car yourself yet?' Quartermaster asked amiably as they made their way along a magnificent passage.

'Shortly. A man named Austin has been recommended to me. I understand he used to be a coachman, and then turned to making bicycles, but is doing very well supplying and mending motor cars instead. We are indeed living in a wonderful age. I have heard that a man named Henry Ford is producing motor cars faster than anyone else. His aim, I believe, is that everyone should be able to afford one. I dread to think of the increase in traffic. Whatever next, I wonder? We already have flying machines and I myself have a telephone.'

'Indeed. When Sir Avis heard you had a telephone, he decided at once that you were the doctor whose opinion he would value.'

Doctor Miller nodded. The statement satisfied him very much. 'A wonderful age indeed.'

Quartermaster stopped outside a pair of double doors, solemnly shaking his head. 'I cannot see the devilish contraptions ever replacing horses. What will we do with all the unwanted creatures?'

'I've no idea, but it's the price of progress,' said Doctor Miller, gratified that he had had the foresight to purchase a telephone. In doing so, he had acquired a very illustrious patient indeed.

The kitchen door was a miniature edition of the

grand front door only having six panels instead of eight. It was also not so wide.

Seeing no doorknocker, Lydia rapped on the door with her fist, very hard, because her fist was small. Even the matron at the hospital where she trained had remarked on the delicacy of her hands.

'Excellent for rolling bandages,' she had remarked.

Lydia had grimaced at the prospect of rolling bandages for the rest of her life just because her hands were small. Surely, she could do more than that.

'Hello Miss,' said the maid who opened the door, a plain-faced girl with large brown eyes and a turned-up nose.

'I didn't think you heard me.'

'I didn't need to hear you, Miss. The butler phoned down to say you were here. Even if he hadn't you could have pressed the bell,' she said chirpily.

Lydia looked round for a bell pull. She could not see one.

'There,' said the maid, pointing to a white button sitting like a mushroom in a polished brass surround. 'You press that. It's electric. This house is all electric.' She was amiable and confident, as though she knew all there was to know about electricity and how to use it.

Lydia followed the maid past the scullery and into the kitchen, a warm, glorious place full of good smells and sounds.

'There you are, Miss. Cook will be with you in a minute,' said the maid. 'You'll have to excuse

25

me. I've got potatoes to peel for tonight's dinner.'

The girl disappeared through a doorway, closing the door behind her.

The smell of things cooking drew Lydia further in. A leg of mutton sizzled and spat on a spit in front of the glowing coals of a traditional range. A kettle and a number of saucepans boiled above bright blue flames on a gas range next to it.

Copper saucepans gleamed from hooks along one wall; a dresser full of meat platters, cheese and butter dishes, tea plates, breakfast plates and dinner plates took up another wall, the crockery so shiny it reflected the light from the window opposite.

The clattering of pots, pans and dishes came from the scullery where a young woman was up to her elbows in soapy water.

'It's a gas range in case you didn't know.'

Lydia started. Sitting at the far end of the kitchen table was a girl of around her own age. She had been so engrossed in admiring the kitchenware she hadn't noticed her.

The girl was quite striking, her look forthright, her eyes a startling amber. A plate of biscuits and a glass of milk sat on the table in front of her.

Lydia stood at the opposite end of the table and introduced herself. 'Hello. My name is Lydia. I came here with my father.'

The girl said nothing but took another bite of biscuit, her amber eyes never leaving Lydia's face as she chewed. A mass of dark blonde hair framed a face as pale as porcelain.

Lydia shifted her weight from one foot to another. The girl's eyes were disconcerting, her atti-

26

tude intimidating. She felt like an intruder.

She wondered who she was: perhaps the daughter of Sir Avis? No. He was old. Her father had said so. A servant's child perhaps or a ward like in *Jane Eyre*, a story she had read where a mad woman lived in the attic and a young girl married a much older man.

She discarded the idea; things like that only happened in books.

Whilst the girl chewed and drank, her eyes stayed fixed on Lydia. She did not introduce herself. She just sat and stared.

Some of the patients Lydia nursed could be intimidating and she dealt with them all, just as she would this person.

She pulled out a high-backed Windsor chair at the other end of the table. On receiving no hostile reaction, she began explaining her reason for being there in as friendly a tone as possible.

'I've been sent down here while my father treats Sir Avis, the gentleman of the house who is presently very ill. My father is a doctor, a very good doctor in fact. We came here in a motor car. It's the first time I've ridden in a motor car. The butler said that the cook had just made some biscuits and that I should try some. Are those the ones you're eating?'

'I've ridden in a motor car many times.'

The comment had nothing to do with biscuits, but Lydia sucked in her lips and carefully considered what to say next. She decided to stick to food, but be light-hearted, jovial about it.

'Those biscuits smell very nice. The cook must be very good. I expect she is very fat. Good cooks are usually fat. Have you noticed that?'

The girl's shoulders stiffened.

However, encouraged there had been no tart response, Lydia pressed on. 'I expect that it is so. It usually is. All the best cooks are fat. Fat as fat can be!'

The sudden sound of footsteps beating on a flagstone floor preceded the return of the cook who entered, blowing her nose, her apron flapping and her movements quick and sure.

The girl grinned and her eyes slid sideways. 'Cook,' she said, as though that one word said it all.

She was not fat and neither did she have a red face like Mrs Trinder, the cook at the Miller house. In fact she was really quite good-looking.

A coif of pale blonde hair that might have once been a shade darker framed a strong but handsome face. The eyes were the same colour and shape as those of the girl eating biscuits. Mother and daughter!

Lydia felt a fleeting embarrassment.

At first, the cook didn't notice her.

'The doctor says that Sir Avis is going to be all right... Oh,' she said, stopping abruptly on seeing Lydia. 'I do believe you're here to try my biscuits. I'm to tell you the doctor – your father – won't be too much longer.' She turned to her daughter. 'Agnes. Where are your manners? You should have given Miss Miller a glass of milk and some biscuits.'

Agnes tossed her mane of springy hair and lifted her tilted nose that bit higher. Her jaw looked as solid as the salt block sitting at one end

28

of the table.

'Just because she's the doctor's daughter doesn't mean to say that I had to wait on her. I'm not her bloody servant.'

'Agnes!' The cook flipped a hand in her daughter's direction. 'I'm warning you right now; no more of that gutter language. Whatever would Sir Avis say if he heard you?'

'He'd laugh.'

'No he would not! Miss Lydia is a guest in this house. It costs nothing to be polite. You're not too old yet to get a clip round the ear if you don't mind your manners.'

'Sir Avis only had Quartermaster call him because he was one of the few doctors nearby with a telephone. But he doesn't even have a motor car.'

The cook tossed her head in the same manner as her daughter had done. 'Lydia's father also happens to be a doctor with a very good reputation.'

'Quite right, Ma. Came quick 'cause he had a telephone, didn't he?' Though the girl smiled, mischief shone in her eyes. 'Lovely biscuits, Ma. Best you've ever made. Can't stop eating them.' Her voice cajoled and flattered.

As if to back up her statement, she reached for another, popping it into her mouth whole.

'Lovely,' she murmured between a splattering of flying crumbs.

The cook sighed and rolled her eyes heavenwards but there was no mistaking the fact that Agnes could wind her mother around her smallest finger.

'Right,' said the cook, smoothing her skirt before pouring milk from the jug and placing four crispy coconut biscuits on to a gold-rimmed tea plate. 'Do it yourself, Sarah Stacey. If a job's worth doing and doing well, do it yourself.'

The girl Lydia now knew as Agnes was unmoved except that her grin had widened and the amber eyes she turned on Lydia were catlike and cunning.

Lydia thanked the cook for the glass of milk and a plate of warm biscuits that were set in front of her. The biscuits were sweet, and the milk creamy and straight from the churn.

Lydia felt obliged to show the cook's daughter that she was not easily intimidated by an over-sharp tongue.

'I have to agree that they are wonderful biscuits...' she said.

The cook beamed. 'Mrs Stacey. You may call me Mrs Stacey.'

She had a musical lilt to her voice, which made her sound as though she were on the verge of laughing lightly at something subtle and sweet that had amused her.

Positioning herself behind the girl at the end of the table, she patted the spongy mass of hair before both hands fell to the girl's shoulders.

'Let me introduce you properly. This is Agnes Stacey, my precocious, headstrong but very beautiful daughter.' The girl laughed as her mother ruffled her hair and planted a kiss on the top of her head. 'Agnes, say hello to Lydia, Doctor Miller's daughter. Lydia, meet Agnes.'

Agnes nodded. 'Hello Lydia. I won't call you Miss Lydia. I will only call you Lydia. You may call me Agnes.'

Lydia nodded back. 'Hello.'

She didn't care that Agnes ignored the formality of one class for another. She was mesmerised. Agnes was an amazing creature. It wasn't just that she was wildly beautiful with her unruly hair and dancing eyes, her pale skin and the brace of freckles across her nose. Her outgoing personality was breath-taking. Lydia sensed that Agnes had strong views about everything and anything and always did as she pleased.

'Right,' said Mrs Stacey with an air of finality. 'I must be getting on.' In the process of tying her apron strings, she called to the girl in the scullery. 'Clara! Has Megan finished peeling those potatoes?'

'I have, Mrs Stacey.'

A glass partition divided the scullery from the kitchen.

Lydia turned her attention away from the scullery where Cook had gone to inspect the work the two girls had done.

Agnes, who was chasing crumbs around her plate with her finger, raised her eyes though not her face, eyeing Lydia from beneath a frizzy fringe.

'Megan is a fool.'

'Why?'

'Because she thinks she's in love. My mother says she'll get herself in trouble if she goes on the way she is and that will be that. Her young man won't marry her because she's seen his sort before. He flirts with every maid at every house in the street.'

Lydia nodded sagely. 'Our maid Doris canoodles

31

with the postman when he comes round.'

Agnes pulled a face. 'I don't know whether Megan canoodles, but she's in love with the coal-man. Personally, I do not know what she sees in him. He's very black.'

Lydia pointed out that coal dust does wash off.

Agnes adopted a pert, cheeky expression. 'Who said it was coal dust? He's got black skin. Ma says it's because his mother met a lascar from a ship loading at the East India Dock. It was a very dark night.'

'I see.'

Lydia eyed the girl at the other end of the table, the almond-shaped eyes, the tousled mane of hair. She sensed there was more to Agnes than just being attractive. Agnes seemed a little younger than she was, though she exuded confidence and attitude way beyond her years. It made Lydia feel childish in comparison.

In an effort to gain some equilibrium between them, Lydia tried to think of something clever to say, but no matter how hard she tried, nothing clever or comic came to her. She ended up asking how long Agnes had lived in this house.

Agnes's look was forthright. 'All my life.'

'Does your father live here too?'

For a moment, she thought she detected anger flashing in the amber eyes. It went as swiftly as it had come. 'No. He was a drunken bastard so my mother got rid of him before I was born. Sir Avis is my guardian now, so kind of my father.'

Lydia felt a great wave of relief wash over her. This was the common ground; they both had only one parent.

'I too only have one parent. My mother died when I was born. On Christmas Eve as a matter of fact.'

Agnes's eyes narrowed. 'My mother could have married anyone she liked, but she didn't. She stayed here in the position of cook to Sir Avis. I stayed with her.'

Lydia nodded solemnly as though everything Agnes was saying made absolute sense to her. Why shouldn't her mother marry anyone she liked? Whom else would Agnes be with except her mother?

The joint turning in front of the fire chose that moment to blister and spit with juices causing the fire in the range to flare up and smoke. Both girls turned their heads towards it, chewing biscuits, sipping milk, the glowing coals warming their faces. The smell of roast meat hung heavy in the air and blue smoke curled like fine muslin towards the ceiling.

'I've decided to like you, Lydia, mainly because you have a telephone. That makes you modern. I think everyone should have one and one day everyone will,' declared Agnes.

'I'm not convinced,' said Lydia.

'Absolutely. They're quite easy to use although watching some people trying, you'd think the phone was about to bite them. My mother's not afraid of the telephone though; it was her who phoned for your father to come.'

'Really?'

Surely, it must have been the housekeeper. Alternatively, the butler? Cooks were very much 'below stairs' people, seldom appearing above stairs unless invited to do so.

'We could phone each other.'

Agnes sounded as though there were no argument about it.

'I'm not sure that's very likely. It's for patients; people who are sick can phone and ask my father to call no matter what time of the day or night. It saves a lot of time.'

'Of course it does. That's what new inventions are meant to do, make things easier for people.' Agnes tilted her head sideways, her strange amber eyes glinting behind half-lowered eyelids.

'Anyway,' Lydia went on. 'I'm not at home that much. I'm training to be a nurse at a big London hospital. Do you work here in the kitchen?'

Agnes's eyes blazed with indignation.

'Certainly not! I drive the motor car when Thompson's not available. That's what I'm going to be. A chauffeur, certainly not a cook.'

'You can drive a car?' Lydia was very impressed.

Agnes nodded. 'Yes. I learned how to drive while staying at Heathlands, Sir Avis's country estate.'

Lydia felt instantly tongue-tied. Was this girl telling the truth? She wasn't sure. However, driving a car seemed far more exciting than being a nurse.

'These biscuits are lovely,' she said again after taking a bite.

'You could become my friend if you want to. Do you want to?'

Agnes stated it as though being her friend was a great prize not offered to all and sundry.

Lydia thought about it carefully whilst nibbling another biscuit. It was still hot and oozed butter on to her tongue. She decided it did not matter that Agnes was only a cook's daughter. She couldn't help wanting Agnes to like her and it appeared she did.

'Good. I'm glad you agree. Now come along,' said Agnes sliding off the big Windsor carver chair she was sitting in. 'Let's go outside. I'll show you the garden and everything.'

Lydia didn't know what 'everything' meant, but it sounded intriguing the way Agnes said it. Besides, the girl amused her.

However, there was the possibility that her father might need her assistance. She told Agnes this, but Agnes waved aside her concern.

'If you're needed, someone will come and fetch you. The house is full of servants. They're paid to do things like that.'

The air outside was so cold it took Lydia's breath away.

'Look,' said Agnes, huffing her breath into the air. 'Just like a steam locomotive.'

Lydia aped her new friend, blowing a stream of steamy breath into the cold air.

'I like this time of year. I was born in the winter-time, January as it happens. Did you say you were born on Christmas Eve?' asked Agnes.

'Yes,' Lydia replied, somewhat glumly.

'All those presents. Lucky you.'

Owing to her circumstances, Lydia did not believe herself lucky, but refrained from saying so. It was unfortunate to lose your mother at birth and even more unfortunate for it to happen on Christmas Eve.

'So where will you stay for Christmas?' Agnes asked.

Lydia shrugged. 'The same place as every year. Home. In Kensington.'

Apart from the small Christmas tree, the festive season would be no different from any other day of the year. The presents would be sensible, the Christmas lunch shared between herself and her father.

'I shall be spending Christmas at Sir Avis's country house,' Agnes said loftily. 'We always spend Christmas there. Sir Avis holds wonderful parties for all his friends. Would you like to come?'

'I suppose so. As long as I'm not needed at the hospital. Student nurses have to work the same hours as those already qualified.'

It occurred to Lydia that it was not appropriate for Agnes to invite people to a house that didn't belong to her, yet she did so with total confidence.

'Then that's settled. You shall stay with us at Heathlands for Christmas! Now come on. It'll be dark before long.'

A red brick wall encircled the kitchen garden. The smell of wood smoke overwhelmed that of rotting cabbages and damp earth.

Lydia pulled her hat down over her ears.

A man wearing dark clothes and big boots, his face the colour of burnt sienna, was prodding a heap of burning twigs and hedge trimmings. His prodding caused the smoke to swirl into eddies before spiralling upwards into the naked branches of fruit trees.

He looked up from beneath a mud-coloured cap. 'What you doin' 'ere?'

Brown eyes twinkled in a face criss-crossed

with plum-coloured veins. The pipe clenched in the corner of his mouth jiggled when he spoke as though it were preventing a smile.

'I'm showing Lydia around. She's the doctor's daughter. He's attending the master. Sir Avis has not been well,' replied Agnes.

'Hope the master regains 'is 'ealth.'

He went back to tending his bonfire in a desultory manner.

'I'm going to show Lydia how easy it is to drive a motor car so I've invited her to Heathlands for Christmas. I'm sure she'll enjoy it.'

Lydia looked at her in surprise. 'I'm not sure I can.'

'Of course you can.'

The gardener looked at her with one eye half closed as though in warning. 'Children and women ain't supposed to go messin' wiv motor cars.'

Agnes laughed. 'Don't be silly, Mr Matthews. Why ever not?'

'Because it's so,' replied the old man, the corners of his eyes wrinkling with amusement, the half-closed one now totally shut. 'Though the way things are goin' p'raps it won't always be so. Not if you grows up like one of them suffragette women. Some of 'em even wears trousers so I 'ear.'

'I shall wear trousers,' Agnes exclaimed. 'And I shall smoke and drink and I shall drive a motor car. I might even fly an aeroplane. You see if I don't.'

The cracked face broke into deep wrinkles as he smiled, shook his head and went back to tending his fire.

'We'll go to the garage now,' said Agnes, taking long strides whilst Lydia ran to keep up with her. Agnes, Lydia noticed, was about two inches shorter than she was but had longer legs.

Tossing her auburn hair, Agnes opened a stable-style door just a few inches and slid through the narrow opening. Lydia followed.

The building had clearly once housed the carriage horses and the hacks useful for riding along Rotten Row on favourable Sundays. The smell of hay, horse sweat and the lingering odour of manure still hung in the air, but the more pungent stink of oil and axle grease was slowly taking over.

A circular window was set high at one end. The overhead hayloft was as empty as the mangers still attached at regular intervals along the wall.

Agnes went round to the front of the bright yellow car sitting in the centre of the garage.

'Sir Avis has two motor cars. There's the one you came in and this one. It's a Rolls-Royce.'

The car had shiny brass lamps and a horn made of rubber and brass, perched next to the windscreen. Lydia was amazed.

A man Lydia recognised as the chauffeur who had driven them to the house looked up from sweeping a hand brush over the running boards.

He had round eyes and stuck-out ears, which looked too big for his long face. His thin lips formed a tight, straight line. A cigarette dangled from the corner of his mouth.

Without asking for permission, Agnes opened the car door, climbed up into the driver's seat and spread her hands over the steering wheel.

'Thompson, I'm going to drive to Brighton today. Lydia is coming with me. Climb in, Lydia.'

Lydia looked nervously at Thompson who just stood there, his big hands hanging at his side.

'Well, come on!' Agnes sounded impatient.

The man jerked his head, took the cigarette from the corner of his mouth and spat on the floor. 'Go on. Best do as her ladyship tells you.'

After dislodging a scrap of tobacco from his lip, he stuck the cigarette back in position, grunted something about interruptions to his work, and then returned to what he was doing.

Lydia got in beside her new friend.

Agnes reeled off each part of the car whilst pointing with long, strong fingers.

'Now this is the steering wheel. This is the brake. You have to squeeze the clutch tightly to ease it off. That thing there is a damper...'

'Are you really going to earn a living driving a car?' Lydia asked, her eyes shining with admiration.

Agnes eyed her haughtily. 'This is the twentieth century. I can do whatever I want. I can be whatever I want. I had my first driving lesson when I was only nine years old. Thompson showed me how.'

'He showed you?' Lydia was now seriously awestruck.

'Yes. I had a go.'

Thompson looked up at them from the job he was doing on the running board.

'I told you not to tell.' He sounded displeased.

'Where did you drive?'

'At Heathlands. Sir Avis's country estate. We don't just stay there for Christmas. We stay there at other times too. There's a drive, a piece of road with no other traffic on it except for the odd farm cart. Acres and acres of grass to drive on if I wish, and there are deer and a lake.'

Lydia had visited the house owned by her mother's family in the town of Wareham in Dorset, a stout building adjoining the shops they owned, but it was nothing like the house Agnes was describing. The main street was dusty during the summer and slick with rain or ice in the winter. The green hills surrounding Wareham were within walking distance and sometimes they had gone there for a picnic or taken the train to nearby Weymouth.

'I've been to Weymouth,' she exclaimed in an attempt to match Agnes's experiences. 'I saw the sea.'

Agnes was not to be outdone.

'I've seen the sea too. Sir Avis also has a house in Brighton though we don't go there now. Lady Julieta lives there.'

'Who's she?'

'Sir Avis's wife. They don't like each other so they don't live together.'

'I see.' Lydia nodded solemnly as though the fact that two married people lived apart was perfectly understandable.

'If you like you can come to Heathlands in the summer too – that's if you like it at Christmas. I can show you how to drive a motor car; perhaps not for Christmas, but at some other time. Sir Avis often has friends and family to stay – mostly friends. He only invites those members of the family that he's on speaking terms with. He prefers servants and friends rather than family. Some people call him eccentric because of that. But he's not. He's just a humanist. That is how he describes himself. A humanist.'

Lydia nodded. 'A humanist,' she repeated, as though that too was as understandable as not living with a despised spouse.

'I'm hungry,' Agnes said suddenly. 'Let's see if there's some sliced ham in the kitchen. I'll make sandwiches. With pickle. Do you like pickle?'

It seemed rude to say that pickle upset her, so Lydia nodded and said yes, she was quite fond of it, though not too much please.

The garage had been warm and cosy; outside the air had turned sharp.

'Frost tonight,' shouted the old gardener as they made their way past the shed where he kept his tools.

'Good for the parsnips,' shouted Agnes. 'He always says that, so I've said it for him,' she giggled.

Lydia giggled with her.

'You've quite away with you, Agnes Stacey.'

The two girls hurried back to the kitchen, Lydia hampered by her hobble skirt, Agnes striding as though she had no skirt on at all, though she did; a navy blue one that billowed like a tent around her. The maid who answered the door was wearing something similar, Lydia noticed.

Back in the garage, Thompson straightened and rolled his shoulders before standing back and eyeing the car's bodywork.

'Bloody lovely,' he exclaimed, his smile threatening to split his face in half.

He was in the process of lighting another cigarette, when the door in the far corner of the garage opened and attracted his attention. He smiled as Megan Rogers brushed the damp from her shoulders and shook her umbrella.

He grinned at her and held his arms open. 'Give us a kiss.'

Megan tossed her head. 'You might not deserve one.' She was always ready to tease him.

'Why might that be?' he asked. He ran his fingers through his wiry light brown hair, his legs apart, waiting for her to come to him.

'You've been entertaining other women. I know you have. I heard them.'

Her tone condemned but her lips were smiling.

'Lady Agnes has found herself a friend.'

'Shhh!' Megan hissed, her finger held in front of her lips. 'You know you shouldn't say that. What if somebody hears?'

He shrugged. 'What if they do? We all know that she's the old man's kid.'

'She's the cook's daughter. She don't know the way things is herself. So you watch it, Ted Thompson. You just watch what you say.'

Chapter Three

It was Sarah Stacey's habit to visit her mother on the other side of London two weeks before Christmas. After that there was too much to do at Heathlands what with all the guests Sir Avis invited. Even with a household of experienced domestic servants, plus Agnes, she would be too busy.

Agnes was the biggest problem, the sulkiest kitchen maid ever to don an apron.

'I don't want to go into service. I want to fly, or drive, or make useful things. I don't want to wait on people.'

'So, if you wish to make things, how about being a milliner?'

Agnes's sulky expression turned even sulkier. 'I don't mean hats. I mean useful inventions.'

Sarah rolled her eyes, sighed and hustled her daughter out of the door and into the car. Thompson was driving them to Myrtle Street. Once the visit was over, a few days later, they would get a cab and a train to Heathlands, Thompson picking them up the other end.

Sarah's mother Ellen Proctor lived in a red brick terraced house in Myrtle Street, not far from the docks in the East End of London. Originally built for rope makers, coopers and carpenters in the days when sailing ships had been made of wood, the houses were flat fronted and basic. They had a door at the front, one sash window on the ground

43

floor and one above it. There were two bedrooms, a living room and scullery plus an outside privy at the end of the garden. Most of the people who lived there had poorly paid jobs, or in some instances, none at all.

The terraced street was one of many arranged in lines along cobbled streets where kids played, women gossiped and the sound of cranes swinging from ship to shore screeched and clanged for most of the day.

Agnes's mood was still on her when they were offloaded in a deserted street some way from the house in Myrtle Street. Sarah did not like being dropped off at the door in case the neighbours would accuse her of being snooty.

'You should consider yourself lucky, my girl,' snapped Sarah Stacey to her daughter. 'At least you have a position.'

'I don't want to be a kitchen maid or a house maid. I want to drive a car,' Agnes repeated.

'Don't be ridiculous! You're a girl. Girls do not drive cars.'

Sarah Stacey looked and sounded exasperated. She had always hoped that her daughter would stay in the house where she worked, a domestic servant on better pay and enjoying better conditions than most. It had never occurred to her that Agnes might not want that and it had certainly never occurred to her that Agnes wanted to drive a motor car.

'Damn Ted Thompson! He had no business teaching you how to drive. No business at all!'

Sarah had never liked Ted Thompson, a man who considered himself attractive to women with

44

his smart uniform and leather gloves that squeaked when he pulled them on.

She knew he was having a fling with Megan and had cautioned the girl.

'He's not the settling type,' Sarah had said to her.

In return, Megan had smiled knowingly and said, 'Neither is Sir Avis.'

The barb had hit home and a bright flush had flown over Sarah's handsome face. Deep down she knew it was Sir Avis she had to blame. He'd encouraged Agnes to aim above her status. It wouldn't do. It just wouldn't do.

'Sir Avis thought it was a brilliant idea,' said Agnes, instantly confirming the truth that her mother found hard to face.

Sarah was speechless. Sir Avis had very modern ideas that she herself found difficult to come to terms with. She'd laughed the day he'd declared that at some point in the future men would take to the skies in flying machines.

'Nonsense,' she'd said to him. That was some years ago before Agnes had been born. Since then she'd had to eat her words, but still she found it difficult to believe that the lot of the domestic servant and the working class in general would ever change.

The rich man in his castle, the poor man at his gate. God ordained one's lot in life according to the words of the hymn. Not that she needed a hymn to tell her that. Some things would change but not everything.

'Remember to say don't instead of do not, and drop a few aitches. Otherwise your Gran might think that we're both getting ideas above our station and the neighbours will make fun.'

'So why teach me how to speak properly in the first place?'

'For the benefit of your betters. Rich folk like to have servants who speak properly.'

'I've already told you. I don't want to be in service. If I did I would be a chauffeur.'

'Well, you can't. And that's an end to it.' Sarah sighed. 'Well, in the meantime you'll have to accept your lot in life until something else turns up. If you meet a nice young man and get married, you won't be working for long anyway.'

Agnes smiled to herself and whispered a long drawn out 'Yesss... That might be different.'

'Don't even think about Robert Ravening,' hissed her mother. 'Mark my words; marrying him is something that will never happen.'

Agnes pouted. 'That isn't necessarily so...'

'No!' snapped her mother, a warning finger raised in front of Agnes's face.

'If that's the case, where does my father fit in?' she'd asked but her mother had just walked on.

Agnes was determined to hold on to her dream. Some day she would get to do what she wanted to do. Like the doctor's daughter, she too wanted to do something useful, not cleaning and cooking for rich folk no matter how good to her they were.

Agnes followed her mother past Jarmans, the shop on the corner of the street where they sold everything from enamel jugs to fresh bread, Colman's mustard to Cherry Blossom shoe polish.

Sacks of cabbages, potatoes, carrots and onions

46

took up half the narrow pavement in front of the shop window. An enamel sign advertising Sunlight soap filled the gap between shop window and the living space above the shop. Brushes and mops hung from the wall in the narrow shop doorway making it necessary for customers of wide girth to turn sideways to enter. Inside the shop smelled of lavender polish and strong tea.

A bell jangled and the door opened as they passed. Mr Jarman came out wearing a brown apron that reached to his ankles. He had a broad face, kind eyes and a black moustache that curled over the corners of his mouth. His hair too was black, plastered down with hair cream and parted in the middle.

His face lit up when he saw Agnes's mother, the ends of his moustache seeming to curl up closer to the corners of his eyes.

His voice boomed in welcome. 'Good day to you, Sarah.'

'Good day to you, George.'

'My offer still stands,' he called out to her.

Wearing a slightly bemused smile, Sarah swept on by over-the hopscotch squares chalked on the pavement, almost skipping by the time she reached the threshold of her mother's house.

It wasn't so long ago that George Jarman had asked her to marry him. He made a point of asking her every time she visited her mother. He'd even offered to adopt Agnes as his own. 'Seeing as that wastrel of a husband has never given the child the time of day,' he'd pronounced.

Sarah had turned him down. She'd given him no reason as such except to say that she was managing quite well, thank you, and that Tom Stacey might still be alive somewhere, and if she married George, she would be committing bigamy.

Being an upright man who scorned the public house and attended the Methodist chapel on Sundays, George had nodded sadly on each occasion she'd delivered her answer.

'A man can hope,' he'd said to her.

'You're hoping my husband is dead, George,' she pointed out to him.

'So be it,' he'd said. 'I'll keep hoping and keep asking.'

Number one Myrtle Street was right next door to the shop and the first on the right in the street. It was also the only one with a brass step, all the others having cold, white marble.

Henry Proctor, Agnes's grandfather had been responsible for that. He'd worked in a turning mill in Bristol, shaping metals for various uses. Brass was one of them, and this particular piece, left over from a job, had arrived miraculously at number one Myrtle Street when they'd moved there.

He was dead now, but Ellen Proctor lovingly polished that step twice a week.

'In his memory,' she was fond of saying. 'I keep it shining so his memory will always shine. He'd come back and haunt me if I don't keep it polished.'

Agnes followed her mother into the cramped little house, her nose tingling, her eyes beginning to fill with tears.

The smell of stale food and mothballs mingled with that of old drains and cats.

Agnes began to scratch.

'For goodness' sake,' whispered her mother. 'Not already.'

Agnes shrugged. 'I can't help it. I don't dislike cats, but my body does. My eyes do. And my nose.'

She began to sneeze.

Sarah Stacey frowned as she began unbuttoning her coat. 'You do it on purpose. I know you do.'

'I can't...'

Agnes sneezed again, a big almighty one into one of Sir Avis's old handkerchiefs she'd thought to bring with her.

Sarah Stacey took off her hat and coat. Agnes followed suit without bothering to argue further about the cat thing. Her nose was tickling; her eyes were watering and just the thought of being close to those cats again was making her itch.

'Is that you, our Sarah?' called a voice from the back of the house.

'Yes, Ma,' Sarah called back.

'I'm out back, mangling.'

Sarah Stacey's sharp eyes took in the amount of cleaning she would have to do whilst she was here. The fact was her mother was getting on in years and not up to doing other folks' laundry and keeping on top of her own housework. They were only here for a few days, just the other side of London from the house in Belgravia. Between the two of them, she reckoned her and Agnes could sort things out. By then Agnes would have stopped scratching and sneezing. Once they'd seen Ellen all right and had a pre-Christmas party of their own, then they would leave Myrtle

49

Street behind and get the train to Heathlands, Sir Avis's country estate lying to the west of London. The house in Belgravia was already locked up for the Christmas period.

Sidestepping a glossy black cat with orange eyes, Agnes followed her mother through the scullery and out into the back yard.

Three separate washing lines each carrying a line of limp laundry and leaving barely enough room to move, criss-crossed each other.

Ellen Proctor, Agnes's grandmother, was turning the wheel of a cast-iron mangle with one hand and feeding through a grizzled-looking shirt with the other. The fact that she had few remaining teeth showed when she smiled.

'All right, my babs? A few bits more and we can have a cup of tea. Got to finish it though. That old skinflint Mrs Bennett is only paying me half a crown, but that's better than nothing. My cupboard's as bare as that Mrs Hubbard's is. How's you, Agnes?'

Agnes was rubbing each arm in turn.

'Fine, Gran. What are you going to buy with that half a crown?' she asked with a smile.

The fat red arm that turned the wheel of the mangle never faltered. Bright blue eyes, half-hidden by plump cheeks and drooping eyelids, twinkled.

'Pork cuttings, onions, potatoes, bread, butter and cheese. What the 'ell doss thee think I was going to buy? Fur coat? Frills and frippery fer wearing to the ball?'

Her accent was Bristolian, her tone teasing but oddly serious. When work had dried up at the

50

Bristol docks some years before, this is where Agnes's grandfather had come to find more work. The River Thames had less of a tidal surge than the River Avon flowing through Bristol, thus ships could come and go more easily. Also, as a capital city, it attracted more trade and Henry Proctor had been tempted by a more plentiful supply of work.

No amount of teasing from her grandmother could dampen Agnes's spirit. She was ready in an instant with a cheeky response.

'I thought you might be splashing out on a new cap? Or a new pipe?'

'Cheeky thing! Me cap's nice and greasy. Keeps off the rain. And as long as there's baccy in me pipe, it suits for me.'

She said all this without looking up, without slowing the process of feeding the laundry through the rollers. The mangle squeaked with each turn and the water poured down, splashing her feet and trickling down the drain.

As she spoke, she clenched the clay pipe in the last of her teeth, sucking it in with each downward turn of the mangle and blowing out on the upward stroke. No more than three teeth, two at the top and one at the bottom, gripped her pipe.

Her mother read her mind and nudged her arm in warning.

'I've brought you a few things, Ma,' said Agnes's mother. 'Leftovers, but all good. Half a leg of cold lamb, a knuckle of cooked ham, a chocolate cake and a veal and ham pie. That should keep you going for a while.'

'Lovely,' exclaimed Ellen Proctor. 'If you put the

51

kettle on, we can have a piece of that cake with our tea. This pair of coms is the last,' she declared as the legs of a pair of men's combinations came through the rollers and dropped into the laundry basket.

Agnes watched with interest as her grandmother wiped her meaty hands in her apron. She didn't know how old her grandmother was, but guessed at sixty. Her hair was white as Old Man's Beard growing on the hedgerows around Heathlands; her face was wrinkled and plump, and her body as round as a cottage loaf.

'Me back aches fit to break in 'alf,' Ellen Proctor grumbled while massaging the small of her back with both hands. 'I'm gettin' too old fer this lark.'

'How old are you, Gran?' Agnes asked, seized with a sudden urge to know exactly.

Her grandmother winked, her wrinkled face only inches away from that of her granddaughter. Agnes and her mother helped hang out the washing before going into the kitchen.

'Too old. Know this, me girl, that it's better to be young though youth is wasted on the young. And I used to be young. I weren't born this age. Theese oughta know that.'

Just like Agnes and her mother, Ellen Proctor's eyes were amber and tilted upwards at the outer corners. It was difficult to deduce what her features had been before they became bloated with age and scarred with hard work. The hair beneath the man's cap was thin and white. Her figure had long gone to seed and she was shorter than both her daughter and granddaughter.

Agnes's grandmother, who was giving herself a good scratch, her flesh wobbling beneath her faded dress and patched apron, noticed her prolonged stare.

'What you looking at, girl?'

'You don't wear stays do you, Gran?' Agnes asked.

Her grandmother threw back her head and belted out a hearty laugh.

'Agnes!' exclaimed her mother, who had just put the kettle on to the hob. 'That is rude. This is your grandmother. You should have more respect.'

Agnes shrugged. 'I was only asking. It doesn't look as though Gran does wear stays, and I was wondering...'

Ellen Proctor's eyes twinkled as she took it all in.

'Well, wonder no more. You're getting too big for your boots, young lady.' Her mother chided her.

'Leave the girl be, Sarah. I likes to be comfortable and I don't care who knows it. She's curious. It don't hurt being curious. Anyways, I don't wear stays. They itch and I feel like a horse in harness. Why should I be constrained like a horse just 'cause I'm a woman?'

'Men don't,' said Agnes, pleased with her grandmother's response. 'And I don't want to. I mean, what's the point?'

'So, what do you like to wear?' asked her grandmother whilst tipping the contents of her teacup into her saucer.

'Trousers. And goggles. I like driving. I want to be a chauffeur when I grow up.'

Her grandmother slurped back some tea, her eyes never leaving her granddaughter's face. Shaking her head, she said, 'No. That's no good. You want somebody to drive you around, not you driving some bigwig around.'

Sarah bristled. 'Don't encourage her, Mother. She's difficult enough as it is.'

Agnes beamed from ear to ear. 'I'm going to learn to drive a motor car and a motor bike. Then I'm going to fly like the Wright brothers. They flew high above the ground in an aeroplane at Kittyhawk and now everyone's doing it. Their exploit will go down in history. That's what Sir Avis told me.'

While her mother stood looking dismayed, her grandmother laughed even heartier than before and told her she could be whatever she wanted to be.

'Please yourself,' she said, her broad smile enabling Agnes to count every tooth in her head. 'Please yourself, my girl! Before long, girls will be doing whatever boys are doing.'

'That's what Sir Avis says,' Agnes proclaimed, her complexion brightened by the sparkle in her eyes, her pink lips slightly parted. 'He said in this modern world I could be whatever I want to be. He told me to reach for the sky and I might end up sitting on the roof. And he'd help where he could.'

'He would,' said her grandmother, a knowing look passing between her and Sarah, and her daughter.

Agnes looked at her mother who was hanging her head over her cup and saucer and sensed that

54

her red cheeks had nothing to do with the hot tea.

The sound of heavy footsteps came from the passageway that led to the street.

'Mrs Proctor? Are you there?'

Agnes's grandmother put down her cup and got to her feet. 'I'm out in the scullery,' she shouted back.

'Harry Allen come for his mother's laundry,' she exclaimed while wiping her hands down her apron. She winked at Agnes. 'At least she ain't mean with the money, like Mrs Bennett.'

Harry Allen, a young man of seventeen, with blue eyes and a shock of corn-coloured hair, breezed into the scullery. On seeing Agnes and her mother, he took off his cap.

'Hello, Mrs Stacey. Hello, Agnes.' His eyes lingered on Agnes. 'My, but you're growing up. Nice dress. You're even beginning to look pretty.'

Agnes didn't like being reminded that she was a girl and had to get used to wearing dresses with lace and frills and bobs and bows; even being called pretty irritated.

'I am not a child and I hate wearing dresses.'

He laughed as though she were even younger than she actually was which irritated her even more.

'Well, I think you looks lovely. If you keeps on going as you are, I might even ask you to marry me when you grows up.'

Agnes was speechless. She eyed the fresh-faced boy with his glossy hair and happy countenance. She should feel flattered but instead felt even more irritated.

'Oh no, you will not! Whatever makes you think I would marry a stupid boy like you?'

Her mother sighed with exasperation. 'Would you like a slice of chocolate cake and a cup of tea, Harry?'

Agnes was in no doubt what her mother was up to; Harry liked her and was available. But she didn't want Harry. She wanted Sir Avis's nephew, Robert. She'd known him since they were both two lonely children, one without a father and one whose parents spent their time overseeing a sheep station in Australia or touring the world with a fashionable set.

Robert was the love of her life and if she couldn't have him, she'd never marry.

Harry accepted the cake and tea, his eyes hardly leaving her face as he pulled a chair from beneath the kitchen table and sat down.

'There's one of them picture houses opened down Lambeth way. How about I take you there?' He turned abruptly to Agnes's mother. 'If you've no objection, Mrs Stacey.'

Agnes cringed when her mother answered that she had no objection at all.

'I think you'd enjoy that, wouldn't you Agnes? They're so modern, these moving pictures.'

'I don't think so,' Agnes replied tartly. 'Watching a stage in the dark gives me headaches. I think I've got one coming on now what with the travelling and the cats. I itch you know,' she said to Harry. 'I itch because of the cats and get rashes all over me. Quite ugly rashes in fact. Now, if you'll excuse me, I'm quite tired. I need a lie down.'

Aware of her mother's harsh looks, she took the

creaking narrow stairs that led to her grandmother's bedroom two at a time. Once there, she
flung herself on to the patchwork quilt that
smelled of stale snuff and damp.

Cradling her hot cheeks in her hands, she stared
out of the window: not that there was much to see;
just the window of a room much like this and roof
after roof and chimney after chimney beyond that.

To think that Harry Allen entertained the idea
of marrying her! What a silly idea that was. It was
Robert she loved; Robert she would always love.

They'd come across each other in the orchard
at Heathlands, a shady place of gnarled old fruit
trees and long grass.

Robert had been riding Copper, his chestnut
pony, and had almost trotted over her until she'd
popped up out of the grass in front of him.

The pony had shied and Robert had ended up
beside her in the grass.

Footsteps pounded up the stairs. The smell of
violets came into the little bedroom along with
her mother. Her mother closed the pine plank
door tightly behind her. Her expression was tense,
the little cameo brooch at her throat moving in
time with nervous swallowing, as though she were
rehearsing the words she wanted to say.

'Agnes Stacey, you were rude to that young man.
Harry likes you. He's always liked you. I think you
should go down immediately and apologise.'

Agnes sighed and cupped her face in her hands.

'I wouldn't want to lead him on. He's not the
one for me and...'

'Don't say that you're not curious about the
picture house. I know my own daughter. I know

57

you'd love to go.'

'I don't want to go with him. I don't want to build up his hopes. I won't ever marry him. I'm going to marry Master Robert. I think I'll ask Lydia if she'd like to go to the pictures.'

'Lydia?'

'The doctor's daughter. I can telephone her.'

Her mother did what she always did when she was agitated and not quite sure what to do. She began moving swiftly around the room, rearranging ornaments, straightening pictures, opening a drawer, tidying it, slamming it shut again and moving on to the next.

She shook her head before peering into the water pitcher sitting in its matching bowl on the washstand.

'This room needs a thorough spring clean,' Sarah murmured, mostly to herself.

Agnes sighed and clutched her chin more tightly. 'I have to have feelings for someone and I don't have any for Harry.'

'Think carefully, Agnes.' Her mother's gaze was intent and her brow furrowed with concern.

'I have thought about it. I only have feelings for Robert.'

Her mother spun round to face her.

'Well, you can get that idea out of your head, young lady. It will do no good you setting your sights on the likes of him. He's of a different class. He's gentry and we're working people. Nothing is ever going to change that unless the world itself changes. Get it into your head that the highest you're likely to achieve is ending up as a cook like me. That is all you'll ever be to

Robert. Just a servant.'

She sounded angry, breathless and her neck was flushing red above the high collar of her cream lace blouse.

'That's not fair!'

'You'll learn as you get older that the world isn't fair. That's the way it is.'

Her mother turned from brushing away dust with her bare hand, dragged her off the bed and on to her feet.

Agnes winced. The redness of her mother's neck had travelled up to her face. Her expression was unreadable and oddly guarded and when she began to speak, she drew in her breath as though she were afraid of the words she had to say.

'You're not listening.' She delivered her words slowly and precisely. 'You have to understand that he won't ever marry the likes of you. He won't. You should know that. I know he won't. I know it for sure because...'

Sarah Stacey, Agnes's mother, stopped herself from saying anything more and turned her face towards the window, seemingly watching the brisk wind that was blowing dead leaves up and over the rooftops.

She hated to disappoint the daughter she loved so much, but it had to be; not that she could tell Agnes the whole truth. A dreadful secret lay behind her warning, a secret few were privy to and she had sworn never to reveal. The truth was Sarah Stacey had difficulty dealing with Agnes; Sir Avis dealt with her far better.

'She's just like my Aunt Peridot,' he was fond of saying to Sarah. 'She was a wild one when she was young. So was I, come to that,' he'd added with the boyish grin that had first seduced her.

Sarah Stacey knew Sir Avis far better than most. She knew he'd been a wild young man, an out and out womaniser and pursuer of pleasure. Sarah had been one of his pleasures, but there had been others, quite a few others.

'I don't believe anything you say,' shouted Agnes as she bolted for the door.

There was a swishing of layers of petticoats as her mother headed after her.

'Come back here, young lady. Come back here this minute,' she shouted.

The vibration from the slammed door shook loose plaster from the ceiling.

Sighing, Sarah sank on to a chair and rubbed her aching forehead with her long, white fingers.

She eyed the closed door. It had not been easy bringing Agnes up, and not at all easy deciding to keep her. Sir Avis had been good about it all. Few would have been so generous to a servant like her. Women who got pregnant by the master of the house usually had a bleak future. They lost their position and the income that went with it. Some ended up in workhouses, some on the street. The lucky few were paid a fee for their silence and were taken in by their families.

Sarah had been very lucky. Sir Avis had genuinely cared for her, and paid for her lying-in at a handsome nursing home in the country. He'd also had her back to work for him. Sir Avis was genuinely fond of her just as she was of him. They were closer than many a man and wife no matter their class or status in life.

60

Sarah fiddled with the cameo brooch at her throat, gazing out to where a blood-red setting sun barely peered over the rooftops. She couldn't help feeling unnerved. Agnes was no longer a child. The time was coming when she would have to be told the truth.

Sarah looked down at her fidgeting fingers. There had been instances when she could have told, but her courage had failed her.

On her daughter's birth certificate, in the space reserved for the name of the father, were the condemning words, *Father Unknown*. There was no Tom Stacey. Sir Avis had promised her nothing. 'I cannot even acknowledge the child as mine whilst Julieta is alive,' he'd said to her. 'Should my wife die, then I will reconsider.'

He never spoke of marriage, but then he wouldn't. Despite his professing to be a modern, forward-thinking man, he knew society would shun both him and possibly his family if he married his cook.

Unfortunately for Sarah, Julieta appeared in the very best of health. It seemed there was nobody to place his name in that box marked *Father Unknown*. Yet she desperately wanted there to be a name, even if it meant marrying someone willing to insert their name, even if they were not Agnes's natural father. So far, George Jarman was the only candidate worth considering. However, she'd got used to being unattached – at least in the accepted meaning of the term.

The last rays of the setting sun finally disappeared. Sarah sat and took deep breaths. It had

61

hurt her to quash any aspirations her daughter had towards Master Robert, but very necessary. Firstly it was Sarah's dearest wish that her daughter should benefit from her own experience. Secondly, she was privy to a very dark secret she had sworn never to reveal.

Sir Avis freely admitted that he loved women. The fact was that they loved him too. He could charm the haughtiest woman off her feet and into his bed. Lady Julieta, his wife, had been one of many; a vibrant, black-haired creature, daughter of an American industrialist of Hispanic descent sent to England to find herself a titled husband.

Besides her beauty, her fortune had been the key to Avis's heart. However, it had not altered his habits; one woman was never enough.

'But I will never share a house with any woman save you. But then, you are the best cook I've ever had,' he'd said to Sarah.

As usual, she had swallowed the stinging comment, accepting that cook and mistress was all she would ever be to him.

She loved him with all her heart, but had no wish for her daughter to fall into the same trap, although with Robert there was no question of them marrying.

Sarah was no fool and was in no doubt as to who Robert's father really was. She'd seen Sir Avis exiting Lady Jacintha's bedroom whilst her husband, Avis's brother, was still in Australia. There had been no issue up until that stage, no son to carry on the name or daughter to marry well. Robert had been born almost nine months later.

In time, Robert would marry a young woman of his class and approved by his family. Agnes would find somebody of her own class to marry and the secret would stay a secret.

Chapter Four

During winter, it was the duty of the student nurses to crack the ice on the water used to wash the patients and to add a little hot water to the bowl.

'Just enough to take away the chill. Too hot is as bad as too cold,' instructed their matron, a heavy woman named Sister Bertha who was a deaconess in the Lutheran church as well as being a highly qualified nurse.

The women's wards occupied the east end of the building, the men's wards at the other end. In between were the children's wards, Lydia's particular favourite. At the very far end of the east wing was the nursery for the few new-borns that were born at the hospital.

Lydia had asked why the new-borns were not next door to the children's wards. Sister Bertha had drawn herself up to her loftiest and widest before informing her that small children carry infection and were best kept away from babies.

'Babies have little resistance to infection during their early years. We must do the best we can to help them achieve some immunity before they go home to mix with older children.'

The main thing Lydia learned in those early days was that the regime at the hospital was strict, but their attention to detail and their attitude to modern medicine was quite astonishing.

In order to retain what she learned, Lydia didn't just study, she kept notes on her patients, sticking them into an exercise book for future reference.

One of the other nurses asked her whether she would have a bonfire of those notes once she'd passed her finals.

Lydia shook her head, her eyes sparkling and a faint smile on her wide pink mouth.

'They might come in useful. I might need to refer to them in future. Isolate infection. That's what Sister Bertha says.'

The nurse, Sally Hoffman, shrugged. 'You are the most dedicated student here. I'm only going to be a nurse until I marry.'

Lydia laughed. 'I might marry too, but still, if I have children it pays to know how to keep them healthy. Whooping cough, measles and chicken pox can kill the very young. If I can learn something about isolation, I will.'

Although founded by Lutherans in the nineteenth century ostensibly to cater for the German community in the East End of London, the German hospital offered treatment to anyone.

One of the deaconesses, Sister Ursula, was a midwife who made home visits. Only the more difficult births were hospitalised, mothers preferring to give birth at home.

Lydia felt extremely privileged to be chosen to accompany her on a home visit. This was the sort of thing she wanted to do, reaching out in the wider community, to those crammed into the narrow, damp tenements in the East End of London.

Sister Ursula flitted around, adding the things they would need to her bag. To Lydia's surprise, forceps were included. Sister Ursula noticed her surprise, keeping up her speed of preparation as she explained their presence.

'I know that only doctors are supposed to use forceps except in dire emergency. I have a mother who has been in labour for twenty-four hours. The father is worried. It would be good if both the forceps and you came with me.'

Sister Ursula stopped tipping things into her bag to eye her sceptically, almost as though she might or might not tip her into the bag too.

'I hope you will be up to this. The place we are going to is not Kensington. It is not pretty and not very clean.'

'I'll be fine,' Lydia declared, aware that Sister Ursula was studying her, though in truth she had visualised a cosy bedroom, a mother's joy on bringing a baby into the world.

Sister Ursula was weighing up whether her confidence might dissolve once faced with dire reality. Finally, she nodded. 'All right. We will now go. Come along.'

It was no surprise, of course, that most mothers gave birth at home, usually attended by a midwife who might or might not be qualified. Some mothers to be did not send for someone qualified, but preferred 'a woman that knew', someone from their own community, which might mean the next street, or could just as easily mean of the same nationality, someone who spoke their language. In their hour of need, they didn't care about the law that had been passed in 1902 specifically stating that only qualified midwives should attend a birth. The habits of centuries were hard to break – together with the financial considerations.

The house they went to was at the very end of a series of squat-fronted houses in a narrow street, squashed up against the wall of a railway viaduct. At the passing of a train, the windows of the house rattled in their frames and steam fell in thick clouds.

Ragged children stopped playing with marbles or at hopscotch, and followed on behind, asking them if they had any sweets or a penny to spare.

Women, their faces etched with the lines of poverty, their bodies worn out with too many pregnancies and too many mouths to feed, came out on to doorsteps, nodding an acknowledgement and warning the children to leave them alone.

Even so, Lydia glanced nervously over her shoulder.

'Take no notice. All will be well,' Ursula assured her. 'They are poor but they respect and appreciate what we do for them.'

The moment they entered the house, Lydia knew that the smell of poverty would stay with her for the rest of her life. Bare boards, boiled potatoes, clothes worn for at least a week and washed in carbolic, ash smouldering in the fireplace, and children with that peculiar smell of sticky jam mixed with peed pants.

The father excused himself, telling them he was on night shift at the docks and had to get some sleep before he clocked on.

'If I get picked,' he told them.

Lydia didn't know what that meant and this must have shown on her face.

'The dockers have to stand in a row and wait to be selected,' explained Sister Ursula. 'Sometimes they are picked and get to earn some money, and sometimes they are not. It depends if your face fits; if the ganger favours you.'

She told Lydia all this as they ascended the uncarpeted stairs, their footsteps clumping all the way to the top.

'In 'ere,' somebody called out from one of the two bedrooms.

A double bed took up most of the room in which a woman was propped up against a striped bolster. Lydia noticed it didn't have a cotton slip and two pillows with it like the one on her bed at home. Just the bare bolster.

The woman looked to be in her late thirties, perhaps even her early forties. Two young girls, one of about twelve and the other ten, were at the washstand, a rickety piece with dented woodwork and broken tiles. Besides the bed, it was the only other piece of furniture in the room. They were pouring hot water from a jug into the basin.

'We got everything ready for you, Sister,' said the eldest in a forthright manner.

Lydia followed Sister Ursula's lead and began pulling off her gloves and unfastening her cape.

'We will need more water. Can you get some from the pump please?' Sister Ursula asked the two girls.

The two girls looked at their mother. 'Ma, we can't.'

Their mother, her straggly hair clinging in wispy fronds around her pale face, shook her head. 'Sorry, Sister. They 'ave to go to work, Sister. Our Lil's got a job in the sugar factory and our Flo's 'elping out at the greengrocer's.'

'Never mind. If one of your girls can show Nurse Lydia where the water pump is...?' Sister Ursula asked. 'Whilst you're doing that, I'll get started here,' Sister Ursula said to Lydia.

Flo, the youngest, guided Lydia back down the stairs and out through the rear door into the back yard and along a path to an ancient water pump.

'You need to give it a good tug,' said Flo with the no nonsense manner of someone three times her age. 'You 'old it and I'll give it a pull.'

Lydia eyed the skinny girl with the long arms and eyes that seemed far too big for her face. The poor child; she looked too thin and weak to walk let alone battle with the water pump.

She suggested an alternative. 'I'm older, bigger and stronger than you, so how about I tug the handle and you hold the jug beneath the spout?'

Flo shrugged her bony shoulders, prominent through the threadbare bodice she wore.

'Up to you. 'Ave a go if you like, but I'm warning you, this pump 'andle's got a mind of 'is own.'

'I'm sure I can manage,' said Lydia feeling too smug for her own good.

Flo folded her arms across her chest, a faint smile on her face as she moved aside to make room for Lydia.

Lydia took a deep breath, and using both hands gripped the handle tightly and gave it a mighty tug. The handle rebounded, jerking upwards. Lydia's hands went with it, her aching arms feeling as though they'd been pulled from their sockets.

Flo regarded her with her big, soulful eyes and shook her head.

'You hold the jug. I'll pump,' she suggested. This time Lydia didn't argue. The water glugged and gurgled into the jug.

'I'll leave you to it, then,' said the girl. 'If the birthing of all me other brothers and sisters is anything to go by, it shouldn't be long now.'

Lydia was of the opinion that the birth of the latest member of the family would be some time yet, but kept her opinion to herself. It wouldn't do to be proved wrong again.

'How many brothers and sisters do you have?' she asked the girl.

'Three brothers and three sisters. Our Lil's the eldest. Then Toby. Then me. Teddy, Walter and Vi are all younger than me. There used to be an Olive and Dorothy as well but they went with the whooping cough and the scarlet fever. They was only little. Still,' she said, as she fastened the one and only button on her cardigan, 'must be going. Ta ta, Sister.'

On her return along the stony lane, Lydia worked out that Mrs Kinski had given birth to eight children, the eldest of whom was twelve. Two children had died. That worked out to one a year over eight years and four years to spare. It appeared that Mrs Kinski had produced a baby every eighteen months or so, far too many for the strongest of bodies. Poor woman. Poor children.

The wood of the door back into the house was

white with age. Here and there were chips of dark green paint, but most of it was gone. Warped through lack of attention, the door took some tugging before it opened.

She gasped at a sudden scuttling across the floor in front of her. The house being ill lit it was difficult to see whatever had scurried across her path. The creature was probably more terrified of her than she was of it, she told herself, so she kept going and made the stairs without spilling a drop.

On reaching the tiny square of landing, she thought she heard a mewing sound. The sound escalated into the unmistakable cry of a new-born infant. The girl had been right. She had been wrong.

Sister Ursula was wrapping the baby up in what looked like the pillowcase missing from the bolster. Glancing at the washstand, Lydia noticed the water in the bowl was rose coloured. She also noticed the forceps.

'It's a boy,' declared Sister Ursula on seeing Lydia. Her eyes flickered between Lydia and the bloodied forceps before fixing on Lydia with a mix of warning and pleading.

'Boy or girl, it makes no difference. It's still another mouth to feed,' murmured Mrs Kinski.

Lydia emptied the bloodied water out the back window of the second bedroom, though getting to the window was not that easy.

Mattresses covered the floor, leaving only the smallest avenue to get through.

As she threw the water out of the open window, Lydia contemplated all that had happened and all

70

that she had seen today. No more would she ever expect a cosy home in this part of the world or a mother feeling immense joy at the birth of a child. Poverty and pain dictated a mother's response.

On the way back to the hospital, Sister Ursula said to her, 'You will not mention the forceps.' She spoke in German, having been delighted to discover that Lydia was familiar with the language, given her parentage. 'I had no choice.'

Lydia frowned. Wasn't it true that only a doctor could use forceps? Doctors possessed greater skills than nurses or midwives and using forceps was a task that also required great responsibility.

'I know what you are thinking,' Sister Ursula continued, sticking to German so her comments could not be overheard. 'For the most part I believe it best a doctor uses forceps. However, there are times when one must do what one can quickly and without recourse to a doctor.'

'But if anything had happened, I mean, I've heard the baby's head can be crushed when forceps are used,' said Lydia in German, the language she and her father had used when she was a child.

Sister Ursula stared straight ahead, as she spoke. 'Yes and there are instances of a baby's body coming out in bits. The truth of the matter is that, yes, I did take a risk in not summoning a doctor, but you see, a doctor would not have come. Mrs Kinski could not afford to pay for one. There was no choice. We have a live mother and a live child. That is payment enough. This is a secret between us, yes?'

71

Chapter Five

On a Friday evening, just after six o'clock, Lydia left the ward after a long day. It had occurred to her to go for a walk. A glance out of the window to see a fresh wind fettering female legs with billowing skirts tempted her.

Somebody knocked at the door just as she was putting on her navy blue coat plus a matching hat with silvery grey pompoms on the side.

Sally, with whom she shared a room when she was on duty, looked at her and shrugged. 'It's not for me.'

Lydia wasn't expecting anyone either, but seeing as she was already dressed for going out, she opened the door.

Agnes Stacey, her hair a glorious halo of unruliness around her face and dressed in olive green from head to toe, stood at the door.

'My word,' she said, eyeing Lydia up and down. 'You've already got your hat and coat on. You must have guessed I was coming.'

'Hardly...'

Lydia was speechless. Normally she might not have recognised a person on only meeting them once, but Agnes was more memorable than most.

'I was just going out for a walk,' Lydia began.

'I came round to take you to the pictures. Have you seen the moving pictures yet?'

'No. No, I have not, but...'

'It's my treat. Are you coming or not?'

Lydia finally agreed to go with her.

'It's only a short walk,' Agnes said to her as they braced themselves against the wind, quickening their steps when it came at them face on between gaps in the buildings.

'How did you find me?' asked Lydia.

'Easy. I telephoned your house. Some old battle-axe answered and said you were at the hospital. I told her I was a friend of yours, another nurse who wasn't sure you were on duty tonight or not. She told me that you were but believed you finished at six. That was right, wasn't it?'

Lydia shook her head and laughed. 'Oh you are clever!'

Agnes looked pleased.

'I spoke to an ambulance driver while I was at the hospital. He told me they were doing away with the last of the horse-drawn ambulances and replacing them with ones driven by petrol engines. I wondered...' Agnes paused. Lydia thought she had a vague idea what was coming. 'I wondered whether you could put in a good word for me. I can drive an ambulance. You know I can.'

Lydia was stunned, but also impressed by Agnes's ingenuity. On the other hand, she wasn't sure her recommendation would get her new friend what she wanted.

'I could try, but do bear in mind that I'm only a student nurse.'

'Perhaps we could devise a plan when you stay with us at Christmas.'

Lydia stopped in her tracks. 'Where did you get this idea that my father and I would be staying with you at Christmas?'

Agnes's wild hair was all over the place, half of it hiding her face. Sitting precariously on her thick head of hair, her hat looked in severe danger of slipping sideways.

'Didn't I tell you?' she said, pushing past her and into Lydia's room. 'Sir Avis has invited you and your father to Heathlands for Christmas. I fully admit I had a hand in it; I told Sir Avis that I liked you and he thinks your father is a very good doctor. My, my,' she said, her eyes darting from side to side and up and down as she gave the room due scrutiny. 'What a miserable room. Like a cell for prisoners or nuns or something.' She turned suddenly after cuddling a cushion then flinging it aside as though it were a bad-tempered cat.

'You will come, won't you? You do celebrate Christmas?' Agnes asked brightly, her reddish-blonde hair glowing like autumn beneath her dark green hat.

Lydia was wearing pale grey kid gloves, but still she shoved her hands deep into her pockets, clenching her fists tightly. If she hadn't been wearing gloves, her fingernails would have dug into her flesh.

'Well?' demanded Agnes when she didn't answer.

'We usually have a Christmas dinner – just the two of us though sometimes Aunt Iris, my mother's sister, comes up from Dorset.'

'Well,' said Agnes, full of exuberance. 'It couldn't possibly compete with a Christmas at Heathlands. Everyone comes: staff, guests and even a few relatives whom Sir Avis is still speaking to.'

She laughed then, but halted on seeing the awkward tension on Lydia's face.

'Is there something else?'

'My birthday's on Christmas Eve,' Lydia said hesitantly.

'Well, that's wonderful. We can celebrate that too.'

Lydia stopped and turned to face her new friend. 'You don't understand. We never celebrate my birthday. My mother died when I was born. My father still grieves, or at least I think he does. My father doesn't really like my birthday to be mentioned.'

Agnes looked horrified. 'It was hardly your fault. You didn't ask to be born.'

Lydia shrugged. 'What you've never had, you never miss, though there have been times when I've wanted to alter things.'

Agnes cocked her head. 'Would your father turn down the invitation?'

Lydia sighed. 'My father is very ambitious. Since my mother's departure, he's thrown himself heart and soul into furthering his career. German men of science – and that includes doctors – are very well respected all over the world.'

'So you're half German? Do you speak the language?'

'I was brought up to speak it. My father thinks it will stand me in good stead.'

It was true. Her father had big ambitions; he wanted to become a truly middle-class Englishman with lofty connections. He'd wanted that the moment he'd come to England from Germany, a gifted doctor who had fallen in love with Emily

75

Wilson, a girl from Dorset.

Agnes turned thoughtful. 'I have a grand idea. You *will* come to Heathlands for Christmas and seeing as it's your birthday on Christmas Eve, we'll have a birthday party – just us young folk – you, Robert and me. I suppose we'll also have to invite Siggy, Robert's cousin. There has to be one cloud to spoil our day.' On seeing Lydia's puzzled face she added, 'Siggy's full name is Sylvester Travis Dartmouth. Sir Avis's sister married an older man who happened to have a son by an earlier marriage. For some strange reason she dotes on him. Nobody else does!'

'Sylvester Travis Dartmouth! That's a mouthful. And this Robert, who might he be?'

Agnes hid her blushing face as they walked on into the wind.

'He's Sir Avis's nephew and the most wonderful young man in the world.'

On noticing Agnes blushing, Lydia surmised that Agnes was in love.

Printed in black on sparkling white card with gilded edges, the invitations duly arrived courtesy of a special messenger.

Lydia's father was over the moon.

'We are indeed privileged,' he said to her, sliding each card from hand to hand and back again, his face beaming with delight. 'This will certainly be a change from just the two of us dining here, or three if your Aunt Iris deigns to impose on us for another year,' he added with a frown.

'You need to write to Aunt Iris and tell her we are indisposed. Quickly,' Lydia advised.

It wasn't so much that she didn't welcome her aunt's company over the festive season; it was just that she would much prefer to be with Agnes at Heathlands.

'This Agnes. She's the cook's daughter?'

'She is.' Lydia thought of Agnes's manner in that warm kitchen; her haughtiness, her unreserved confidence. Almost as though she owned the place, she thought to herself. She smiled at the thought of it.

'I like Agnes. She's fun,' she said. 'And Heathlands. Imagine a country estate. I think Christmas there will be quite wonderful.'

She said nothing about Agnes's plans for a birthday party but entertained a childish excitement. She was quite looking forward to it. Although she was only two years off twenty-one, she still yearned to celebrate her birth, no matter what her father might think.

'Lydia,' her father began in the kind of tone he always used when about to speak his mind, 'I wouldn't want you getting too fond of her. She is after all merely a cook's daughter.'

Something about his tone, hijacked from his wealthy English patients and friends, irritated.

'I like Agnes. I don't care where she's from. You wouldn't want to offend Sir Avis, would you?'

She knew the answer to that. Of course he wouldn't! Sir Avis was something of a feather in his cap.

He stood tapping the invitations against his fingers, frowning at her whilst he rearranged his thoughts.

'You haven't known her for very long. There are

77

things you don't know about her,' he grumbled.

'Am I likely to be contaminated by these things that I don't know about her?' she asked sharply.

'Her status is … questionable…'

'You mean the status of her birth?'

'Yes. There are rumours,' he said slowly.

Lydia shook her head, feeling a growing unease, or perhaps even nausea, with regard to her father's attitude to class and pedigree.

'I don't care about rumours. What I know beyond doubt is that Agnes is a very intelligent girl. Unfortunately, she's likely to end up doing the same job as her mother simply because of the circumstances of her birth. I must say I think that's unfair, as unfair as women giving birth to children year after year, expected to feed and clothe them on next to nothing, and men seeming to think…'

Her voice trailed away. She looked down at her hands, studying their softness and imagining how red and blistered they would be if she had to skivvy for a living. The Kinskis' house was still vivid in her mind, its smell seeming to be lingering at the very top of her nose where the olfactory nerve ran into her brain.

'You sound as though you have allowed sentimentality to overrule professionalism. It doesn't do to fall into that trap, Lydia, certainly not in a world where the little you can do to help is just that; too little.'

'I still think I can try.'

'Of course you can and I much admire you wanting to change the world. I hope you will.'

'So we are going to Heathlands for Christmas?'

He jerked his chin in a single curt nod. 'If Sir

78

Avis has seen fit to honour me with an invitation, I feel obliged to attend.' He grimaced and his eyes twinkled. 'More fun perhaps than Christmas with your Aunt Iris.'

'*Wunderbar!*'

Her father's sudden grin lit his face, like a naughty boy planning to play truant. 'Let's look at the alternative.'

'Aunt Iris descending on us for the festive season!' said Lydia.

'Not if I can help it,' he said with a rueful grimace.

Placing the invitations behind the mantel clock, her father sighed, took out a handsome pocket watch from his waistcoat, a look of great satisfaction coming to his face as though the time – seven o'clock – gave him great pleasure.

'Time I was going.' He went on to state his intention to change clothes and go to the theatre. 'I may eat at my club,' he added.

'Like a true English gentleman,' said Lydia, whilst thumbing through a recent edition of *Harper's Bazaar.*

She raised her eyes, regarding him with amusement.

Women loved her father, and her aunt was no exception. She wondered at his relationships with other women. He never mentioned anyone; neither had he introduced her to any of his female acquaintances. Perhaps there had not been anyone of note, not until now. She had lately detected a gleam in his eyes. Someone had touched his heart. It was a matter of time before she found out who that was.

Chapter Six

Five days before Christmas, uninvited and un-announced, Iris Wilson arrived on the doorstep surrounded by bulky luggage, namely three brown leather bags and one trunk.

When informed by the housekeeper Mrs Gander that his sister-in-law had arrived, Doctor Miller looked up in dismay from the article he was writing entitled 'Contraception and Family Stability'. The pen dropped from his hand.

Iris breezed in wearing a new coat, a new hat and for the first time he could recall, looking as though she were wearing rouge on her cheeks and dark lines around her eyes.

'Darling Eric. Merry Christmas. I thought I would come early and get things organised. Mrs Gander, you do a wonderful job, but you are ever in need of help are you not?'

'Well, I wouldn't say that...' said Mrs Gander, looking slightly affronted, her chin seeming to recede into her neck.

'Iris,' said Eric, pushing down on his chair arms so that he rose more quickly. 'I sent you a tele-gram telling you not to come and that we – Lydia and I – would not be at home for Christmas.'

No matter how bright her cheeks, Iris's com-plexion seemed suddenly to turn a pale mauve, her lips dark purple.

'Telegram? What telegram?'

'You know very well what telegram, Iris,' said Doctor Miller, gritting his teeth at the same time as trying to wear a welcoming smile. 'I sent you a telegram telling you not to come.'

The fact was he could barely keep his temper; not that Iris made him angry as such. What she did do was irritate, behaving as though she were flighty and empty headed, when in fact she was totally the opposite.

She spread her hands and looked surprised. 'Where are you going? Where else could possibly be as welcoming as home with the family on Christmas Day?'

'This year will be different. We – Lydia and I – have been invited to spend Christmas in the country. A very influential patient of mine owns the house and estate. I cannot turn him down.'

'How important?'

'He's a baronet.'

'Eric! I don't know what to say. This is so unexpected. We've always spent Christmas together – you and I – and Lydia of course.'

Looking to be on the verge of hysterics – which Doctor Miller didn't believe for a minute – she took out a lace-trimmed handkerchief and began to dab at her eyes.

'What shall I do?'

'So why was it you didn't receive my telegram? Were you somewhere else?'

He knew very well that Iris spread herself around in the Christmas season. She visited one relative or friend after another before finally settling with her brother-in-law and niece for Christmas.

'I was with Celia. She hasn't been well.'

Her eyes suddenly took on a contemplative look, as though something about her visit to Celia had been quite pleasurable.

Eric didn't know it, but she had attended a large dinner party at the house of a widower, a friend of Celia's who had paid her court all through the meal. Well, if Eric didn't want her here... Still it always paid in one's personal life as well as in business to hedge one's bets, and she wasn't about to give in too easily.

'Are you sure this is what you want to do?' she asked. Her eyes seemed to fill her whole face and her voice was tremulous – which relieved Doctor Miller; he couldn't possibly have coped if she had burst into tears and fallen to her knees.

In a bid to soothe her disappointment, he suggested they sit down, take a sherry and discuss the matter in greater depth.

Lydia, who had followed them into the study, standing there without saying a word, excused herself, saying she was meeting the friend she'd gone to the theatre with the night before. She'd thought it best to say theatre rather than the picture house, which was acquiring a bad reputation in some quarters due to the amount of courting couples locked in tight embraces in its darkness.

'I'll see you both later.' She beat a hasty retreat before either of them had the chance to ask her to join them; her aunt for some kind of female affinity she did not feel, her father as a shield against his sister-in-law's romantic notions.

'Leave the door open,' her father called after her.

Lydia smiled. Her father wasn't often nervous, but he was when Aunt Iris was around.

Lydia could see into the study from the safety of the first floor landing. Being careful his sister-in-law didn't see, her father looked up at her and grimaced.

'Now, Iris,' he said, adopting his very best bedside manner. 'I do apologise, but that, I am afraid, is the way it is. Lydia and I have a previous engagement.'

Iris Wilson's generous chest heaved with an equally large sigh.

'The thought of catching another train and travelling all the way back...'

She rolled her eyes in his direction before tipping the sherry down her throat.

Unable to suggest how the journey might be improved, Doctor Miller instantly poured her another.

'As I said, Iris, you should have sent a telegram or telephoned to say you were coming. I know you are more in tune with modern inventions than you make out.'

Iris sprang to her feet. 'I quite understand, Eric! My company is not required. I have no option but to catch the next train back.'

'I'm sorry, Iris, but if you had contacted me I would have told you not to come.'

'I do not use telephones. I do not use any of these newfangled devices if I can possibly avoid it. Anyway, they'll never last.'

'People said that years ago about the steam train, but you managed to get on that.'

Her jet and marcasite earrings jangled with

indignation. 'Don't be facetious, Eric. And by the way, my glass is empty.'

Eric apologised and refilled her glass. After replacing the decanter in its tantalus, he paced up and down the room. It was something he couldn't help doing when Iris was around, afraid she might pounce on him if he dared to stand still.

If he could read her mind, he would see he wasn't far wrong.

'I haven't got a tantalus,' she said, eyeing the wooden contraption that locked the three bottles within its grasp so the servants wouldn't be tempted. 'I think I should buy one. Servants are so dishonest. Food, drink, linen and silver; they'll steal anything if they can.'

Eric gulped back his drink. If he hadn't done so, he would have lost his temper. She talked about servants as though they were another species of human being; similar but different.

When Iris Wilson looked at the man her sister had married, something inside her melted. If only he'd listened to what they were *truly* saying all those years ago, he wouldn't have married Emily, the wild one, Emily, the rebel; perhaps, just perhaps, he might have married her instead.

She pushed the upstart thought away, determined to keep her composure. No matter her true feelings back then, she had erected a barrier between herself and the outside world. A woman running the family business had to be better than the men she dealt with. Men for the most part expected women to be docile, intent only on marriage and having children. Rarely did they come across an independent woman who could wheel and deal with abundant confidence and quite regularly beat tough tradesmen at their own game.

When eventually she realised that her unfeminine attitude put men off, youth and marriage had passed her by. Not that she'd cared much for any of the men who had attempted to woo her. Besides, she'd never forgotten that first fluttering of her heart when she'd set eyes on her sister's fiancé.

When he was left with a young child to bring up, she had entertained the hope that Eric might consider her as a suitable companion for himself and a mother for Lydia. But Eric had been devastated at the loss of his wife and even though Iris had suggested she could bring the child up in Dorset, Eric had refused. Iris had entertained the hope that having joint care of Lydia might have warmed his heart to her. Alas, it didn't happen.

Becoming a little light headed, she accepted another sherry, and looked around her. Eric's study reflected the kind of man he was; the chairs were of dark green leather, the desk strong, hard mahogany. A bookshelf ran along the far end of the room, the books' titles etched in gilt down their spines.

A black slate fireplace graced the other end of the room and midway between them two matching windows framed by dark green curtains overlooked the street below.

The room had no curving lines, no fancy lace to impede the light coming through the windowpanes. It was a handsome room, a man's room and even though he was now middle aged, Doctor Eric Miller was still handsome and eminently masculine. No wonder her wild sister had mellowed at the sight of him – though only long enough to marry and produce a daughter.

It occurred to her that even though her looks were more rugged than Emily's were, they might still be a painful reminder of her charming sister. Perhaps that was why he kept pacing up and down, only stopping to replenish her glass.

However, there were compensations for not being the more beautiful daughter. Her darling father had depended on her to run the rank of shops and the lemonade factory they owned and she'd risen ably to the challenge.

'Your health,' Eric said to her, raising what must have been his third drink. She did the same before gulping back half the sherry, feeling it warm the back of her throat.

'Eric, are you sure you're doing the right thing spending Christmas at this country house? Are you sure you won't be overcome with melancholia seeing as it's the time of year when Emily...' She licked her bottom lip and let her gaze fall to her half-empty glass. 'What I mean to say is ... what about Lydia? I have been seriously considering my niece's future. She is also of an age, my dear Eric, when a young girl needs a mother's guidance. There are certain physical aspects...'

Suddenly she felt her face burning and immediately began fanning her face with her hand. She was not comfortable pronouncing the fact that Lydia was now a young woman with a woman's desires.

Eric knew exactly what she meant and almost laughed. 'I am a doctor, Iris, and Lydia is a nurse.

86

She is also a very independent young woman. Do you have any idea how long she nagged me to let her enter the nursing profession? She never gave up. It was what she wanted to do and she's now studying hard. Frankly, I think she will make a splendid nurse. She is also fully aware of what happens between a man and a woman. If the medical books still leave unanswered questions in her mind, she can ask me. After all, my dear, I am in a position to know! More so than you, my dear Iris.'

Iris's indignant expression froze on her face. 'If you are saying that I am not, then that was quite cutting, Eric. And cruel.'

'I'm sorry, Iris. I didn't mean to sound...' He had always tried hard to be polite to her whilst holding her off.

Iris heaved her bosom again and downed the last of her drink. Her cheeks, he noticed, were turning a soft shade of cerise.

'It's all right. I know what you mean,' she said, looking everywhere but into his eyes. 'I have never been married, so am in no position to give advice, but I am a woman, Eric. I am a woman.'

She lowered her eyelids, afraid he might see the longing in her eyes, her desire to know a man's body – his body.

He drained his glass, and poured himself another. He offered her one too. This time Iris declined.

He took a sip, looked thoughtfully into the glass then looked at her.

'Eric,' she said, rising from her chair, the beautiful mauve muslin dress she was wearing lifting

87

softly away from her body as she moved closer to him. Panels edged with purple embroidery fluttered and fell against the taffeta lying beneath. The dressmaker had told her that it was most becoming. She hoped Eric would notice. 'Do reconsider about Christmas. I would not want you to feel sad at this time of year. Send me a telegram if you change your mind and need me to come. You will do that, won't you?'

He nodded thoughtfully and glanced briefly at her before tipping the contents of his glass into his mouth.

She wondered if in that glance he had seen how lovely she looked in this dress. The widower she'd met at dinner had said so. He'd even gone so far as to propose marriage, but she had asked him to give her time. She had to give Eric one last chance first.

Even if all Eric wanted to do was get her out of the house and on the next train back to Wareham!

Chapter Seven

'Christmas,' muttered Sarah Stacey as she bustled around the kitchen, stirring sauces, basting the turkey, making sure the custards and jellies were the right consistency to set firmly.

Peggy, one of the women from the village roped in to help with the preparations, dipped a wooden spoon in and out of the custard she was stirring. She frowned because it wasn't dropping off the spoon, and it was supposed to drop off – wasn't it?

Sarah Stacey's confident tread was near at hand.

'Is that all right, Mrs Stacey?' Peggy asked, wooden spoon poised over the pan.

Sarah took the spoon, dipped it in then held it out. Her eyes narrowed as she waited for the reassuring plop of custard returning to the pan.

'That's it,' she pronounced when it plopped on cue. 'Sir Avis is always pleased by firm custard.'

And firm flesh, she thought as she scanned her steamy kitchen, her thoughts returning to the first time she'd stepped into the house as nothing much more than a drudge, a girl to clean out and lay the fire grates at five in the morning before the rest of the house rose.

She had been fourteen years old, a pretty girl with a fresh complexion, a forest of dark blonde hair, and a body that was filling out with womanly curves faster than most other girls of her age.

Sir Avis Ravening had noticed her bending over the grate and the coalscuttle, her cap slightly askew and smudges of coal dust on her cheeks.

She hadn't known he was there and had hit her head on the cowling once she realised – he'd startled her that much. Despite knocking her head, she sprang to her feet and bobbed him a curtsey.

'Did you hurt your head?' He'd sounded genuinely concerned. 'Here. Let me see.'

Sarah had been terrified, not just of him taking off her cap, his fingers tracing the big bump that was forming on her temple.

'I think you should get Cook to put some butter on it,' he'd said to her. 'Better still, come down to the breakfast room with me and I'll put it on. How would that be?'

With a mind for what Mercer the butler would say, she'd protested, though weakly. Sir Avis seemed such a nice man, far nicer than her own father whose drinking habit had ruined his body and mind as much as the hard work he did.

'Do you want to glaze these sprouts with more butter?' asked Megan, breaking into Sarah's daydream.

'Yes. Butter,' she responded. 'Butter has a lot to answer for,' she muttered as she added a little to the vegetables.

To give Sir Avis his due, though he'd admired her from the start, he'd waited until she was sixteen before he'd seduced her.

'Merry Christmas, Mrs Stacey,' said Quartermaster, popping his head round the door.

'Same to you, Mr Quartermaster,' said Sarah.

His name wasn't really Quartermaster but everyone knew he'd been called that in the army at the same time as the master, and that was what the master still called him so everyone else did the same. It had been either that or inheriting the name Mercer from the previous butler. 'A cup of tea, Mrs Stacey? I've mashed a brew.'

'I'll be right with you, Mr Quartermaster.'

'Ow, that's good,' said Sarah, crossing her slim ankles after sinking into a chair. 'I've been up since four this morning and don't mind telling you my feet are due for a holiday. I can't remember them

90

aching like this last Christmas.'

'Too many Christmases, Mrs Stacey,' said Quartermaster, with a laugh.

He'd been cleaning the silver, his hands suitably coated in white cotton gloves. He refused to entrust this task to any of the housemaids whose job it strictly was. He'd taken these off in order to drink his tea.

Suddenly he sighed.

'I wonder where we shall be next Christmas,' he said, his face drooping with sudden sadness.

When Sarah's eyes met his, she knew immediately that the pair of them were thinking the same thoughts. The lives of domestic servants were inextricably tied up with the people they worked for. That's the way it had always been, and that's the way it would remain. They were like the furniture in the house and could be used or discarded at will.

'Here. I hope,' she said quietly. 'Though I have to say, the master is not well. Not well, at all.'

Pondering her words, Quartermaster studied the process of turning his cup around in its saucer, for no reason other than he was worried, not so much for himself. He was old and had saved what little he could for his retirement. He hoped to move in with his sister who lived not far from Sarah's mother in the East End of London. His savings weren't excessive, but enough to save him from the workhouse.

However, Sarah wouldn't be so lucky. Sarah would be dismissed from her position as cook when the master died, his widow would see to that.

91

With a view to brightening their mood, he said, 'Doctor Miller seems to have done better for him than the others he's had.'

'Yes. There's that,' said Sarah though she only half believed it.

It was true Sir Avis had been a little better since being treated by the new doctor, but Sir Avis had been at death's door prior to Doctor Miller's arrival. His sunken cheeks and his strangled breath still woke her in the middle of the night. (Not that she could admit to Quartermaster so overtly that on occasion she still shared the master's bed, though not since he'd been ill. Even so, she still regularly looked in on him to see if he was all right.)

'I don't know what I shall do when he's gone,' Sarah whispered, her voice cracking with emotion. 'Live with my mother if I can't get another position.'

She looked down into her cup as though she might really see her future there. But it won't be, she told herself. The future was not readable.

Quartermaster reached across and patted her hand. 'Be brave, lass. Be brave. With a bit of luck the master will live a few more years. With a bit more luck her ladyship might reach the pearly gates before he does – or t'other place,' he added with a wishful grin. 'Fact is we'll all benefit if young Mr Robert inherits.'

Sarah smiled warmly and thanked the butler for his kind optimism. 'I was only fourteen years old when I came here, two years younger than Agnes,' she said, her eyes downcast as she considered the passing of the years and all that had happened.

Quartermaster nodded. 'She's like you in looks, but like her father in attitude. Just as when he was young... I'm sorry... I shouldn't 'ave been so bold...' he stammered, suddenly aware he'd crossed an unspoken threshold. He knew of Sarah's history. He also knew his master, his old colonel, so very well.

Now it was Sarah's turn to reach across and pat his hand. 'I know my secret's safe with you – if it ever was a secret. Now,' she said, getting to her feet and smoothing down her apron, 'I'd better get back on the treadmill. I've a Christmas spread to organise, the like of which this old place has never seen before!'

Agnes looked out from behind the curtains in the breakfast room and held her breath. There he was! He didn't leave the servants to deal with his luggage, but joined in with them, slapping them on the back, wishing them the seasons' greetings and asking who was coming and whether they were here yet.

Robert had finally arrived.

She fancied he looked a little taller, more mature, more masculine than the last time she'd seen him. Then he would, she counselled, seeing as he was now at Sandhurst, a capable young man destined to be a capable young officer. If there was ever a war that is, possibly in some far-off land where British soldiers were needed to quell a native revolt.

She was out of sight, hidden behind the curtain, yet she could tell when he smiled in her direction that he knew she was there. Then he was gone.

Another car pulled up behind that in which Robert had arrived.

The corners of Agnes's mouth turned downwards at the sight of Robert's cousin, Siggy, Sylvester Travis Dartmouth; a mouthful of a name for a thickset young man who had hair that was almost white and ice-blue eyes. Unlike Robert, he left the unloading of his luggage to his valet, a short-legged terrier of a man, who scurried along behind him loaded with baggage.

Siggy was also at Sandhurst but might not have been if his family had not paid his way, unlike Robert who would have got there on his own merit if he'd needed to.

The French clock on the mantelpiece chose that moment to remind her that time was getting on, tinkling like a bunch of spoons as it struck the time.

Agnes spun out from behind the curtains. Her heart was racing, her cheeks were pink and all she could think of was finalising her duties as fast as she could.

She'd checked the welcoming snacks laid out on the sideboard, simple things by the standards of many grand old houses: strips of cold pheasant, cheeses, game pie, pigeon breasts stuffed with apricots, apples and sultanas in pastry cases, chocolate truffles covered in coconut, fruits, breads, cold sliced sausage and peeled prawns wrapped in smoked salmon.

She'd also retrieved the port, brandy and whisky from the tantalus, plus port, a dark-red Burgundy and a crisp German white that Sir Avis hoped would please his new doctor.

'There,' she exclaimed with a sigh of satisfaction. Everything was in place, the glasses sparkling, the silver spotlessly clean, the porcelain plates gleaming as though shiny and straight from the kiln.

As she turned to leave, she spotted her reflection in the huge mirror above the marble fireplace. The face and figure looking back at her was something of a surprise. She was wearing her dark blue dress, her white apron and cap. Normally she hated her uniform, as she'd never really noticed how good her pale complexion looked when she wore a dark colour. Her hair was always wild, so it was no surprise to see escaped tendrils curling around her pink cheeks and falling below her jaw line.

It had been her plan to change into something more alluring and less like a uniform once she'd done all she had to do.

She scooped off her cap that had slipped sideways thanks to the thickness of her hair. On a whim, she also removed her white apron. The dress was of good quality and made her complexion look luminous. Her eyes sparkled. Her pink lips parted to reveal pearl-white teeth.

The navy blue dress was simple, but very effective. As an afterthought, she took out the locket Sir Avis had given her. Once again, she studied her reflection, liked what she saw and smiled. A rose needs no gilding, her mother had once told her. For the first time she thought she knew what that meant.

Chapter Eight

It was the twenty-third of December. The guests for Christmas were arriving by car and carriage.

A chill mist drifted over fallow fields, through copses clinging like gauze around the railway station and farm labourers' cottages.

Lydia sat looking out of the window of the taxi that had brought them from the railway station at Ravening Halt and decided that Heathlands was exactly as Agnes had described it.

'Lots of rooms, lots of trees and lots of grass around it.'

'It's very grand,' she said to her father.

'And very old,' he responded. 'It has a lot of history, as does the Ravening family.'

He didn't see her knowing smile. Her father viewed the English upper classes with awe-struck respect. As he never tired of telling her, Queen Victoria was mother or grandmother to most of the crowned heads of Europe.

Lydia was wearing a dark green velvet coat with black braiding at the cuffs and around the hem and collar. Beneath it she wore a white blouse and a green skirt that matched the coat and a red silk bow at her throat. She was feeling good about herself and the outfit had been chosen carefully to match the time of year. It had been a pleasure to leave off her nursing uniform, if only for a few days.

The house dated from Elizabethan times, its facade weathered to a glowing redness, its towering gables seeming to scrape the sky. Diamond-shaped windowpanes looked out on a vista of trees and parkland that had not changed for centuries. Smoke curled from a forest of chimneys, each one different from its neighbour, the brickwork twisted into amazing patterns.

'I feel as though I'm about to curtsey to Good Queen Bess,' Lydia said to her father, her voice bubbling with amusement.

'I think Queen Elizabeth would find you very suitably dressed for the occasion,' he responded. 'That is a very fetching outfit.'

The gravel drive lisped to silence, instantly reawakened as a footman, attired in livery of dark green jacket, white shirt and black pinstriped trousers, rushed to open the car doors.

Quartermaster, the butler, awaited them.

The reception hall glowed by virtue of overhead chandeliers; tiers of lights piled one on top of the other. Lydia held her breath. It was exquisite and like nothing she'd ever seen before. A massive Christmas tree stood straight and tall between two separate curved staircases sweeping down from a mutual landing; like welcoming arms to either side of the tree. Glass balls hanging on the tree re-directed a rainbow of colour around the room.

A footman carrying their luggage followed them in and asked them if they would be so good as to follow him up one of the curved staircases to the landing, where they followed the jewel colours of Turkish rugs along a wide hallway to their rooms.

Affected still by her visit to the Kinskis' house

97

in the East End, Lydia tried not to be impressed, though she was. Sir Avis's London house was splendid enough, but Heathlands astounded her.

'You're next door to each other but there's a bathroom in between,' the footman stated proudly.

She thanked him. Somehow she'd expected the bathroom to be at the end of the landing, or even on another floor. Bathrooms weren't usually given high priority and neither was heating. All she could have expected was a coal fire.

She found herself entering a room that was uncommonly warm, quite the opposite of what she'd expected. Grand country houses were famous for having big, draughty rooms.

Placing her tasselled reticule on to a velvet-covered chair, she stood in the centre of the room, taking in the rose-patterned wallpaper, a massive bow window and the pale pink roses of a Chinese-style carpet, the latter almost covering the dark oak floor.

A dressing table with cabriole legs and a triple set of mirrors stood against one wall, a chest of drawers against another.

Pale silk curtains of pink and green hung in front of the windows and a huge painting of a country cottage surrounded by a rambling garden was set over the fireplace where a coal fire shed its glow over a set of brass fire irons hanging from a tripod to one side of the grate.

Lydia's first thought was to take a bath once she'd unpacked. The footman told her that a maid named Alice would be along shortly to do the unpacking for her.

'I wouldn't want to trouble someone with a task I can do myself,' she informed him.

He had the look of a young man with loftier aspirations than carrying out the tasks he presently undertook. His jaw clenched when he smiled, as though he could be more outspoken if given the chance.

'It's no trouble at all, Miss. It's her job. She expects to be made use of.'

Lydia disliked the comment. 'You make her sound like a pair of coal tongs; useful to convey coal from scuttle to fireplace,' she said to him.

His expression was conciliatory as though he had not noticed her sarcastic tone.

'She is here to be of service – as am I, of course.'

He inclined his head before closing the door behind him. Lydia stared at it while she considered how she was feeling.

She was standing in the middle of the room, unable to dislodge the plight of the poor family she had visited in East London just a few days before. The contrast was frightening: so much opulence for some and such terrible poverty for others. When would it change? What was likely to change it?

Agnes stood at the bottom of the servants' staircase tossing a coin in her hand at the same time as asking herself a very important question.

'Heads I go to Robert's room. Tails I go to Lydia's.'

The result was tails. Agnes turned up her nose, slid the coin back into her apron pocket and headed for the library. Neutral territory. Not Robert's room and not Lydia's either, though she suspected he would be there. He always headed for the library, especially at this time of the year when the gilded lettering on book spines glowed and danced in the flames from the fireplace.

Fir branches, laurel, mistletoe and holly decorated the mantelpiece, their scent mingling with that of apple. It was traditional at Christmas that apple logs burned amongst the coal, filling the house with their pungent aroma.

Robert was stretched the full length of a leather Chesterfield, one foot on the floor, one balanced on the sofa's arm. He was reading a book, one arm folded behind his head, his trouser legs straining against his strong thigh and calf muscles, the result of playing rugby and riding spirited hunters.

He looked up and smiled before his eyes went back to the book.

'Do you live in the breakfast room?' he asked her. 'Or just hibernate in there around Christmas time?'

She sauntered across the room, resting her hands on the back of the sofa so that her shoulders hunched, and her breasts squeezed together. She had a cleavage. Surely, he would notice it.

'Of course not,' she said tartly, annoyed that his eyes were still fixed on what he was reading.

'Never mind. I depend on you being in the breakfast room when I arrive. It means nothing's changed.' He sounded amused though showed no sign of it in his expression.

'Nothing has changed,' she said to him

A slight frown creased his brow when he looked

at her.

'Should you be here?'

'Of course I should.'

'I would have thought your mother would have need of you in the kitchen – you don't have time to spend with childhood friends.'

'I will always have time to spend with childhood friends,' she said hotly, not wanting to face where this was going. 'Unless you want me to go. Unless you want me to spend the rest of my life in the kitchen.'

'Nonsense. That wasn't what I meant.'

'You should be more careful what you say.'

'Oh dear. I sound quite selfish, don't I? Sorry. I suppose I am. I hate the thought of things changing. I'd like us to stay the same forever, but that's not possible. Oh well. Never mind. Now put me out of my misery,' he said, putting the book down and chucking her under the chin. 'So who's here this year besides Terrible Travis?'

Agnes laughed. Robert tolerated his cousin, even making the effort to include him in everything they did, but he didn't especially like him.

'Siggy is here.'

'Don't keep me in suspense.'

Your eyes are so blue, she thought to herself. What are you seeing when you look at me? Are you as enraptured with me as I am with you?

'Who else?' he asked again, sounding as though he suspected she had a reason for hesitating and would prefer not to know what it was.

'The new doctor's here. And his daughter, Lydia. Sir Avis likes this doctor and hopes he might cure him. And I like Lydia. She's a nurse.

Very friendly. Not at all stuck up.'

Robert laughed, his voice a full-blown baritone that made her toes tingle. Even the sight of his neck when he threw his head back like that was oddly erotic, with something vulnerable and almost naked about him even though he was still fully clothed.

'Everyone you might wish to meet will be at supper this evening.'

He frowned. 'How many courses?'

'Seven.'

'Then my decision is made. I hate huge meals of many courses. Please arrange for something light to be brought to my room.'

'I'll bring you something special.'

'Whatever.'

His casual response was disappointing. She wondered if he might be warmer when she took supper to his room. In her heart of hearts, she wanted him to desire her, to lock the door and not let her out. It had never happened, but she lived in hope that one day it would. In the meantime she would contrive to be in his company as much as possible over the Christmas period.

'I thought we could all go for a walk tomorrow,' she said to him. 'You can meet my friend Lydia then. It's her birthday on Christmas Eve and she's never had a party. Sad, don't you think?'

'Very.'

'I think she deserves one,' said Agnes. 'Will you come?'

'Of course I will.'

'Just a small party. Lydia, me, you and... I suppose we'll have to invite Siggy – Terrible Travis,' said Agnes.

Robert heaved a big sigh and went back to his book. 'If there's food and drink involved, just try and stop him.'

'You will come, won't you?'

'Of course I will,' he repeated, settling himself deeper into the padded Chesterfield.

'Then that's settled. I'll arrange everything. We'll have a wonderful time.'

Agnes smiled as she thoughtfully played with the locket at her throat. Time with Robert was always precious. Absorbed in her plans and excited they'd have some time together, she didn't notice Robert's glance and his secretive smile.

'Is she pretty?' he asked suddenly.

'What?'

'This new friend of yours. Is she pretty?'

Out of the corner of his eye, he saw her lips part, her pink tongue licking nervously along her bottom lip.

'I suppose she is.'

'Only suppose?'

Agnes shrugged. 'I'm not a man! I wouldn't know.'

Her tone was sharp. Robert smiled to himself. He knew Agnes cared for him, and he cared for her, though only as a brother might care for a sister. He could never foresee her being anything else.

Robert smiled into his book.

'Very well. Let me know what time this party is happening and I'll be there.'

Agnes stayed by the door. There was something she wanted to say, something she just HAD to say.

103

'Robert. You mustn't fall in love with Lydia.'

Surprised, Robert looked up from his book.

'Good grief. That's a tall order. Do you mind telling me why I shouldn't?'

'Because...' For one bold moment she had been going to say 'because you must fall in love with me', but she couldn't do it. 'You have to establish a proper career before falling in love.'

Robert threw back his head and laughed uproariously. 'I will take your advice, my sweet.'

She smiled, wishing she could stroke the back of his head when he bent back to his book. He'd called her my sweet. She tingled from head to toe.

Feeling warm all over, she began to take her leave.

'Agnes,' called Robert, his attention still speared into his book. 'I have to say you look very fine. Very fine indeed.'

Agnes flushed furiously, though she managed to say a rushed thank you before closing the door.

Once the door had closed behind her, she leaned against it and shut her eyes. Her heart was racing and every inch of flesh tingled. How she ached for him to touch her bare flesh, for his hand to seek out her most secretive places...

She consoled herself with the knowledge that he had noticed what she was wearing. He loved her. She was sure of it.

On the other side of the door, Robert Ravening raised his eyes from his book and frowned. Agnes had indeed looked very fine, the darkness of her dress complementing the delicate pallor of her skin.

He'd also noticed her fingers playing with the silver locket she was wearing. Agnes wore it quite regularly. It was only now it occurred to him that he'd seen that locket, or a similar one, before, hanging around his mother's neck. Perhaps they were two of a kind, he thought. He frowned as another thought took root. Had they been given as a present by the same person?

Chapter Nine

There was a sharp rapping at Lydia's door followed by Agnes floating in and stating that she was here to help her unpack and put her things away.

'I was expecting someone called Alice,' said Lydia, 'though I'm very pleased to see you.'

'I happened to drop a hint with Sir Avis. It's quite easy to put an idea in his head if you know how to go about it. Not that he needed much urging. He has a high regard for your father. I hated to think of you sitting down to Christmas dinner with just your father for company.'

Lydia grimaced. 'No need to. I would have stayed at the hospital. There are never enough staff over Christmas. People still get ill at Christmas or have accidents or have difficulty giving birth...'

'Shall I make a start?' said Agnes, cutting in across her statement whilst eyeing the luggage Lydia had already opened.

'So, what about Alice?'

'I swapped. I told her to help out in the kitchen

where my mother is running around like a headless chicken.'

Lydia eyed her new friend with interest. 'Does everyone in this house always do what you tell them to do?'

Agnes grinned. 'Not always, but Alice prefers to be where the food is. She likes her food, does our Alice.'

'Now listen. A footman will come for the portmanteaus and your trunk once everything is put away. They'll go into storage downstairs until you're ready to leave,' added Agnes, stroking one of Lydia's dresses as she shook out the creases.

Lydia looked towards the window and the gracious parkland beyond. The white mist had thickened, hovering among the top branches of the trees. The sky was leaden, heavy with snow.

'It looks very cold out there.' Agnes went over to the fireplace, picked up the poker and gave the coals a poke until the sides that glowed red were upended and giving out their heat.

'There you are. That should keep you warm.'

'It's a lovely fire and a lovely house. I've never stayed in such a grand house before. Now tell me what I can expect,' said Lydia, flexing her fingers towards the flames. 'There won't be any lords and ladies will there, or royalty? I've never met people like that.'

'Of course not,' said Agnes, shaking her head and laughing. 'First there's high tea in the drawing room or in your room if you're feeling too tired to face company,' she added, counting on her fingers. 'Dinner is at seven and supper is at eleven, if you're still hungry, that is, after a seven-course dinner...'

'Wait! No. I don't think so,' said Lydia, laughing and holding her stomach. 'My corset would give way if I ate all that.'

'Just a light meal in your room?'

'Yes please.'

Agnes continued putting things away, hiding her expression as she did so. She didn't want Lydia to see the look in her eyes, the sudden suspicion that either Lydia and Robert were alike in their tastes, or that they had met before.

'Breakfast is from seven-thirty to nine-thirty,' Agnes went on, hurrying around the room, putting away stays, skirts, blouses and hats. Lydia was dealing with underwear, opening drawers and wondering at the amount of storage she had – certainly too much for the amount of clothes she'd brought with her.

'Lunch is from twelve-thirty to...' Agnes stopped. 'Ah! But you won't be wanting lunch. You're invited to a birthday party.'

'That's very nice,' said Lydia as she unbuttoned her boots, then stopped when she saw Agnes's pixie-like grin. The penny dropped.

'You haven't!'

Agnes's grin grew wider. 'I have. I've organised a birthday party – for you, of course.'

'All this food!' Lydia exclaimed, both hands now resting on her stomach as though she'd already eaten the promised feast.

'You can walk it off. We can go down to the lake. I promise you, you'll love it. And it will do you good. In fact, it will do us all good. Just think of how lovely it will be to return to a warm house

107

with the air smelling of mince pies,' Agnes said brightly.

Lydia thought there was little chance of bumping into anyone at breakfast the next day, spread out as it was over two hours.

A little old lady, wearing a lace cap over silver hair, was huddled at one end of the table scrutinising what looked like a copy of *The Times*. She nodded silently in response to Lydia's good morning.

Her father came down for breakfast after first visiting Sir Avis to check how he was bearing up. He did not wish her a happy birthday; he never had in the past so it came as no surprise that he did not do so now.

'So what are your plans?' he asked after helping himself from the array of dishes set out on the sideboard.

He seemed in an extremely good mood, his cheeks quite pink and his manner cheerful as he attacked a plate of kidneys, bacon, sausage and mushrooms.

'I understand I'm having a birthday party,' she told him, her eyes bright with glee.

He looked slightly taken aback, but recovered quickly. 'Please note that I will not be attending.'

'I'm not sure you're invited. The young people are arranging it,' she added with a smile.

Her father raised his eyebrows in mock surprise. 'Are you insinuating that I am no longer one of these young people?'

'Yes, I am.' She kept smiling, eyeing him sidelong to see how long he could hold out before his face broke into a smile.

At last, it happened; his face cracked with amusement.

She excused herself before rising from her chair.

'Take my advice and don't eat too much cake,' he said to her.

'Don't worry. I'll go for a walk afterwards.'

After she'd gone, he sat looking over the rim of his coffee cup to the French doors on the other side of the room without actually looking through them. Old memories had surfaced when Lydia smiled at him, her head held to one side, eyes shining. Dimples appeared when she smiled. She looked so like her mother, the same laugh, the same lively manner. He missed her mother and hated Christmas Eve.

Lydia retired to the conservatory with a good book. Conversations were all very well, she thought to herself, but there are times when I like being alone.

She was roused from her book at around midday.

Agnes came dashing in, her white apron flapping and her cap perched at a jaunty angle.

'Happy birthday, Lydia. Are you ready?'

Pleased to see her friend, Lydia responded that she was hardly dressed for going to a party.

'There's no time for you to change. Everything is ready. Robert and Sylvester are already here, and if we don't get there right away, your cake will be gone. Come on.'

Lydia followed her out of the conservatory, through a long passage up a flight of stairs, another passage and then another flight of stairs. Portraits and landscapes hung from every wall, gaslights flickered and thick carpet muffled their hurrying footsteps.

Lydia reckoned she was on the third floor of the building.

'Are there no guests in these rooms?' Lydia asked.

'Not bloody likely,' said Agnes. 'This is where the nursemaid, the governess and the children used to live. Children should be seen and not heard, that's what they used to say.'

Agnes stopped dead before one of the doors leading off the passageway.

'This is the old nursery,' Agnes whispered, her eyes bright with conspiracy. 'I shall go in first. Count to ten, then follow me in.'

The door slammed in Lydia's face before she could say another word. She sucked in her lips, wondering whether to run away in case it was all a joke.

She decided that it probably was a joke. If she was so bold as to try the handle, the door would prove locked and everyone inside the room would laugh at her. Perhaps they would keep her waiting here and, in an hour or so, somebody would pop their head out, shout boo and hoot with laughter.

'I really could be doing more interesting things,' she said to herself.

She turned to go, and then paused. Count to ten, then open the door.

Believing she had counted to ten, she clasped the ivory doorknob. It turned. The door opened.

'Happy birthday to you… Happy birthday to you…'

110

Balloons and paper chains fluttered from the ceiling and a hand-painted banner wished her a happy birthday. Better than that, the table in the middle of the room groaned with food, pride of place going to an iced cake.

'Can we eat now? I don't mind telling you that I'm damned famished. That I am!'

The speaker was a young man with the most extraordinary mop of snowy blonde curls. He looked her up and down, muttered something that sounded like 'very nice', and then turned his attention to the food and wine.

It was down to the third person in the room to chastise him.

'Siggy. Be a gentleman and introduce yourself first.'

'Sorry,' said the snowy-haired young man and offered his hand. 'Lydia Miller, isn't it? It's an honour to meet you. I understand your father is administering to dear old Uncle Avis's needs. Quite a doctor so I'm led to believe. Now please, allow me to feed my face and I in turn will pour you a glass of wine. Agreed?'

He didn't wait for her agreement, but went ahead, filling his plate before pouring wine into two glasses – his and hers – leaving out the other people in the room.

'My cousin, who is in a perpetual state of starvation and therefore omitted to mention his name, is Sylvester Travis Dartmouth, otherwise known as Siggy.'

The voice was notable, as in unforgettable and easily brought to mind even when that person was no longer present. She found herself looking up into the most striking pair of blue eyes she had ever seen. The young man was a little taller and a little older than she was. His hair was warm blond and his features firmer and more regular than those of his cousin.

The young man introduced himself as Robert Ravening. 'Cousin to Sylvester there,' he added. The smile he exchanged with her was conspiratorial as if their opinion of his cousin agreed.

Siggy, otherwise known as Sylvester, handed her a glass of wine.

'Happy birthday, old girl. Would you like to cut the cake now? I'm very fond of birthday cake.'

'I suppose so,' said Lydia feeling both amazed at the feast and ashamed she'd doubted Agnes.

The young man with the honeyed voice, Robert Ravening, shook his head. 'Sylvester, you're a pig.'

Agnes handed Lydia the cake knife. Sylvester grabbed the first piece she cut. Robert intercepted it and passed it to Lydia. 'Ladies first, Siggy. Ladies first.'

'Sorry. Forgetting my manners,' said Sylvester who was now eyeing Lydia with far more attention than before.

Robert passed the second slice to Agnes, his fingers accidentally brushing hers. To Lydia's surprise, Agnes blushed. It is apparent, she thought to herself, that the intriguing Agnes likes Robert very much.

Between mouthfuls of food, Robert explained that Agnes had done them proud. 'And we did our best to help things along – at very short notice might I add. I for one thought it was jolly mean that you've never properly celebrated your birthday just because it's the day before Christ's birthday.'

Lydia thanked him graciously. 'I didn't do it on purpose,' she added.

'I doubt you did, dear girl. Your mother must have been miffed at the time too. Imagine wishing for all those presents and being incapacitated and not able to open a single one,' Sylvester remarked as he took another piece of cake and poured himself a second glass of wine.

Agnes turned on him. 'Siggy! You are so inconsiderate. Her mother died giving birth to her, for goodness' sake. I suggest you apologise.'

'Sylvester! Master Sylvester to you!' Sylvester screamed at her.

'Please,' said Lydia, embarrassed at being the cause of the harsh words. 'Please don't. It's all right. He wasn't to know.'

Sylvester glowered at Agnes who, in turn, eyed him haughtily, refusing to look away.

He finally beamed at Lydia.

'You're a true sport, old girl. Quite a looker too. No offence meant.'

'None taken.'

Sylvester rebounded quickly. It was in his nature not to dwell on anything that disturbed him. Sylvester Travis Dartmouth lived to have fun.

'Here,' he said, his joviality totally restored. 'We've made presents for you. I do hope you like them. They're actually Christmas decorations for you to hang on the tree. We made them years ago when we were children and each year we vote for who has the honour to hang them on the tree.

This year we voted for you. It's a great privilege. I do hope you'll accept.'

The mood that had descended on her melted away as Lydia perused the three objects her new friends had made.

'I'm honoured,' she replied, her voice bubbling between words and laughter. 'What do I do? Oh Lord, I don't have to give a speech?'

'No need. Just do as instructed,' said Robert. 'Place the one you like best first on the tree. And just so there won't be any mistake, I made this one.' He handed her a silver star made from cardboard and tinfoil.

Agnes gave her a snowman made out of white cardboard and cotton wool. Sylvester handed over a robin made out of balsa wood. He'd neglected to paint in the features so it was only vaguely bird-like.

'The star's for the top of the tree,' said Robert. 'Hope you can climb up there all right, but if you can't I'll do it for you.'

Sensing this to be a great honour, Lydia took a deep breath before she could say a word.

'Thank you. Thank you all very much.' She hung her head over the gifts. 'They're lovely.'

'I'm not sure they're terribly lovely, certainly not as lovely as you ladies, of course,' said Robert, including Agnes in his compliment but his smile was warm and kindly and aimed solely at Lydia who blushed deeply.

There had been other men who'd looked at her like that, but she'd never felt the same stirring inside before, the feeling that they had known each other forever. She'd read of love at first

114

sight, but surely that only happened in novels?

Stuffed with food and red-cheeked from the heat of the room, Agnes suggested they leave hanging the decorations on the tree until later. Her manner had turned less amiable, more abrupt, though instead of aiming her hostility at Sylvester it seemed to be directed at Lydia. Agnes was in love with Robert but Robert had favoured Lydia with his smile.

'We need some fresh air,' Agnes added.

'I second that,' said Robert.

Agnes's face turned rosy with a grateful blush.

'We could all do with some fresh air. Muffins when we get back I think. Oh, and mulled wine,' Robert added.

Sylvester, whose eyes seemed to be devouring Lydia with as much fervour as he had the food, clapped his hands in appreciation of the plan.

'And when we come back, Lydia will oblige us by placing the decorations on the tree. And if you put my robin on first, my dear Lydia, I insist on kissing you beneath the mistletoe.'

Lydia smiled sweetly, though she wasn't sure whether she'd welcome his kiss.

'But if you choose the star first...' said Robert, 'I shall leave the option with you. All I can do is hope.'

Lydia laughed. 'I will need more than one glass of mulled wine first.' The star, she thought to herself, secretively studying Robert from beneath lowered eyelids. I definitely favour placing the star on the tree first.

Agnes seemed preoccupied in clearing things away.

Lydia began helping her.

Sneering at Agnes, Sylvester couldn't help but make a comment. 'Lydia, you don't need to do that. It's not your job.'

The insinuation was clear; Agnes was just a servant.

'We can all help,' said Robert. He began stacking plates and scraping waste food into a bowl. 'The quicker we get this done, the quicker we can go for a walk and get back to hang our decorations on the tree.' He shot his cousin Sylvester a warning look. 'Don't forget we made those decorations that first Christmas. We played together back then. All three of us. You, Agnes and me. We shall continue to be friends – with, I hope, a happy addition.' He flashed Lydia a magnificent smile.

'I was only saying...' said Sylvester.

'Oh for goodness' sake,' muttered Agnes. 'I'll ask Peggy in the kitchen to clear up. She won't mind. Now come on before it starts to snow. Let's go.'

Chapter Ten

'I swear it's going to snow,' said Robert, sniffing the air as they tramped along a gravel path. 'Never mind. We'll head towards the lake before this mist comes down more heavily. We'll circle it then head past the stable yard and home. Everyone in agreement?'

Lydia declared that she would go where everyone else was going.

'The new girl agrees,' stated Sylvester, a small cigar gripped at the corner of his mouth. 'What a treat you have in store, my dear.'

Lydia wasn't sure whether he was being sarcastic or really meant it.

'I'm sure she'll enjoy the experience,' said Robert. 'Don't you think so, Agnes?'

'Of course she will. There's nowhere in the world like Heathlands. It's heaven on earth – even in winter,' said Agnes, who seemed to keep as close to Robert's side as she could, sneaking a peek at his face, her cheeks rosy and her eyes shining.

Yes. She's in love with him, thought Lydia. Does he love her? She hoped not. Such a short time and, already, she felt the first stirrings of jealousy – and guilt too, given that Agnes had clearly been sweet on Robert first.

Robert's face was harder to read, partly because his white-haired, blue-eyed cousin Sylvester placed himself so that Lydia was always one or two persons removed from Robert.

Sylvester, she decided, had a purpose. She couldn't help the feeling of unease. He struck her as spoilt, the child who had been denied nothing. The selfish child who had grown into a self-centred man.

The path they walked along wound through bushes and down over steps, through an avenue of shrubs that turned this way and that before sloping down to a lake.

Sylvester nudged Lydia's arm. 'We go swimming here in the summer. All three of us. No costumes of course.' He grinned at her salaciously. His

117

implication was clear. He was saying that Agnes too bathed naked with them.

'That was when we were children,' said Agnes flashing an angry glare in Sylvester's direction.

'No swimming today,' declared Robert.

'I hear you're a nurse,' said Sylvester. 'I must say I love to see women in uniforms. There's something very appealing about all that starched linen and being ordered around. If you ever fancy giving anyone a bed bath, I'm your man.'

Lydia felt her cheeks burning.

Robert grabbed his cousin's shoulder, jerking him backwards so they were level, Robert's handsome face looking down into his.

'Siggy, old chap.' He used his cousin's nickname in the same way as a knight might once have thrown down a gauntlet. 'Do you see that lake? Can you imagine how cold it is?'

Sylvester looked dumbly at the lake. It was quite large and fringed with bulrushes. A stone-built grotto bearing more than a passing resemblance to a Greek temple stood at one end.

'If you do not apologise immediately, old chap, I will throw you into that water. No doubt, you will emerge a lot cooler once I do that. Do you understand me, Siggy? Do you?'

Sylvester managed a weak smile. 'No harm meant, Robert. I admire nurses. They do a grand job. A very grand job.'

'Apologise,' said Robert, his fingers now entwined in the thick woollen scarf wound around his cousin's neck, tugging it backwards as though he would throttle him.

'I apologise, Lydia. No offence intended. Do

you forgive me, my sweet?'

His expression was congenial; the look in his eyes was not.

Feeling discomfited and something of an interloper in this group, Lydia made a decision.

'If it's all the same to you, I think I'll make my way back to the house. I didn't tell my father I was going out. He'll be wondering where I've got to.'

Robert offered to go with her. 'You might not be able to find your way.'

'She's not helpless, Robert,' Agnes pointed out.

Lydia sensed Agnes wanted her to go. She wanted Robert to herself.

Lydia shook her head. 'I'm sure I'll be fine. I wouldn't want to spoil your walk. Besides, you three are old friends. There must be lots of things you want to discuss without a stranger listening in.'

Robert smiled kindly at her. 'Lydia, from what Agnes has told me, I don't think you're going to be a stranger to us for very long.'

'I hope not.'

'If you're sure you will be all right?'

'I'm sure,' she said in her most resolute manner. 'And thank you for the birthday party. You especially, Agnes. It was very thoughtful of you.'

She walked briskly away, thinking more about Robert's smile than either Agnes or Sylvester and his silly comments.

She really had felt like an interloper; no matter that Agnes was only the cook's daughter, these three had known each other since they were children. They were close. She, Lydia, was the outsider.

Being the outsider was never easy; her father had

119

told her that. He'd come to England in pursuit of her mother whom he'd met at that lakeside hotel in Austria. Emily Wilson was the reason he'd ended up practising medicine in England.

From the very start, he had made great efforts to fit in and become an English gentleman. He had concluded that to do so he needed to court middle- and upper-class patients. He'd most certainly made his mark with rich patrons without neglecting his poorer patients.

The German hospital in London catered for those of German extraction, mainly sugar workers and Jewish people fleeing from oppression in Europe who had settled in the East End of London.

The East End was a melting pot of ethnic diversity and on those days of the week when he administered there, he slipped easily back into the German tongue. Those he treated worked hard and although they didn't earn much, they maintained that the country they'd settled in was the greatest and most tolerant in the entire world.

He still feels like an outsider, she thought with some surprise as she wandered along the path she considered would take her back to the house. He feels like an outsider, just as I did back there with Agnes, Robert and Sylvester.

The house seemed further away going back and the late afternoon was turning colder. The last leaves were blowing from the trees, scuttling like wingless birds across the ground.

Fearing that the path she was on might not be the right one after all, she looked around her.

The white mist that was earlier hanging like

torn veils from the trees had thickened.

The sensible solution was to go back the way she had come, get her bearings and set off again.

She rounded a stone balustrade, past a huge urn overflowing with dark green ivy and went down some steps. As well as the mist thickening, the afternoon light was fading. She had to hurry.

A sound carried through the mist. She stopped, craning her neck, and called out.

There was no answer.

The cry of an owl, out early for a night of hunting, startled her. She backed into a box hedge, looking from side to side. Agnes had said something about a maze. What if she'd wandered into the maze? How would she find her way out?

Except for an infrequent, shrill cry from something unseen, the beating of her heart seemed the only sound left in the world.

The sudden splash of something landing in water suggested to her that she had come full circle and was back down by the lake. A patch of clearness appeared in the mist. Ahead of her, dark, rocky and overhanging the lakeside path, she espied the grotto.

'Lydia!'

She jumped as a dark figure loomed out of the mist on the side furthest away from the lake. She recognised Sylvester, his hair bright as a candle.

'It's you,' she said, sighing with relief. 'Thank goodness. You frightened me.'

He grinned boyishly.

'Typical girl. You got yourself lost.'

'I didn't mean to. I mean, this is the first time I've been here.'

'So it is. Good for you that I'm around to rescue you.'

'Yes. Yes it is. I don't mind the mist, but I don't like these places.' She nodded towards the dark opening of the grotto.

He laughed and a strange look stole across his eyes as though a sudden thought had come to him.

'Nothing to be frightened of. Nothing at all. Have you heard of the Great God Pan?' he asked, his broad chest only inches from hers, his blue eyes, a blue as deep as that on a willow-pattern plate, looking down into her face.

She nodded, maintaining a brave expression, though quite honestly she didn't trust him.

'One of the old Greek legends.'

'That's right. Pan. Priapus,' he said, his voice almost drooling over the word. 'He was half goat and half man – and he drank a lot. Wine mostly I believe. I do hope it was always a good vintage. I can't stand mediocre wines, can you?'

'I'm not a connoisseur. My opinion wouldn't mean much.'

'Oh, my dear,' he said, his perfect teeth sparkling white in the gathering gloom. 'I think it would. Now, before we go back to the house, I really must give you the guided tour of my favourite place. Don't be afraid. It's only a grotto built by my great grandfather, a very interesting place. I guarantee you'll enjoy it, my dear Lydia.'

She looked around her and saw nothing except mist. It made sense to stay with somebody who knew this place. She followed him along the path they'd walked earlier.

The patch of lake she could see through gaps in the mist looked dark and flat as pewter. Close to the bank, bulrushes rustled in petrified clumps. The rocks forming the grotto towered above them and she jumped when something rattled from within the entrance that yawned as black as an open mouth.

'Don't be frightened, my dear. Just a water vole. I'm with you. Come and see.'

His fingers found hers, his palm hot and clammy as he dragged her closer to the gaping entrance.

'I think we should go back,' she said, digging in her heels.

'Not yet. I want to show you this place. This is where he's supposed to live; Pan's grotto – that's what this is called,' Sylvester proclaimed. 'Oh, sorry. Have I already said that? Well, no matter.'

His grip tightened. He dragged her into the stone building that looked as if it were carved from the solid rock behind it.

The interior was gloomy and an iron grille spanning the interior rang like a bell when Sylvester shook it.

'Would you like to look inside? It's terribly interesting. I did hear a rumour about buried treasure. Uncle Avis knows all about that. He likes your father, you know. Thinks he's the best doctor he's ever had. Did you know that? I wouldn't wonder that he'll be recommending him to all his friends. Now wouldn't that be a feather in your father's cap?'

Sylvester's eyes were bright with intelligence – and something else. When he smiled the corners of his eyes tilted upwards like a fairy creature or

123

a cat about to pounce on a bird.

Calm yourself.

She suddenly spotted the stout padlock holding the gate shut. She gave it a tug, the cold tackiness of the metal apparent even through her woollen gloves.

'It's locked. We can't get in. We'll have to go back.'

'That's right,' returned Sylvester. 'We need a key.'

Out came an iron ring with keys hanging on it. 'I took it from behind Maynard's door when he was showing my mother some flowers. Maynard's the gardener here. Bet I can return them before the old fool notices they're missing.'

Lydia gasped. 'It could get you into trouble.'

Sylvester suddenly burst out laughing, the sound echoing off the cold stone. 'I only took the keys from a servant. Servants don't count when it comes to honesty.'

Lydia was appalled. 'Of course they do.'

Sylvester shook his head. 'I don't think so. But never mind. Are you brave enough to enter Pan's grotto?'

The key turned. The grille creaked open.

The smell was rancid and a dark dampness came out to meet them.

Lydia shivered. 'It's cold.' She wrapped her arms around herself. The Kinski family came to mind. How cold would their house be if Mr Kinski wasn't taken on in the docks?

'A penny for your thoughts,' said Sylvester, the heat of his body palpable and close to hers.

'I was thinking of a family I met recently. A big

family all crammed into a tiny house. It was cold and damp, just like this.'

'Well, that's the working classes for you. Live in a place the size of a rabbit hutch and breed like rabbits. Can't control themselves.'

She turned on him angrily. 'And what do you know about the working classes?'

He leaned closer, his chin resting on her shoulder. 'I know which I would prefer to be, and that's rich and privileged. Which would you prefer to be?'

She moved forwards into the grotto so that his chin fell off her shoulder.

'It smells in here. And it's cold.' She shivered as she took in the gloomy details.

Moss hung like green hair from narrow crevices between rocks coated with watery slime.

'Can you see him?' Sylvester's voice rang like a bell, echoing off the rocky interior. 'Can you see the Great God Pan?'

'Don't be silly, Sylvester. I think it's time to leave...'

She spun round on her heels attempting to brush past him.

'I don't.'

He was a barrier between her and the arched entrance.

'I do,' she said with a determined thrust of her chin. 'I want to go. My father will be missing me.'

'I missed you too. That's why I came back.'

She could barely see his features; his face was in darkness, his eyes no more than deep pits, his head towering over her.

'Humour me. Come into the grotto with me. I

promise you'll find it interesting.'

He took hold of her hand, leading her back into the darkness. Her heart was racing, and the further in she went, the gloomier, the colder it became.

She stopped abruptly just inside.

'This is it. No further. Now what is it that's so interesting?' she asked, her heart pounding against her ribs.

'You are!'

He grasped her face and kissed her fiercely, his fingers digging into her cheeks.

'No!'

She pushed at his chest with both hands, but still he held on to her face.

'You don't mean that,' he said, his voice muffled, his breath upon her face. 'Women never mean that.'

His mouth smothered hers. One arm now hugged her close. Spreading his free hand over her breast, he squeezed – hard.

She beat at him with her fists, but Sylvester Travis Dartmouth had bulk on his side. Hitting him with her fists did no good at all and his hand was reaching for the hem of her skirt.

'You know you want this,' he hissed against her ear. He was preparing himself, spreading his legs and attempting to fumble for the buttons of his trousers with one hand whilst trying to scoop up the hem of her dress with another, using his weight to pin her against the cold, wet rock.

Lydia knew she had just one chance to hit him hard – exactly where it would hurt the most.

First, catch him unawares.

It must have seemed to him as though she was giving in when she stilled and smiled up into his face.

The smile turned into a grimace. 'This is for you, Sylvester.'

In one swift movement, she raised her knee, bringing it up swiftly and solidly between his legs.

He doubled up.

'Bitch!' he shouted, both hands covering his crotch as he staggered backwards through the iron grille.

'Hah!' Lydia's eyes glowed with triumph. 'Women are not chattels, Sylvester. They're not creatures to do with as you please.'

'You led me on!'

'I did not, Sylvester Travis Dartmouth. You tried to force me! You're a cad!'

Even in the gathering darkness, she knew he was looking at her in fury, probably wanting to beat her if he could. She'd heard stories of what rich men could get away with. Some of those women who had been attacked found their way to her father's surgery or the hospital, along with the money for their treatment and some extra to pay for their silence.

The only thing stopping him doing similar to her was the fact that her father was an educated man with friends and patients in high places, notably Sir Avis Ravening, Sylvester's uncle.

A dark, brooding, bent-over figure, Sylvester suddenly grabbed the grille and slammed it shut.

'No!' Lydia wrapped her hands around two of the bars of the grille and shook it.

'I've locked it,' crowed Sylvester, holding the

127

bunch of keys in front of her face but out of reach of her outstretched arm.

'Sylvester, this is stupid. Let me out.'

'You're too hot blooded. You need to cool down.'

Lydia shook her head. 'I won't say anything. I promise. Nobody will be the wiser and my father won't press charges.'

Sylvester laughed. 'What charges? I am a gentleman. All I have to say is that you led me on.'

Lydia closed her eyes and counted to ten. She had to think. If he was so heartless as to leave her here all night, she could die of pneumonia. Like the street people found frozen to death in the doorways of abandoned buildings or children found up on warehouse roofs or ruined cellars, huddling together, only in her case, there was no other body with whom to share mutual warmth.

She also knew from some of the victims of rape brought into the hospital that convictions for rape were rare. *'She led me on'* was considered a fitting defence, even if the victim was little more than a child.

Resting her forehead against the iron grille, Lydia took a deep breath.

'It's going to be cold tonight and this place is running with water. I could be dead by the morning. There would be nobody to blame except you. Have you considered that?'

She tried desperately to gauge his response but couldn't. His face, his whole figure, was now melting into darkness.

Finally overcoming the pain she'd inflicted on his groin, he straightened and re-entered the grotto. He stood close to the bars. She could smell his breath, his sweat and the pungent cologne he wore.

'I'm only leaving you long enough to cool down and consider what we might be to each other.'

'I don't understand.'

'You don't need to understand. You just need to submit. I always get what I want in the end, dear Lydia. Always.'

Fear was like an iron hand gripping her heart. Give in or what?

She rattled the bars of the grille with both hands, screaming and shouting for him to let her out.

'Not until you kiss me.'

'I can't kiss you. I'm in here and you're out there.'

Shaking his head, he wagged a finger in front of her face.

'Naughty, naughty. You think that I need to let you out so I can kiss you, and then you can run away. Now this is what I want you to do. Lean up against the bars and pout. Then I shall kiss you. Now isn't that easy?'

'Then you'll let me out?'

'That depends on how enthusiastically you kiss me.'

She did as he said, resting her face against the bars. He did the same, their lips just about touching in a surprisingly gentle kiss.

It might have been bearable if his hands hadn't also come through the grille to grope at her breasts.

Lydia sprang backwards.

'You disgusting creature!'

He laughed and took more steps backwards until

he was yet again in the entrance arch, the doorway between the interior and the exterior of the grotto.

'I see you need a little more time to consider. Unless you'd like to swear an oath to the Great God Pan?'

Lydia frowned. 'I don't know what you mean.'

'It's quite simple. Just say that you believe in Pan.'

'No. I will not. That would be blasphemous.'

'No, it would not. This is his place, his grotto.'

'Rubbish,' shouted Lydia. 'He was a Greek god. He can't be here! He's dead. He's stone dead!'

'I won't let you out until you say he's real.'

'He is not real! And you, Sylvester, are quite mad!'

Sylvester looked taken aback. It wasn't often that somebody denied him something or refused to do as he wished.

'Then you can bloody well stay there!'

He stalked off then stopped, turned round and flung the keys on to the floor.

Horrified, Lydia shouted after him. 'Sylvester. Come back here this instant!'

Sylvester had made up his mind; shoulders hunched, arms crossed, he set off towards the path that ringed the lake, the bulrushes rustling as he passed.

He stopped at the top of the incline where he'd found Lydia lost by the box hedge. Earlier he'd seen Robert make an impression on Lydia Miller. It was always Robert who made an impression, always Robert who had people – both adults and children – taken in by his charm. Take the cook's daughter for instance; it was obvious the girl doted on him. Well, it was time somebody looked up to him; he was grateful to him. He'd like Lydia Miller to dote on him. He wanted her to admire him, to want him as a woman always wanted a man. He certainly wanted her.

His plan was to let her stew awhile then rescue her. The fact that he'd imprisoned her there in the first place was unimportant. She'd be grateful when he got back to her. She would throw herself into his arms and he would undoubtedly get what he wanted. He always did. He was Sylvester Travis Dartmouth; brave, wealthy and used to getting his own way.

Chapter Eleven

The darkness intensified. Lydia could see little, but she could hear things scurrying into the undergrowth, the splash of rats entering the lake outside. Daytime noises – rustling bulrushes, flapping birds' wings and trout leaping for flies – were different when darkened by night. Even the distant lowing of cattle driven to the milking shed seemed more monstrous when the light began to fade.

From somewhere behind her, deep in the cave, she heard the fluttering of leathery wings.

She'd memorised the spot where Sylvester had thrown the keys, about three feet in front of where she had stood when he'd kissed her. Even in the darkness, she was sure that if she had a stick, she could use it to reach out and draw it back to where she was.

For that, she needed some kind of tool, something long enough and strong enough to reach out and pull the keys towards her.

There was nothing. Everything she touched was wispy and fragile, bits of dried bulrush stalks blown in by the wind.

It was getting colder. Stamping her feet kept her circulation going. Damn that man! Who did he think he was, leaving her like this?

Getting angry helped less than stamping her feet. The truth was that she would freeze if she stayed here much longer. She pressed herself against the bars. Surely someone would come! Someone would miss her, hopefully before Sylvester came back.

Fear as much as cold lurked in the darkness. It crossed her mind that the Great God Pan might really exist, lurking somewhere in the grotto behind her. On the other hand, was he outside, watching for someone to get trapped in his grotto like a fly wandering into a web? She'd read about ancient sacrifices. Did they sacrifice to Pan in ancient times?

'Get a grip, Lydia,' she said to herself. 'Never mind Pan. It's Sylvester you've got to worry about.'

Wishing her hands were around his neck rather than the bars of the iron grille, she gave them a good rattle, hoping that someone might be out there, somebody might hear.

'Help! Help me! Let me out!'

Somewhere a rabbit screamed, an owl hooted and a vixen yelped to her mate.

Lydia leaned her forehead against the iron grille, her fingers clenched around the cold metal.

'I won't cry. I won't cry,' she told herself. Despite her intentions her bottom lip trembled.

Then she heard a sound, faint at first, footsteps disturbing the gravel on the path that circled the lake.

Sylvester! It had to be Sylvester come back to see if she would give in to him. It crossed her mind that for the sake of release from her imprisonment, perhaps she should do that.

'Absolutely not,' she murmured resolutely, then more loudly, so that he could hear and know he had not defeated her. 'Absolutely not!'

'Hello! Is someone there?'

Not Sylvester's voice. That beautiful baritone; once heard, never forgotten. With some surprise, she realised she had already stored the timbre of Robert's voice in her head.

She shouted again. 'Help me. I can't get out.'

The flickering of a storm lantern fluttered like a butterfly around the grotto entrance. And there was Robert's form, taller and more lithe than Sylvester's.

The light was puny, but it was enough to see that it was Robert.

'Don't ask why and how. When I couldn't find you, I beat it out of him.'

'Sylvester locked me in.'

Even in the meagre light, she saw Robert's jaw clench.

'He's nursing a black eye for Christmas.'

Lydia shoved her hand through the bars of the grille, pointing out the whereabouts of the keys.

'The keys are on the floor, just there, right in front of me.'

His sharp eyes found the keys; he swooped on to them and unlocked the grille.

Lydia almost fell into his arms.

'Thank goodness you came.'

'You look frozen. Here, take my cloak.'

The cloak he placed around her shoulders still held the warmth of his body. She snuggled herself into it.

'I take it you got lost on your way back to the house.'

'I did get lost. The mist thickened suddenly and I lost my bearings. I decided the best course to follow was to retrace my steps and start again. That's when Sylvester found me and offered to show me something special. I didn't really have much choice.'

'Oh. Perhaps I misunderstood. Sylvester said you came willingly, kissed him almost breathless and bared your breasts to him.'

Lydia was aghast.

'That's disgusting.'

'You wouldn't be the first.'

'Let us get something straight, Mr Ravening. My father and I were invited here by Sir Avis, not by your cousin. And I think Agnes had a hand in it. If I'd known this sort of thing was likely to happen, I would not have come.' She glared angrily at him. 'Unless this whole thing was contrived by both of you.' The light of the lantern threw patterns on to his face. Robert looked stunned.

'Please believe me. I had no idea.'

He sounded and looked sincere, almost as

though she'd offended him in fact. It came as something of a relief. She didn't want him to be guilty of anything. If that was part of falling in love, then so be it.

They began walking back to the house, their breath steaming from their mouths, fading into the mist. She shook so much her teeth chattered, not from cold but because of what had just happened.

The aftermath of her frightening experience did not go unnoticed. Robert insisted she took his arm.

'We don't want you getting lost again,' he said genially whcn he saw her hesitate.

She pensively linked her arm through his, glancing up at him sidelong, studying the strong jaw, the high cheekbones, the dark blond hair that framed his face. She felt safe with him and there was also something else; a stirring she'd never felt for any man before.

Their clothes were thick and heavy; she found herself wondering how much of Robert's body she would feel if both of them were more lightly clothed ... or even... Suddenly she felt overly warm inside. She needed to curb her imagination.

'Where's Agnes?' said Lydia.

'Helping her mother.'

'You seem very close to her.'

'I've known her all my life. We used to play together when we were children.'

'You didn't mind that she was just the cook's daughter?'

He shook his head quite vigorously. 'Agnes was the only other child living in the household. Sir

Avis paid for her education...'

He stopped as though something had just occurred to him. 'He's very fond of her. He's always been fond of her, having no family of his own.'

'That was very good of him.'

'I think he felt sorry that her father had deserted her mother.'

'She's great fun, and quite ladylike at times. Has she always been like that?'

He laughed. 'Hardly. She's quite a tomboy actually.'

As they approached the house, they espied a figure, hair flying, running along the parapet at the front of the house. The figure, unmistakably Agnes, came to an abrupt stop at the bottom of the steps leading to the front door. She looked alarmed.

'Lydia! Where have you been? I was coming to find you but Robert said that he would.'

'Sylvester locked me in the grotto.'

Agnes grimaced, sniffed and tossed her tangled mane. 'He did that to me once when I was a child. Sir Avis gave him six of the best. He never did it again.'

'I think he's too old to be given six of the best now,' Lydia responded with a grimace of her own.

Sylvester was standing in front of the Christmas tree when they entered the house.

'Lydia,' he said, beaming at her as though they were the best of friends, 'ready to decorate the tree, my sweet?'

'I couldn't reach the keys,' Lydia responded sourly though she couldn't help smiling a little at the sight of the bruise below Sylvester's right eye.

'Another of your little games,' said Robert to Sylvester. 'I swear you get stupider year by year.'

'The girl should be flattered that I paid her such attention. She's only a doctor's daughter after all, and he's a foreigner at that! Anyway, no harm done. All I did was give her a bit of a squeeze!'

Sylvester didn't see the fist coming. It hit him squarely on the jaw. Arms flailing, he tottered backwards, his legs finally folding under him so he lay splayed on the floor.

Robert stood over him, his body trembling with anger, his hair flopped across his face. He pointed down at his cousin.

'Never again, or I'll black your other eye. Do you hear me? Never again.'

Chapter Twelve

'Did you know that Sir Avis's Aunt Peridot is a suffragist? She was one of the very first in fact. I think I might become one too, though I think I could be one of the more violent ones. I quite fancy smashing a few windows and chaining myself to the railings shouting for votes for women,' whispered Agnes.

It was around four in the morning and still dark outside. Agnes and her mother were getting up in plenty of time to prepare everything for the Christmas feast.

Sarah Stacey sighed and shook her head. 'A

suffragist! Whatever next?' She too kept her voice down, keen not to wake anyone until she had everything under way.

Agnes was pulling on her simple navy blue dress followed by a large white apron and cap. 'Then, after changing the world, I'm going to explore it. I think I might even take Lydia with me. We're going to do all the things men do, only better.'

Sarah drew in her chin and placed her fists on her hips. 'I see. Might I remind you that young ladies are not considered ladies if they do the things young men do.'

'But they will. In time. Aunt Peridot has arrived. She's Sir Avis's aunt. It's quite amazing really. He's old, but she's a lot older. Somebody told me she's in her nineties, not that it stops her from getting in trouble. She told me all about the suffragists when I was unpacking her things. Do you know a stupid man can vote on who goes into Parliament, but an intelligent woman cannot? Aunt Peridot thinks it's wrong, and so does Sir Avis. I think it's wrong too. That's why I think I might become a suffragist. I expect Lydia will become one too. Who knows, one of us might become the first woman to enter Parliament. One of us might even become Prime Minister. Imagine that.'

'I can't.'

Sarah Stacey shook her head. If there was one thing guaranteed to both amuse and worry her, it was her daughter relating how she saw her future. However, not this morning, and not just because there was so much to do.

'I dare say you will make your mark on the world, Agnes,' she said merrily, though still speaking quietly. 'Though I think a woman being Prime Minister is hardly likely to happen in this century or the next. In the meantime we have things to do. Puddings to steam, a stuffed turkey to put in the oven.'

The kitchen smelled of rich fruit steeping in brandy, the aroma coming from six cloth-wrapped puddings, all awaiting the steaming pan.

'That's a lot of puddings, Mother.'

'Four or five for the staff party. I think one will be enough for the family.'

'There,' said Agnes with a satisfied sigh as she lowered the first pudding into the first of three steaming pans big enough to take two at a time. 'If Sir Avis is feeling a bit better, perhaps he'll have some too.'

Sarah looked away so her daughter could not see the worry in her eyes.

'I dare say he might, depending on how he's feeling,' she said. 'Now give me a hand putting this turkey in the oven.'

Agnes looked sidelong at her mother. She'd always darted around the kitchen at breakneck speed, but today her movements had quickened. Once one task was finished, she immediately started on another. It was as if she didn't want to waste a minute talking or thinking about what she had to do next.

'Slow down, Mother. There's plenty of time,' said Agnes.

'I'll be the judge of that,' her mother snapped. 'Now get on with those sprouts.'

Agnes could not read her mother's mind, but if she could, she too would have been worried.

139

Sarah Stacey was no doctor, but she knew Sir Avis well. She knew how healthy he used to be, how frail he had become.

The appointment of Doctor Miller had given some respite, but in her opinion he'd come along too late to do anything except make the old man's last days comfortable.

And there was something else.

Late the night before, the sound of somebody, at the front door came as something of a surprise, despite the time of year when all manner of guests and staff were coming and going.

Quartermaster, looking forward to dousing the lights once Master Sylvester had drunk himself into a stupor, and then getting himself to bed, heard the front doorbell reverberating through the house, and went to investigate.

Earlier that day he had been feeling quietly optimistic that this would be the best Christmas ever. He'd just taken a cup of hot chocolate laced with brandy up to Sir Avis and had been delighted to find him still sitting upright in bed, almost his bright and perky old self.

There was something about that bell. Perhaps if it had been the old-style bell, a cast-iron monster, he might not have heard it. However, the old master did so love modern inventions, especially anything electrically driven.

The electric bell made a soulless sound, a thin buzzing noise that wasn't remotely like a bell, more like the buzzing of a giant bee caught in an equally giant spider's web.

'Who the devil is it on a dirty night like this?' he'd muttered, thinking as he slid back one large bolt at the top, one at the bottom, that no one of any good travelled on nights when the mist was thick as a pea soup.

'Good evening,' he said in a far brisker manner than he normally used. 'Ah! Mr Credenza. We weren't expecting you...'

He had been hoping that the traveller – who-ever it was – had lost their way.

The moment he saw the dark man at the door, he knew his worst fears had come true.

'Good evening, Quartermaster. Would you tell Sir Avis that I'm here and would discuss business with him?'

'Certainly, Mr Credenza. Do you have luggage?'

Rudolfo Credenza, Sir Avis's brother-in-law, boasted dark Spanish features, heavily hooded eyes and a nose that looked big enough to peck the meat off a dead hare.

Moreover, thought Quartermaster, that is ex-actly what he's come for. He's heard the master is dying and, given the chance, he'll pick the bones clean.

Quartermaster had found Sir Avis still awake and asking who was at the door.

'Your wife's brother. He says it's regarding a business matter.'

Sir Avis's brown eyes, still bright with intelli-gence despite his debilitating illness, looked up. Whereas his hair was white, his eyebrows had remained dark, a fitting accompaniment to the velvet brownness of his eyes.

His smile was thin but sincere. 'It's Christmas. We'll put up with him, won't we Quartermaster?'

Once Lady Julieta's brother was supplied with a

141

room and supper of oxtail soup, cold chicken, bread and butter, cake, coffee and brandy, the old butler stomped along the landing meaning to inform Sarah. He found her halfway up the stairs, on her way from the kitchen to her bedroom.

'Rudolfo is here.'

It was all he said. All he needed to say.

Fear gripped Sarah Stacey's heart like cold fingers squeezing the life out of it. What would happen to her when her benefactor – Agnes's father – was gone?

She shook herself back into the present and the preparation of the Christmas lunch and, stabbing the wooden spoon deeper into the mince pie filling, she stirred afresh. Concentrate on the here and now. Let the future bring what it may. She'd cope with it when it came.

Looking up at the ceiling of the ballroom at Heathlands was like gazing at a star-spangled sky.

'Splendid, isn't it?' said the doctor, his noble head tilted backwards so he could better behold the spectacular ceiling.

'It's like Ali Baba's cave in *Tales of the Arabian Nights*,' Lydia whispered.

She had to agree with Agnes that Christmas at Heathlands was quite magical. Every room in the house sparkled with light from the overhead chandeliers. The smell of the apple logs piled high in the fireplace of each reception room vied with that of oranges, rich fruit puddings and freshly picked greenery.

A second Christmas tree, far larger than any normal house could cope with, gleamed with balls of coloured glass, each one reflecting light from myriad candles rising in tiers to the very top where Robert's silver star looked slightly shabby but oddly fitting.

'It's beautiful,' she whispered, gazing at the sheer opulence of the room and its decorations. 'And yet it makes me feel guilty. So many people have so little. I live a life of contrasts.'

Her father, this man who mostly looked dour with his sad memories at this time of year, agreed that it was beautiful. 'Lydia, please remember that only a fool worries about that which he or she cannot change,' he added.

Through the warmth and glitter, her eyes met those of Sylvester. He smiled and raised his glass. Lydia's smile vanished. The nerve of the man, smiling as though what he'd done was just a joke.

She'd weighed up the consequences of telling her father what had occurred in the grotto, but had decided against it. This Christmas was so different from those in the past. They were together in a jolly environment and Doctor Eric Miller's star was rising. Rich and influential people would follow where Sir Avis led. Besides that, she had never seen him looking so happy. It cheered her immeasurably.

No, she decided. Let it be. Sylvester had behaved badly. Robert, on the other hand, had rescued her and in doing so had stirred her emotions in ways she had not experienced before.

They learned that it was traditional for the staff to have their party before sitting down for a late dinner. Household staff and estate workers were enjoying themselves dining on rich food and cups of mulled punch served from a silver bowl big enough to bathe a baby in. A barrel of cider made from apples picked from the Heathlands orchard had been set up in a half-hidden corner tended by men with ruddy faces and stiff white collars. Everyone was dressed in his or her best.

Lydia was wearing a mint-green dress decorated with tiny seed pearls. The neckline exposed her shoulders and enough of her décolletage to be enticing but still decent.

The eyes of staff and guests had flickered in her direction when she'd entered the room. Sylvester was the first in line to greet them, acknowledging and saluting her father like an officer and a gentleman before turning to smile down into her face.

'You look quite enchanting, my dear. Good enough to eat in fact.'

He licked his bottom lip, making Lydia decide that he had every intention of devouring her if he could. She would not put herself in a position where he could take advantage of her again.

'Oh, I don't think you want to get quite as close to me as that. I think I may be coming down with a cold,' she murmured, glaring up at him.

'Is this the young man responsible for you being late back last night?' asked her father.

'Yes,' she responded sharply, but did not elaborate. Her father had been content with only half the story.

'I hear he's of good family, Sir Avis's nephew in fact.'

'By marriage only.'

Her father grunted. She fancied he was impressed, perhaps even thinking Sylvester might possibly be a suitor for her hand.

The room was wide, glistening with light and packed with people.

Even before she saw Robert, she knew he was there, as if he was longing to see her just as she was longing to see him.

Somehow, she'd known exactly where to look for him. Now all she had to do was get to him, but the room was crowded.

Staff and estate workers were milling around on the dance floor, all laughing and chattering at once. There was no break in the crowd, no sudden surging aside to let her through. At times, it seemed as though the crowds were no more than blobs of colour, subdued pieces of their surroundings. There was only the two of them, the light in each other's face. Lydia smiled at him. He smiled back, raising his glass in a soundless toast.

The conversation and jolly songs erupted into three cheers welcoming the arrival of Sir Avis Ravening. Quartermaster pushed his bath chair in. The bath chair had been sitting in a corner of the house for weeks, but Sir Avis had shunned its use until his weakness had finally outstripped his pride.

He waved to everyone, his hands pale as weathered bones, and a rug across his legs. Unlike some patients Lydia had encountered in her brief nursing career who were close to death, his face was not skull-like, his smile stretched across his teeth. On the contrary, his eyes were merry in his broad face, his mood jovial, but his complexion was as pale as unbaked bread.

'It's like the old family Christmases I used to

know,' he cried in a voice that cracked between words. The laughter that followed was short lived, replaced by a bout of phlegm-filled coughing that only receded once he'd downed a brandy. Sir Avis had insisted that the Christmas feast would be exactly that; there would be no cutting back simply because his stomach wasn't as strong as it used to be.

'No milky puddings and eggnogs for me,' he declared as Quartermaster wheeled him to the head of the table.

Crooking his finger, he beckoned his new doctor. 'As for you, Doctor Miller, please do not tell me to drink only water or weak tea. Pour me another brandy, Quartermaster.'

Doctor Miller shook his head. 'Sir Avis, I would advise that you adhere to the prescribed diet.'

Sir Avis waved away his advice. 'It's Christmas. I am over three score years and ten. I am on borrowed time. I shall enjoy these last years doing the things – most of the things – I have always enjoyed doing...'

His eyes misted with memories and his lips spread in a thin smile as he whispered in the doctor's ear.

'I have loved life, and I shall continue to do what I can,' he said finally.

The cook, Sarah Stacey, Agnes's mother, took Quartermaster's place standing behind the wheelchair, her smile a little too tense to be one of happiness. Out of sight of prying eyes, the tips of her fingers brushed his shoulders. He was slipping away. She wondered how long it would be until he was gone, and prayed he would be around a little longer, long enough to ensure that she and his daughter were taken care of.

Sir Avis's Aunt Peridot, a doughty woman with weasel-like features and chips of agate for eyes, who wielded an old-fashioned pince-nez as if it were a decorative fan, was the first to wish him a Merry Christmas.

'Same to you, Perdy,' he responded as she kissed his cheek.

'Make the most of it. I may not be here for the next one,' she shouted at him.

'Don't shout, Perdy. You're the one who's deaf, not me, and anyway, you said that last year. You're still here. And so am I.'

'Good God, man. What are you saying? Do you want me to promise not to be here next year? If that's what you want, you need to have a word with the Good Lord above. He's the one in charge of whether I'm on earth or in heaven – or elsewhere,' she added with characteristic gruff wit and a flicking and clicking of her pince-nez, though the clicking could just as easily have been her arthritic wrist.

The pince-nez was gold rimmed and loose at the joints, snapping shut when she least expected it to. When a person or occurrence took her eye, she snapped it open with a flick of her wrist. She did that now, peering at her nephew then slamming it shut with an air of finality.

'It's far too stuffy in here. I'm off to the conservatory; red cheeks are only for young girls.'

Out of sight of those present, she swiped a tear from her eye whilst muttering that old age was not for the faint hearted.

Sarah Stacey stood pale faced and shaking behind Sir Avis's wheelchair, watching Rudolfo Credenza prowling the room like a caged tiger looking for a meal.

Unexpected and uninvited, the man had bowled into the house late the previous night. Sarah was in no doubt that he wasn't there to wish the old man the greetings of the season. Like his sister, Sir Avis's wife, he never did anything unless there was something to gain by doing so. The reason had to be that news of the master's illness had spread to Brighton where Lady Julieta was biding her time until Sir Avis died.

Husband and wife had neither seen nor communicated with each other for years. Sir Avis tolerated being married to her, but preferred her at a distance. He didn't like her and that was that.

'So perish the thought of loving her. And who,' he would ask with a twinkle in his eyes, 'would want to go to bed with a woman who prays her husband will depart from sin?'

Aloof in both appearance and manner, Rudolfo circled the ballroom, carefully avoiding estate workers and household staff for whom he had nothing but loathing.

Of all the most outlandish ideas, he thought, holding a party for the estate workers was the most outlandish of all. Let them eat their own Christmas dinner bought with the wages they earned. He had always entertained the view that his brother-in-law was too generous by far.

He sought out the few guests who didn't have work-worn hands or smell of carbolic soap.

Robert, Sir Avis's nephew, Rudolfo thought was

148

polite but not over friendly. Sylvester he regarded as 'promising company', in that he was very much like himself. His main ambition in life was to feather his own nest, though at this stage, Sylvester did appear to have some scruples left. Rudolfo surmised that as he got older, the young man would become more self-indulgent, vainer and ultimately more vulnerable to his own vices. Sylvester Travis Dartmouth was a typical son of the English upper classes, a man living in an insular environment, the ugliness and poverty of the outside world kept firmly at bay.

Tiring of conversation with Sylvester, his dark Spanish eyes searched the room for more interesting company. He principally wished to meet Sir Avis's doctor. He knew immediately he had found him when his gaze landed on a tall, distinguished figure, impeccably dressed and smiling a lot. The young woman standing beside him was quite striking, a vision in a pale green dress.

Out of the corner of his eye, he saw Sarah Stacey. She had strayed from the protection of Sir Avis, who was presently slumped in his wheelchair, halfway between wakefulness and absolute fatigue.

'Mrs Stacey. You are still here.'

Sarah eyed him as though she wished she could kill him with one look from her violet eyes.

'Yes, Mr Credenza.'

She nodded a brief welcome, one she didn't feel. 'An odd time for you to arrive,' she said to him. 'Your business with the master must be very urgent indeed.'

'My business with Sir Avis is none of your concern,' he said coldly.

149

'The master's health *is* my concern.'

'Mine too. And my sister's.'

'I don't doubt it. I'm sorry to disappoint her, but he's been better of late and likely to be here for quite a while yet,' she said, though she didn't believe that to be the case at all. Still, she would not give Julieta the satisfaction of knowing that Sir Avis was growing weaker day by day and close to death.

Rudolfo's face, a structure of angular cheeks, a long chin and deep-set eyes, stiffened. His nostrils, like black pits of indefinable depth, flared in anger.

'My sister's husband has invited me to stay and as for the urgency of my business that is for him to judge, not his cook!'

Sarah's voice trembled and a terrible coldness came over her, as though her skin had been touched with frost.

'I care for the master's health as well as his stomach...'

'And warm his bed too!' Rudolfo's eyes narrowed, his black hair gleaming beneath the lights of the room, as though it were one expanse painted on to his skull.

'I will say only this to you, Mrs Stacey,' he hissed. 'My sister never forgets or forgives and neither do I. Do I make myself clear?'

The coldness Sarah felt intensified. 'You make yourself very clear, Sir. I wouldn't expect anything else from someone who knows no better. Breeding will out, as they say over here. A lady has to be born a lady; marrying into it is not enough.'

She saw his jaw clenching and knew she had gone too far. But she couldn't help herself. The arranged marriage between Sir Avis and Lady Julieta had been destined to fail. Sir Avis was by nature a philanderer who loved women – all women; he was not and never had been husband material. Sarah understood that but loved him and accepted him as he was.

The moment when she thought Rudolfo might shout, or hit her, passed. He collected himself, drawing in a deep breath as though he were swallowing all her comments, digesting them for future reference.

Eventually he said, 'Let's hope there's not too much of a scandal when he passes. I take it the stately looking gentleman over there is this Doctor Miller that I've heard so much about.'

She nodded, her warmth returning, her blood seeming to flow and warm her veins again. 'Yes. Doctor Miller, Sir.'

'And the girl? Who is she? His daughter or his wife?'

A wave of supreme satisfaction swept over him when he heard the young woman was his daughter.

'Pretty. For an English girl.' His black nostrils flared over his thick, dark moustache.

'She's half German. Doctor Miller is from Dresden.'

'Really?'

'His daughter is a nurse.'

Rudolfo turned back to make another sharply observed comment, but Sarah Stacey, having no wish to spend another minute in his presence, had fled.

As she always did when she tired of the big

151

parties and a host of invited guests, she headed for her kitchen. The heat from the ovens would keep the kitchen warm all day and through the night too.

Still shaking following the confrontation with her ladyship's brother, she opened the door from the kitchen to the scullery where she slumped on to a stool, covered her face with her hands and cried.

'My dear.' Rudolfo Credenza took hold of Lydia's hand and kissed it.

Lydia felt the coldness of his lips through the fine cotton of her elbow-length gloves.

Eyes that dissected as much as looked at a person, studied her further, even when he was speaking to her father.

'I hear you have done a very good job of keeping my brother-in-law alive, Doctor Miller. He sings your praises regularly.'

The truth was that the first time he'd heard Sir Avis sing the doctor's praises was tonight, but Rudolfo had never been a man to let truth get in the way of expediency.

Lydia felt her flesh prickle beneath the gaze of the dark eyes that were so hungrily devouring every inch of her.

Rudolfo might be darkly handsome and elegant of manners, but she instinctively didn't like him. He was, she decided, a man who used flattery to inveigle himself with those he wished to trust him, an arrogant man who possessed a high regard for himself and contempt for others.

'My dear Sir,' said her father, preening his own

thick moustache with one hand, whilst holding a wine glass in the other. 'Your compliments are very much appreciated. I have done the best I can for Sir Avis, though as you may or may not be aware, he is very poorly.'

'No doubt Sir Avis will trumpet your good services among the upper classes and your fame will spread far and wide as a result of that.'

Lydia noticed her father positively bloomed in response. He was making inroads with the landed gentry, and that could only serve him well. 'I am glad to be of service.'

Rudolfo jerked his chin at Lydia. 'A skilled man with a beautiful daughter. Perhaps we could dance later.'

'Do excuse me, but not tonight. I have a headache.'

She felt her father eyeing her in disbelief; the dashing man with dark eyes and long chin looked disappointed.

'Never mind. Another time perhaps.'

His attention went back to her father.

'I feel we have met before. The theatre perhaps?'

Doctor Miller sipped at his sherry. 'I do go to the theatre on occasion, although of course I am a busy man...'

Lydia detected a distinct change in his expression, a dot of red rising on each cheek. He looked suddenly boyish as though rightly accused of raiding an apple tree.

He had indeed been attending the theatre a lot more of late. Was something – or someone – attracting him there?

'Of course,' said Rudolfo. 'Perhaps somewhere

153

else. I like the theatre very much. I like the pretty actresses, so refreshing I think.'

Doctor Miller looked unsure how to answer. 'I wouldn't really know,' he said at last. 'Do excuse me. I must have a word with my daughter in private.'

'Come,' he said to Lydia, his hand resting on her shoulder.

'Who is that man?' she asked.

'Sir Avis's brother-in-law.'

'What did he mean about seeing you before? About the theatre?'

'You know I like to attend the theatre.'

She noticed the flush had spread slightly.

'Do you know any actresses?'

'No! No! Of course not!'

They left the heat of the room for the coolness of the conservatory where he dabbed at the sweat that had broken out on his brow.

Lydia regarded her father carefully as she realised the likely cause of her father's embarrassment. 'Who is she?'

'What?'

He looked astounded.

'The actress.'

'How dare you?'

Again the flushed cheeks, the denial in his voice, but not in his eyes.

Lydia sighed. 'Father, it's none of my business. If that's what you want, then so be it.'

Robert, who had come in to ask her for a dance, interrupted them.

She went with him gladly, though not before throwing her father a tight smile and a comment about doing whatever made him happy.

Doctor Miller stood there once she'd gone, thinking about how he should deal with this.

Rich patients were the lifeblood of his profession. They had the wealth but they were also fickle, determining that the lower classes should abide by a moral code they themselves were more likely to break.

Rudolfo Credenza worried him. His face was familiar. He had an inkling that Rudolfo knew his actress friend Kate. Perhaps he was even one of the many admirers she had been friendly with before taking up with him. Eric grimaced. He knew how narrow minded and superior people could be. The fact of the matter was that he couldn't give her up and neither could he hurt her feelings. He was infatuated with her and that, he realised, was a damning fact.

The party for Sir Avis's employees had ended, the estate workers returning to their homes to while away their evening in front of a fire, stupefied by food and drink.

Following a brief respite, the domestic staff was back on duty, catering to the needs of their employer and his guests.

A cold buffet was laid out in the dining room. Satiated, Lydia only picked at it. Only Sylvester piled up his plate and went back for a second helping.

At last, even he was full, sprawled out in a chair by the fireplace, legs akimbo, loud snores coming from his mouth whilst his aunt played cards with the other invited ladies.

Eric Miller had asked if anyone would like to play a game of snooker.

The last person he expected to join him was Aunt Peridot. He looked somewhat alarmed at the prospect of playing a woman.

'She'll beat you,' said Robert, his eyes shining with amusement, his smile directed at Lydia.

Once they were gone and while Sylvester was still snoozing, Robert took hold of Lydia's hand.

'Ghost stories. A piece of pie down in the kitchen and ghost stories.'

'You tell ghost stories?'

'It's traditional.'

With her hand clasped tightly in his, they ran all the way along the passage on the first floor landing.

He stopped in the shadow of a large armoire, its carved frontage swirling with leaves and clusters of acorns.

Before Lydia could think, Robert's lips were pressed on hers.

'I couldn't help myself,' he said to her. 'I've wanted to do that all day.'

Lydia stroked his face. 'And I had to wait all day.'

'Come on,' he said, grabbing her hand again, dragging her down the stairs through the servants' hall and into the kitchen. The air was still thick with the rich smells of turkey, gravy and vegetables and the range was still hot, the room warm and cosy.

Agnes was sitting in an armchair to one side of the fire with her feet up. She smiled directly at Robert, though she froze on seeing that he was

156

holding Lydia's hand.

Sarah, her mother, who had been hard at work since early that morning, sat dozing in an armchair, her head resting on her hand.

'Ghost stories, Agnes!' Looking pleased with himself, he pulled up two more chairs and settled down, his fingers linked across his trim waistline.

'We always tell a ghost story at Christmas,' he explained. 'Sylvester's usually here with us, but at present he's in the land of nod. You know him,' he said to Agnes with a wink. 'Too much food and too much drink. I didn't have the heart to wake him.'

'I bet you didn't. So who's first?' said Agnes. Her features had turned quite wooden in her effort not to show her hurt. Robert looked at Lydia quizzically. 'This is how it goes. I tell a ghost story, then Agnes tells one, and then you do.'

'You do this every year?'

'We do,' said Agnes, 'though it's usually only the two of us, three if you count Siggy,' she added, almost as though it couldn't possibly work with more than that number. 'You first,' she said to Robert.

Robert took a deep breath, sat back in his chair, crossed one leg over the other and began his tale.

'There was once a lordly knight who lived in an old house like this. He was having an affair and deeply in love with his best friend's wife, but wouldn't hurt him for the world, and so they carried on in secret.

'Everything might have continued like that, until a murder occurred in the local town. Witnesses said the murderer looked just like the

157

knight. At his trial, he said nothing in his defence, but looked as though his thoughts were elsewhere. The truth was he'd been in his lover's arms that night. She had not stepped forward to give him his alibi but he loved her so much, he would not betray her.

'He went to the gallows without saying a word in his defence. He would not declare the truth; he'd been in the arms of his best friend's wife. And so he was hanged.'

Robert leaned forward, his eyes looking into Lydia's, his elbows resting on his knees, his hands reaching for hers.

'When the night is dark and the wind wails forlornly, his lover still visits his grave to this very day, asking his forgiveness for not speaking up, and declaring she will love him forever.'

'Scary,' said Agnes, barely suppressing a shiver. 'Now me. The old master of this house, centuries ago, once seduced a lowly serving maid. In fact, she had a child by him, but when he decided to marry a rich American heiress, he had the maid and the child walled up, down in the cellars. And there they are to this day, nothing left of them except skin and bones. Every so often, you can hear the baby cry and the woman beg for something to eat. But the poor things, it's too late. Sylvester is staying and he's gobbled everything up.'

'Ha!' cried Robert, throwing back his head, his laughter loud enough to wake the dead.

Tears of laughter trickled down Lydia's face.

'Now you,' said Agnes. 'Can you tell us a ghost story?'

Lydia didn't regard herself as much of a story-teller. 'I don't know. I'm no good at telling stories.'

Robert smiled at her, bending forward so that she could smell the brandy on his breath and see little flecks of silver in his eyes.

'Just tell us something to scare us. Something we don't know much about.'

So she told them about the Kinski family she had visited in the East End of London, of bugs walking up the walls, of children with no shoes, ragged clothes and little to eat.

'They're not ghosts,' Agnes protested.

'Not yet,' said Lydia, her expression sad as she gazed into the fire.

She could feel that Robert was eyeing her silently. She didn't raise her eyes to meet his gaze because she wasn't sure what she would see there. He might think she was weak in the head. What was it her father had said? Only a fool worries about what they cannot change.

'You're very brave,' said Robert. 'I don't know what this world would be like if it wasn't for people like you.'

'I think you're brave too,' said Agnes, gazing up into Robert's eyes, her hand resting on his knee.

Chapter Thirteen

The following morning the white mist that had been as diaphanous as a curtain thickened. The parkland, the trees, the green, and even the stable-yard clock, became shadows, grey forms in the breathless white.

It had snowed during the night. This morning the world was hushed beneath a blanket of whiteness; no birds sang. There was no wind, no sound of cattle lowing or movement over the gravel drive. It was as though the mist had drowned everything in silence.

Quartermaster stalked along the landing, his footsteps light, despite his bulky frame. Every morning he did the same, carrying Sir Avis's breakfast tray with both hands. The contents of the breakfast tray never varied; porridge liberally laced with sugar and brandy, a boiled egg, one piece of bread and butter, plus a little marmalade. A pot of tea would follow on a separate tray, though not until he had eaten whatever he could manage and given it time to digest.

Setting the tray down on a convenient side table just outside his master's bedroom door, Quartermaster raised his fist and knocked.

There was no answer. The butler did not consider this to be unusual as Sir Avis was a heavy sleeper and hard of hearing.

Following his usual routine, he knocked on the door for a second time and turned the knob.

'Breakfast, Sir,' he said as he always did, holding the silver tray before him.

Again, there was no response.

After setting the tray down on an oak coffer used to store blankets, Quartermaster flicked the light switch. Nothing happened. No electricity. He didn't question why, but lit the oil lamp that was sitting on the bedside table, a box of matches beside it.

'Sir?'

Leaning over the bed, he reached for his master's shoulder. Shook it.

The flesh was cold. Hard.

He straightened slowly. The moment he'd long dreaded had finally come.

It was hard not to break down. Quartermaster was a man for whom duty to Sir Avis ranked alongside breathing to stay alive. They had served in the army together, a bond had been created, and the old man had made him his butler even though he'd not been born into the role. They'd been brothers in arms. That was all.

'Goodnight, old friend,' he said softly.

Doctor Eric Miller was called from his room some minutes later. After donning his dressing gown, he grabbed his medicine bag and rushed along the landing.

The first sign to the rest of the household that something was wrong was Mrs Stacey running through the house and down to the kitchen.

The second was Agnes banging on Lydia's door, falling into the room when Lydia opened it.

'He's dead,' she said, sounding as though she couldn't comprehend people dying at all. 'Sir Avis is dead.'

'Oh, my darling,' said Lydia feeling instantly sorry for her friend. 'Come in and sit down.'

Agnes's vibrant expression was absent, replaced by a stillness born of shock and disbelief.

Lydia bit her lip as she considered what to say next. 'I'm so sorry. He was such a nice man and very good to you.'

'He won't be here any longer. My future is in

161

ruins. I don't know what I'll do now.'

'Everything you always wanted to do.'

'I'm not sure,' said Agnes biting her bottom lip. 'I certainly don't want to remain in domestic service. At least I got to drive the car now and again when Thompson was off. Sir Avis thought it marvellous that I could. But now…?'

Lydia thought about what might be best to say at such a time. What were the right words? Where would she find them?

'Where will we go?' said Agnes.

Lydia clasped both Agnes's hands. 'What are you talking about, you silly goose? You'll still be here. I don't suppose your mother will mind working for somebody else too much.'

Agnes pulled her hands away from Lydia's and began picking at the embroidered roses on the bedspread.

'It won't be the same.'

'Lydia.'

His voice sounded hollow, as though he were shouting to her along a low, narrow tunnel.

He had caught her running along the gallery, a landing of oak-panelled walls that would have seemed menacing if not for the plasterwork ceiling of leaves and roses in the Tudor fashion.

The gallery was long, lined with doors on one side and lead-paned windows on the other. Persian rugs muffled the sound of her footsteps, so he couldn't have heard her coming. Robert had been waiting for her.

He beckoned her from a doorway, his body blanketing the details of the room behind him.

162

'In here,' he whispered.

The atmosphere at Heathlands had changed, and because of this, she looked up and down the landing, thinking somebody might appear and tell her she was doing wrong; tell her she had no respect for the dead, entering a room in which she knew she would be alone with him, with Robert Ravening.

Thick curtains prevented any light entering the room. Only the white dustsheets, greyish in the subdued light, were noticeable.

Robert wore an expression of sadness.

They stood there with about a foot between them, both searching for the right words to say.

'Are you packed?'

They were not the words she'd expected from him, but she answered in the same, dull tone.

'Yes. I am.'

With the exception of family, everyone was leaving Heathlands.

'When are you leaving?'

'Within the hour. My father has done the necessary. The funeral directors...'

She stopped herself from saying that the funeral directors were dealing with the embalming of Robert's uncle.

'Lydia. I do know what happens next. My uncle enjoyed his life and I want to enjoy mine. I think I want to enjoy it with you – no – I *know* I want to enjoy it with you.'

Lydia folded her arms across her chest and regarded her fingers. 'I don't know what to say. We hardly know each other and this isn't really the right time...' She also worried about Agnes's

163

feelings. It was clear her friend had a crush on Robert.

'My uncle said that first impressions count. He also said that I should grab an opportunity with both hands. Never wait for tomorrow in case it never comes.'

Lydia felt her fingers tapping at her elbows and still refused to look up into his face.

'Look, your uncle has just died. Don't you think...?'

'Uncle Avis would approve. I've just told you why. You know what he also said to me? That the most exciting moment of one's life is that moment you think you're going to die. He said it happened to him when he was in the army on a number of occasions. That's why he was so keen on living life to the full and grabbing the moment.'

Moved by the passion in his voice, Lydia looked up at him. 'We are not at war, Robert. And you are not in the army.'

'No. I'm joining the Royal Flying Corps. Haven't you heard the rumours? Germany is arming herself, ready to take on the British Empire and wanting to dominate Europe.'

'Germany?'

Lydia thought of her father; a worldly yet kindly man. A man who had settled in England for the love of her mother. She'd heard rumours, seen her father's worried frown as he'd read the headlines in *The Times*. When she'd asked him what was wrong, he'd commented that France was worried and so was Russia. He'd looked shaken and a little puzzled. It had occurred to her that he might wish for them to go to Germany.

'This is all so unreal,' said Lydia. 'Like in a fairy tale.'

He smiled. 'I quite like the idea of being Prince Charming. I don't know about you, but I feel that we've known each other all our lives. We were just waiting to meet.'

'I'm not so sure about Cinderella.'

'Perhaps you're the Sleeping Beauty and I'm the passing prince, immediately taken with you. Was he called Prince Charming too?' he asked with a laugh.

Lydia shook her head. 'I'm not sure.'

'You don't have somebody else, another admirer tucked away somewhere?'

She shook her head again. 'No. I thought you were in love with Agnes. I mean, you two have known each other all your lives.'

'Darling Lydia. I knew from the start you were a compassionate sort of girl. Agnes has been my dearest companion since I was a child. All three of us grew up together, me, Agnes and Sylvester, though quite honestly we could have got along well enough without him. We would probably have got fatter for a start.'

Lydia threw her head back and laughed. Clearly Robert must be unaware of Agnes's interest in him. That, however, didn't stop her feeling a frisson of guilt as Robert ran his thumb down her exposed neck. She knew the kiss would come even before she felt his lips on hers. All thoughts of Agnes flew out of her head as he kissed her. She also knew he was speaking the truth when he murmured something in her ear about love at first sight.

'Permit me to call on you,' he whispered once their kiss had broken apart. 'Once we leave here.'

She agreed, of course.

Not wishing to be indiscreet, she left the room before he did, walking briskly along the gallery wearing a stupid smile. Anyone who came across her might think her uncaring at the death of Sir Avis, or even drunk. She was, in a way: Robert felt the same for her as she felt for him. He'd even suggested becoming engaged. In the past, she might have questioned such a hasty proposal, but now she didn't. Life was there for the living, and she intended to live it.

Her smile faded when she considered his comment about going to war with Germany. He didn't know her father was German, or if he did, he didn't care. However, that was now. What would happen if they did go to war? What would happen to her father? What would happen to them?

Chapter Fourteen

Agnes awoke, blinking into the darkness. What time was it? She knew what day it was. New Year's Day. The master's funeral and less than a week since his death.

Her mother made a point of waking her up every morning, but not today. She had not called or shaken her from her slumbers, and yet it must be late.

She glanced at the curtains. Even though it was

winter and still dark, it was possible to judge how long she'd been asleep and what time it was.

Seven, she decided, swinging her legs out of bed. It had to be seven and way past the time she usually got up.

Things had changed at Heathlands since the master's death. The servants whispered amongst themselves and Thompson, the chauffeur, was less guarded than he used to be, sniggering and blowing puffs of smoke in her direction, even though he knew she hated it.

'Making the most of your last days 'ere,' he shouted out to her as she wandered down to the lake.

She didn't bother to answer him. Deep down she knew very well that the world she had always known was about to change, but then, the master himself had told her when she was very small that the world she knew would change as she grew up. He hadn't said anything about his dying, but then he hadn't needed to.

Robert, Sylvester and their respective families had returned the night before. So had Lady Julieta and her brother.

One of the maids waiting on table had re-marked how the mood at dinner was black.

'As black as her ladyship's brother's hair. Mind you, he didn't seem too sad if you judged him by the amount of port he was knocking back.'

Quartermaster had warned her to watch her tongue. She was there to be of service to the family, not to gossip about them. 'The atmosphere will improve once this is all past,' he said.

His tone was confident, but Agnes had seen the

167

worried look he'd exchanged with her mother.

The hearse pulled up outside the main door of Heathlands pulled by four black horses. Feathered plumes bobbed between their ears and black velvet cloth covered their flanks. The day was cold and their breath steamed in the cold air. A horse-drawn hearse, not a motorcar, would convey the remains of Sir Avis Ravening to his final resting place.

Agnes thought he would have preferred a motorcar. Rumour had it that his wife, now his widow, was responsible for the ostentatious show of mourning, the ornately carved vehicle with its etched glass and jet black japanning that gleamed like satin even on a dull day like today.

The older members of the family would travel to the church in the car, younger members and staff walking behind the hearse.

In the kitchen, Agnes watched her mother fussing nervously over the funeral luncheon. Sarah Stacey was pale faced and bleary eyed above the stiff blackness of her collar. Her hat was already on her head, bobbing around like a stuffed bird as she went about her duties. Between overseeing the kitchen and checking that the dining room sideboards were suitably groaning with food, she checked Agnes.

'Oh, dear, oh dear. Why do you never look lady-like in a dress?'

Agnes rolled her eyes upwards and sighed. 'I'm not made that way.'

'Of course you are. You can look really pretty when you try.'

Agnes pouted. She didn't want to try. Anyway,

what was the point of looking pretty at a funeral? Sir Avis wasn't there to see her and nobody else would care.

Her mother was embroiled in the battle of getting Agnes's collar to lie flat when she spotted the locket and recalled that it had been a present from Sir Avis. He'd given it her for her seventh birthday.

'Nothing that glitters,' she said, her fingers already searching for the catch. 'It's not seemly.'

'Sir Avis gave it me for my birthday. I'm sure he wouldn't mind me wearing it to his funeral,' Agnes said tartly.

Sarah Stacey was about to insist, but changed her mind. If people saw the lovely locket with the Ravening coat of arms, they would know it meant something, especially if they heard that Sir Avis had given it to Agnes. A seed planted in those minds in which gossip had not yet taken hold. The locket would confirm that Agnes was indeed his daughter.

'Why not indeed? It's Sir Avis's funeral and the locket was a present from him. That's what we will tell those who notice it.'

As she turned away she muttered, 'Let them see. Let them all see and know.'

Agnes felt a sense of foreboding. There had always been comments whispered behind cupped hands, always smug asides that hinted at the status of her birth, that the 'husband' her mother spoke about was a made-up person, someone unreal.

The kitchen was empty, but even so Sarah Stacey seemed to fill it with her buzzing around, with her need to be occupied so she wouldn't break down, so her grief wouldn't show.

169

Agnes felt her mother's anguish and it saddened her.

Lighten her spirits. Make her think of something else. Make her retaliate about something less important.

'I suppose I have to wear that dreadful hat. The black straw one with the elastic under the chin?' she said, sounding as though the hat was some kind of torture device – which it was in a way.

She knew she had to wear the itchy, wide-brimmed hat, but she wanted to get back to mundane things, to have her mother back in the routine of complaining about Agnes's unfeminine foibles.

The ploy might have worked if it hadn't been for what happened next.

'You know very well that you have to...'

The kitchen door swung open, instantly extinguishing weak squares of sunlight falling from the panes of the adjacent window.

A dark-eyed woman, her hair frosty white and fashionably coiffed, stood in the doorway. She was clad in a black dress scattered with jet beads that sparkled when she moved. The collar of her blouse was high and stiff, black like the collar on Sarah's blouse. Rigid like the one worn by Queen Mary.

The hawk-faced Rudolfo Credenza stood at her shoulder, half a head taller. His eyes and brows were as dark as those of the woman and so was his hair.

All thoughts of hats and lockets flew from Agnes's mind. She followed her mother's lead, nodding at them and wishing them good morning.

'You look quite lovely,' she said to the woman,

170

then bit her lip. It wasn't what she'd been planning to say, but too late, it was out.

Never mind. It was still far superior to a plain old hello or good morning. All women liked being flattered didn't they?

The woman's eyes, black as the jet beads glinting on her dress, glowered in her direction before fixing on her mother.

Reading pure venom in that look, Agnes instinctively felt duty bound to protect her mother no matter what. If she'd been made of milder stuff, she might have shuddered or hid behind her mother. She did neither. She wanted to know who this woman was and what she'd read in that dreadful look.

'Pack your things, *Mrs* Stacey. I want you and your child off the premises by noon,' said the woman, her voice as cold as the wintry day.

Sarah Stacey swayed and reached for the edge of the table in order to keep herself upright. 'But I have the food to deal with...'

The face and voice of the woman in black remained frosty. 'Other members of the kitchen staff can deal with that. I want you out of here. Now!'

'But the funeral... Surely, you wouldn't begrudge me paying my last respects?' Sarah Stacey held one hand over her breast as though she were suddenly having trouble drawing breath.

'Under the circumstances, I begrudge it very much! I want you gone from here. And take your brat with you.'

Her foreign accent, a mixture of Spanish and American English, served to make her tone even sharper.

171

Agnes's mother shook her head in disbelief. 'He wouldn't have liked this. It isn't right and you've no right... I will see Master Robert... He wouldn't treat me like this.'

The woman in black stepped forward, her face flushed, her eyes fiery with hate. They faced each other, both scowling, each harbouring great resentment towards the other.

The woman in black tossed her head. Her nostrils flared widely, just like those of her brother.

'Heathlands and the town house have passed to me. They will be mine as long as I live. They will pass to Master Robert on my death. In the meantime, I will do with them as I please; that includes dismissing and hiring what staff I please. You do not please me, Mrs Stacey. Go. Go now. And take your bastard child with you!'

'How very informative,' Agnes piped up suddenly. 'You have just confirmed what I'd started to suspect, what clearly everyone around me has always known, that I was born out of wedlock and that Sir Avis was my father. I thank you for that! However, I will not have you speaking to my mother like that. It is totally uncalled for.'

The dark, furious eyes stared unblinking, the corners of the woman's mouth twitching as she sought to regain the higher ground. Frightening as her presence was, Agnes did not flinch.

The twitching lips finally spoke. 'Get out of my house, the pair of you. Get out now before I send for the constable and accuse you of stealing the silver. I'm sure you have stolen things over the years. My husband would not have noticed. He was a fool. Nothing but a fool who had this insane

172

belief that everyone was equal. Well, I know they are not. A servant is a servant. A slut is a slut. Now get out!'

Mother and daughter moved closer together, an act defining their solidarity.

'I am not a slut,' muttered Sarah, gritting her teeth so hard they hurt.

'And you are a harpy,' yelled Agnes.

Lady Julieta's eyebrows rose almost an inch. 'Harpy? What is this harpy?'

Agnes took great delight in explaining. 'A mythical creature with the face of a woman and the claws of a monster. And leather wings and a beak to tear a man's heart out.'

Round eyed and blustering for breath, Lady Julieta exploded. 'Get them out of here. And oversee their packing. I want everything accounted for. They will take nothing that isn't theirs.'

With their luggage loaded on to the back of a cart, they headed for the railway station. Sarah's request for a lift to the station was denied. Sarah was in no doubt that Lady Julieta was exacting revenge in any way she could, her treatment meant to put Sarah firmly back in the lower orders where she belonged.

Agnes and her mother trudged tiredly beside the cart, eyes downcast, their black-gloved hands clasped tightly in front of them.

Agnes sensed her mother's tears, though there was no sound of sobbing, and no wailing that she didn't know what would happen next.

She reached out and squeezed her mother's arm.

173

'We will survive. I can work. You will see how I can work.'

'She won't give us references. Can you believe that? That old bitch would sooner see us starve.' Sarah felt she was choking with despair.

'But Robert will. I have his address. He'll give us a reference.'

She heard her mother blow her nose. There was quiet for a time as Sarah Stacey digested what she had said.

Finally, after mulling it over, she managed to speak.

'It's worth a try. Of course it might mean we end up in different households...'

'That isn't what I was thinking. I thought we could both live with Gran in Myrtle Street. And I wasn't thinking of being a kitchen or parlour maid. I want to drive a car.'

Her mother shrugged herself down into her shoulders and said that Agnes would never get a job driving. 'You're a woman, Agnes. You will only get women's work, looking after a household, laying tables, cleaning silver...'

Agnes was fierce in her response. 'No. I will not do that. I will get a job driving, you just see if I don't. Sir Avis said I could do it.'

Sarah covered her eyes with splayed fingers, rocking backwards and forwards as though that would console her. 'He shouldn't have told you all those things...'

Agnes sighed and transferred the bag she was carrying from one hand to the other. Her mother would grieve for some time, wishing she'd done things differently perhaps, even to wishing she'd

174

married a respectable man who worked hard for a living and didn't inflict modern ideas on his children.

'Know your place,' she'd often said to Agnes.

Agnes knew what it meant, and it bridled her sorely. The world of servants and masters was close to disappearing; Sir Avis had told her that. Her mother couldn't see it. Much as Sarah had loved him, she had never really understood that Sir Avis had had foresight.

It was different for Agnes. They had talked together, just the two of them in the conservatory. He had been the biggest influence on her life and she would always remember him.

'They all think our world of privilege and possessions, the British Empire and all that, will go on forever,' he'd said to her. 'They all think that women will never get the vote or own property in their own right or do all the things that men do. But it will all happen, my darling girl. So never be afraid of change, Agnes. Your life will be full of changes.'

Still thinking her own thoughts, Agnes fell behind a little as the cart swung between high, unclipped hedges, the road narrowest here before widening again.

The crispness of the morning air pinched at her cheeks as she regarded her mother's rigid back, as tight as a corset holding everything in.

She's gone through a lot for me, Agnes thought to herself. She never gave up on me, nor on Sir Avis. We were both dependent on her. Now she's dependent on me. I have to get a job. I will get a job, but one of my choosing.

175

The road widened. Agnes caught up and slid her hand into that of her mother's. 'It'll be all right, Mam. You see if it isn't.'

Sarah Stacey swiped at her eyes.

'Yes. Of course, it will. Everything will be fine.'

Chapter Fifteen

Eric Miller watched as Kate Mallory pulled off each garter and then her stockings. A true actress, who knew her audience well, she did it slowly, meticulously, bending this way then that, allowing him delicious views that even married men seldom had of their wives.

Soon she was dressed in nothing but stays and drawers; he helped her off with both before leading her to the bed. His bed.

'And now,' she said, her voice husky with promise as she lay full stretch beside him.

He had initially felt guilty at having another woman in the bed he'd once slept in with Emily and had suggested using the guest room.

'Your servants will know,' she said to him. 'Do you want them to know?'

Of course he didn't.

'We'll be careful,' she said to him. 'We'll leave no evidence and I'll be gone before dawn. Your servants will come back from their day off completely unaware that your ... paramour...' she said, clicking her tongue between her teeth, 'was ever here.'

The arrangement was working out wonderfully

well, thought Eric as he drew Kate into his arms. They only went to bed at his house on the servants' day off and when Lydia was on duty at the hospital.

Kate had reawakened something in him that he'd thought was dead. Yes, she was an actress and his colleagues in the medical profession would no doubt condemn him as immoral to consort with her. They would suggest he give her up before society was scandalised and no longer sought his services.

Kate caught him grinning as he stroked her naked back, his chin resting on the top of her head.

'What's so amusing?' she asked.

'I was just considering how an old lady once said that she greatly appreciated my skills in the bedroom. She was actually referring to my bedside manner.'

Kate snuggled up to him, her lips brushing his chest, her eyes bright with desire.

'I rather think she had it right in the first place. Your skills in bed are very good indeed!'

Sister Gerda leaned over the woman lying there so white and so still.

'She collapsed on the steps outside. She also left a trail of blood behind her. I have detailed a porter to mop it up.'

The senior sister's eyes met those of Lydia, a young nurse who had made her mark here and not just because she was the daughter of a doctor. All the senior sisters had agreed that she was a good nurse. They also liked her, as did the patients. It helped with the latter that she was pretty.

'It makes our patients happier when a nurse is pretty,' Sister Ursula had said.

Sister Bertha had rolled her eyes in an indulgent rather than exasperated fashion.

The three women looked down disconsolately at the pale-faced woman lying bloodless and spent in the bed.

On the stand beside her, pink-tinged water floated in an enamel bowl.

Sister Bertha addressed Lydia. 'You know what caused this.' This was not a question but a statement.

Lydia swallowed and nodded. 'Yes.'

Sister Gerda shook her head. 'Poor woman. I cannot condemn her, and I will pray for her in chapel.'

Lydia sighed. 'A woman has to be desperate to destroy the child she is carrying.'

She felt angry. How could a woman do that? *She* wouldn't. Even if the man refused to marry her, she would not destroy her child.

Sister Bertha's sigh brought her back to reality. 'She's lost a lot of blood – and the child too of course. Will you speak to her when she comes round and ask for her name and address? We have to let somebody know.'

Lydia's eyes met hers. Without her saying a word, Sister Bertha understood and shook her head.

'No. We will not tell the police.'

The sentence for aborting a child was harsh, for both the abortionist and the victim, the loss of the child recorded as a miscarriage, but murder

178

in the eyes of the law.

Lydia checked on her patient all that night, creeping along the ward in semi-darkness, mopping the poor woman's damp brow, changing her dressing when necessary.

Placing her age at around forty, it was a foregone conclusion that this was not her first pregnancy. Nobody liked to hazard a guess, but the average for a woman of this age and class was four. It would come as no surprise if she had more children than four, but until she came round they couldn't know for sure.

The sad thing was that nobody had come looking for her, yet it was no secret that women in a delicate condition quite often made their way to this particular hospital.

It was around three in the morning when Lydia heard a weak call for water.

Getting up from her desk in the middle of the ward, Lydia went to the woman. Her eyes were deep set and bloodshot, her jowls hanging from her jaw like an elderly matron.

She was looking up at Lydia, her mouth opening and closing as though she was desperate to say something.

'Shhh,' said Lydia, smoothing the woman's brow. 'You've lost a lot of blood. If you'll give me your name and address, we'll let your family know. Can you do that? Can you tell me your name and address?'

The woman's voice was barely above a whisper. Lydia got closer, turning her head to one side so the woman could whisper into her ear.

'My name's Edith Allen...'

It was eight in the evening, the end of a long day, when Lydia was told she had a visitor.

'She's waiting by the front door,' said Sally, the girl she roomed with when working the night shift. 'Fiery sort, your friend. All reddish-blonde hair and insisting she wouldn't be moved until she'd seen you. Even Sister Bertha backed off and you know what a tartar she can be.'

The fatigue Lydia had been feeling lifted at the news that Agnes was here. She'd heard from her father that Sir Avis Ravening's widow had fired both the cook and her daughter. Lydia saw the familiar figure immediately. Her hair was still as wild as ever and she was neatly dressed in a navy blue suit with a white collar, a fox fur nestling around her shoulders, a navy blue hat decorated with blackbirds' wings ungainly on her vast expanse of hair.

'Agnes! I thought I would never see you again. What are you doing here?'

'You don't mind me coming here, do you?'

'Of course not. I heard what happened. Where are you living? What are you doing?'

'I'm living with my mother at my grandmother's house, and as for what I am doing – as in for a living – well, that depends on you.'

'On me?' Lydia shook her head. 'How? What?'

'I'm looking for a job. Not in service. I certainly don't want to do that. I've got the chance of a job at a factory – better pay than domestic service, but I have my heart set on driving. I was wondering ... perhaps your father might know of someone?'

Lydia considered the prospect of asking her

180

father. 'He may do. I will ask him. I promise...'

'I thought I might ask Robert, but it isn't easy. Not now we're no longer in service to Sir Avis.'

Lydia said that she thought that was a great shame. She made no mention of her conversation with Robert following the death of Sir Avis. Neither did she mention her subsequent meetings with him for lunch, for tea, for dinner, any way they could meet. Any mealtime. Any event. Soon she would have no choice, but for now, she put it off, telling herself that the right moment would come when Agnes wouldn't be hurt so much.

'Sister Lydia!'

The voice of Sister Bertha boomed across the arched atrium followed by her formidable presence.

'I'm just going off duty, Sister. My friend Agnes...'

A curt nod went by way of greeting. 'Good day.'

Agnes did the same. 'Good day.'

Lydia sucked in her lips to prevent herself from smiling. Agnes was as forthright and cheeky as ever.

'Edith Allen. Has she gone home yet?' said Sister Bertha.

'No, Sister. She's given us her name, but not where she lives.'

'Edith Allen?' Agnes looked from Sister Bertha to her friend Lydia. 'I know an Edith Allen. She lives in the same street as my gran. Myrtle Street. Next door in fact. What's wrong with her?'

'She's had a miscarriage,' said Lydia before the senior sister could say anything else. 'She's still weak. We have to get her out of her bed and home.'

'Now would be best,' said Sister Bertha. 'Only she has no taxi or bus fare and we have nobody here to drive the ambulance.'

'Well, that's no problem at all, Sister,' exclaimed a bright-eyed Agnes, her fingers visibly twitching at the thought of getting behind a steering wheel again. 'I can drive her home in the ambulance if you like. I am qualified,' she said when Sister Bertha's plump forehead fell in a lumpy frown.

'I'm not sure we can allow that.'

'So how else will the poor woman get home?' asked Agnes.

Sister Bertha looked from one young woman to the other. The young woman who had offered to drive the ambulance was unknown to her. However, she had a very open mind about what jobs women could or could not do. She also had a very flexible approach to getting things done.

'Doctor Miller will vouch for me,' Agnes declared in a very refined manner. 'He attended my late benefactor, Sir Avis Ravening. I have great faith in Doctor Miller's skills, as he has in me.'

Sister Bertha's frown lessened. 'Very well. I have no objection if Doctor Miller can vouch for you. I'll phone him right away.'

It was apparent from Edith Allen's expression that she was not happy to see Agnes. Her features, already washed out, went paler and her eyes filled with alarm.

'You won't tell, will you? I collapsed. I had the flu and passed out. That's what you have to say.'

'Of course,' said Agnes, too excited at the prospect of driving the ambulance to worry about

182

Edith's troubles.

She helped Lydia get her into the back of the ambulance where Edith lay down gratefully.

Lydia pulled a blanket from one of the overhead lockers and placed it over her.

'There. You'll be back with your family before long and they'll be none the wiser,' she said.

'How 'bout 'er?'

She managed to bob her head at Agnes who was tucking the end of the blanket beneath Edith's feet.

'She's sworn to secrecy,' said Lydia. 'Aren't you, Agnes?'

'Not a word will pass my lips,' Agnes stated in a dour manner that Lydia would never have thought her capable of managing.

Lydia declared she would stay in the back with Edith while Agnes drove. 'We'll catch up with our news at the end of the journey when you take me and the ambulance back.'

'I would love to keep the ambulance you know,' said Agnes. 'I don't suppose there would be any chance of a job...'

Lydia sighed. 'It would be lovely to have you working here. I can't promise, but I will try.'

Lydia settled herself in the back of the ambulance opposite Edith. The poor woman wasn't too well and had no idea how close she had been to death. Whoever had performed this abortion was breaking the law. Someone said there had been another woman with Edith helping her up the front steps.

'Looked like a flower seller. She was carrying a big basket over her arm – a trug – a big trug like what flower sellers have.'

Lydia had some questions to ask.

She started by calmly stroking Edith's forehead and telling her that everything was fine now.

'You had a nasty experience. You could have died. The person who did this has to be stopped. The next time they do it, somebody might die. Who was she, Edith? What was her name?'

Edith rolled her head to one side so Lydia could not see the look in her eyes.

'I daresn't tell you. I promised.'

'Have you any other children, Edith?'

Her nod was barely perceptible.

'How many?' asked Lydia.

'Seven.'

'How old are they?'

'Albert's thirteen. He's just started work. Told them he was fourteen. Beatrice is eleven, George is ten, Oswald is eight, Teddy is six, Gertie is four and Gladys is two. Then there's our Harry. I had him years ago before I met Cyril.'

'So that's ten of you.'

Edith nodded.

Lydia didn't know the exact size of the house Edith lived in, but guessed it wasn't big – no bigger than the one lived in by the Kinski family.

'And this woman, the one who helped you get rid of your baby. Does she live in Myrtle Street too?'

Edith's eyes stared up at her, the alarm that had abated now returning.

'No! You won't tell anyone, will you? I had to do it. I couldn't cope with another mouth to feed. I really couldn't.'

184

Lydia persisted. 'So where does she live, this woman?'

She hated to upset Edith, but she'd heard at the hospital how many women came in following abortions carried out by someone with little knowledge. Not all of them survived the ordeal. Some carried the scars, both physical and mental, for the rest of their lives.

The very thought of money changing hands for what was murder by any other name made her angry.

Edith shook her head. 'I can't tell. I just can't.'

'Listen,' said Lydia, leaning closer so she could speak in a whisper. 'Someone may die, Edith. If we don't stop this woman, someone, someday, may die.'

Edith kept her head turned resolutely away.

Lydia sighed. Nobody told. That was the way it was.

She'd thought that was it, until suddenly Edith said, 'What would we do without somebody like Daisy. There's nobody else.'

Daisy! The woman's name was Daisy.

Lydia tried to coax her into telling more, but Edith had closed her eyes, feigning sleep, unwilling to betray the woman who had almost killed her.

The house where Edith lived was in darkness, but flickered into life when they knocked at the door. A young man looking as though he hadn't slept for days filled the doorway, almost whooping with joy the moment he saw his mother.

'Mam! Where have you been? Jack's out looking for you.'

Agnes explained that Jack was Edith's husband. 'Works on the docks,' she added.

Lydia might normally have added that almost everyone around these streets seemed to work on the docks or in warehouses hereabouts, but she was too preoccupied, too consumed with anger.

Edith threw her arms around her eldest son, telling him she'd collapsed and been taken to the hospital.

'But I'm all right now, my lovely boy,' she said, gazing up at him in adoration and stroking his face. 'I'm all right now. Have you had any supper, our Harry?'

'No Mam, I've been too worried...'

'I'll get you some now. Don't you worry. Can't 'ave my boy going to work on an empty stomach...'

Lydia looked at Agnes, amazed at Edith's sudden surge of energy and the adoring way she looked at her son.

'She dotes on him,' said Agnes, who was running her hands over the bonnet of the ambulance, eyeing it almost as adoringly as Edith had Harry. 'Isn't it wonderful?'

'Very commendable,' replied Lydia, presuming her comment was with regard to the scene they'd just witnessed. 'I would still like to know...'.

She stopped what she'd been going to say. It wasn't right that Agnes should know. Edith had a right to privacy.

Agnes sighed from her position draped over the bonnet of the ambulance.

'You haven't turned it off.'

'I know. If I turn it off you'd have to turn the starting handle, and I'm not sure whether you're up to it. That's why I haven't invited you in for a cup of tea before we take it back.'

'Are you sure of that?'

Agnes's expression gave nothing away. 'Yes. Of course.'

They might have left right away if Sarah Stacey hadn't suddenly opened the front door.

She looked astounded to see the ambulance. 'Where did you get that?'

Only when she saw Lydia in her uniform did her expression change, a sigh heave from her chest and a girlish smile tremble on her lips.

'Miss Lydia. Well, I never. Would you like a cup of tea?'

Agnes had no option but to turn off the engine. 'It'll be a devil to start when it's time to go. It's getting cold out here,' she grumbled.

Lydia found the house warm and welcoming, the opposite to the Kinskis' house and others like it she'd visited since. The furnishings were simple and either worn but clean or home made with an eye on detail and matching one colour to another.

A lump of a woman, short and snoring loud enough to do better to the fire than a set of bellows, lay sprawled in an armchair, legs akimbo, face huddled against her shoulder.

'My mother,' whispered Sarah Stacey. 'Best not to wake her.'

Sarah Stacey made them tea and insisted they eat a slice of fruitcake.

'Your grandmother made it this afternoon,' she said to Agnes. 'It's still warm – well, warmish.'

From her spot sitting in a fireside chair, Ellen

187

Proctor, Agnes's grandmother, opened one eye.

'So what have you been up to, our Agnes?'

'What makes you think I've been up to anything?' countered Agnes, her mouth full of cake. 'I've been with Nurse Lydia Miller here, helping her get Mrs Allen home. She's been at the hospital after fainting on the steps outside.'

'Has she indeed?' said her grandmother, now sitting straighter in her chair, all signs of drowsiness gone. 'Pleased to meet you,' she said to Lydia before turning her attention back to her granddaughter. 'So what was it all about?'

'I told you. She fainted and was taken to hospital.'

'You said she fainted on the steps outside the hospital,' Ellen Proctor pointed out, her narrowed eyes pinpointed on Agnes.

Agnes shrugged, her chin almost disappearing into her collar. 'I don't know. Lydia knows more about it than I do,' she said. 'I drove the ambulance. That's what I did,' she said, her eyes shining with delight. 'I'm good at it. Really good at it.'

Lydia knew immediately what that look meant. 'I'll ask at the hospital. I think a female ambulance driver would be really useful.'

As they talked it through, Lydia felt Ellen Proctor's eyes on her, still narrowed, almost as though she were trying to see beyond the intelligent eyes and into the depths of her brain.

'Now we'd better get this ambulance back to the hospital.' Lydia glanced at the mantel clock. 'It's late. I think you might have to stay the night with me at the hospital,' she said to Agnes.

Agnes jumped at the idea.

188

'Goodnight, Mrs Proctor,' Lydia said before leaving.

'I suppose she bin to see the flower seller again,' said Ellen Proctor, a sly, knowing look in her small, spangling eyes. 'Edith Allen. I suppose she bin to get the flower seller to put 'er right.'

Startled by both her searching gaze and the reference to a flower seller, Lydia asked who this person was. 'The woman must be stopped before she kills someone,' she stated.

'Bah,' exclaimed Ellen Proctor. 'What else do you expect a poor woman to do? You don't know enough.'

Lydia realised Ellen Proctor was suggesting she was being naive, when in fact she felt quite sure of herself, confident of the difference between right and wrong.

'It's against the law,' said Lydia, suddenly feeling she didn't belong here, was nothing but an interfering outsider. Again, the outsider.

Ellen Proctor shifted in her chair so that she was sitting upright, her eyes fixed on this neatly uniformed nurse with her clean face and bright grey eyes.

'I s'pose Edith was 'avin' another and did what any woman with too many, mouths to feed 'as to do. She sent for the only 'elp there is for a woman. And don't look at me like that, girl. Nobody can know 'ow it is unless they've been through it. It's an 'ard decision and that's a fact, but better that than giving away yer baby to Granny Smith.'

Lydia was knocked totally off guard.

'Who is this Granny Smith?'

'Well, she ain't a bleedin' apple, that's fer sure!'

Mrs Proctor snapped, her jaw clamping shut so sharply a loose tooth flew out into her lap.

'Well, would you look at that,' she said, pulling the tooth out of the fold of her skirt where it had landed and eyeing it as though it were a lump of gold. 'At this rate all I'll be eating is porridge and milk sops!'

Nothing more was said about the flower seller, or about Granny Smith. Sarah Stacey had steered the conversation away to discussion about finding a job Agnes would really enjoy.

'Don't get your hopes up too high,' Sarah Stacey said to her daughter. 'One step at a time and think of the future. What do you think, Lydia?'

Lydia's thoughts immediately went to Robert. 'I think you should grab the opportunity if it comes along.'

Something flashed briefly in Agnes's eyes and then was gone. It occurred to Lydia that Agnes already knew about the attraction between her and Robert.

'I think it's worth me asking at the hospital to see if there's a driving job available. I for one think it's a great idea to have a female ambulance driver. Women sometimes prefer another woman to be close by, especially when it comes to babies.'

Whilst in that warm, cosy living room, she promised she would do all she could to get Agnes the job she wanted. She promised once again on the drive back to the hospital.

Settled down with Lydia in her room at the hospital, Agnes talked excitedly about her prospects for half the night.

Lydia listened and made the right noises where

needed. In her mind, however, she was thinking about finding the flower seller and what she could do to stop her aborting other babies. Eventually she told Agnes she planned to find the woman and have her brought to justice.

Agnes fell into silence as she thought it through. 'You're not Sherlock Holmes, Lydia, and besides, it's as my gran says, women who seek Daisy's help are at their wits' end; too many mouths to feed. You should leave things alone. Who knows when one of us might be in the same predicament ourselves?'

Lydia clamped her lips tightly together before saying, 'I can't see that ever happening. I won't let it happen.'

'Goodnight,' said Agnes.

Lydia heard her turn over in bed and knew Agnes disapproved, but the law was the law. Something had to be done.

Chapter Sixteen

April, 1914

Lydia smiled up at Robert. 'You're going to announce it?'

'The time is ripe. Have you told your father?'

She shook her head. They had been discussing getting married since shortly after Sir Avis's death. Now Robert was forcing the issue, desperately wanting to declare their intentions.

'They'll say we hardly know each other,' said Lydia, though she felt as though she'd known him all her life.

'What they say is irrelevant,' he responded. 'It's up to us to decide when the time is ripe. It's just that we reached that time a lot sooner than most people do.'

'I think,' said Lydia, looking down at her hands, 'that we should tell my father together. Kill two birds with one stone so to speak.'

'I've written to my parents in Australia. It'll be a while before I get a reply. In the meantime, perhaps we could meet at my aunt's house in Belgravia?'

'As a surprise to my father?'

'As a surprise to my aunt too,' he responded.

It came as no surprise to Lydia when her father asked her to accompany him on a visit to Lady Julieta Ravening.

'The town house in Belgravia of course, not Heathlands. Robert will be there. I'm hoping he might have persuaded Lady Ravening to avail herself of my services. And anyway, he'll be overjoyed to see you.'

'Of course he will,' thought Lydia, dimples appearing in her cheeks as she smiled up at him.

This was to be a very special occasion. In her mind she was already running her fingers over the dresses in her wardrobe, heart racing as she sought the right one, the best one to wear.

'Did you hear what I said?'

Lydia's mind jumped back to reality.

'I did, Father. I think Robert probably has been doing exactly that, singing your praises to his aunt. Why else would he have invited us?'

Her father was leaning on the mantelpiece, one hand hanging carelessly down.

'Yes,' he said, thoughtfully, the other hand resting on his waist, still trim despite his advancing years. 'Yes. I think that is exactly what he has done. What a corker of a chap. Better than that other fellah who locked you in that rocky pile, don't you think?'

'I like Robert. I like him a lot.'

Lydia eyed his high forehead, the straight nose and eyes that darkened when he was thinking deep thoughts. Her father was still a handsome man, who had not gone to fat and had never taken much notice of the latest fashions. Medicine had always mattered most to him and yet today he was well dressed, quite sleek in fact. His jacket was grey, his waistcoat dark, his shirt very white and his trousers very black. They looked new.

Where had the new clothes come from and when had he acquired his new tailor who made things fit him so well? It wasn't just about new clothes; when was it he'd begun smiling more? He'd always been such a serious man, content to stay at home, studying his medical books or writing some piece on a particular surgical procedure that few had yet undertaken.

She tried to pin down the time when his expression had changed. When had he first started singing in the morning? When had he first flicked his newspaper open at breakfast time, smiling at the articles, even laughing aloud and declaring that some of what was written was quite preposterous.

The house in Belgravia Square had a pediment

above the door supported on two stout white pillars. An apron of black and white tiles lay before a brass step, so polished it reflected the sky. Lydia recalled coming here and meeting Agnes for the first time.

Robert came striding across the hall to meet them, his hand held out to Lydia's father, his teeth flashing white in a smile of welcome. He was wearing his newly acquired uniform of an aviator in the newly formed Royal Flying Corps. Flying was all that Robert had ever wanted to do.

'My dear Sir. I am so glad you could make it. Lydia,' he added, his eyes gentling as he gazed at her, 'I'm so glad you could come. My aunt has organised tea in the drawing room. Cakes and sandwiches too, I notice. I'm sure they're good.'

Lydia didn't want them to be good. Lady Ravening had hired a new cook, but not before dismissing Agnes's mother.

Light flooded into the drawing room from the garden at the rear of the house.

Lady Julieta was sitting in a chair at the side of the fireplace. Light coming in from the window picked up the details on the brass implements heaped in the grate: a pair of bellows, tongs, a brush, a dustpan and a poker decorated at one end with the head of an Indian chief.

Robert sat next to Lydia. Lydia's father remained standing. Reading his body language, Lydia surmised it was his way of asserting himself, looking professional at all times, even if he wasn't feeling that way.

They made small talk whilst pouring tea and eating the cakes and sandwiches.

Lady Julieta ate like a bird. 'I have a delicate disposition. It is what comes of living in a damp climate and wed to a dissolute man. I will retain your services whilst it pleases me to do so. But, I warn you, I am very demanding and insist on the very best of medical care from a physician of impeccable reputation – both personal and professional I might add. I do not like scandals, Doctor Miller. I do not indulge in behaviour likely to result in a scandal. I trust you too behave in an appropriate manner.'

'I am at your service, your ladyship,' said Eric, bowing slightly from the waist.

'As regards the other matter of your daughter and Robert, well, what can I say...'

Lydia looked at her father's face. She'd said nothing of Robert's proposal because she was still coming to terms with it herself.

'I'm sorry?' Her father's jaw dropped as his gaze swooped to each person in turn before he beamed with pleasure.

'It appears my nephew wishes to marry your daughter. My sister-in-law and my brother are abroad, but they've been informed. Not that Robert can be dissuaded and he is over twenty-one.'

'So. It seems we're engaged,' said Lydia, her eyes sparkling, and feeling the happiest she had ever felt in her life.

Robert gazed down into those sparkling eyes feeling as though he might explode with joy.

'Only a very short engagement. I want us to marry as soon as possible so that you can join me wherever I happen to be posted.'

'Delighted!' boomed Lydia's father. Lady Julieta

195

gave no sign of what her opinion might be. Not that Robert and Lydia cared what anyone else thought. They were too wrapped up in each other.

They excused themselves from the doctor and Lady Julieta. Robert led her into another room. There was a piano in front of the window, pale cream curtains draping in big swathes on to the floor.

They kissed long and hard, and in that moment, Lydia actually believed that she could leave her vacation and follow him all over the world. There was just one thing that stopped her. She wanted to find the flower seller, the woman who aborted babies.

'Robert, I don't want to give up nursing just yet.'

His expression was one of disbelief.

'But why not? You won't need to earn money. You'll be my wife.'

He wrapped his arms around her and held her close. 'You'll be mine. All mine. I told you it was love at first sight, didn't I?'

Lydia could no nothing to stop the wave of different emotions and thoughts that suddenly swept over here. Was she being foolish to think there really was such a thing as love at first sight? She hadn't thought so. She'd really felt a great surge of feeling as though her heartbeat had doubled and wings grown out of her heels. She felt like flying – without the benefit of an aeroplane.

'Can't we be engaged for a while until I feel ready to leave nursing?' she asked timidly, her cheek against his neck so that he surely felt her lips moving.

'I want you to be my wife,' he said to her, a slight

frown creasing his brow. 'I don't want to share you with a ward full of aching patients. I want you to ease the ache I'm feeling, this pain, right here,' he said, patting in the general area of his heart. 'Feel my heartbeat,' he said, placing her hand on his chest. 'Take my pulse,' he added, pulling back his cuff and placing his fingers on that part of his wrist where he thought his pulse might be.

Lydia laughed and moved her fingers to where his blood throbbed through his veins. She loved this man and had no wish to hurt him or turn down his proposal. However, she had inherited an independent streak from somewhere. The marriage had to be equal in all things, including her profession.

'I love being a nurse. I need time to adjust to this.'

The arms that had held her so tightly slackened and the small frown deepened.

'You need time to think about marrying me?'

She shook her head vehemently. 'That's not what I said. I just want to finish off some of the work I've been doing.'

She didn't mention Edith Allen and the abortion that had almost killed the poor woman.

'A little time to give notice. I love my vocation and I'm going to find it hard to leave.' She wrapped her arms around him so that he had to come back to her. That was when she became acutely aware of the points of her breasts touching his chest. She tingled at the feel of him against her, and her breath seemed tight in her throat.

'I will marry you, Robert. I don't think I could ever marry anyone else.'

Chapter Seventeen

'Kate, Kate! I don't know what I'm going to do without you. Do you have to go?'

Normally in total control of any given situation, it wasn't often that Doctor Eric Miller begged anyone for anything. Up until she'd mentioned Paris, he had been admiring Kate's glistening shoulders and the creaminess of her bosom. Now he was holding on to her fingers as though that alone would prevent her from leaving.

Her eyes sparkled and her laugh was one of reassurance.

'It will do both of us good to be apart for a while. Absence makes the heart grow fonder. Anyway, I've always wanted to visit Paris, and this is my chance to make a name for myself there. I understand the theatre is of good quality. I wouldn't be going if it were anything but.'

Her commentary on her proposed visit did nothing to lift Eric's spirits. Kate catered to his personal needs very well indeed, besides which he liked her. He knew very well she was closer to middle age than she made out, but her vivaciousness made up for the few wrinkles she had. Theirs was a relationship not based entirely on physical attraction. They shared many likes and dislikes, laughed and were saddened by the same things, had the same taste in theatre, music and art. In short, they suited each other. He tried to persuade her of this in the hope that she wouldn't go to Paris.

'I'm sorry,' she said, her eyes looking up into his. 'My agent has signed the contract. I have no choice, but...' She smiled in a way that from the very first had beguiled him into letting her into his bed. 'I will be faithful to you. I never dally with more than one man at once.'

His dark eyebrows rose almost high enough to reach his hairline.

'A dalliance? Is that all I am to you?'

She noted the peevishness in his voice and, still smiling, attempted to stroke his frown away with her fingers, her voice as soft as silk.

Her eyes sparkled when she took his hands and smiled up into his face.

'No, Eric. Far from it in fact. We will never marry I think, but we will always be ... together. Anyway,' she said, disengaging herself from his arms, 'I'm sure there are aspects of your social life that have been neglected of late. Perhaps you should take up those invitations you have declined in the past. I'm sure you must have some...' She fastened a finger against his mouth before he could utter a word.

'Don't deny it. I know there are places you wouldn't dream of taking an actress. Please don't take me for a fool.'

Eric closed his mouth. Kate had a knack of hitting the nail on the head, pointing out things to him that he'd neglected or failed to notice. He found himself wondering how he'd ever lived without her. He'd been dead before he'd met her, or at least not as full of life as he was now.

'Anyway, Lydia would appreciate your company for a while. You rarely take her anywhere. She's your daughter and I think you should.'

He didn't take criticism that well and couldn't help clenching his jaw. There was no doubt that he'd neglected Lydia, but his daughter didn't seem any the worse for it. He thought about voicing this truth, but Kate was already talking about something else. Paris and Lydia were settled subjects.

They left the theatre to dine at a new place recommended by some young man in the cast of the latest play. Eric hesitated at the door and looked through the plate-glass window. The tables were crowded and there was much laughter. He searched for familiar faces; just one and he would beat a hasty retreat.

It had long been their habit to choose out of the way, less popular places where they were not known. He discerned that perhaps Kate was getting tired of the subterfuge.

His worst fears were realised when he saw a tall figure he recognised, resplendent in evening dress, a black cape and carrying a silver-topped cane. Rudolfo Credenza, Lady Julieta's brother.

'Damn,' he muttered. He began to back out of the man's line of sight immediately but he was taken aback by the youth of the woman accompanying him. Stones as red as rubies glistened from the necklace she wore and matching droplets dangled from her ears.

A faint glow of rouge warmed her fresh young face and glistened on her lips. Her eyes, outlined in black, lids shaded blue, sparkled with what he could only interpret as excitement coupled with upward glances of adoration for Rudolfo Credenza.

Although only lightly applied her makeup looked somewhat incongruous on so young and fresh a face. It crossed his mind that she was barely more than a child, in his judgement no more than fourteen.

If that were my daughter, he thought, clenching his jaw...

'Is everything all right, Eric?'

Kate's voice jerked him back from his deepest fears and to the moment, the restaurant and the haughty expression on the face of Rudolfo Credenza.

'I think we should leave.'

'But...'

She was about to say that they had only just arrived, when she too noticed Rudolfo Credenza. Her smile faded.

'If you say so, my love,' she murmured.

Arm in arm they left the establishment, both entertaining their own opinions of a man they had had dealings with and whom neither of them liked.

Chapter Eighteen

The starched aprons of house maids and parlour maids cracked in the breeze as they ran to the lower meadow, one hand holding on to their caps.

People from the village, labourers from the estate, chattered excitedly, their eyes scanning the sky for their first glimpse of a flying machine.

The crowd gathered in the lower meadow at Heathlands was the biggest since old Sir Avis had died. Everyone was making the most of the day seeing as his widow was not one to socialise with either the local gentry or the ordinary folk thereabouts.

Robert had also sent an invitation to be passed on to Agnes, so when she went off duty, Lydia decided to catch the tram to the end of Myrtle Street.

'Off to see that Agnes Stacey, are ya?'

The speaker who accosted Lydia as she passed the corner shop was Arthur Truelove. His father owned most of the properties in the street, Arthur collecting the rents on his behalf. Because of this, he fancied himself as a man of means, a cut above others of his age in the neighbourhood.

Lydia replied that she was indeed paying her friend a visit and did her best to skirt around him.

'There's a lot of comings and goings in that house,' he said. 'Not that it's my business, just so long as the rent is paid. Must be getting a bit crowded though seeing as there's only two bedrooms.'

'I don't know what you're talking about.'

Lydia knew that Sarah Stacey and her mother sometimes took in lodgers to help make ends meet, but would not enlighten Arthur Truelove, though they would only let one of the attic rooms. Agnes had the other one, her mother and grandmother having the two bedrooms on the first floor. Not that it was any of his business. Besides that, he smelled of mothballs so the less time spent near his tweed jacket and stained waistcoat, the better.

She did a sideways step, but Arthur still kept pace.

'We are very great friends. Sometimes Agnes is a guest at my father's house.'

'Is that so? Well, I never. I hear your dad's a doctor,' he said, wheezing slightly as he attempted to keep pace with her. The fact was Arthur was a big, broad lad, but not the most active or agile thanks to a huge appetite turning the firmness of youth to fat.

'Yes,' she answered tersely.

'Hand you're a nurse.'

Lydia smothered a giggle. Arthur considered himself a gentleman and as such added aitches on to words beginning with vowels.

'I ham.'

It was so easy to mimic poor Arthur who really did think himself a cut above everyone else in the street.

'Must have a big house then. Where might that house be situated, might I hask?'

Lydia just managed to get out the word 'Kensington' without bursting into a more vigorous giggling fit.

She eyed the distance to go before she could safely pop through the front door where Agnes lived. About thirty more feet and...

'Excuse me if hi ham speaking hout of turn, Miss Lydia, but could hi be so bold has to hask you to accompany me for a repast at Sampsons

203

in Hosborne Street?'

The door to the house in Myrtle Street loomed like a cool lake.

Lydia barely broke step. 'I'm sorry, Arthur. I'm already spoken for.'

She was gone before Arthur Truelove suggested she reconsidered his invitation. Persuading her would include his personal résumé: how much he earned and how much he would be worth once his father had 'passed over', as he put it when describing death.

Arthur Truelove Senior and his family, as great exponents of the afterlife and spiritualism, didn't die, they only passed over.

The moment she was through the front door, Agnes swung out from the front room, grinning from ear to ear.

'I saw Arthur was keeping you close company. I take it his father hasn't passed over yet, but he's still telling you how much he'll inherit when he does.'

Lydia leaned against the closed door and shook her head. 'We didn't get that far. Thank goodness!'

Agnes giggled. 'One of these days it'll happen. We'll look up and see old Mr Truelove passing over – floating past the chimney pots.'

Suddenly, Agnes saw the look of glee on Lydia's face.

'You're grinning like a Cheshire cat. Something good has happened. What is it? For goodness' sake, what is it, Lydia?'

Lydia gave her the crisp white envelope containing the gilt-edged invitation.

'From Robert,' said Lydia, her eyes shining.

204

Agnes bit her bottom lip, glanced at Lydia and then down at the card.

'Did you ask him to invite me?'

Lydia sighed. Agnes hid her feelings well. There had been no real understanding between Robert and Agnes, but Agnes had been hurt. She'd always loved him and probably always would.

'No. I did not ask him to invite you. He asked me to bring this to you and for us to pick you up in my father's new motor car.'

Agnes considered it for a moment. Lydia held her breath.

'All right,' she said at last, the old confidence returning and glowing in her eyes. 'But only if I can drive.'

It wasn't too hard for Lydia to persuade her father to let Agnes drive.

'Just think. A chauffeur-driven car and nobody will suspect it's a woman driving. Agnes wears goggles, a leather cap and trousers. Nobody will be any the wiser. Lady Ravening and her friends will be very impressed.'

He'd been won over. It was now a case of keeping Agnes out of sight. Lady Ravening was likely to boot her off the premises on sight.

'Keep to the crowds and the old lady won't see you,' Lydia advised her friend.

Agnes was her usual rebellious self.

'I won't hide from that old cow. I'm not afraid of her.'

'Agnes, please remember my father's position in this. Wealthy patients don't grow on trees.'

Agnes burst out laughing. 'She'd look good hanging from a tree.'

'That isn't funny.' Lydia was adamant. Grabbing Agnes by the shoulders, she gazed solemnly into her face and made her promise to behave herself.

Agnes stifled her laughter and adopted what she considered a serious expression, her lips constantly stretching into a wide grin.

'I promise I won't flaunt my presence. I'll mix with the blokes when she gets close, with my goggles and scarf hiding my face. Will that suit?'

Lydia said that it would. Sighing with relief, she looked around her. The excitement in the air was palpable, like electricity before a thunderstorm.

Lydia wondered at her father taking the time to be with her; they rarely spent time together. It was someone else he took to the theatre, someone else who had made him happier than she had ever seen him.

This special someone was never mentioned. Lydia wondered – it was definitely a woman – but had never asked questions about her. To her knowledge he had not brought the woman to the house, or at least not when Lydia was there. Perhaps he cared more for her feelings than she'd thought, or perhaps this woman was just a companion and not a replacement for Lydia's mother.

I wonder, she thought as she watched him, his caped tweed coat flapping like a dark gold wing. On the journey to Heathlands, he'd asked Agnes how her mother was keeping and what she, Agnes, intended to do with her life.

'Drive motor cars, then aeroplanes,' said Agnes.

Agnes had commented on the performance of the doctor's brand new motor car.

'It smells of new leather and the seats are very comfortable,' she exclaimed. 'It also smells of violets,' she said. 'Just like the perfume my mother wears.'

Some of the crowd gathered had brought sandwiches, great doorsteps of crusty bread and thick wedges of cheese. Some of the men had brought beer and children ran and played, shrieking with excitement even before the arrival of the aeroplane.

Not even the arrival of Lady Julieta could dampen their cheerful voices or curtail their youthful energy.

Lydia managed to study her while at the same time keeping Agnes safely hidden behind the large pink hat she was wearing. The hat, she decided, was a wonderful buy, ably killing two birds with one stone; firstly to hide Agnes and secondly Robert would be able to see it from the air.

She hid a smile behind a gloved hand as she watched the old lady's progress. Her ladyship was the sort who wore helplessness like a shield. In actuality she seemed quite fit and undoubtedly formidable.

Neverthless, Quartermaster pushed her bath chair over the rough ground, the small figure bouncing each time one wheel caught on uneven ground while the other remained level.

The continual bouncing resulted in her sour expression turning even sourer.

The elderly butler stumbled here and there thanks to the uneven ground and the state of his knees, which had become more bowed and unsteady with time.

The pastureland they were traversing had been nibbled short by the sheep that had been grazing there just a week or so before.

'There she is,' murmured Agnes, her scarf wound up over her nose, her goggles pulled down over her eyes. 'By the looks of her face she's either been sucking lemons or licking a cat's rear end.'

Lydia had long realised that Agnes could be quite rude at times and that there was no point in admonishment. Agnes did and said more or less what she liked.

'Agnes! Get back,' Lydia hissed. 'Otherwise she'll order you from the premises and our day will be ruined. I'll never forgive you if it is.'

She caught sight of Agnes's eyes narrowing from behind the thick goggles.

'Listen to Lady Lydia! So you won't forgive me? How about me never forgiving you for becoming engaged to Robert? And I bet you'll save yourself until your wedding night. I wouldn't. The quicker I could get him into bed the better. I'm made of flesh and blood, that's me.'

'I will not be a slut, Agnes!'

'Are you calling me a slut because I have a passionate nature?'

Lydia saw the tears in Agnes's eyes; her friend didn't really mean it. Because of that she would not argue. Agnes had become a dear friend. 'Of course I'm not.'

'It's through passion that I came to be. We all did. Even you,' snapped Agnes.

Lydia turned away and purposely looked skywards.

'Where is Robert?' she murmured.

208

Her outspokenness forgotten, Agnes pushed her goggles up on to her forehead. 'We should be able to see him, surely.'

They both strained their eyes but saw only cumulus clouds sitting like giant meringues in a clear, cold sky.

'I can't see him yet,' Lydia said breathlessly whilst holding on to her giant hat. 'It's quite amazing though, isn't it? Robert flying a plane. Robert an officer in the Royal Flying Corps.'

The very thought of his strong hands propelling the machine up into the air made her fear and made her wonder.

'I'm going to ask him to take mc up in it,' stated Agnes, in the process of tying a red silk scarf around her neck. 'I've heard there are women aviators who are just as good as men. I think I would make an excellent aviator and now's the time to get in some practice. And by the way, that's a formidable hat you're wearing. It's not your usual style.'

'Yours is very typical, Agnes,' Lydia responded, the argument forgotten. They looked at each other and laughed.

Lydia admired her friend's rebellious nature, her determination to be different and to prove that whatever a man could do, she could do it too.

Despite the initial hurt at Lydia and Robert's engagement, Agnes valued Lydia as a friend. Lydia was a friend who had not abandoned her when she'd fallen on hard times as others might have done and had done.

'He'll be coming from the west; out of the sun,' said Agnes knowledgeably.

Lydia raised a hand, shielding her eyes against the brightness of the sky. She looked in the direction everyone else was looking, while standing between Agnes and the place where Lady Julieta sat, one blanket tucked around her knees, another around her shoulders and a thick shawl over her head. Lydia decided there was little chance of Lady Julieta peering through that lot and seeing Agnes.

Towards the west, the setting sun had gilded the fluffy clouds with gold and its rays were still strong and warm.

Lydia craned her neck. There seemed at first to be nothing to see except gilt-edged clouds and a blinding brightness. Agnes did the same.

'I can't see him,' said Agnes, sounding thoroughly disappointed.

Lydia kept her hand shielding her eyes. Robert was coming and she was desperate to see him before Agnes did.

'There,' said Lydia, shrieking so loud that heads turned in their direction. 'I see him; at least I think I do. See? It's no more than a black dot, but it's getting bigger as he gets closer. I'm sure of it.'

'You're seeing things!' Agnes snapped, annoyed that Lydia had seen Robert's plane first. 'Here. Let me borrow those.'

She snatched a pair of opera glasses from the hands of a junior butler, thinking to herself that the great house must be empty of staff. It seemed the whole household and half the village besides was out here to see an aeroplane land.

'Remember to keep out of Lady Julieta's line of sight,' Lydia hissed at her.

210

'Damn the old bat!'

Lydia sighed and shook her head. Agnes was incorrigible.

The dot got bigger and bigger; first, it looked like a plus sign and without any defining features. Nearer and nearer it came until the plus sign was like a dragonfly with one wing on each side only and spindly legs ending in fat tubular tyres.

A chorus of exclamation went up as the fragile craft swept over the field only some fifty feet or so above the ground, an oblong mix of string, canvas and strips of iron framework.

'I can see him,' cried Lydia and waved for all she was worth.

Robert waved back, his white silk scarf streaming out behind him.

Agnes was jumping up and down beside her, waving both hands and clapping above her head.

'Hooray, hooray, hooray,' she shouted amongst other sounds that were pure enthusiasm rather than actual words.

'You're attracting attention,' Lydia hissed at her, nudging her in the ribs. 'The old bat will see you.'

Agnes took no notice so Lydia positioned herself to block the old lady's line of sight, hoping she'd forgotten to bring her opera glasses or her spectacles.

A few men recruited from the village to hold back the crowds got between them and the likely landing strip, their arms outstretched – as if that was enough to hold back such excitement.

'Keep back,' they shouted, their voices almost drowned out by the noise of the aero engine.

Despite the competition of sound, the cry passed

211

all along the line, the crowd dividing obediently, some tripping backwards over clumps of stubble, unwilling to take their eyes off the fragile craft descending from the sky in case they missed its landing.

Everyone gathered there gasped with one voice when the wheels bounced once, twice, three times before the plane levelled out to bump along over the bumpy ground.

Agnes attempted to duck beneath the stretched out arms and suddenly found herself whipped off her feet by the strong arms of John Filer, the gamekeeper.

'Oh no you don't, young fellah, no matter who you are!'

'Let me go. I'm an aeroplane mechanic,' she shouted.

'Is that so? Then what are these?' He grabbed Agnes's breasts, laughing as he jiggled them and made lewd suggestions.

Agnes brought one foot back then the other, both connecting with his shins.

Lydia took advantage of the situation, popping through the human barricade, stumbling as she ran across the field towards the aeroplane. Breathless, she stopped some distance from where the propellers were turning until they slowed and finally stopped.

Face slick with sweat, Robert shoved the goggles up on to his head and wiped his face with his scarf. The moment the scarf left his face, he spotted her and his eyes lit up.

'Lydia!'

Heaving himself out from the aeroplane, he

212

swung his legs over the side, landed on the grass and ran towards her.

'Lydia. Did you see that? That was the best landing I've ever done.'

'You bounced a bit,' she said, relishing the feel of his hands holding her shoulders.

He smiled into her face as though the crowds around them didn't exist. The smile was for her and her alone.

'It was the best landing because you're here,' he said to her. 'Better than any awards I must say. I could fly the Atlantic if I knew you would be there at the end of my trip.'

'I would be,' she whispered, her cheeks pink with both joy and the crispness of the evening.

He kissed her, his lips hot on her mouth, and then broke off, grinning as he tapped the brim of her hat.

'That's a thoroughly cunning hat you're wearing.'

'Cunning?'

'No one can see me kissing you.'

Lost in his embrace, loving the feel of his muscular arms around her, his lips on hers, the rest of the world faded away.

Standing a few hundred yards away, Agnes pulled her goggles back over her eyes. Nobody must see the moistness in her eyes. Nobody must suspect she was close to tears.

Her mother's voice echoed in her ears. 'Know your place, my girl. Theirs is to live in big houses and have all the good things of life; yours is to wait on table, cook for them or scrub the floors.'

She felt a fool for loving Robert. Blinded by her

213

own infatuation, she had chosen to ignore the loving looks he and Lydia had exchanged from the very first moment they'd met, the colour in Lydia's face, the obvious way their hands brushed together, the closeness of her hip against his.

Seething with bitterness, she realised that everything her mother and grandmother had warned her about was true. There was a big divide between the classes. The world had not yet changed enough to alter that despite all the assurances given her by Sir Avis. And perhaps it never will, she thought to herself.

On a whim she headed for that part of the stable yard used as a garage, pulling her helmet off and sliding her scarf down from her face.

She hadn't expected anyone to be in the garage, everyone having headed for the field and the landing of the aeroplane.

Tears threatened and her face was hot. It wouldn't take much for her to burst out crying. She ground her teeth in an effort to keep the tears at bay whilst telling herself that only sissies cried and she wasn't a sissy. She never had been. Never would be.

The door of the garage was heavy and it took a lot of effort to push it open. She eyed the one remaining car with sadness. Sir Avis had kept three cars. His widow saw no point in keeping three. She didn't love cars; to her they were merely a convenience for getting around. One sufficed.

The air inside the garage no longer held any vestige of the smell of horse fodder. There was only the smell of oil and grease, smells that she breathed in with great pleasure.

Running her hand along the bonnet of Sir Avis's favourite car, she reflected on all the things he'd said to her, how she could be anything she wanted to be if she applied herself with dedication and determination. She'd hung on to his every word and regularly reminisced about those precious moments he'd spent with her. Sir Avis had made her feel important and fired her up with dreams of what she could achieve. On reflection, never once had he mentioned marriage to Robert being achievable. Everything had been about her being independent and rising above the circumstances of her birth.

He'd never admitted to being her father, but then he didn't need to. She knew now that her mother had never been married to anyone called Thomas Stacey; in fact, he'd never existed. All she did know was that Sir Avis had filled that particular spot in her life and she would never forget him.

A slight sound, another smell and a shadow moved just to the right of her peripheral vision. She looked in the direction of the sound.

'I've just finished polishing that car and would be obliged if you removed your mucky hand.'

Thompson the chauffeur emerged from the shadows. Agnes scowled at him. 'I see you're as welcoming as ever, Thompson. Been drinking, have you?'

News that Thompson had turned to drink following Megan the maid's having ended their relationship after meeting and marrying a soldier had reached Myrtle Street. 'None of your bloody business.'

He jammed a cigarette into the corner of his

mouth and lit it.

'Better be careful, Thompson. Petrol and fire are a dangerous combination. Worse still when alcohol is added.'

'What you talking about, you silly cow?'

His voice was slurred, his eyes glazed and yellow tinged. The lips that held the cigarette were wet and his jaw sagged slightly.

Agnes thought how grotesque he looked – untidy too. 'I'm saying you're likely to set the whole place on fire if you're not careful.'

'None of your bloody business,' he said again.

'No. Perhaps not. But it is Mr Robert's business. This house will pass to him when the old girl is dead and buried.'

Thompson sneered. 'Well, you won't be 'ere, now will ya? The old lady don't want you 'ere, you and yer mother. I'd get going if I was you.'

Agnes folded her arms and stood with legs braced, holding her chin defiantly.

'You gonna throw me out, Thompson?' she asked, her eyes glaring fiercely. 'You and whose army?'

His sneer widened.

'No point in bein' 'asty. That's what I says. You ain't so precious now the old man's not around. Not his darling little girl anymore.'

'If he was still around, he would have sent you packing by now.'

Thompson shook his head and chuckled. 'Well, you was the one sent packing. Bet that surprised your mother. I reckon she was bankin' on the old man leavin' you a bit in 'is will then you and 'er would 'ave been set up for life.'

Agnes felt her face colouring up. She was grateful Thompson had taught her to drive the car when she was very young, but that was only under forbearance. Sir Avis had instructed him to do so.

'You wouldn't speak to me like that if Sir Avis was still alive!'

'Course I wouldn't. That was back when we was all expectin' 'im to admit you was 'is daughter. But 'e didn't, did 'e? Never said a bloody thing!'

The smell of engines, petrol and cigarette smoke all combined to make a heady brew that was suffocating.

'Hey. How about you stay and we can talk about motor cars. I'll give you a cigarette. Give you something more besides if you fancy it. So! Do you fancy me, Agnes?'

Agnes paused by the door, turned and threw him a look of utter contempt.

'I would never stoop so low.'

'Excuse me, but I think the boot should be on t'other foot! My father married my mother. Yours didn't!'

Chapter Nineteen

June, 1914

Sarah Stacey was at the range stirring a mutton stew when Agnes arrived back at the house in Myrtle Street.

On hearing the door open, she looked over her

217

shoulder, wearing a surprised expression on her face.

'So what was it like? Did you see Master Robert land?'

When Agnes didn't answer, she straightened and turned round and was alarmed to see her daughter looking pale as a waxwork mannequin, both hands resting on a chair back, eyes downcast.

'Are you ill?' asked her mother, while holding her wooden spoon as though she would smite whatever was afflicting her daughter.

Agnes shook her head and swallowed the lump that had been sitting in her throat.

'Robert Ravening and Lydia are a ravishing couple, don't you think?'

Sarah's jaw dropped. So did the hand holding the spoon.

'Oh my darling,' she said, her eyes filling with tears. 'I won't say I told you so. But I did, so there's an end to it. Just be happy that it's yer friend that's landed him. Yes,' said Sarah Stacey.

'Yes,' she said again with a resolute nod before briskly turning back to the saucepan. 'They make a very fine couple.'

Something about the way her mother said what she did upset Agnes. She couldn't help but feel that her mother was almost happy that Robert had fallen for somebody else.

'You don't like him, do you?' she said petulantly, her fingers tightening around the chair back.

Her mother kept her face averted, the stirring of the stew now seemingly of great importance

'I like him well enough, Agnes, as the nephew of my ex-employer, but that's as far as it goes. He just isn't for you and never was. He's of a different class.' She looked away as though reluctant to meet the despairing look in her daughter's eyes.

'Sir Avis was right for you, wasn't he?'

Cheeks bright red, Sarah Stacey rounded on her daughter. 'How dare you...'

'Mother!' Agnes's sudden shout brought her mother up short. 'I am no longer a child. I know that you and Sir Avis were very close – too close to be just a cook and the master. There was more between you; anyone could see that.'

The slap was fast and fierce; Agnes hadn't seen it coming and neither, by the look of it, had her mother.

Sarah's expression was instantly regretful. 'Agnes, I didn't mean...' she whined, the offending hand now clenched into a fist, so tight her fingernails were cutting into her flesh.

'It seems I was right,' Agnes said bitterly.

Her mother opened her mouth to protest that she had it all wrong, but no words would come out. Besides, Agnes only had it half right. Should I tell her the whole truth, Sarah wondered? She was tempted to, but something held her back.

Agnes, her cheek red and tears stinging her eyes, left the room, headed along the passageway and out of the front door. She didn't look back, walking the streets without working out where she was going, not turning to left or right, not acknowledging anyone who cared to say good day to her.

Three days later, Lydia left the nurse's hostel to take the tram to Myrtle Street. All the way there, she rehearsed what she would say, picking on

219

phrases then discarding them as inappropriate.

She looked out of the window at the passing scene while telling herself that she had nothing to be ashamed of: she hadn't purposely gone out of her way to fall in love with Robert; it had just happened.

Not even the street newspaper vendors shouting something out about an assassination could deter her from her mission. Although she loved Robert, she would not let it ruin her friendship with Agnes. She valued it too highly and she wanted Agnes to know that.

The dreadful Arthur was standing on the corner of Myrtle Street licking the end of a pencil before making notes in the little blue book in which he recorded rents due and paid. The moment he saw Lydia he stuffed everything into his coat pocket, blobs of red flush bursting over his fat cheeks.

'How lovely to see you on this fine evening,' he called, his feet swiftly covering the distance between them. 'You are just the person I wanted to see.'

'I'm in a hurry, Arthur. Perhaps some other time?'

Either he didn't hear her or chose not to; he continued to head her way, his plodding footsteps hurrying to keep up with her.

'I really think we could enjoy a little repast together. Shall we say Thursday night?'

'I think not,' returned Lydia without halting her pace.

'I'm very sorry to hear that, though on reflection I am perhaps aiming above myself. Perhaps

220

I should lower my sights and enquire of Agnes Stacey?'

Lydia came to an abrupt halt. 'I beg your pardon?' Her eyes were blazing when she turned to confront him. 'My friend Agnes has had the benefit of a good education and her mother is a hard-working woman. How dare you consider asking her out to be a lowering of your sights!'

She hadn't realised her voice was so loud and her manner so threatening until she saw Arthur take a step back, his expression alarmed.

'I meant no offence... I ... meant that she's...' His eyes rolled from side to side as though he were looking for the right word. 'Different!'

'Just as well for you that I'm in something of a hurry, Arthur, or you'd be getting the sharp side of my tongue!'

She turned on her heels and left him there looking as though she'd smacked both sides of his face. As she neared the house, she began to smile and then to laugh. It wasn't like her to lose her temper, but in doing so a lot of the tension seemed to have floated away.

Thank goodness, she thought, and breathed a sigh of relief. She could speak to Agnes sensibly and calmly.

As was usual in most of the houses in Myrtle Street, the front door was open.

Lydia did what everybody else did. She went in. 'Hello. Is anyone there?'

Her voice seemed to roll down the passageway to the room at the end, the kitchen and scullery where Agnes, her mother and her grandmother were enjoying a pot of tea, bread and butter and

221

jam sandwiches seeing as it was four o'clock.

Agnes came out of the kitchen. She was wearing a dark-coloured dress with a white collar and cuffs. She touched her hair nervously, an action uncharacteristic of her; Agnes, Lydia thought, was never nervous. She was the bravest person she knew.

'I wasn't expecting you,' said Agnes.

'I thought I should come. I thought I should see how you were...'

Agnes shrugged. 'There's really no need, Lydia,' she said with a brightness Lydia thought a little false. 'I'm quite all right. Are you staying for supper? Ma's done pigs' tails. They're a mucky meal to say the least, all that fat sticking to your fingers. She only cooks them 'cause Gran likes them, though it's a wonder she manages to gnaw on them like she does seeing as she ain't got many teeth.'

Relieved at her reception, Lydia smiled and said she would.

The kitchen smelled of cooked meat and potatoes. Globules of condensed steam hung from the ceiling and ran down the windows. Opening a window was the only way to dispel the moisture but it took time to get rid of all of it.

Sarah Stacey was picking up a pig's tail from the roasting tray with two fingers.

She gave her mother Ellen Proctor a warning look. 'Mother, I'm giving you the meatiest. And don't suck on the bones.'

She looked up and smiled at Lydia. 'Nice to see you, Lydia. Got a spare one if you want one.'

She held up a small pig's tail. Lydia wasn't

keen, but decided it would be rude to refuse.

'My, my. It looks good. I've never eaten one before.'

Ellen Proctor swallowed what she was chewing to ask, 'So when's the wedding?'

Lydia fidgeted nervously. 'We don't know yet. I favour next year, but Robert would prefer us to marry as soon as possible. He thinks we might have a war. I told him that if that were the case, nurses would be in short supply. I have to do my duty.' Then, her eyes scanning the table, she said, 'I don't appear to have a knife and fork.'

'You use yer hands,' said Ellen.

Somewhat defiantly, Agnes reached for a pig's tail and proceeded to bite large pieces from the bone. Lydia knew she was being challenged. To her surprise, she found the meat tender and tasty.

'It's lovely,' she said while chewing a small portion. 'Better than I expected.'

She caught the amused smirk on Agnes's face and noticed the grease on her chin. Presumably, her chin was just as greasy and shiny. She resisted the urge to swipe her hand at it.

'Use the bread,' said Agnes's grandmother, swiping a chunk of bread across her chin as some might a linen napkin.

Seeing that it seemed to work on Mrs Proctor's face, Lydia did the same.

'Eat while you can, my dears,' said Mrs Proctor. 'Who knows what tomorrow might bring. So eat while you can.'

'So it's really war,' murmured Lydia. She shook her head. 'How foolish. How very foolish.'

'You're right there,' said Ellen Proctor, puffing

223

on her pipe. 'I read that the Queen 'erself reckons it's foolish. Worst thing ever to happen to this country if it 'appens.'

Lydia agreed that indeed it was; Robert would be flying into combat and her father'd be regarded as an enemy alien. Things couldn't be worse.

Chapter Twenty

On her return from Paris, Eric told Kate Mallory all about Lydia's engagement to young Robert Ravening.

'A young man of good family, good prospects and property, Kate. I am very happy,' he said as he laid down his outer coat, hat and cane.

They were at Kate's house, a pretty place in Wimbledon with roses round the door and iron trelliswork forming a first-floor balcony.

Kate's drawing room held more knick-knacks than Eric himself favoured, but it seemed to reflect her character. Stylised Chinese chrysanthemums in rich shades of deep pink and yellow blossomed against a dark background on the walls. Chairs and cabinets had clean lines except for a single tulip of minimal design on a chair back or a cupboard door, all of it totally lacking the over-elaboration of the Victorian years.

Kate paused in the process of pulling a pin from her hat to peer at him through her arched arms via her reflection in a copper-framed mirror.

'Is your happiness for your daughter being in

love or for the prospect of joining the landed gentry?'

Although she appeared to have returned to the process of removing her hatpin, she watched him carefully, noticing how he seemed to hold his breath as he considered what she'd said. As though I've punched him, she thought wryly.

'What do you mean?'

After withdrawing the pearl-ended pin, she took her hat from her head with both hands, setting it down on the dressing table in front of her.

'These people – the gentry as we so glibly call them – rarely marry for love. They marry for money and for alliances.'

'Lydia is a very intelligent girl and it's not as though we're paupers...'

Sensing his hostility, Kate swung round on the stool. She eyed him seriously without even the hint of a smile on her lips.

'I know you are not paupers, Eric. You are a very good doctor with an enviable reputation. You are well patronised by the wealthy, but you also treat the poor at that hospital. And what of Lydia's mother's family?'

'They have a number of businesses in Wareham ... very successful businesses... They are well thought of...' He delivered the statement falteringly, knowing what she was getting at but loath to do the same.

'They are in trade?'

Eric thought of the haberdasher's, the grocery store, the factory bottling lemonade.

'Yes. They are in trade. Good honest people working hard to make a living. Is that so bad?'

'It might not be. Has nobody mentioned your relationship with me yet?'

'No!' He looked severely affronted, straightening his shoulders, consternation locking his jaw. 'No. They have not.'

Kate stood up, cupped his face with both hands and looked deeply into his eyes.

'They will check everything is to their liking; both your background and your personal behaviour – and that includes your relationship with me.'

Eric shook his head and smiled, as though the whole idea was too amusing to be true.

'Kate, Kate, Kate. I believe your fears are groundless. Lydia will marry Robert. His family will raise no objections. I am sure of this.'

Kate's lips, that seemed always to smile even when she had nothing to say, began to smile again.

'Perhaps you are right and I am being foolish. Perhaps.'

Doctor Miller convinced himself that indeed he was right and pushed all fears to the contrary aside – until yet again he saw Rudolfo Credenza at the theatre, this time in the company of another very young woman. She had pale skin made even paler by the acid green of the silk dress she was wearing, the hint of adolescent bosom showing above the plunging neckline. Her hair was fair and baby fine, eyes blue and her lips were a Cupid's bow of rosebud pink.

Eric and Rudolfo exchanged a respectful nod, yet Kate Mallory, well used to the behaviour and foibles of male machismo, saw the look in

226

Rudolfo's eyes.

'He will make trouble,' she whispered. 'I am sure … I know … he will make trouble. I think we should dine elsewhere.'

'You were less wary of him before. What makes it different now?'

'That girl with him is the daughter of an old friend – deceased sadly. Once the girl turned twelve, she was left to her own devices. She wants to be an actress. Credenza is her sponsor – though there are many words to describe what he truly is. I warned the girl of him. I told her that what appeared to be kindness was really the worst kind of flattery and that there would be a price to pay. It appears young Flora is willing to pay whatever it takes for the pretty clothes and fancy baubles he gives her. I shall be glad when the man returns to America where he belongs.'

On seeing Kate, a mischievous smile twitched at Flora's rosebud lips before she stood on tiptoe to whisper into her escort's ear, her gloved hand held in front of her mouth.

'I fear you could be right,' Eric said quietly.

Kate attempted to smooth away his frown lines with her cool fingers.

'I suppose we should look on the bright side. This Lady Julieta is hardly your only client, Eric,' remarked Kate.

He shook his head. 'The woman has influence. Although she does little entertaining herself, she does frequent many a social gathering of the rich and influential. She could ruin me if she had a mind to; that's if her brother tells her he's seen us together.'

'He may not.'

'I'm sure he will.'

'So! Is this goodbye?' She sounded petulant.

Roused from his brooding thoughts, Eric jerked up his head. He looked appalled at the prospect of parting from her.

'No!' he said, her comment finally annihilating the persistent frown. 'I couldn't live without you, Kate. You know that.'

Kate tossed her mane of auburn hair teased upwards tonight into a full style forming a halo around her lovely face. 'Then let us forget about Rudolfo and his sister. Maybe he will keep his mouth shut.'

Doctor Miller smiled though he remained concerned. 'Maybe.'

Now she looked thoughtful, her eyes carefully avoiding his.

'What is it, Kate?'

'Paris,' she said with a sigh. 'It was a beautiful day, so typical of late June in Paris. People were marching up and down, waving flags. Eric, they were baying like dogs for war. Welcoming the prospect of men dying.'

Eric shook his head. 'Let us hope it never happens. It is so needless. All these ridiculous treaties with one country and another, and all over the Balkans. I cannot see our leaders being so foolish as to lay men's lives on the line for the Balkans.'

He shook his head, imagining how terrible it would be and how pointless. He was no expert on weapons, but knew enough to surmise that modern weaponry and traditional tactics could be a lethal combination.

Kate had fallen into silence. On raising his eyes, he saw that hers seemed too big for her face, and her skin – her complexion – had turned incredibly pale.

'What is it, Kate?' he asked gently. It crossed his mind that she might be ill. He hoped not. Kate had made a huge difference to his life. She made him feel alive again.

'What will you do if war is declared on Germany, Eric?'

Her voice was huskier than it normally was, as though the words were catching in her throat.

He stared at her at first, wondering what she could possibly mean.

He shrugged. 'I will continue to practise medicine. What else should I do?'

Kate's expression never wavered. Her eyes stayed fixed on his and were full of meaning.

He blinked as that meaning hit him. If Britain went to war with Germany, he would be an enemy alien.

Chapter Twenty-One

On the following Thursday he was summoned to the London house in Belgravia where Lady Julieta had taken up residence in plenty of time for the London season.

The interior was unchanged except there were flowers and tubs of tropical plants everywhere.

The perfume from a bunch of arum lilies came

from a large urn. Doctor Eric Miller attempted to take shallow breaths in order not to breathe in an overabundance of their scent. Lilies were greatly favoured by funeral parlours to mask the smell of decaying bodies and he hated them.

He had brought his medical bag, though he suspected the old girl wished to discuss more than just her health. At the back of his mind he wondered if he was about to be dismissed because of the situation with Germany. He reminded himself that, although of Spanish ancestry, she was an American by birth and the Americans preferred to distance themselves from European squabbles.

Quartermaster, his shoulders more stooped than ever, wheeled her ladyship into the room. She looked frailer than usual; her small frame encompassed in a pale mauve stole run through with silver thread. Tendrils of fine, grey hair clung like feathers around a thin face. He supposed her hair was growing sparse, which explained why she was wearing an old-fashioned cap covered with black lace – as though she were grieving for her dead husband – a fact he disbelieved.

Her eyes glittered like chips of colourless glass. The colour of her lips matched the stole.

A tartan blanket covered what other clothes she was wearing, tucked tightly around her knees and down into the sides of the wheelchair.

The suffocating perfume of the lilies intensified when the butler left, closing the door behind him, having given her ladyship her walking stick.

Although it was early July and the weather outside was warm, a banked-up fire of glowing coals threw out an intense heat.

The doctor helped her ladyship into a comfortable armchair positioned to one side of the fire.

'Would you like me to open a window?' he asked, aware of sweat breaking out on his forehead. 'The fresh air will be good for you.'

Her lips curled with contempt. 'English air is damp. I need sunshine. I should never have come to this country. If I could, I would return to California. Even New York was better than this and of course New York society helped me cope with its cold winters and humid summers.'

'As you wish.'

He wanted to say that there was no baronet in New York and in the last century rich American families had wanted their daughters to marry men with titles.

Her gnarled hands gripped the chair arms; her skin as thin as rice paper and speckled with spots – like a mottled egg. She pursed her lips, staring into the fire whilst choosing her words.

'On the death of my husband I took you on as my physician.'

He nodded attentively, taking the liberty of sitting himself in the chair opposite hers even though she had not invited him to sit. 'I trust you are satisfied with my attention.'

Her tiny nostrils disappeared when she sniffed and tossed her head.

'On a medical level, yes. You have suited me very well.'

'I do hope so.'

He contemplated the service he had given her. Lady Julieta had a weak chest. On one particular occasion, she'd been at death's door. Following a powerful prescription and prescribed rest, she had improved greatly and assured him that she would have died without the treatment he'd given her.

However, she had a reputation of being a fickle woman. Sir Avis, her late husband, had confided to his doctor that his wife was as changeable as the English weather. 'Prepare yourself for a storm and you get sunshine; prepare yourself for sunshine and there's thunder in the air.'

Bearing Sir Avis's judgement in mind, he braced himself for the deluge to come.

'Your reputation as a doctor is impeccable and you have served me well enough,' she said in a voice that was as thin as she was, a whine like something that lacks strength but keeps going anyway. 'I have to consider my disposition to a weak chest of course. However, I have never patronised the services of those lacking in basic morals. I now find myself questioning yours. Rumours have reached my ears regarding your personal life. I am of strict morals, Doctor Miller. I abhor men who consort with loose women.'

Eric stiffened as fury rushed through him and got up from the chair. This was not what he'd been expecting, but he was ready to defend both his reputation and that of Kate Mallory. If the old girl wanted a battle, then she'd get one. He wouldn't give information freely; damn it, but he'd make her worm it out of him bit by bloody bit.

He stood with his legs slightly parted, hands clasped behind his back and his head held high.

'Loose women? To whom do you refer, your ladyship?' he said through a smile that hid his gritted teeth.

Strings of tiny diamonds swung from her ears as she turned her head this way and that, the wrinkles in her neck deepening.

She also pulled out a handkerchief trimmed with lace and smelling of perfume, and dabbed it at one nostril then the other.

'I hear this woman is an actress. I also hear that you are not married to her but are seen in her company on a regular basis.'

And you are an actress too, thought Eric, recognising that the dabbing of her nostrils had been a delaying tactic, a ruse that had given her time to think. If she had not married well, Lady Julieta might have achieved a passable career on the stage.

Eric kept his anger under control, though God knows he felt he could quite happily place both his hands around her scrawny neck and throttle the life out of her.

'How does your brother know this for sure – that I am in this woman's company on a regular basis?'

Lady Julieta's head jerked round to face him at the mention of her brother. 'You do not deny this?' she said.

Eric cleared his throat in an effort to swallow the spiteful words he really wanted to say, but he wished to keep her on as a patient. Her patronage was worthwhile.

'I am denying nothing. It is my business surely, not that of either my patients or their relatives. I am a grown man, not a young fool who doesn't know what he's doing.'

233

Black eyes inherited from the Spanish side of her family darkened with disapproval.

'Your morals matter to me, Doctor, especially seeing as your daughter, and my nephew are unofficially engaged. Anyone who marries Robert must be of the right family and impeccable reputation. I'm sorry, but you have to tell her that Robert is not for her. Either that, or I'm afraid I will have to find another physician.'

Doctor Eric could hardly believe what he was hearing. The effort to control his anger caused his voice to tremble. 'Are you trying to blackmail me, Lady Julieta? If so, I fear you are going to fail miserably.'

He read arrogance in the toss of her head, the thin meanness about her mouth as it stretched in a malevolent grimace. Her ladyship loved the power her status and title had bestowed on her. That's what these American heiresses had married into: the wealth and rank of centuries, the superiority of having a title even though Sir Avis's was of the lower order – not a duke or earl.

The old lady was unrepentant. 'Of course I am. I have the power to do so and, frankly, if you wish to retain my patronage, I think I'm being very fair. So far, I have not dismissed you as my physician despite your dalliance with a common actress. Robert is a different matter. You have to understand that your reputation has damaged your daughter's prospects. She cannot have Robert if you persist in your relationship with that sort of woman.'

In the past, Eric would have gone out of his way to pour oil on to troubled waters, but that was in the days when he'd strived to better himself. To do so had meant sucking up to the upper classes because they were his betters. Although it came as something of a surprise, he realised things had changed since he'd met Kate.

Standing there, towering over her, he noticed, with unrepentant glee, that she had to tilt her head back to look up at him. He hoped she had an aching neck tonight.

'Mrs Kate Mallory and I are of an age when we both know what we want. We both have chosen careers that we love, but dedication to one's career can be lonely. We have chosen not to be lonely.'

'A career! Do you call acting a respectable career?' she trilled, sounding as though acting was as bad as admitting to being a professional murderer.

'Respectable enough, though fortunes have been made from far more reviled professions than acting. There's a saying in the north of England that where there's muck there's money. I hear the same can be said for things in America.'

He saw that the barb had hit home. He'd heard that Julieta's family had made a fortune gathering up scrap metal following the American Civil War. Men, women and children, they'd scoured every battlefield, taking scrap metal to be smelted down, until they'd set up their own smelter, buying scrap metal from other lowly immigrant families. In time, they became very rich.

Realisation flashed into her ladyship's eyes then was gone. Her pale mauve lips set into grim resolution.

'What matters is that you flaunt your relation-

235

ship in public...'

Just as she had resolved to attack him, Eric had resolved to defend himself regardless of the outcome and he had not lost sight of that resolve.

He glanced at the vase of flowers, his nostrils dilating in response to the heady perfume.

'As I have just pointed out to you, Mrs Mallory and I are around the same age and are great friends. Ours is not just a physical relationship, Lady Julieta. Or perhaps I should take a leaf out of your brother's book and pursue freshly cut lilies?'

He could tell by the puzzled frown that she knew nothing of her brother's tastes.

She eyed him indignantly, her chin receding into the frilled collar of her blouse.

'What do you mean?' she demanded. Her voice was crisp and shrill.

Feeling as though he had the upper hand and meaning to play one last card, Eric headed for the door.

'I like mature women of my own age, your ladyship. Unlike your brother who prefers very young girls. Ask him the age of the young girl he was with the other night, a child made up to look like a woman. I do believe investigation might prove his habits illegal.'

'I say again, what do you mean?' bellowed Lady Julieta, her pale eyes suddenly dark and frightened.

Eric turned the door handle, opening the door ever so slightly, just enough that anyone outside – especially the servants – could overhear.

'I believe her name is Flora and that she is little more than thirteen years old. Let's put it this way, I would not leave my daughter in the same room as Rudolfo Credenza!'

He bid her good day and headed for the front door where Quartermaster was waiting with his hat and coat. It was obvious from his expression that the servants had heard the remark about her ladyship's brother. Servants, thought Eric, are not stupid and docile. On the contrary, they know everything their employers would prefer they did not know.

Halfway along the passageway from Lady Julieta's room, he almost collided with a maid bearing her ladyship's tea tray. The maid had given him a nervous smile then averted her eyes. He guessed she'd heard what he'd said. He also guessed everyone in the servants' hall would know before the day was out.

The anger continued to boil inside of him. Damn the English upper classes! Did they think they could dominate forever?

Suddenly he felt the outsider, the foreigner who belonged elsewhere. Why had he assumed acceptance into this insular society? The only spark in it had been Sir Avis, a clear-sighted man of deeper scruples than people gave him credit for.

Quartermaster was his usual solicitous self while handing the doctor his hat and coat, his head slightly inclined.

'Do have a good day, Doctor. It's been so very nice to see you again. I know the old master always looked forward to seeing you. He liked the little chats you had once the more serious business was over.'

Eric noticed the look in the old man's eyes and

237

knew he was not content with how things now were.

'How long have you been here, Quartermaster?'

'Thirty years plus ten – the ten were with the master when we were both serving in the army. I was his batman.'

'And how much longer here?'

Bending slightly from the waist, Quartermaster looked down at his polished shoes before raising his eyes.

'I retire shortly. There's a time for everything, and everything is changing. My day is done. I will go soon.'

'Let's hope your day is not entirely over,' Doctor Miller said thoughtfully. 'You deserve a peaceful retirement. However, I have to agree with you that things are changing, but then, some things need to change.'

Chapter Twenty-Two

June, 1914

Just before the assassination of the Austrian archduke and his wife on the twenty-eighth of June, Agnes had dared to telephone the hospital to tell Lydia she would be outside, waiting for her when she finished her shift.

'I've got splendid news,' Agnes had said. 'It concerns my future, my wonderful future.'

That was as far as it got; Agnes refused to tell

her what the splendid news was.

'Not until I come to collect you from the nunnery,' she declared.

'It's not a nunnery, Agnes, it's...'

'A hostel for nurses. But they do look a bit like nuns, all starched aprons and stiff bonnets.' She paused.

Lydia guessed what was coming.

'Have you heard from Robert?'

'He wrote saying he's going to try and get away, but if he can't then I am to take you and have a rare old time. His words I assure you. He's been learning how to fly some new aeroplane. All I hope is it stays up in the sky and docsn't come crashing down.'

'Lydia, you have no faith in modern inventions. They're getting safer all the time.'

Lydia said that she was probably right, but the catch in Agnes's voice was noticeable. She still loved Robert.

It was her weekend off and although she loved being a nurse, the prospect of spending the weekend with Agnes gave wings to Lydia's feet. Not that it seemed to make the time go any quicker.

Mr Trimble, a local man whose chest rumbled with noxious fluids and whose pasty skin seemed the only thing keeping his bones in place, watched her with amusement.

'The hands on that clock ain't going to movc any faster no matter how often you look at it or rush around this ward like a blinkin' greyhound.'

Lydia smoothed and tucked in his bedding. Although she attempted to adopt an innocent expression, she couldn't help smiling.

'Now who said I was looking at the clock, Mr Trimble?'

He winked at her, his pale hands fragile as birds' wings sticking out the sleeves of his pyjamas. His beady eyes stayed fixed on her face.

'Yer own clock's looking bright as a button, Nurse. I mean yer face. Off somewhere nice the weekend are you? Deserting old Sam Trimble for a lovesick young man who's promised you the world?'

'Of course not. I'm spending the weekend with a friend.'

'Not a boyfriend? Well bless my soul. Pretty girl like you without a sweetheart. Can't believe it, but there. If you want a sweetheart, call Sam Trimble. He'll be your sweetheart any day of the week.'

Lydia laughed – quite the wrong thing to do as it turned out. She felt Sister Bertha's eyes landing on her from beneath a beetled brow.

At the end of her shift, the German deaconess, a substantial woman of purposeful bearing and iron-grey hair, called for Lydia to come into her office.

'Close the door.'

Lydia did as ordered. Divided from the ward by a framework of green painted timber filled in with frosted glass panes, the room held a large desk, a filing cabinet and a profusion of potted plants, mostly along the window ledge.

The swivel chair creaked in protest when Sister Bertha's wide rump landed on its seat.

Lydia stood with her hands folded in front of her, eyes downcast. All the same, it was hard not to smile; Sam Trimble was such a cheeky beggar

– but funny – really funny.

Sister Bertha's square jaw set firmly.

'I see that you were smiling, Nurse Miller. You were smiling earlier. You were also flitting from bed to bed like a nervous butterfly.'

'Yes, Sister. Sam... Mr Trimble made me laugh. He's a bit of a character.'

The solid face in front of her bore no sign of amusement.

'There is no room for characters in this profession, Nurse Miller. Above all else, it is a nursing sister's duty to be efficient and professional, not a source of entertainment. Is that clear?'

'I...' She thought about saying that her father believed laughter was a good antidote to disease, but perhaps that would seem too superior. One thing she had learned since becoming a nurse was that it was better to fit in with those she worked with. A nurse was a member of a team. It was best if they all regarded each other as equal and worked as one.

'You were going to say something, Nurse?'

The small, searching eyes that fixed on her face were unsettling.

Lydia cleared her throat. 'No. Just a tickle in my throat, Sister.'

Sister Bertha lowered her eyes to the manila folder in front of her, opened it, surveyed its contents, and then looked up.

'You have a wilful nature, Nurse Miller. I am not tolerant of nurses with wilful natures. I wish only for nurses with dutiful natures because I know they will do as I tell them without thinking. I am also of the opinion that you are too familiar with

241

the patients. It is not professional. You should not call a patient by their Christian name.'

'Yes, Sister, but...'

'But?'

It was no use. Being professional means putting the patient first. She had to say what was on her mind.

'My father says that being friendly towards a patient helps put them at their ease and may even contribute to their recovery.'

Sister Bertha had a fleshy face. Two deep grooves ran downwards from the corners of her mouth, moving in line with whatever she was thinking.

'Your father's opinion is greatly respected. However, this hospital has been here in the East End of London longer than your father has. In fact, there has been a German hospital here since the last century, catering for the many ex-patriot German speakers living in England. Not that we treat only German speakers. We make no distinction between race, religion or colour. Our duty is to serve.' She paused, her gaze falling on the open folder.

'However, I have to admit that your examination marks are admirable. Seeing as you speak fluent German and English, you are likely to prosper and gain swifter promotion here than in an English hospital. However, a little serenity would not come amiss.'

'No, Sister. I'm sorry, Sister.'

'No matter.' Sister Bertha closed the file. 'We cannot stop patients from upsetting our decorum. And I suppose a little humour when mixed with medicine has to be beneficial.'

Lydia nodded. 'Yes, Sister.'

Sister Bertha sucked in her lips, her gaze dropping back again to the closed folder. Her fingertips beat a mild tattoo in time with her thoughts.

When she finally looked up, Lydia saw the concern in her eyes.

'If it does come about, war is a very bad thing, Sister Lydia. Our nurses have the option of going home to Germany. They do not have to, but...' She sighed deeply, her large breasts thrusting against the full bib of her apron. 'There is the possibility that we will be driven from the hospital simply for being German.'

'That would be terrible,' said Lydia, shaking her head in disbelief. 'The hospital does such good work.'

Sister Bertha nodded as she leaned back in her chair.

'It may not be enough, not for those who call themselves patriots.' She raised her face and looked directly into Lydia's eyes. 'Patriotism is never enough. We are here to serve the whole of mankind.'

'I cannot believe you'll be treated badly; not nurses or doctors.'

'You too are a nurse, Lydia. You also have a German father. Will you both be staying in England?'

'Yes. I think so. I have a fiancé. He's an aeroplane pilot. We're going to get married.'

The senior sister looked surprised. 'He will still marry you? Even though your father is from the country with whom England might go to war?'

'It hasn't mattered up until now and my father

has lived here for a very long time. Robert knows my father was born in Germany, but it won't make any difference to him. It made no difference to anyone before this ugly war started. He will still marry me. Yes,' she said again, nodding as though her firm conviction would melt away if she were to stop. 'Yes. He will still marry me.'

Old Mr Trimble winked and smiled at her when she came back on to the ward.

'She didn't eat you then,' he said to her.

Lydia tried adopting a coldly professional approach, but it was no good. Mr Trimble might be sick, but he'd clung on to his sense of humour. He made her laugh. She couldn't help herself.

'I have to be more professional,' she whispered to him.

'You're a right tonic. That's professional enough fer me,' he said, chuckling as she patted his bedding tidy and plumped up his pillows.

Lydia was ready with a witty riposte, but something outside of the window caught her eye. At first, she thought it was a flock of birds flying far off in the distance. Coming round from the side of the bed, she leaned closer to the window. They were a long way off, but she had no doubt that what she thought had been birds were aeroplanes.

Lydia's hand went to her throat in which a lump had suddenly formed. Were they already on their way to France? Was Robert with them?

'You all right, Nurse Miller?'

Lydia's eyes followed the small shrinking dots until they were no more. She tried to work out

244

where they were going. South? East? Yes. East.

'Nurse Miller? You ain't gonna faint are you?'

She jerked her head round to face one of her favourite patients.

'Mr Trimble. I think it's nearly time for your medicine.'

'That's good. I thought it was you might be wanting medicine.' He bent his head to one side. 'Something upset you out there, did it?'

Lydia closed her eyes and took a deep breath. 'I saw aeroplanes. My fiancé is a pilot. He might have been piloting one of them.' She looked down at her hands clasped as though in prayer, something done unconsciously.

The humour that helped Mr Trimble cope with his illness was no longer there. Numerous wrinkles, so deep they seemed gouged into his flesh, drooped and quivered.

'This war if it comes ain't gonna be nothing like the Zulu wars, the Boer wars and such like. Nothing like the kind of wars I was ever in.'

He sounded very fearful for a man who had fought many times for his country.

'It's all so strange,' said Lydia. 'The world is talking about war yet so far nothing has changed. I hope it doesn't. I hope everything stays the same.'

The look of fear left the wrinkled face. 'I hope so too, me dear. I hope so too. Get out and about this weekend and enjoy yourself. 'Opefully that young man of yours might not be in that there flying machine.'

'I'm staying with a friend for the weekend. We're going down to the country. My fiancé has

245

given us the key to his cottage.'

The cottage was a godsend, left to Robert by his uncle and not far from the airfield. It was a slight hope, but Robert might still be there and Agnes had agreed to go with her.

'Going on the old chuff chuff?' he asked her. She knew he meant the train.

'No. My friend is picking me up in a motor car.'

Mr Trimble's many wrinkles lifted in unison.

'My word. Fancy being picked up in a chauffeur-driven car at your age! Very posh I must say.'

'She won't be using a chauffeur. She's driving the motorcar herself. She *is* a chauffeur.'

Mr Trimble looked even more amazed before he brought his grizzled eyelid down in a wicked wink. 'Better not tell Sister Bertha. She'll be shocked out of her stockings, that she will!'

The vision of Sister Bertha looking shocked out of her stockings stayed with Lydia when she was in her room washing and gathering up her things into a tapestry-weave bag.

Mr Trimble always said the right words to make her smile. So did Agnes for that matter, with her outspokenness and her ability to shock people.

She was just finishing her packing when a message came to say she had a visitor.

'A gentleman,' said the auxiliary nurse who had brought the message. 'He's waiting for you in the library. Sister Bertha said that as he looks to be an officer and a gentleman she will not insist on you being chaperoned.'

The young nurse blushed. Lydia's eyes sparkled. It had to be Robert.

She closed her eyes. She hadn't consciously

246

prayed for a miracle, yet it seemed she had one; Robert was here!

The packing left for later, she hurried off to the library, impatient to feel Robert's arms around her and to tell him that she'd give everything up for him. They would marry as soon as possible.

Before he's no longer here. Though pray God he will be.

As it was mid afternoon, the library was not much used, nurses preferring to study in there early in the morning before they began their shifts, or late evenings after they'd finished. Today it was empty except for one stalwart figure wearing the uniform of the King's Hussars. Captain Sylvester Travis Dartmouth.

Lydia's high excitement crumbled. 'I was expecting Robert.'

Sylvester turned away from studying the spines of a fine set of medical books.

'He gave his note to a subaltern to deliver. I took it from him. Pulled rank. Thought we should keep all this in the family. Anyway, my dear, how lovely to see you.'

He kissed her cheek in greeting. His lips were cold and his breath smelled as though he'd just eaten Dover sole with lots of lemon.

'What's happened?'

'I've already more or less told you. Robert is detained.' His fingers attempted to grasp hers as he handed her a note. Lydia snatched her hand away, along with the precious message.

She read it swiftly, loving to see his words at the same time as feeling immense disappointment.

'How are you, Lydia my dear?' Sylvester said.

247

'I'm fine.' She knew he wanted to know what Robert had written, but she wasn't going to tell. Robert's words were for her and her alone.

'More than fine, I think,' said Sylvester. 'In fact you look very fine indeed for a woman who works for a living.'

He was doing his best to sound amiable, but somehow his air of superiority always won through.

She felt him eyeing her condescendingly from head to toe. Her head held high, she gave him the same look back. Hair that had once been very light blonde was now darker and trimmed close to his head. He was clean-shaven, crisp and despite her comment, she had to admit he was splendid to look at. The trouble was, Sylvester being the way he was, he knew it.

'Yes, and I wear a uniform, just as you do.' She looked him up and down in the same way he had looked at her. 'A fine uniform, Sylvester. I take it both that and your commission as an officer cost a pretty penny.'

She saw him wince at the insinuation that he'd purchased his commission without having to earn it. The rich could do that. You could buy anything if you had enough money.

'I expect you were looking forward to seeing my dear cousin. Shame he couldn't make it.'

His sympathy didn't match his expression or his tone. He sounded as though he were well pleased with the fact.

'Yes. It is,' she said, smiling as she folded the message and put it into her pocket. She would not disclose what was in the message. 'Never mind.

248

There'll be other weekends when he can make it.'

'I dare say, though not always in such fine weather, don't you think? He's taken one of his flying machines down to Dover. The whole shebang will be setting off from there, all those intrepid young men in their flying machines. Must say I don't rate their chances of crossing the Channel without losing a few. String, canvas and little else. And if that engine fails ... whoosh...' He did a diving motion with his hand. 'Into the drink!'

'Robert is a very capable pilot.'

'Of course he is, but is the flying machine capable of flying all the way across the Channel? That's what you have to ask yourself, dear girl. That's what you have to ask yourself.'

He stepped close enough for her to smell his hair oil, his mannish sweat and the fish he'd eaten. The buttons on his uniform gleamed, no doubt polished and buffed by some lowly batman. In time that same man who took care of Captain Travis Dartmouth would be given a rifle and shoved into battle-fodder for the big guns.

She found herself repeating the kind of things Agnes had told her.

'Robert knows what he's doing and aeroplanes are improving all the time. Anyway, he's doing his duty and I have to do mine.'

'How about I take you out this weekend? We could go to a music hall. That Kate Mallory woman is performing in something at the Prince of Wales. I hear she's lovely, loud and of loose morals, but a damned good performer. How about it?'

She shook her head. 'I don't think so.' All she

wanted was to get away from him, to drive off with Agnes and stay at the cottage anyway. Agnes had been going along as chaperone. Now it would be just the two of them.

Sylvester seemed loath to leave.

'Shame you're not wearing your uniform. I was hoping you would be.'

'I've already changed.'

'So I see. I do love women in uniform,' he suddenly said. 'I think I told you that once before. It brings out the brute in me.' He reached out and cupped her cheek.

Lydia stepped away, her worst instincts about Sylvester urging her to flee. 'I beg your pardon?'

'The caveman instinct I believe it's called. Come on, old girl. Robert's not to know. I won't tell him if you don't. How about we step out on Saturday night? We can go wherever you wish. We'll make a good pair.'

'I don't want to go out with you.'

Sylvester's expression darkened. 'You think too highly of yourself, Fraulein Miller – or, should that be Muller? Who do you think you are? You should think yourself lucky to be going out with a commissioned officer. I usually only favour titled ladies of good breeding from excellent *English* families.' He stressed the word English so she was in no doubt that he knew her father was German, and knew he had her at a disadvantage.

'Then you should call on one of those ladies,' she said, her words becoming more and more clipped.

She kept moving backwards, but he kept coming until the edge of a table was digging into the back of her thighs.

'Do you recall when I locked you in the grotto at Christmas? I would have come back later. I would have set you free. We could have had such fun together. Shame Robert got there before me. He has got there before me, hasn't he? You and him have done the dirty deed, have you not?'

'No,' she shouted. She slapped his face. He grabbed her wrist with one hand and grabbed her breast with the other. With her free hand, she scratched his face.

'Bitch!' He fingered the marks she'd left behind; long enough for her to step sideways then back until she was safely behind one of the armchairs with which the library was furnished.

'Get out of here!'

He stood there smiling, looking down at his hand. 'What a lovely feeling that's left.'

Lydia's grey eyes flashed with anger. She had been looking forward to this weekend. Sylvester had managed to ruin it.

'I shall tell Robert what you did,' she said.

He shrugged. 'Not until he gets back from flying his little machine. Anyway, you're hardly off limits, my dear Lydia. I mean, it's not as though you two are *formally* engaged is it? I mean, you're only a nurse and half foreign, whereas my dear cousin is heir to a great fortune. What a waste. Do you know that if he dies I get to inherit? No doubt your attitude will change towards me then. I know your sort. Nothing but a little gold digger.'

Lydia picked up a heavy book, raising it above her head ready to throw.

'Get out!'

He grinned. His lips were wet. His face glistened with sweat.

'Feisty. I do like that, but obviously, the time is not yet ripe. I'm sure at some time in the future you and I will come together, one way or the other. I'm willing to wait. In the meantime, I have other fish to fry. Very tempting fish in fact. Nevertheless, do bear me in mind. If ever you need a man, I'll be there for you. Toodle pip for now.'

Once he'd gone, she leaned against the armchair to catch her breath, the book falling to the floor with a loud bang.

The door opened and Sister Bertha entered. She frowned at the sight of Lydia's flushed face and the tendrils of hair that had escaped to fall in wisps around her face.

'Are you all right, Miller?'

She nodded. 'Yes. I'm fine.'

'I take it the fine young officer was your sweetheart?'

'No,' she said, shaking her head. 'Definitely not my sweetheart.'

Captain Sylvester Travis Dartmouth frowned at a stubborn stain that his batman had failed to remove from the cuff of his jacket. A poor job indeed. The man would have to go. He'd given him a chance and he'd blown it. The likes of him, working class with a horde of children, were best off holding the front line so their betters wouldn't have to.

Sylvester believed in spending on himself. In his opinion, servants should work for their keep, just enough to keep them clothed and fed. The new

Labour movement that had sprung up thought otherwise, but their protests were weak and easily suppressed. They really had to accept that the plight of labourers and servants in general had not changed for centuries and it wasn't about to change now. Not in his opinion anyway.

Stepping away from the main entrance to the hospital, he took a deep breath before lighting a cigarette. My God, but he needed a smoke. The fresh air was an added benefit. He couldn't stand that sterile smell of carbolic and whatever other stuff they used to clean the wards and treat people. Obnoxious smell whatever it was.

The road outside was noisy and crowded with trams and horse-drawn trade vehicles, street vendors pushing two-wheeled carts, and flower sellers offering posies to passers-by. He wished he could sweep them all away and leave only the buildings, some of which he would delight in knocking down, and some he could almost worship.

He turned and looked up at the imposing entrance to the hospital. He thought the building excellent and wasted on sick people. It would take a few more cigarettes and a cab journey to his club to get rid of the stench of sick people in poor clothes. Moreover, more were coming in.

Two children were helping a thin woman up the steps to the hospital entrance. Her face was sunken by sickness and her clothes were as black as her hair, clean but shabby. He assumed she was Jewish from Russia or Germany, a peasant victim of persecution that had sent the Jews fleeing in terror. As if we haven't enough of our own peasants, he thought to himself.

The woman nodded to him, a courteous nod that he was used to getting from anyone from the lower classes.

He grimaced in response and said aloud, 'Damn it, there will be more peasants and foreigners in this country than us before long.'

Chapter Twenty-Three

August, 1914

The weather was fine and things would have been wonderful if only Robert had been able to get away to see her.

Staying in the cottage had been her idea; he'd looked surprised when she'd suggested it.

'Well. If you're really sure, though I think your father would prefer you to have a chaperone. Unless he comes too.'

She'd shaken her head. 'I think not.'

They'd both fallen into silence. 'I want to be alone with you, but for the sake of propriety I'll bring Agnes,' she said.

'I'm not sure her presence will be enough to control how I feel – if you know what I mean.'

'You mean sharing a bed,' said Lydia with a sigh. 'It's the war,' she said to him. 'The war is barely begun, yet is altering everything.'

'As long as you're sure.'

'I think there comes a moment in everyone's life which defines them entering adulthood.

That's how I feel now,' she'd told him. 'This is the moment when we shall all grow up. Agnes will come with me. I can meet you there. She can drive me down.'

Robert's weekend cottage was in Sussex, not far from the airfield. They, of course, did not stay there very often themselves. They had investments, land and sheep in Australia. They owned a logging company in Canada and a rubber plantation in Malaya.

Robert had mentioned it having roses around the door and a garden he considered overgrown, though in reality it was typical of a cottage garden, with hollyhocks, roses, lupins, gladioli and delphiniums all jostling for space like a crowd at the Derby or a football match.

Agnes had jumped at the chance of an outing, especially considering she got the opportunity to drive her employer's car. She still wanted to become an ambulance driver, but nobody would give her the chance. In the meantime she continued to drive an old lady around. It looked as though she would have to do so for some time.

'I told her it was for the war effort,' she'd told Lydia cheekily when she'd asked how she'd managed to wangle it.

The car, being of the sedan variety, had a roof. Although Agnes preferred to wear her leather cap and goggles when driving, today she'd made an exception. She wore a hat; a very large hat made of straw with an enormous brim.

'You look like Little Bo Peep,' said Lydia as she got into the car after first strapping her luggage on at the back.

'How would you know what Little Bo Peep looked like?' asked Agnes, peering out at her from beneath the battered brim.

'I had a picture of her in a nursery rhyme book when I was a child.'

Agnes grinned. 'You had just about everything when you were a child!'

Although the comment needled her, Lydia chose to ignore it. She accepted that she'd had a privileged childhood, but Agnes had not really known poverty. Even the house in Myrtle Street was comfortable compared to some, and, of course, she had spent much of her childhood in one or the other of Sir Avis's houses.

Agnes was wearing a silk scarf over the big hat, fastened beneath her chin with a large bow. Consequently, the large brim was bent and covered both sides of her face.

Lydia stroked the walnut panelling lining the interior of the car door. 'This is amazing. Your employer must be worth a fortune to run something like this. What an amazing stroke of luck.'

Agnes tipped her head sideways and grinned at her. 'Not for much longer. I have something to tell you. I've got a new job.'

Agnes was keeping her eyes on the road ahead, so Lydia was unable to read her expression, but she sounded quite exuberant.

'What is it? What's happened? Whatever it is, you sound very excited.'

'Guess!'

'Judging by the way your voice is bubbling over, I would guess that you're going to be doing something you really enjoy, and there's only one thing you really enjoy. You're going to be driving a motor car. Am I right?'

Agnes laughed and shook her head. Fronds of hair showed from beneath her straw bonnet; like fine horsehair, wild and completely uncontrollable.

'I already drive a motor car. It's an ambulance. I'm joining up – in a manner of speaking. I can't be a soldier of course, but I can be in what they call a supporting role.'

Agnes felt herself swelling with pride. What she wasn't telling Lydia was that the people doing the recruiting had turned her down for the more mundane jobs, preferring instead to hire vicars' daughters, girls with parents of note with cut-glass voices and the confident air of those in receipt of a private income, certainly not the daughter of a cook, an illegitimate one at that.

Lydia congratulated her. 'That is simply amazing. Where will you be based?'

'Here and there, though I'm hoping I might get to France. The army is heading there. Everyone.'

Lydia knew instantly that everyone meant Robert. Agnes was going to follow Robert – if she could.

'Robert's already there; at least I think he is.'

'Under the circumstances, I'm not surprised he couldn't get away to the cottage,' said Agnes. 'But you still want to go? Just the two of us?'

Lydia nodded. 'Just the two of us.'

'Right.'

Agnes released the clutch, took off the brake and eased the car out into a gap behind a horse and cart.

'Have you seen him?' Agnes asked.

Lydia shook her head. 'I may have done.'

She told Agnes about the flying machines she'd seen from the window of the hospital.

'I hope he's not in France just yet. Not yet, not until we've had the chance to at least say goodbye.'

'At least,' agreed Agnes, sounding as though she were swallowing something, a cough, a sigh, or perhaps a sob. 'I would have liked to say goodbye to him too.'

They drove in silence for a while, Agnes supposedly because she was concentrating on driving, though in actuality her heart felt like lead. She would never get over Robert; there would never be anyone else.

Lydia was silent, buttoning down her seething resentment for Robert's cousin.

'Sylvester brought me the message,' she said to Agnes.

'Oh! How was he? His usual gluttonous, selfish self?'

'All of those things and looking well. He's a captain now.'

Agnes grabbed the horn and gave it a good blast. A startled delivery boy on a bicycle veered into the kerb.

'I got the impression he tried to force himself on you. You're not the only one. It happened in the library when my mother and I were still at Heathlands. I was dusting some of the old books. Sylvester found me there and threw himself at me. I fought like an alley cat, which seemed to surprise him. Told me I should be grateful that such as he

258

was interested in the daughter of a cook as he was kind enough to point out. I bashed him with a copy of *The Peloponnesian Wars*. It was quite heavy.'

Lydia laughed. 'Well, there's a coincidence! He tried something similar in the library at the hospital. I threatened to hit him with a copy of *Modern Medicine for the Nursing Profession*.'

Pedestrians stopping to watch the car go past looked amazed to see two young women, laughing and waving as they drove past.

'He'll never forgive you,' said Lydia once the laughter had diminished.

'I think he might. I laughed afterwards and told him not to be such a fool. Did he really want to get his brains bashed out because of a cook's daughter? He seemed to see the funny side at first, and then he said something about me having missed my chance to be respectable. He went on to say that if I didn't end up as a domestic servant, I would end up as a whore. I told him that would be better than ending up like the fat barrel of lard he was likely to become.'

Two hours later, after getting some directions in the village of Melton Wendell, they came to a halt outside Rose Cottage.

Even if she hadn't noticed the name etched on the gate, Lydia would have guessed it was the right one. Pink, red and white climbing roses tumbled over a trellis fence and petals fluttered along the grass verge.

'It is so pretty,' Lydia exclaimed as she got out of the car. 'And that perfume!'

Agnes took a deep breath. 'It smells wonderful, not as good as roast beef and vegetables, but good all the same. I'm going to enjoy staying here.'

Lydia didn't voice her disappointment that Robert wasn't here. Although she hid it well, she knew Agnes must be hurting. I'll not mention Robert, she decided. Best not to mention him at all.

'It's a shame that Robert couldn't make it,' said Agnes, taking Lydia unawares. 'Let's hope he's all right.'

Lydia paused at the gate, her hand resting on the rough wood.

'I shouldn't have brought you, Agnes. Knowing how you feel about Robert, it was thoughtless of me.'

'Don't be silly,' said Agnes, who was facing the cottage, her expression hidden behind the bent brim of her yellow straw hat. 'Someone had to act as chaperone – or gooseberry – however you want to look at it. If I hadn't agreed, your father would have locked you in your room. Come on. Let's explore this place.'

Pushing through the gate ahead of Lydia, she marched up the path to the front door.

A thick thatch frowned over whitewashed walls and square windows with green painted frames. Half hidden beneath a canopy of wisteria that hummed with the sound of bees was a solid front door painted the same shade of green as the windows. A handwritten sign of welcome, in a childish scrawl, hung on a black chain beneath the knocker. Above that, lodged firmly into the upper right-hand corner of the door surround, hung a cast-iron key around which somebody had tied a red ribbon.

Lydia, being the taller, reached for it. 'Well!

Let's see if the three bears are at home.' The key grated but the door didn't budge.

Agnes pushed Lydia aside. 'Let me do it.'

Lydia accepted that Agnes could work wonders with anything metal or vaguely mechanical. The door lock fitted into the latter category.

'Open Sesame!'

There were three rooms on the ground floor plus a scullery. The main living room had a huge ingle-nook fireplace. An oak Welsh dresser, dark with age but shiny with copper and brass and blue and white crockery, took up one wall. A sofa with squashy cushions and chintz upholstery matched comfortable chairs to either side of the fireplace.

'I love this room,' exclaimed Agnes. 'I love this cottage in fact. Time to make myself at home!'

Off came the yellow straw hat, Agnes's hair flying around her head in tangled skeins as she whirled around the room.

Lydia laughed and clapped her hands. Agnes was so spirited, so full of life. If this was an act to hide her feelings, it was a good one.

Lydia went to the small square window deep set into the thick wall of the cottage. After a short struggle with the window catch, she opened the casement. 'Let's have some of that perfume in here,' she said and breathed deeply.

Beyond the garden, she could see houses in the nearby village plus the grey tower of a Norman church. The sky was mostly blue, but beyond the village, grey marbled clouds were rolling in from the east.

From the east, where war had finally begun.

The bedrooms were a good size and they had

261

one each. A pretty washstand with flower-patterned tiles graced each room and someone – possibly the woman who looked after the cottage for the family – had placed a cut-glass bowl full of roses on each bedroom windowsill.

The clouds were visible through these windows too, though closer now.

'Lydia? What are you looking at?'

'Clouds. Over to the east.' Lydia's voice cracked with emotion.

Agnes reached out to touch Lydia's cheek. It was quite cold and the look in her eyes had nothing to do with the weather.

'He'll be all right,' she said calmly. 'The war may not come to anything, and everyone is saying that they'll all be home for Christmas.'

'I hope you're right,' said Lydia with a huge sigh. 'I do hope you're right.'

With Lydia feeling only slightly reassured and Agnes burying her pain beneath her natural exuberance, they scuttled back down the stairs and outside.

Agnes undid the straps holding their luggage in place on the car, passed Lydia her shiny brown suitcase and lifted down her own more scuffed affair.

'I'll come back for the hamper,' said Agnes.

'I bought a new dress,' said Lydia, decanting a pale pink lace dress from beneath wads of crisp white tissue paper. 'I thought Robert would like it.' She bit her lip. It shouldn't have slipped out, but it had. She looked to see if Agnes had noticed.

'Sorry, but there's only me to impress. In fact as your chaperone this weekend, I might not have let you wear it if Robert had been here. Much too revealing!'

Agnes laughed and Lydia laughed with her, relieved that they were still friends despite both of them loving Robert.

At the bottom of the stairs, Agnes paused to bite back the aching in her throat. Muffled by carpet, her footsteps sounded hollow within the narrow stairwell, as she went upstairs. Everything had been manageable up until Lydia showed her that beautiful dress, a dress she could never afford. The dress she had bought for her meeting with Robert underlined the fact that she, Agnes, was of a different social class. Her love for Robert had been in vain. Robert loved Lydia. They would get married but would still be her friends and she should be grateful, but she wasn't.

'I'll fetch the hamper,' said Agnes, and dashed outside, tears stinging her eyes.

Sunlight peering from behind a silvered cloud caught the chrome of the car headlights, making them glint as though they were exploding with light.

Gladdened by the sight of the car, Agnes sniffed back the threatening sobs. She had achieved so much in her short life; she had trodden where other women feared to tread, venturing on to male territory.

With the failing sunlight warming her bare head and shoulders, she swore an oath, repeating it in her mind until the power of her oath replaced the pain she'd been suffering.

I've lost Robert and there will never be another man in my life. I will achieve wonderful things, but marriage and having children will not be one of them.

Heaving a sigh big enough to send her shoulders almost up around her ears, she went to the car, opened the door and found … nothing.

The hamper! Her mother had baked cakes, bread, cooked ham, sliced cheese, and made all other sorts of delectable things, wrapping everything in red and white check cloth before placing it all in the hamper. The hamper had been sitting on the kitchen table, ready to place on the back seat of the car. She'd taken her luggage out first. She'd forgotten the hamper.

Agnes covered her eyes and groaned. Behind her hands she could see the honey-coloured basket weave of the hamper and smell the delicious aromas, could even visualise what she should have done and what she hadn't done; she had left it behind.

Lydia was filling up a copper kettle from the outside pump when Agnes returned.

'I thought you might be more successful getting the range working than...' On seeing Agnes's glum expression, her blood ran cold. 'What? What is it? What's happened?'

Agnes sucked in her bottom lip and said tearfully, 'I forgot the hamper. We've got no food.'

Lydia shook her head. 'Is that all? The world will not end, Agnes. We'll just have to go into the village to buy food. Unless you want to go home?'

It had occurred to Lydia that forgetting the hamper might not be true but only an excuse to go home seeing as Robert wasn't here.

Agnes was adamant. 'We'll go into the village.'

The car decided to be temperamental about re-starting.

'It probably thinks it's gone far enough already,' commented Lydia.

'Cars do not think,' said Agnes, sweat dripping from the end of her nose as she once again heaved on the starting handle in an attempt to turn the engine over. 'They're just stupid lumps of metal!'

Agnes's legs left the ground as the starting handle kicked back, catching her in the ribs. The engine rumbled into life.

'That hurt,' said Agnes. She frowned as she rubbed her ribs with one hand and wiped smears of oil from her face.

'You shouldn't have called it a stupid lump of metal,' Lydia remarked.

'Get in,' scowled Agnes.

The village shop sold everything from buckets to bacon. Buckets piled one inside the other ob-structed the door, just as they did in the corner shop at Myrtle Street. The bacon, a slab with yellowing fat and meat only a shade or two above purple, was slammed against the side of the slicing blade with its sharp teeth and easy action.

The woman behind the counter was a typical country person with pink cheeks and brown hair turning to grey. Her eyes lit up at the sight of them.

'Visitors are ye? Oh, that is nice. Visitors are always welcome,' chirped the woman behind the counter, her speech bubbling with subdued laugh-ter. 'I do like 'aving strangers to serve. Bacon is it?'

Her pink face stilled whilst her strong hands patted the bacon, as though placating it before

265

slicing off a few rashers.

The woman asked one question after another as she weighed bacon and cheese, counted eggs and slapped a loaf of bread on the counter.

'Where are you from?'

'Where are you staying?'

'How long for?'

'Any relation to the Ravenings?'

Agnes blurted out that Lydia was informally engaged to Mr Robert Ravening.

'Ow!' said the shopkeeper, her whole face seeming to form a solid circle of amazement.

Lydia blushed. 'Agnes!'

Agnes was unrepentant. 'It's true.'

By the time they got outside, their purchases packed into a cardboard box, the first drops of rain were falling.

Agnes caught a penny-sized droplet in her outstretched hand.

'I think we're going to have a thunder storm.'

Lydia gasped. 'Oh no. I forgot to close the windows. Quick. We have to hurry.'

Once the box of groceries was sitting on the back seat, Agnes hurried round to the front of the car to do battle with the starting handle.

'Now, you beast!' she muttered, gripping the starting handle with both hands.

Lydia wasn't sure exactly what happened, but the starting handle gave an almighty jolt. Agnes flew through the air, landing ignominiously in the centre of the dusty road where she lay sprawled, her eyes closed and blood trickling from her temple.

'Agnes!'

Lydia ran into the middle of the road where she fell to her knees beside her friend, checking her pulse, feeling her face, ultimately concluding that Agnes was not dead, just unconscious.

The woman from the shop had seen everything and came running out, her apron flapping around her body.

'Is she dead?'

'No,' said Lydia, her expression strained, eyes wide with mute pleading. 'But she does need a doctor.'

Chapter Twenty-Four

The doctor examined her and then advised that Agnes should go to the cottage hospital, which turned out to be exactly that. It had six beds in the women's ward and another six in the men's ward. Four of those in the women's ward were empty; one woman asleep, the other an elderly patient with twinkling blue eyes that followed their every move.

'You don't have many patients,' Lydia remarked.

The doctor seemed offended. 'That's why it's called a cottage hospital. It's mostly pregnant women and injured farm labourers who come here. Rest assured, your friend is only concussed, but I'll keep her in until she wakes up. It doesn't hurt to be careful. You go on back to wherever it is you're staying.'

'Rose Cottage,' Lydia informed him, adding

267

that she was a nurse and could stay and look after her friend.

'No need. I have a nurse. My wife, you see,' he said in a Welsh accent of the kind that bellows from the pulpit. 'It's our hospital. You drive on back to Rose Cottage. Your friend will be fine.'

'I'm afraid I can't drive a car. I'll have to leave it here and walk back,' she explained.

'There's a storm coming. You'll be soaked through by the time you get back to Rose Cottage. I'll arrange a lift in a pony and trap. Will that be all right?'

Lydia told the doctor that it would suit her fine.

The weighty clouds let loose their rain, it poured down.

Hair dripping water, droplets falling from her nose, Lydia held on to the cardboard box of groceries on her lap with both hands. The brim of her hat was becoming sodden, raindrops falling off like crystal pearls and running down her neck. Her clothes were wet through.

She wished she could have stayed with Agnes regardless of the doctor's reluctance, but she'd left windows open back at the cottage. Agnes is resilient, she reminded herself.

She'd barely darted inside the front door before lightning flashed and a peal of thunder rolled overhead. Startled, she let go the bottom of the box, soggy and soft now thanks to the downpour. Cheese, bread, bacon and a mix of eggs and brown paper bag fell out and on to the floor.

Soaked through and tired, Lydia sat down on a chair, buried her face in her hands and howled. Nothing had gone right with this trip. She had come here hoping to be with Robert before his posting came through. Would she see him again before he went to France? She dearly hoped so.

Lightning flashed and thunder rolled again before wind-driven rain lashed the window.

Lydia leapt to her feet. She'd closed the down-stairs window, but the one upstairs in her bedroom was still open. She ran up the stairs, not relishing the prospect of sleeping in a sodden bed – before remembering that Agnes's bed was empty. So much for her friend acting as a chaperone. Not that it mattered. Robert had been unable to come anyway.

Saved by the overhanging eaves, the bedroom was quite dry except for a few windblown rose petals.

Taking a deep breath, Lydia sat herself half on to the window ledge, leaned forward and stared at the sky. Thunderstorms had always fascinated her, the way the lightning flashed across the sky, the thunder crashing like great waves upon a rocky shore.

Fear had replaced fascination. She knew little about cannons, but the comparison was obvious. A cannon flashed then a thunderous crack occurred before the shell was despatched. That's what it would be like when the guns opened up on the other side of the English Channel.

Supper was bread and cheese washed down with hot milk. Worrying about whether Robert was already in France, and with Agnes in a hospital bed, she didn't have much of an appetite.

After stripping off her wet clothes, she sank thankfully into bed. She lay with her arms crossed behind her head thinking. The bedside candle threw flickering shadows over the lime-washed walls. Some of those shadows thrown by ordinary objects, a jug, a vase, a hairbrush, turned into something else, something more frightening.

She imagined them as machines of war, crawling over the ground. She reminded herself that Robert would be flying and safe from all that.

Just as she was about to put out the candle flame, a moth flew into it. Its wings burst into flame. It fell, twitched and moved no more.

The storm abated and she fell asleep. Dreams came and went and for a moment she thought that Robert was there, standing at the side of the bed, telling her he wouldn't go to France unless she went too. 'I will,' she said in her dream. 'Yes. I will.'

Someone called her name.

'Lydia? Lydia?'

She woke up in an instant. The wind. The thunderstorm was over; it could only be the wind.

Raising herself on to one elbow, she looked around the room but the darkness was impenetrable. It was as though somebody had placed a black screen before her eyes, or painted the room and everything in it with black paint. No light seeped through the curtains because there was none; no street lamp, no light from a neighbour's window. The cottage stood alone at the end of a narrow track.

There was a creaking sound, perhaps an opening door, perhaps the branch of an aged oak moving in the wind.

She pulled the bedclothes up higher whilst telling herself not to be frightened. It *was* only the wind, just the wind whistling round the house.

Another creak, then another. She held her breath. The sound was coming from the stairwell. Footsteps!

The door creaked open, the sudden fluttering of a candle lifting the total blackness.

'Who is it? Who's there?'

A dark figure came into view, the light from the candle accentuating his jawline, high cheekbones and deep-set eyes.

'Lydia! I called you, but when you didn't answer, I thought you were asleep. I took off my boots before climbing the stairs. I didn't mean to scare you. I just wanted to see you, look at you one last time before I leave.'

It wasn't a dream. It was really him.

'I saw flying machines in the sky over London. I thought you were already gone.'

She gave him no time to answer, flying from the bed, flinging her arms around Robert's neck.

'Careful,' he said, holding the candle as steady as he could.

He quickly set it down. A spot of wax dripped and he cried out when it burned his finger.

'What is it?'

'Just wax.'

'I'm sorry.'

His smile was wide and brave. 'It's worth the pain, my love. Well worth the pain.'

He wrapped both arms around her, hugging her tightly and burying his face in her hair.

'Didn't you hear my car?'

'No.'

'Better be careful we don't wake Agnes. I didn't

see your car outside.'

'She's not here,' said Lydia, shaking her head, not realising that just the sight of her loose hair, the smell of her body so warm inside her long linen nightgown, was the most erotic thing he'd ever encountered.

He stroked her face as she told him about what had happened.

'She's going to be all right?'

Lydia nodded. 'She'll be fine.' She paused. 'We're here alone.'

She said it softly, huskily and full of meaning.

He looked down into her face. She felt his biceps tense as though he were hesitating whilst he thought through exactly what she was saying.

Waiting for him to make the next move was sheer torture. She realised she'd to make it plain.

'I have no chaperone,' she heard herself saying. Reputation, her father and everyone else no longer mattered. There was only today. Tomorrow might never come.

Gather ye rosebuds while ye may...

Every contour of his body was discernible. The candle flickered over his muscles, the line of his shoulder.

He ran one hand down her arm, over her breast and over her hip.

The moment his lips crushed hers, she knew there was no going back. He couldn't – wouldn't – resist her. She herself was beyond resistance. She felt light headed, not just because she'd feared those noises in the night, but because she knew this was the man she wanted and would not resist. The attraction was too strong.

He took off his jacket, slung down his braces and unbuttoned his trousers, all done with his lips still clamped to hers.

She unbuttoned his shirt and, trembling, helped him remove his vest. His smell too was somehow familiar, a sweet maleness that when she breathed it in almost made her dizzy.

The message got through, the pressure of his hardening penis almost painful as well as exciting.

Echoing her excitement, he tugged at the six small pearl buttons fastening her nightgown. In his haste, one button popped off.

'Sorry. I'm too clumsy,' he murmured, his voice thick with desire.

'Let me.'

She pushed his fingers away, her own trembling as she undid each button in turn, pulling the sleeves halfway down her upper arms so her shoulders, her breastbone, and then her breasts were exposed.

The nightgown tumbled in tiers around her ankles. The heat of his chest, a sprinkling of hairs dividing each breast, surprised her, and yet she relished it.

He cupped each of her breasts, lowering his head, his voice smothered with groans of desire and exclamations of how beautiful she was. The touch of his hands, large hands with warm palms and sensitive fingers, made her skin tingle.

She felt his breath on her body as his lips moved upwards, dotting her flesh with fiery kisses, licking the dip beneath her throat whilst stumbling sideways in his attempt to remove his trousers and underwear.

Laughing, Lydia held on to him to stop him from falling. They stood like statues amongst the discarded clothing, two lovers who had been instantly attracted to each other, now about to venture further, to claim the final prize.

He wrapped his arms around her and clasped her tightly to his chest, breast against breast, belly against belly, thighs against thighs.

'I can feel you all the way down,' he whispered.

'I can feel...' She took a deep breath, arched her back and pressed closer. 'You!'

Tentatively, she reached down between them, touching the tip of his penis with her fingers.

Robert groaned and closed his eyes.

Lydia whispered in his ear, 'The bed's getting cold.' Without another word, he picked her up and set her down in the middle of the feather mattress.

The candle cast a subtle light, not that they had need of light. They had looked at each other long enough to know what they were getting.

'I love you, Robert Ravening,' she said to him. The words came out without warning but were heartfelt.

He smiled down at her, drinking in the expressive face, the round breasts, the narrow waist, the flared hips and the downy patch between her legs.

'I'm going to marry you, Lydia Miller, and don't you forget it.'

The sight of him, the feel of him and this wonderful night; that, she decided, is what I will never forget. And we will marry. When this dreadful war is over, we will marry.

Chapter Twenty-Five

The next morning saw them periodically smiling at each other over breakfast of bacon, bread and tea.

Lydia scraped butter and marmalade across a slice of toast. That would have been all she might have eaten if Robert hadn't arrived.

She glanced around the table at the extra dishes and frowned.

Robert noticed. 'You're frowning. What's the matter?'

Lydia got up, poured more water from the kettle into the teapot and came back to the table, standing just behind him. 'I was thinking of Agnes. I think it best we don't tell her that you were here – under the circumstances. She's had an accident and it's ruined her weekend. She was so looking forward to it,' she stated, studying the back of her lover's head whilst pouring him a second cup of tea. He had a strong neck, solid, like the trunk of a tree. Looking at it, she couldn't resist brushing her fingers through the soft down at the nape of his neck. 'Besides that, she was supposed to be my chaperone. It wouldn't have happened if she'd been here. She might feel guilty – or resentful about it.'

Robert's eyebrows rose as he smiled a lopsided smile.

'Wouldn't it?'

She stroked his hair. 'Perhaps. Perhaps not.'

Robert wrapped his arm around her waist and looked up at her.

'I've known Agnes all my life. She's very capable. I'm sure she'll cope, but... I'll stand by your decision. By the time she gets back here I'll be gone.'

Lydia didn't elaborate that she did sometimes feel a little guilty that she had ended up with Robert when Agnes had loved him so much.

She took the teapot to the sink, then began collecting up the dishes.

'I'll go into the village and see how she is. I'm hoping she's recovered. I think she will have recovered by lunchtime. Anyway,' she said with a knowing grin, 'I doubt she'll leave that car outside unattended for too long. You know what she is like.'

Robert laughed. 'How about I give you a lift?'

Lydia shook her head. 'I think it best if I walk. The woman in the village shop asks questions of everyone and doesn't miss a thing. Questions will be asked. Reputations will be ruined.'

She laughed, not caring whether her reputation was tarnished or not.

The last dishes were placed in the sink. An awkward silence fell between them. It was as though each was concerned that the next word uttered would be goodbye. Both of them were endeavouring to put off the dreaded moment for as long as possible. Tomorrow and all the days after would be very different days from today.

Lydia stayed at the sink, although the washing-up itself was just about finished. Hands clenched over the sink's cold ridge, she stared out of the kitchen window on to a garden of flowers, bees and whispering grass.

The legs of Robert's chair scraped across the uneven flagstones. She closed her eyes when he came and stood behind her. Even though they were both clothed, she could feel the heat of his body. She took a deep breath; she wanted to remember the smell as well as the look of him. It might be all they would have.

'I wish I could stay,' he said softly.

She nodded mutely, knowing that if she opened her mouth to say anything, she would beg him to stay. After that, she would cry.

She steeled herself to him leaving, refusing to wave him goodbye from the garden gate.

'I prefer to busy myself putting these dishes away rather than do that. That way I can pretend you've only gone outside for a smoke or to dig up a lettuce from the garden or a bunch of flowers – anything. Anything rather than say goodbye.'

It was odd the way they didn't touch, but said their goodbyes in the time between washing up and putting the dishes away.

She'd asked him if the bed was turned down. He'd shaken his head and told her be would go up and check, but what did 'turned down' actually mean?

They'd both gone back up to the bedroom, undressing swiftly, carelessly throwing their clothes to the floor, not giving themselves time to get to the bed, but breathlessly, impatiently, falling to the floor, writhing amongst the clothes, too impatient for the formality of a comfortable bed.

And so he left.

She was staring out of the kitchen window again when the sound of the door closing came to her. She was still there when she heard the sound of his motor car starting up and wished he had come on horseback. I might not have heard the sound of horses' hooves she thought, then shook herself, thinking how foolish the notion.

'Where am I? I'm not in heaven, am I?' said Agnes, eyeing the shrew-eyed woman with the big headdress in alarm.

'You had an accident,' said the nurse who appeared to have been taking her pulse.

Agnes tugged up the bedclothes so tightly tucked in around her, and peered the length of her body.

'I've still got my legs and everything, have I?' Her expression was troubled, her voice edging on the shrill.

'Silly girl! Of course you have!'

The nurse snatched at the bedclothes, tucking them back in tightly. Agnes was obliged to remove her arms swiftly before it became a struggle to get them back out at all.

'What did I do?' asked Agnes.

'Something to do with a starting handle, Miss. I understand the car backfired and jolted you up into the air. You landed heavily and the starting handle flew out and hit you on the head.'

Agnes frowned as she tried to recall the sequence of events, namely what had she been doing prior

278

to this. She recalled the smell of earthy potatoes and strong cheese. She'd been in the village store with Lydia. They'd bought provisions to sustain them over the weekend.

She looked around the ward. A dear old soul with china blue eyes was waving to her from across the room. There was a large lump in the middle of the other bed, cocooned in bedclothes. The lump was snoring loudly.

'Is that my friend Lydia over there?' she asked, vowing she would never sleep in the same room as her friend if she were that snoring lump in the bed opposite.

The nurse snorted contemptuously, not unlike the sound coming from across the way, though not so loud.

'That is Mrs Hooker, the parson's wife. She's just had a baby. I'll thank you not to disturb her. She's had a hard time and needs all the rest she can get.'

Agnes thought she'd said Honker, which would have been considerably more appropriate.

'Your friend went back to Rose Cottage. I believe she left the windows open, so Sam Dowding took her there in his pony and trap. She said she would call back lunchtime. You have an hour to wait. It's quite a long walk.'

Agnes's lively mind was already skimming around as normal; Lydia was all right, but there was one other fear tugging at her nerve ends.

'My car. *The* car. It is all right is it? It's not damaged.'

'Not as far as I know,' said the nurse who was now rearranging the contents of an enamel tray sitting on top of an enamel framed table of the same colour as the tray. 'Not that I know that much about motor cars, but... What do you think you're doing?' she cried, her voice shrill enough to cut nerves in half.

'I'm going to sort out my motor car and see where Lydia's got to,' said Agnes, who was already out of bed, tugging her clothes out of the bedside closet and piling them untidily on the bed.

The nurse, Mavis Davis, the doctor's wife, was not amused. 'I really do not think...'

'I'll do my thinking for myself. I have things to do.' She winced as a searing pain shot from her temple along the side of her head. It stilled her, though not for long. She was all action again once the pain had passed, pulling on her clothes whilst cursing anyone who dared damage her employer Mrs Nickleby's car.

Doctor Davis's wife, a strong-willed woman who had determined to keep to her profession despite being married, bustled out after her, all the way protesting that she really should rest, and that Doctor Davis would be very angry indeed, when he found out she had discharged herself.

Once outside the hospital, Agnes stopped to get her bearings. The cottage hospital was at one end of the High Street, but which end?

She turned at the sound of a church clock striking the hour to where a staunchly square Norman tower showed above the roofs of cottages, houses and high street shops. Agnes remembered it was close to the village shop and hurtled in that direction.

Freshly dressed in a pale green dress with wide white collar, white gloves, a cream hat and canvas boots tightly laced up at the front, Lydia walked close to the edge of the road.

The sun was shining and a fresh breeze whipped Lydia's skirt around her legs and blew tendrils of hair across her face.

The green verge was rampant with bright red poppies and pale blue cornflowers. The smell of freshly mown hay was in the air and birds were twittering in the trees lining the road.

She was glad of the fresh air on her cheeks and only wished it would also cool her body. The memory of Robert's muscular torso pressing down on hers was vivid; she burned at the thought of it. Hopefully Agnes wouldn't notice the brightness in her eyes and the tension in her shoulders. She wanted to skip, run and jump, but had a care for her friend's feelings. She would not rub salt into the wounds Agnes tried so hard to hide.

The sudden honking of a car horn burst into her thoughts.

'Agnes! You're supposed to be in hospital,' said Lydia as she climbed aboard. 'What are you doing, out of bed already?'

Agnes grinned. 'Looking forward to breakfast. That old battle-axe out there tried to keep me in bed, but I had other ideas. Have you had breakfast yet?'

'It's nearly lunchtime. I don't have any eggs. The box got soggy in the rain and they fell out of the bottom.'

'Never mind. We bought other things. I fancy bacon in a sandwich with cheese. Have you ever

281

tried that? It's a bit of a luxury back in Myrtle Street, but wonderful if you can afford it.'

I can afford it, thought Lydia who'd bought the supplies in the village shop. Not that she minded, except that talking about bacon reminded her that half of it was gone, and so was the bread. Robert had eaten his fill. Agnes was bound to notice there wasn't as much as there should be. Lydia decided a little preparation would allay suspicion.

'I can't believe how much I ate for breakfast this morning,' she said brightly, her cheeks almost as red as the roadside poppies. 'It must be the country air.'

On arrival back at Rose Cottage, Lydia went ahead, promising to cook the best lunch – or bacon and cheese sandwich – that Agnes had ever tasted.

'Are you going to have one too?' Agnes called after her.

'I'm not sure I've got room,' Lydia called back from halfway down the garden path. Her stomach rumbled in protest. It had been four hours since breakfast, but she had given the impression of eating a man-sized feast. It was best Agnes believed that.

After securing the gear stick, Agnes jumped down from the car, her feet landing in a patch of treacly mud.

'Oh no,' she exclaimed, looking down at her muddied button-up boots. 'These were new boots. I love them as much as my yellow straw hat.'

Her gaze strayed from her boots to the tyre marks running around the patch of lane at the front of the cottage. She thought nothing of them;

they were just tyre marks, though some imprints differed, tracks made by tyres wider than the ones on her employer's car.

She concluded they belonged to whoever had brought Lydia back yesterday.

'Now for that bacon and cheese sandwich,' she murmured, her mouth watering in anticipation.

Lydia had thrown the kitchen windows wide-open. The pale cream curtains billowed in on the back of a gentle breeze.

Lydia was slicing what remained of the bread with an oversized carving knife. Agnes watched her, thinking how ladylike she was, how beautiful with her glossy dark hair and dark grey eyes. Her complexion was creamy, her cheeks a little more pink today than she'd ever seen them. When Lydia caught her watching and smiled, her eyes were dancing, brighter than she'd ever seen them.

'I do know how to slice bread,' said Lydia, presuming Agnes was about to criticise; after all, she was the daughter of a cook, had been in domestic service and knew how to do almost anything in a kitchen.

'I feel such a fool,' said Agnes. 'I'm sorry for spoiling our weekend.'

Lydia paused in slicing the bread and looked at her with those luminous grey eyes; eyes like polished pewter.

'It's not a problem. Honestly, it's not. I'm just glad you're fully recovered. You are fully recovered aren't you?'

Agnes saw the concerned frown creasing Lydia's brow and immediately decided to lie.

'Yes. The doctor said so.'

283

Lydia heaved a sigh of relief. 'And anyway, it was the car's fault, not yours.'

'I suppose so. I really have to be more careful with starting handles.'

'There surely has to be a better method of starting a car,' said Lydia.

Agnes chewed on a crust of bread and shook her head. 'Not in our lifetime. Starting handles are more easily handled by men than women; that alone is a good enough reason not to improve them.'

Lydia laughed at Agnes's comment. If ever Agnes did marry, her husband was going to find his wife to be a very independent and spirited woman.

'Mr Dowding, the man who brought me back yesterday, isn't of that frame of mind,' Lydia said jokingly.

'His car hasn't got a starting handle?' Agnes asked, amazed and intrigued by such a revelation.

'No,' Lydia laughed. 'His vehicle has two ears, four legs and a tail. Oh, and it pulls a two-wheeled trap behind it!'

Agnes stopped chewing the bread and eyed her curiously. 'I thought you came back by car. There are two sets of tyre tracks outside. I suppose I could be mistaken, unless somebody hereabouts has a car.'

'I believe the doctor does,' blurted out Lydia, bending over the kitchen sink to hide her reddening face.

'I suppose so,' said Agnes, but she didn't remark that she already knew that the doctor, like this Mr Dowding, drove a pony and trap.

284

Chapter Twenty-Six

Mrs Nickleby safely dropped off at the shops, Agnes headed for the church hall. The main building was of red brick, its doors and windows trimmed in bricks the colour of Colman's mustard. Although she'd been accepted by the Voluntary Aid Detachment, Agnes wanted to give one more try at becoming a 'proper' ambulance driver.

'If conscientious objectors can drive ambulances, why can't I?'

The car alone provoked amazed expressions on the faces of the men waiting in the queue. On seeing Agnes dressed in jodhpurs, a man's tweed jacket and a leather cap, their eyebrows rose even higher.

A notice outside the hall proclaimed that the proposed British Expeditionary Force were in need of ancillary support in the form of ambulance drivers, clerical and medical staff, stretcher-bearers and field hygiene units. She scanned the notice avidly, her mind ticking like a bomb about to go off. This was what she needed and they needed her.

One snotty-nosed boy offered to give the car a polish whilst she was gone. Two equally scruffy kids stood behind him.

Fists fixed on hips, Agnes looked them over.

'You've got the job. I don't want any sticky fingers over it mind,' she told them.

'I can use me jumper,' he said to her.

Agnes eyed the grey jumper, noticing that the front was full of holes.

'Here,' she said after a deep rummage in her pocket. 'Have a sixpence. You can buy a new jumper with it.'

The boy had freckles and a cheeky smile. 'Spend sixpence on a new jumper? Not bloody likely!'

The administrator in charge of enrolling people for the ancillary services glanced up at her, asked her name, and then looked again.

'You're a woman! In that get-up it's downright questionable! Are you one of those funny women who don't like men?'

There were sniggers from the men in the queue behind her.

One bushy eyebrow dropped over his eye, completely obliterating it from view.

'Not all men. I do have my favourites. One of them just happens to be a pilot in the Royal Flying Corps. I want to follow him to France. I want to do my bit to make sure he stays alive and gets back. If I have to don mannish attire to do so, then I will. Haven't you ever heard that song, "Sweet Polly Oliver"?'

His eyes were liverish, the whites tinged with yellow. The bags hanging beneath his eyes were puffy and purple edged. He had to be in his early fifties, an old soldier with old beliefs and dragged in to fill in forms. He probably didn't much like the job. He would also take a lot of convincing.

'I can see you've never heard of her,' said Agnes gamely and straightway broke into song.

When she came to the lines, *I'll list for a soldier,*

and follow my love, the men in the queue behind her clapped and shouted bravo.

'Well, I suppose pen pushers aren't going to be right up there with the soldier,' said the administrator, his bushy brows seeming to rise up and down independently before levelling out.

'I beg your pardon, but I'm not the sort to put up with inky fingers all day,' Agnes declared. 'I want to drive an ambulance.'

The bushy eyebrows went up and down again. 'And what makes you think you can drive an ambulance, my good woman?'

'I'm a professional driver, my good man. Why else do you think I'm wearing this get-up?'

Agnes returned her employer's car and met Lydia on the corner of Myrtle Street.

'You're still wearing your work clothes,' Lydia said to her.

Agnes usually changed into a skirt before coming home. Today she hadn't bothered. The look on her face said it all.

'You've done it?' Lydia asked, hardly able to believe it was true. 'That's what you wanted to tell me.'

Agnes grinned from ear to ear, lifting her skirts and dancing a little jig while singing 'Sweet Polly Oliver'.

'They weren't going to; that old codger doing the enrolment looked as though he'd fought at Mafeking or in the Transvaal. Not one where women ever went, anyway; not unless they were nurses that is.'

Lydia threw back her head, laughed and clapped

287

her hands.

'Agnes Stacey! An ambulance driver. Who would have ever thought it?'

'I've got to train here first, but I've insisted on going over when the men go over. No point me motoring around back here when the injured are over there, is it now?'

Lydia agreed that it was not. The more she thought about it, the more she wanted to go over there too.

Harry Allen, son of Edith whom they'd taken home in an ambulance, and the eldest of her eight children, caught up with them at the corner. He tipped his cap at Lydia when he wished her good day, but his eyes were for Agnes.

'Yer mam said you weren't home from work yet, but I thought I'd wait around until you were. Still feels funny to think you've got a job driving a car.'

'Well, you'd better get used to it,' Agnes stated, her chin held high and her hair billowing out behind her.

'That woman seems to appreciate you as her driver, and that's a fact. Job for life, I shouldn't wonder.'

'No. It's not going to be a job for life, Harry. In fact, tomorrow will be my last day. I'm off to train to be an ambulance driver after that. Not that I need to learn how to drive, but I do need to learn a bit about first aid and all that. I'm off to the front. That's where I'm going.'

Harry Allen's jaw dropped. 'You're a one, Agnes Stacey. And there was me thinking I'd be leaving you behind. I joined up today. First Middlesex

Fusiliers – or at least I think it's Middlesex. Could be Essex. I never was much good at geography and me memory 'as never been that special. Not that it matters much. Seems to me we might end up seeing a fair bit of each other. If we're lucky, that is. Now wouldn't that be something.'

'Us meeting up wouldn't be lucky, Harry. I shall be driving an ambulance. It's not a good thing if you meet up with me because it means you're injured. Now that wouldn't be lucky, would it?'

Harry looked crestfallen. 'I suppose so.' He switched his enquiring gaze to Lydia. 'Are you joining the military nurses, Miss Lydia? Would I be likely to bump into you over there?'

Lydia had been only half listening. She'd noticed what Agnes and Harry had been saying, thinking that perhaps if she did enrol as a military nurse, it was one way of being a little bit closer to Robert.

'I already work at a hospital. No doubt we'll receive a lot of injured there, that's besides filling in the gaps for those who do leave.'

Harry fell into an awkward silence before saying finally, 'That's a German hospital where you are, ain't it? I mean, it might get closed down...'

'That would be ridiculous,' snapped Lydia. 'We help anyone who comes to the hospital, no matter what their race, colour or religious persuasion. And that's the way it should be. We have to remain neutral.'

Harry looked crestfallen. She offered her apologies for snapping.

'I hate war,' she said to him, her fine eyebrows frowning, her hands clasped tightly, fingers

289

interlocked. 'War is murder, and that's all there is to it.'

Agnes squeezed her arm. 'He'll be all right, Lydia. He's a good flier. The best there is, I shouldn't wonder.'

Although she appreciated her sympathy, it unnerved Lydia that perhaps Agnes could read her mind.

'War! Why is it that men get all excited at the mention of war?' she said, shaking her head disapprovingly.

'Because it is exciting,' said Harry, his calm features animated. 'We'll give them Germans a drubbing, you just see if we don't. I'll be over there giving them what for ... we'll kill a load of them before they kill a load of us! Shoot them down in them Zeppelins and see them frizzle as they fall to the ground!'

He didn't notice Lydia's pallor or the sudden rigidity in her shoulders, but Agnes did.

'Harry Allen, I think we've had enough of this talk of war. We're all going to do our bit, you fighting and me driving an ambulance. But let's not get carried away. It isn't a game. It's a very serious affair and don't you bloody forget it!'

Harry took on the hangdog expression he always did when Agnes put him down. With anyone else he would bounce back immediately, giving as good as he got. Agnes was a different matter. As a lad, he had always followed her around when she came to stay at her grandmother's in Myrtle Street. As an adolescent, he'd been tongue-tied in her presence, and now, as a young adult, his first thought was to impress her, as any young man in

290

love wanted to do. Not that Agnes appeared to have any interest in him. If he could look beneath the surface, he would know she did not love him. Having loved Robert Ravening, she would find it hard to love anyone else.

'Your Mam's cooking roast beef I reckon,' said Harry, war forgotten as he tilted his nose upwards and sniffed. 'Roast beef, potatoes, cabbage and carrots. Lovely. And spotted dick to follow.'

Both girls stopped in their tracks, Agnes bubbling with laughter.

'How do you know that just from sniffing the air?' she asked.

He grinned sheepishly at Agnes, and then winked at Lydia. 'It's a knack.'

'We'll see,' said Agnes. 'Come on, Lydia. I'm starving.'

Harry followed them through the side alley and round the back of the house.

'And where do you think you're going?' said Agnes, slamming her hand hard across his chest before he had chance to pass through the back gate.

'Sunday roast. Yer Mam invited me and whilst I was thinking it over, she told me what was cooking.'

Agnes slapped him playfully. 'Cheeky bugger!'

They all laughed as they made their way along the narrow path through the back yard, dodging the line of washing as they did so. Even Lydia had to admit he was a cheeky so and so, though in her heart there was a strong yearning that had not been there before. Up until the moment Agnes informed her she had joined up as an ambulance driver, she had not considered leaving the hospital and doing the same. It was foolish to think she might meet up with Robert over there, but just the prospect of being nearer to where he was flying made her heart beat faster. She did not regret that night with him, hoped it wouldn't be their last night together, but until then the memory still burned bright.

Although the kitchen was smaller and steamier than what she'd been used to when she worked for Sir Avis, Sarah Stacey had everything under control.

Saucepans bubbled on the old range and the sound of something spitting and sizzling came from the hot oven.

Agnes's grandmother, Ellen, had laid the table with an ill-matched assortment of plates and cutlery. Some of it was her own and some bits and pieces given to Sarah – oddments from the kitchens at Heathlands and the house in Belgravia.

Agnes grabbed a ladle and beat it against the side of a saucepan. Taken by surprise, her mother stopped peering into another saucepan and stared at her daughter, the steam plastering her hair against her forehead.

'Right everyone. I have an announcement to make. Mother? Gran?'

Both women stopped what they were doing, though Sarah did replace the lid on the saucepan and turned her face from the steam.

'I'm leaving my job driving old Mrs Pinchpenny around.' They all smiled at the pet name she'd given her employer; Mrs Nickleby wasn't known for being overly generous. 'I've joined an ancillary unit being sent over to France to take care of the army. It's behind the lines – well, most of the time. I'm going to drive an ambulance!'

Sarah Stacey collapsed on to a kitchen chair with an almighty thump. Ellen Proctor covered her gap-toothed mouth with one hand, eyes wide with surprise.

'Agnes! Whatever made you do it?' Sarah Stacey said in a cracked voice, looking as though she were going to burst into tears at any minute.

'I'm not like you, Mam. I can't settle to a life of cooking and cleaning. You already know that.'

'But you was already drivin' a car,' said her grandmother. 'Weren't that enough fer yer?'

Agnes looked calmer and more confident than anyone had ever seen her. Even her mother felt diminished by the look of her, the set of her chin, the firm resolve that seemed to cover her from head to toe.

'No. I want adventure in my life, and why shouldn't I have it?'

'You're a woman,' said her mother. 'And a very young one at that,' she added, her fingers twisting her apron in her lap, such was her tension and fear.

Unnerved by her daughter's determined stance, Sarah Stacey remembered a time when she too had thought she could conquer the world. Things hadn't worked out like that, but perhaps they would for Agnes? No matter her youth, she looked like a woman who knew what she wanted, some-one in charge of her own life and destiny.

'*He* wouldn't have said that,' Agnes said pointedly, her eyes bright with confidence. '*He*

293

would have encouraged me, told me that in the modern world gender no longer mattered. I could be what I wanted to be if I wanted it enough.'

Sarah Stacey flinched. Agnes was referring to Sir Avis, the man who had fathered her and had been a huge influence on her life. Closing her eyes and muttering something indistinguishable, she covered the lower half of her face with her hands. She might have sobbed if it hadn't been for her own mother, Ellen Proctor, patting her on the shoulder.

'Reap as you sow, our Sarah. I said that to you a long time ago that you reap as you sow; he was always bound to be a force in our Agnes's life. There was always bound to be something of him in her. It's only natural. She gets it from 'im. Could be worse. Could be like he was with women...'

'Mother!' Sarah sprang to her feet. 'Time to dish up.'

Harry Allen didn't have much of a clue as to what they were on about, but put in his penn'orth anyway.

'And I've joined up too. Remember that, Mrs Stacey. I'll be there to protect her.'

'I'm glad to 'ear it, me boy,' said Agnes's grand-mother.

'More like me looking after him.' Agnes grinned as she said it and even her mother managed to laugh.

Lydia ate sparingly. Her thoughts were in tur-moil and she couldn't help feeling an infectious excitement the others had generated in her. Could she bear to leave the hospital? Could she

294

bear to leave her father?

Immersed in her thoughts, she didn't really engage with what was happening around her, until Agnes's grandmother pointed a fork in her direction and asked her what was up.

'Yer father's not ill is he?' she asked quizzically before she popped a roast potato into her mouth whole.

Lydia shook her head. 'No. He's fine, thank you.'

Ellen Proctor beamed, her, cheeks ballooning and falling, as she rolled the potato from side to side in her mouth.

Her liking of Lydia was genuine and she was like a hound on the scent; she knew something was troubling the girl.

When the meal was finished, Agnes and her mother dealt with the washing up. Harry had the job of putting it all away though Lydia would have done so if Agnes's grandmother hadn't asked if she'd give her a hand getting in the washing.

With a mouthful of pegs clenched in the gap in her teeth, Ellen Proctor asked Lydia what was troubling her.

'And don't say nothing's troubling you, 'cause you look as though you've picked up a tanner and lost a five pound note.'

Lydia bit her upper lip with her lower teeth. 'I was thinking about nursing soldiers, you know, over in France. I know there's a call out for good nursing staff to join Queen Alexandra's and others as well, but...'

Ellen looked at her over the sheet they were now folding, noticing the concern in her eyes and

295

the deep frown.

'You're worried about that young man of yours; of course you are. Only natural.'

'Robert? Yes, though that's not all of it.'

Ellen tipped two fingers up under the peak of her cap so it sat further back on her head.

'Our Agnes had a yen for that young man of yours. Course, it could never be. It wouldn't have worked, him being from a different class. I hope it works for you, that I do. You've no airs and graces – you proves that by coming 'ere and staying with us. You accepts us and, I have to say, I hope that you and Agnes remains friends when you marry. That would be nice.'

'Yes. It would be.'

Ellen tipped her head to one side. 'That ain't what's worrying you, is it?'

She shook her head.

'Care to tell me? Promise,' she said, crossing her copious chest. 'I won't tell a soul.'

'I'm not sure what will happen to me and my father. My father's German and my mother was English, so I'm not sure if a military nursing corps will accept me. They may consider my loyalties might lie with my father's country.'

Ellen stuck her broad fists on her wide hips. 'Well, I never. Of course you are anxious, but then, your dad's a doctor and 'as been 'ere for years. Is that not so?'

Lydia nodded.

'And you're a bit of both. Your mother was English. Anyway, aren't we counting the chickens before they're hatched? Your father's a well-respected man so I hear tell. In addition, a nob at

296

that ... begging your pardon, but you're a nob as well. You'll be fine no doubt. Sorry,' she said suddenly, 'I shouldn't have pointed out the obvious differences. You're welcome 'ere young Lydia, and you always will be.'

'Thank you.'

'Anyway, is it only the military likely to be nursing over there? What about Christian organisations and that? What about nuns? What about the Quakers? They always get involved in wars even though they don't fight in them.'

Before Lydia left for the nurses' hostel, Agnes made her promise to meet up the following day.

'My last before I go for training,' Agnes reminded her.

Twilight was falling on Myrtle Street, but in the warm late summer kids still played with bent old pram wheels, attaching them to orange boxes and making them into dandies, as they called them. Neighbours chatted, laughed and made rude jokes that they shouted out from one to the other. Every so often somebody mentioned that so and so's son had joined up, or that there were rumours of rationing.

Some comments were scathing and to the point. 'What do they think we're on now? Smoked salmon and plum pudding every bleedin' day?'

The flypaper man wandered past, a number of his sticky papers hanging from his hat, singing the same old song and thanking God no doubt that the weather was warm and flies were plentiful.

Catch 'em alive, them tormenting flies...

Flies! Dead flies, Lydia thought grimly. Soon it would be men. God help them, their dead bodies wouldn't be as numerous as dead flies.

Lydia made a last-minute decision to go home rather than back to the hostel. She needed to speak to her father about what might be best for her to do. He wouldn't be expecting her, but that didn't matter. They had a lot to talk about.

It was late by the time Lydia got home. The house was dark and cool and there was no sign of her father or of the servants.

She went from one room to another, then down into the kitchen. Nobody was there, not even Mrs Gander the housekeeper who rarely took a day off if she could possibly avoid it. Mrs Gander regarded the house in Kensington as her personal domain. She controlled everything in it, and woe betide anyone who tried to alter her routine or carry out a task in a way that was contrary to her methods.

Lydia considered going to bed, but didn't feel tired enough; besides, if she was going to apply for a posting with the army, she needed to swot up on battlefield injuries; her father was sure to have a book on that.

Because of the bookshelves lining the walls, the library was the darkest room in the house. There was something comforting about the smell of musty paper and dried ink.

Rather than ignite the wall-mounted gaslights with their swan necks and tulip-shaped shades, she opened the drawer, found a box of Vestas and lit the oil lamp her father kept on the table.

Never had she found reading medical books quite so chilling, given her reasons for doing so.

However, it was a means to an end and she forced herself to concentrate on the details, determined to retain everything she learned.

It was because of this enforced concentration that she hardly noticed the regular ticking of the green onyx clock on the mantelpiece. Whereas other clocks ticked time away, this one was a noisy beast, clicking with each motion of the pendulum.

She jerked up her head when it finally struck twelve – midnight.

She'd heard no sound of the front door opening, no sound either of her father's swift, mannish footsteps. It surprised her that he stayed out late, though she didn't begrudge him his love of the theatre and what was to stop him from indulging in dinner afterwards?

The grandfather clock in the hallway struck midnight in a more booming tone than the mantel clock. Her eyelids were getting heavy, so she closed the book and rubbed her eyes back into wakefulness before replacing it on the bookshelf.

She opened the library door at the same time as the front door was opened, feeling the draught coming in from outside. The sonorous voice of her father making some pithy comment preceded that of laughter. There was no mistaking it; the laughter was that of a woman.

Lydia stood at the library door. She heard them talking and laughing as they removed and hung up their coats. Her father's lady friend was in the house.

It was silly to feel so hostile, and for the thought to register that he had no business bringing a woman into the house, not this house, not the house he had shared with her mother. Even when she reminded herself that he was old enough to choose whom he wished to bring home, she couldn't help herself.

As if waking from sleep, she left the library and stepped out into the hall, closing the door behind her.

Her father looked amazed.

'Lydia! What are you doing here?'

Lydia heard him but couldn't take her eyes off the red-haired woman who accompanied him. Of mature years, her clothes were flamboyant but of good quality, purple and edged with black velvet. Dark-lashed eyes shone from a handsome face.

Before she could answer, the bright eyes met hers head on.

'Eric, my dear man. This must be your lovely daughter. Do introduce us.'

A pink flush coloured his handsome features. His mouth hung open before he stammered an answer.

'Ah! Well... Yes... This is my dear friend... Mrs Mallory... Mrs Kate Mallory.'

The two women, daughter and lover, exchanged polite nods.

Eric Miller regained his composure. 'I'm sorry. Did we disturb you, my dear? I wasn't expecting you home...'

Lydia knew without him saying so that Mrs Mallory was an actress; for a middle-aged woman, she was too beautiful, too dramatic in her looks and graceful movements to be anything else.

'No. I wanted to speak to you. Robert's off to

France. I want to go too. I wanted to tell you, and also to ask your advice.'

His forehead, handsome, wide and strong, furrowed. 'You want to go?'

'Yes. I think it's what I should do. Even if I don't get the opportunity to see him, I'll be closer, or at least it will seem that way.'

'Lydia, I'm not sure it's a very good idea. Queen Alexandra's...'

'I know,' she said. 'That's what I wish to talk to you about.' She glanced from her father to the woman with him. 'Under the circumstances, I think it best we speak in private.'

He looked peeved by her suggestion. 'I'm quite happy for Kate to hear anything you have to say.'

'She knows everything about you?'

'Of course!' He sounded agitated.

'They may not accept me because you're German, the enemy. I need to seek another option. I'm sure there must be one,' she said.

Her father and Mrs Mallory – Kate – exchanged looks that said everything and said nothing.

'She's right, Eric,' said Kate, her rich voice soft but extremely expressive. 'They are bound to be biased and the longer the war goes on, the worse it is likely to get. I've seen bunting hanging out of office windows in the city, men betting on which of them will kill their German first. I saw it in Paris and now I'm seeing it here. On enrolment, Lydia will have to give her name and the names of her parents. It's best nobody knows. It's best she stays here.'

Eric Miller's expression was grave. 'That is what

I would wish,' he said softly, looking directly at his daughter. 'I would prefer you to stay, Lydia. Even though the Lutheran governors have advised the nurses of German nationality to return, they are insistent on keeping the hospital open. You will be needed there as much as on any battlefield.'

Lydia shook her head vehemently. 'I know that, Father. Robert will be in France. I have to go there.'

He looked away, rubbing his forehead with two fingers as though trying to remove a blemish of soot from his brow. It was something he always did when perturbed – as he certainly was now.

The red-headed woman swayed back and forth on her heels, looking at Eric as though she could read his thoughts.

'Well. It's getting late. Thank you for supper, Eric. I think it's time I left.'

'No. Kate. Please stay for a nightcap. Just to warm you before you set off home. In fact the cab is still waiting outside,' he added, this comment directed at Lydia. 'Isn't that right, Kate?'

Mrs Mallory raised her eyebrows and looked at him. Lydia saw the laughter in the woman's eyes and knew immediately there had been other plans; a minute or two might very well have become an hour. The ire inside tightened somewhere just behind her stomach muscles. She hadn't exactly taken a dislike to Mrs Kate Mallory, but she had hoped to speak to her father in depth.

Mrs Mallory herself made the decision.

'Actually, Eric, I think I should be going. I wouldn't want to keep the cab waiting. Poor man. He probably wants to get home to his wife and family.'

'What about your family, Mrs Mallory? I expect they might be waiting up for you too,' said Lydia smiling her sweetest smile simply because she wanted her to leave as quickly as possible.

'Oh, I have no family, my dear,' replied Mrs Mallory, her voice deep and gravelly as though she smoked a great deal. 'I'm an actress. Many of us actresses prefer to be known as Mrs even though we've never made it to the altar. Still, there's always a first time, isn't there Eric?'

Lydia's father looked down at his feet, muttering a string of unrelated 'ums' and 'ahs'.

Mrs Kate Mallory looked from one to the other. 'I can see you need to discuss this situation. I will say goodnight, Miss Lydia. Goodnight, Eric.'

She cupped his jaw in a lilac-gloved hand and kissed his cheek.

The sound of the door closing echoed around the hallway. It was a few minutes before either of them spoke.

Eventually, Lydia's father broke the silence. 'Kate and I have been friends for some time.'

'Will you marry her?'

He shuffled a bit from one foot to the other while fingering the brim of his hat.

'Not at this moment, but who knows how things might change. We're both getting older.'

Lydia saw his worried frown. She could see he was happy, but also concerned about her reaction.

'If you married her, she would live here?'

'If I say so.'

She sensed the hardening in his voice. In a way,

it hurt, and in another, it made no difference at all.

She shook her head, resigned to whatever he wanted to do. 'It won't matter to me. I won't be here. Somehow or other I will get to France.'

When her father muttered that he understood, his eyes were moist. She tried to remember the last time she'd ever seen him looking as disturbed as he was now. She couldn't.

'I'm sure I'll be quite safe,' she said as reassuringly as she could.

He swallowed as though he were choking back words he did not wish to utter, but they came out anyway.

'Yes. Thankfully you will be in the service of the Red Cross,' he said softly. 'The Red Cross are neutral.'

Chapter Twenty-Seven

None of them knew exactly what would happen at the hospital. Lydia had noticed strained looks as she hurried up the steps to the main entrance. Sometimes there were ugly mutterings, though nothing direct, nothing too hostile.

Because of this both Lydia and her father believed they could carry on, Lydia at least until her position with the Red Cross was confirmed. Until that happened she did not work late, unless she stayed in the hostel overnight.

Her father would hear none of it. 'I have my

new motor car. I can go backwards and forwards quite safely, therefore if I am attending at the hospital and called to stay late, I will do so.'

It was seven days exactly after that pronouncement before the inevitable occurred.

The child was very sick, the mother very worried.

'Is she going to live, Doctor?'

Doctor Eric Miller adopted his most professional expression. A little hope, a little moderation.

'I will do what I can,' he said to the mother of the child who lay so pale and so sick in the hospital bed.

The child was taking deep rasping breaths, her tiny chest heaving up and down with each one; like a pair of bellows with the hole half blocked, Doctor Miller thought.

'Do you have other children?' he asked.

She nodded at the same time as dabbing at her red-rimmed eyes. 'Three other children, Doctor. They will be waiting for their supper, but I cannot leave this child alone all night. Not my Saskia.'

'You won't be leaving your daughter alone. I will be here – all night if necessary.'

The woman lifted her shawl from her shoulders and tied it tightly around her head, crossing the ends across her breasts.

'You promise me this, Doctor?' she asked, her eyes mute with pleading.

'I promise you this,' he answered her in German.

'Then I will pray for God to bless you. You are a good man, Doctor.'

He knew she would keep to her word, perhaps

305

entering the synagogue on her way home.

Sister Ursula was on duty and looked surprised to see him still there.

'I told your daughter that you had already gone home,' she admonished him. 'Are you leaving soon?'

He shook his head. 'No. I promised Mrs Lehman that I would keep vigil over her daughter. She still has a very high fever. I'm hoping it will break before dawn.'

'You don't need to stay. I can keep an eye on her.'

Doctor Miller shook his head again. 'No. Mrs Lehman has three other children, and a husband come to that, waiting for their supper. I promised her I would sit with her child all night, and I will. Perhaps you can furnish me with a little food and drink?' he asked hopefully.

Sister Ursula smiled girlishly and said that she would. Doctor Miller was her favourite doctor, one of the few who treated the nurses as equals and every patient as an individual. He was a good man and she would ensure that he received the best food and hot drinks throughout the night.

Before she left to tend to other patients, she carefully swabbed Saskia's face with a damp cloth and replaced the bowl of steaming hot water beside her bed. Doctor Miller replaced the wire cage over the child's head, plus the rubber sheet that covered it. The steam from the bowl seeped into the contraption through a rubber tube.

Doctor Miller had used the device a few times before. For the most part it worked, but there had been those who died; he sincerely hoped that

306

Saskia Lehman wouldn't be one.

There was a small table close to the bed where he could make notes on other patients, drink tea, eat cake provided by Sister Ursula, and worry about Lydia and her determination to get to France.

He was her father and it worried him, but also he couldn't help feeling a little proud of her. She was so like her mother, so like the woman he had gone out of his way to purge from his thoughts.

The night dragged on, twilight turning into darkness more quickly now, with autumn only just around the corner. The trees in London avenues still sported green leaves with only the faintest hint of yellow. The weather was still good and news from France at best positive, at worst sporadic. He understood beyond doubt that Lydia would go there.

He knew he would doze during this night vigil, but had asked Sister Ursula to wake him if anything developed.

'And don't let me sleep too long,' he warned her. 'Ten minutes at intermittent intervals should be enough.'

Being a dutiful nurse, who respected him, she made no comment.

He was dreaming of when he was a young doctor, a surgeon with the Prussian army. It was all such a long time ago.

Somebody was shaking his shoulder.

'Doctor Miller! Doctor Miller! You must look at the child.'

Eric blinked open his eyes to see Sister Ursula's face looming over him. It was difficult to tell anything from her placid expression, but he feared the worst.

After rubbing the sleep from his eyes, he noticed she had removed the rubber sheet. All that remained was the wire cage that had held it up off the child's face so she could breathe.

It wasn't the first time he'd approached a patient feeling as though he had just swallowed a lump of iron, and that was how it felt now.

'Turn up the gas,' he said to the nurse, his voice cracking with tension.

Sister Ursula obliged, reaching out her long arm to pull the tiny cord that rotated on to the main gas mantle, causing it to light.

Picked out by the gaslight's glow, a pair of rosebud lips moved weakly; the fact that they were moving at all, the child asking for a drink, was nothing short of a miracle. The fever had broken.

The world outside the hospital was dark and forbidding. Shop windows that were usually bright with lights until midnight, were now in almost total darkness. Not that Eric was too worried about that; his car was close by and he rather prided himself on being able to drive it.

He was even prouder that the sick child had pulled through and was glad he'd stayed.

Sister Ursula called goodnight in German from the top of the steps in front of the entrance. He wished her goodnight in German.

'Hun,' shouted a man on the other side of the road. He had obviously heard the exchange. Eric strode briskly away. He did not look back. Hopefully the man would stagger home without incident and he would get home too.

The sound of his footsteps echoed in the darkness along the wet pavements. Two hundred yards to his car that he'd left inside the iron gates to the side of the main hospital building.

As he made his way along, a smile of satisfaction on his face, he heard rowdy voices coming towards him.

Drunks, he thought, surprised that they were around at this time of the morning. The new wartime licensing laws required all public houses to close by ten-thirty at night in order that workers clocked in on time and not suffering from hangovers. Obviously, these men had acquired drink from somewhere. There were always those ready and able to break the law, he thought.

He heard the sound of their booted feet break into a run at the same time as he saw their shadows appear around the corner. Like some strange monster, they were black and bundled together, their size grotesquely exaggerated by the close proximity of a streetlamp.

The shadows diminished, men of flesh and blood emerging from the blackness.

Their faces were haggard; brawny arms and rolled-up shirtsleeves, waistcoats stretched to breaking point across their gross bellies.

Four of them, perhaps five.

'Good evening,' he said when it seemed obvious they were heading straight for him.

'Good evening? Bloody Hun! Bloody German murderer!'

'I am a doctor! I save lives.'

'You're bloody German! You're a bloody murderer!'

He ducked the first blow, and skipping backwards, managed to avoid the second. Swiftly discarding his bag in which he carried the tools of his trade, and his jacket, he put up his fists and prepared to fight.

'Queensberry rules?' he said in his most superior English accent. It made sense to communicate in the hope of knocking aside their dubious patriotism. Most of all he had to stay on his feet. If he fell to the ground, he was finished. Their hobnail boots would see to that.

He landed a punch on one man's jaw and stepped back sharply as another man stepped forward, running into a jab from Eric's right hand. All the time he kept moving, hoping to keep the four of them at bay until help came.

A heavy fist grazed his cheek close to his eye, followed by another blow to his jaw. They surrounded him now, pounding him incessantly with their fists, their eyes full of hatred and all the most damning, most evil words coming out of their mouths.

The pounding continued unabated, hammering him to his knees.

Blood streaming into his eyes, he reached out, clinging on to the legs of one of his assailants, anything to stop from falling to the ground.

'This is for all them babies you skewered on bayonets,' shouted one of the men.

Eric tried to protest that he'd never done any such thing. That he was a doctor!

The blood streaming into his mouth drowned

310

his words. He groaned as a heavy boot connected with his ribs.

The first Lydia knew of what had happened was when someone came hammering on the door of her room in the nurses' hostel.

Her roommate Sally grumbled that it couldn't be time to get up just yet.

Lydia glanced at the big old clock up on the wall before throwing back the bedclothes.

'Four o'clock. I hope whoever it is has a very good reason for getting me out of bed now,' she muttered as she threw on her dressing gown and flung open the door.

The last person she'd expected to see was the actress, Mrs Kate Mallory, her expression anxious.

'Come quickly, Lydia. It's your father. They're dealing with him now. I said I would fetch you. It's all right. He won't die, but he's hurt. He's badly hurt.'

Lydia felt herself turning cold. 'What happened?'

'He was attacked. Please come. Now.'

Lydia pulled a cape over her dressing gown.

Her father was still in the hospital, bandages wreathed around his bare chest and another around his head, closing one eye. His bandaged hands shook when he looked up at her.

'They called me bad names.' He shook his head. 'I couldn't believe it of this country. I was so disgusted, it crossed my mind to leave her and go to Germany. It is still possible to get a boat to the Hook of Holland and travel by train from there.'

Lydia sat in a chair opposite him, leaning forward so that her worried face wasn't far from his.

'Is that really what you're going to do?' she enquired, the severity of the situation rearing up like a brick wall before her eyes.

He raised an eyebrow. He also raised his hand to cover Kate Mallory's hand, which was presently resting on his shoulder.

'I can't leave. I have patients who depend on me and Kate is here. I will not leave her – unless she wants me to,' he said quizzically, looking up at her for a response.

'I want you here,' she said, clenching her jaw, her hand more tightly gripping his bare shoulder.

'Then I stay,' he said. 'I also must be here for when you get back, Lydia, that is if you are still determined to go?'

'I applied in person, and they accepted me. I'll be going soon, or I was, but with you like this… I'm sorry, Father. It wasn't an easy decision. I leave at the end of the month.'

'Does Robert know?'

'No.' She shook her head and sighed heavily. 'Getting news to him is going to be something of a problem. And I haven't received a letter from him.' She sighed again, not wanting to voice her worst fears; that he'd forgotten her. She didn't want to believe that. 'I hear letters are taking a while to get through unless it's through military channels or from somebody with influence. As you know, his parents are in Australia or Malaya.'

'You'd think they would spend more time in England now the country is at war.'

Lydia shook her head. 'It seems not.'

312

He waited patiently whilst she outlined her plan.

'I thought I would call in on Lady Ravening. I hear she's staying at the house in Belgravia. She loves Robert. I'm sure she'll do her best to let him know.'

'I'm sure she will,' he said, and then stilled. He half closed his eyes as though he were thinking it over. 'Yes,' he said, nodding repeatedly. 'I'm sure she will. I'm not sure how he'll view you being over there, so close to the battlefront. Still, you have your own life to lead, Lydia. You want to be with Robert. I understand that. No need to worry about me.'

'No need at all. I can look after your father very well,' said Kate Mallory. 'Would you mind very much if I moved in with him – in the spare bedroom of course – until he is recovered?'

Lydia studied the fine woman standing at her father's bedside and the way they looked at each other. It wasn't likely that Kate would remain in the spare bedroom for long, but they were both on their own and she couldn't decry their actions – whatever those actions might be.

'I much appreciate your offer. I think it's a very good idea. I also think that we have to grab every precious moment we can whilst this war rages. Who knows what the future brings?'

Billboards invited men to recruit to fight the ugly monster that was devouring Europe. Wearing a German helmet, the monster drawn as some giant hairy ape was depicted feeding women and children into its ravenous mouth.

The people who thronged the London streets cheered the columns of soldiers, fresh recruits to replace those who had already died. Flags waved and people sang 'Rule Britannia', and 'God Save the King'.

Lydia paused to watch, but found it impossible to sing along with the voices around her. One or two nudged her arm as though urging her to join in. It came as something of a relief when the soldiers themselves began singing 'It's a Long Way to Tipperary'.

Anti-German feeling was high and so was support for the government. Lydia spotted women wearing the familiar sashes of the Suffragette movement waving flags and shouting their support for Mr David Lloyd George.

Although she had never been to a bull-baiting spectacle, or a cockfight, or even a boxing match between men, she believed they bayed for blood, just as these people were doing.

There were no crowds in Belgravia, no soldiers singing as they marched off to war. The dignified facades of elegant Georgian houses, and the horse-drawn and horseless transport, with people coming and going, seemed unchanged.

The door, behind which Lady Julieta Ravening lived in splendid isolation, was dust free and the brass knocker polished to perfection.

After knocking, Lydia stood on tiptoe in order to better appraise her reflection in the highly polished door knocker. What she saw pleased her.

Brown suede trim on hem and cuffs took the plainness off her grey suit. She'd deliberated for hours deciding what to wear; something plain but handsome, the grey suit and her brown velvet hat fitting the bill nicely, she thought.

Rogers, the under butler, opened the door, an odd rigidity coming to his face when he saw who was calling.

Lydia had met him once before when Lady Ravening had invited both her and Robert to tea, so she smiled warmly.

'Good morning, Rogers,' she said, remembering the butler's name and supposing Quartermaster was having a day off. The old butler was suffering from poor health and now worked fewer hours.

'Miss Miller, is it?' he asked, a quiet and rather discomforting smile on his wide, languid mouth. Lydia felt an instant unease. On her last visit, he'd greeted her warmly and courteously. She was concerned but put on a brave face.

'Yes it is,' she said brightly. 'I've come to see her ladyship.'

'I'm sorry. Her ladyship isn't receiving today.'

'But I'm Lydia. She'll surely see me. I'm marrying her nephew. You do remember me, don't you?' she asked, her face shining with amiability, her tone challenging.

'Yes, Miss, I do. The fact is that her ladyship has given instructions that you are not to be received.'

Lydia's amiable expression vanished. She shook her head vehemently, still smiling despite everything. 'There must be some mistake. Not me. I'm Lydia Miller.'

'There is no mistake, and under the circumstances...'

'But I'm the daughter of her ladyship's doctor.' A sudden thought assailed her, chilling her to the bone. 'Or has she given orders for him not to be received either?' she added, her smile now completely absent.

Rogers regarded her from pale eyes either side of an aquiline nose.

'That is so, Miss. Under the circumstances, Doctor Miller's services as her personal physician are no longer required.'

She didn't bother to ask what those circumstances might be. The implications were clear; Doctor Eric Miller hailed from Dresden, a lovely old town in Germany. No matter his considerable medical skills and compassion – staying all night with a sick child had almost cost him his life – or her relationship with Robert, they were no longer welcome.

Lydia bristled with anger. 'I insist on seeing her.'

'It's quite impossible. I have my orders.' Rogers was adamant, but Lydia was determined. Shooting forward, she shoved her foot in through the gap in the door.

'If she doesn't agree to see me, I'm going to sit out here on the step, telling a story to anyone that will listen of a family of Mexican refugees whose fortune was based on them scavenging around a battlefield. Robbing the dead, I shall say. Gathering the scrap metal and robbing the dead! How would that go down *under the circumstances?*' she shouted, using the very same words he had used.

Rogers looked horrified. 'Wait here.'

'No. I will not!'

Flinging her arm wide so it slammed against his chest, she brushed past him into the splendid reception hall with its black and white tiles, its columned gallery and ornate staircase with swirling iron leaves sweeping up beneath the balustrade.

She was livid and prepared to do battle. All this privilege, she thought, looking around her and wanting to scream out how unfair things were. *Under the circumstances,* the war might bring out the best in people, but it would also bring out the worst, including bigotry, ignorance and the encouragement of hatred under the guise of patriotism.

Lady Julieta was huddled in front of a fire even though temperatures were above average for the time of year. The last time Lydia had seen the old woman, she'd looked shrivelled inside her fancy clothes and thick rugs. Today she looked even more so, her spine curved into a dowager's hump so that her face poked forward, her sharp nose resembling that of a hedgehog about to spear a tasty grub.

'Rogers,' she shouted, looking beyond Lydia.

Rogers limped in, his arms held stiffly at his side. Funny, she hadn't noticed that before. Well, that should keep him out of the fight, she thought, perhaps a little unfairly.

Newspaper headlines reported that the German army was poised on the borders of neutral Belgium. Already the war was spreading.

It occurred to her that she was about to fight her own battle in this elegant drawing room with its high ceilings, rich furnishings and portraits of

317

long dead ancestors; the Ravenings were used to imposing their will.

Rogers apologised. 'I couldn't stop her, your ladyship.'

The old woman's eyes glittered like chips of ice. 'I'll speak to you later, Rogers,' she said coldly. 'As for you,' she said, turning her poker hard face to Lydia, 'you are no longer welcome in this house. Neither is your father. The Ravenings have a long tradition of service to this country. They cannot be seen taking the enemy to their bosom as they might a viper...'

'We are not enemies,' Lydia responded hotly. 'I was born in this country. My father lived here when he married my mother. He has given both you and this country good service ever since. He is an asset to this country, not an enemy.'

'Please. Stop shouting,' pleaded Lady Julieta, covering her ears with small hands wearing mauve lace mittens.

Lydia took a deep breath. 'I came here because I need to tell Robert that I'm joining the Red Cross. I shall be in the thick of the battle. I want him to know I'll be over there. Who knows, we may even meet up, though I don't think it is likely. I have written a note. Perhaps you could pass it on to him?'

'Certainly not! Do you not hear what I am saying? You are not welcome in this house and Robert can no longer consider marrying you. He is an officer of this country and a gentleman. To marry you would be tantamount to treason.'

A weaker woman might have fainted away on hearing this, but the sight and sound of this dreadful woman only made her more determined to defy everything she said.

'Robert and I love each other.'

'Oh? Is that so?' Lady Julieta sat back in her chair like a Roman emperor about to deliver the death sentence.

'My nephew has already left for France and it seems he did not bother to contact you before leaving. I have also received a cable from his parents in Australia stating that in the present circumstances, they cannot possibly approve of him marrying the daughter of a German.'

Lydia felt her face reddening, her blood boiling with anger.

'I don't care what they say. They have never been there for Robert. All his life they have been absent parents. They hardly know him, but I do know him and I know beyond doubt that he would not forsake me. Not willingly. I demand to know where he's been stationed.'

Lady Ravening grasped the arms of her chair, her chin jutting forward as she raised herself haltingly to her feet. Her pale complexion turned puce.

'The matter is finished and he is beyond your reach. Now good day, young woman. And please, never, ever darken my door again!'

Chapter Twenty-Eight

England, September, 1914

My darling, Robert,

I have joined the Red Cross. Once everything is finalised, I will be heading for a small village near a town named Ypres in Flanders.

Flanders, which is in Belgium, is closer to where you are than England, and although there is only a slim chance of us meeting, to be closer to where you are will be of some comfort to me. I am presuming, of course, that you are still in France. Things have intensified since Belgium was invaded.

I have tried and tried to get a message through to you, but have been told the only way is if you know a family member in the military. With that in mind, and although I am apprehensive of using him, I am entrusting this letter to Agnes to give to Siggy in the hope that he can get it to you via military channels. I trust that under the circumstances he will do so, for after all he is your cousin.

Agnes is coming home from two weeks of training before she goes to France and has agreed to do this.

Your aunt refused to tell me where you are and it is not easy to find out. Besides that, letters can take weeks to arrive and I feel we do not have weeks. I need you to know where I am. I hope that when you see a wonderful sunset painting the clouds pink, you will think of that huge hat I wore on that day you landed the aeroplane at Heathlands. I know it will make you smile and when you do so you will think instantly of me. Wherever you are, my heart is with you. Please, we must try to meet up. I have something to tell you. Something very important.

I'm not sure when I can write to you again, certainly not until I am settled in Flanders, but I will do so at the earliest opportunity.

All my love, Lydia

After putting on her dark pink hat and coat of a similar colour, Lydia pulled back the lace curtain and looked out of the window. Mrs Gander had filled in a broken pane with a piece of cardboard until a glazier could replace it.

Lydia sighed. Egged on by his mates, a young boy had thrown the stone and shouted abuse. Only the intervention of the local bobby, a constable they'd known for years, had saved any more being broken.

'I'm going to see Miss Stacey,' she said to Mrs Gander.

'Everyone seems to be everywhere but here,' she muttered, her features pinched with disapproval.

She sounded more peevish these days because her role had diminished since Kate Mallory had moved in. Mrs Gander was besotted with Doctor Miller, her employer. With her weak chin and protruding eyes, she could not compare with Kate Mallory. However, she is loyal, Lydia decided. You had to give her that.

With the letter secreted in her coat pocket, she sped down the garden path, down the steps and out on to the avenue.

It was Sunday and families wearing their best clothes were leaving church after Sunday morning service.

Lydia hurried along, hoping nobody recognised her as the daughter of the German doctor, the Hun, the horrible monster that was gobbling up Europe.

The tram to Myrtle Street was full of people talking about the war, wistfully discussing when it was likely to be over, how brave their men folk were, but there, the sooner they put an end to such savagery, the better.

'Home by Christmas.' That was what everybody was saying.

Agnes's family had just returned from Sunday mass at St Patrick's Catholic church that nestled amongst rows of terraced housing.

The smells of a summer Sunday hung enticingly in the air; petals falling from cabbage roses, heat rising from the pavements, the slight smell of sweat mingling with that of washed linen.

Sarah Stacey was removing her hat. Her mother was in the kitchen from whence came the delicious smell of a Sunday roast.

'Hello, Lydia. I wasn't expecting you so soon, though we have to make the most of it, don't we? She'll be off soon. More's the pity,' she added shaking her head at the same time as battling with a worried frown. 'Fancy! Our Agnes driving an ambulance. I've told her to be careful. She might be behind the lines, but all the same...'

It was easy to see that Sarah Stacey was far from unaffected by the prospect of her daughter being so close to the battlefront.

'At least she's only driving an ambulance,' said Lydia. 'If she had her way, she'd be an aviator, up there in the sky with the birds.'

Sarah Stacey managed to laugh, though the concern stayed in her eyes.

'She's changing her dress up in her room, love. Go on up if you like,' she said.

Lydia climbed the narrow staircase to the tiny landing, drumming her fingertips against the letter in her pocket.

If she hadn't had things that were more serious on her mind, Lydia would have laughed aloud to see her friend struggling to get out of the dress she'd worn for Sunday service. Her face showed through the neckline, but the dress had jammed around her generous bosom and a button had hitched on her hair.

'Well, don't just stand there, ninny,' Agnes snarled, her knickers showing above her black stockings. 'Get me out of this thing. Undo the buttons or whatever. Do something!'

Lydia stifled her giggles as she assisted the wriggling Agnes until her corset followed the dress on to the bed.

'Thank goodness it's only once a week,' said Agnes, sighing at the pleasure of scratching her freed midriff. 'That's the most insufferable item of attire I own. I'm not taking it to France, I'll tell you that much.' She paused on seeing Lydia's worried expression.

'What is it?'

Lydia slumped on to the bed. Agnes sat down beside her in such a way that she could peer up into Lydia's face.

'You've got the look of a cracked teapot,' she said. 'Come on. Out with it.'

Feeling her eyes smarting, Lydia closed them and took a deep breath before telling her about the attack on her father, and that he was fine now he had Kate Mallory to look after him.

'I don't feel so guilty about joining the Red Cross now Kate's there with him,' she added.

Agnes was nothing if not perceptive. 'Is there more?' Her almond-shaped eyes, as golden as a cat's, looked searchingly into Lydia's face.

Lydia told her that Lady Ravening had forbidden her and her father to set foot in either of the Ravening properties ever again.

'Hmm,' said Agnes, pulling a 'so what' kind of expression. 'That now makes four of us. Can't say I've missed it.'

Although Agnes sounded unconcerned, Lydia knew that both Agnes and her mother missed the great house a good deal. It had been Agnes's childhood home. It had been her mother's refuge, home to both her and the man it had been her fate to love.

'So,' said Agnes, 'you've missed church and you haven't been invited for Sunday lunch, so I presume you have a special reason for visiting.' She paused suddenly, the cotton blouse she was putting on half over her head and sitting on her shoulders. 'I think I've guessed. She's told you Robert will not be marrying you, but it's possible Robert does not know this. Am I right?'

324

Lydia shrugged. 'I don't know for sure, but I have to find out. I've written a letter. That was the easy bit. Now all I have to do is get it to him. Letters travel quicker if they're sent through military channels. Is it possible that you could take this letter to Siggy? He's an officer. He could find out where Robert is and get the letter to him.'

Lydia looked down at the floor whilst fingering the letter in her pocket. 'We're travelling by boat to Holland and then Flanders, to some small town about fifteen miles from a place called Ypres. It's a hospital. That, at present, is all I know.'

Agnes sucked in her breath. 'My word. We're like birds flying south for the winter.'

'Can you get it to him?'

'Yes. Of course, I can. He's in that recruiting place, isn't he?'

Lydia nodded. 'He has an office there. I've checked, but he won't be there until Tuesday, the day before you leave...'

'For the war,' said Agnes, swiftly finishing the sentence. 'I'll take the letter to him before I depart for the war. Is that what you want?'

Lydia nodded and sucked in her lips. 'The letter is very private. I don't want anyone to read it.'

'I wouldn't!'

'I know you wouldn't. But Sylvester Travis Dartmouth... You know how he is.'

For a moment, her friend's eyes turned a deeper grey as though she were weighing up the consequences of that.

'I'll guard it with my life until it's safely flying to wherever Robert happens to be,' she said, her chin jerking in a decisive way. 'There's no question of it. Of course I'll take your letter.'

As she handed over the letter, Lydia felt an overwhelming sense of great relief. She'd half-expected Agnes to be evasive and ready with excuses. After all, she was shipping out in a few days, but at least, she reflected, Agnes did have a few days. All she had was today and half of tomorrow. Time had become more precious from the moment war was declared.

Blown by the wind, leaves rustled against the window before flying onwards. The day was perfect, intermittent clouds rolling across a powder-blue sky. In any other year such a day would be a joy, something worth celebrating. This year was different. This year we are at war and the world isn't the same as it was, thought Agnes, but I'm damned if I'll get melancholy.

'We'll both be off soon and it's a nice day. Fancy a Sunday stroll?'

'Only if you don't mind accompanying a woman not wearing corsets,' said Agnes. 'My grandmother is right. Only horses should wear a harness like that, and they have no choice! My, but I feel liberated! Must tell the Suffragettes that. Discard your corsets and victory is yours!'

Despite everything, Lydia laughed.

The park was full of people enjoying the summer sun even though the clouds of war were darkening its brightness.

Up on the bandstand, a brass band was belting out patriotic marches and some people were waving flags, shouting out 'Rule Britannia' and 'God Save the King'.

'If I was a man, I would join the Flying Corps,'

Agnes said breathlessly.

'That,' said Lydia, 'is no big surprise. I will tend the sick and injured whoever they are and wherever I am needed.'

Their mood had lightened by the time they got back to Myrtle Street, though not for long.

Hunkered at the edge of the pavement, her face buried against her crossed arms, Beatrice Allen, Edith Allen's eldest daughter, was sobbing fit to burst. The bicycle she so loved lay beside her, one wheel spinning forlornly.

Agnes tousled the girl's hat as though there was some kind of joke going on. 'Come on, Beattie, girl. Nothing can be that bad.'

Lydia caught sight of the crumpled telegram in Beatrice's hand and froze. In the absence of enough telegram delivery boys, some being so cheeky as to join up early or take over the jobs of grown men, anyone with a bicycle delivered the dreaded messages.

Agnes's head jerked up when she felt Lydia's hand shake her shoulder. Two pairs of eyes settled on the crumpled piece of paper.

Agnes softened her approach, settling to one side of the girl whilst Lydia settled on the other.

Feeling as though she were freezing from the inside out, Lydia asked her what the matter was.

Agnes had already gone pale and, just for once, she couldn't find her voice. She didn't know which one it was but she knew that somebody – either Beatrice's father or her brother – would not be coming home.

Beattie handed the telegram to Lydia who straightened it and read the name.

'Mrs Allen,' she said, her voice softening as though it would break.

Lydia and Agnes exchanged looks. Telegrams were rapidly becoming the harbingers of bad news.

Lydia bent down.

'Beattie. You haven't opened it. Your mother must do that. We won't know what it says or who it concerns until she reads it.'

'It's me brother. I know it's me brother.'

The poor girl's eyes were red rimmed, the pain behind them too much for one so young.

Lydia felt obliged to reassure her. 'Men are being taken prisoner, which means they are still alive. So dry your eyes.'

Agnes leaned forward, her long pale fingers tucking Beatrice's hair back under her hat, which had fallen to one side. 'It might be better if I deliver it for you. Would you prefer that?'

Beattie's grateful expression lifted her face, though did little to diminish the rigid frown.

'Before you knock on the door, I'm going round to get Gran,' said Agnes.

Their eyes met. Edith Allen adored her eldest son, the child of her youth and a love nobody knew much about. The telegram might indeed say he was injured or captured, but it might also say he was dead.

Ellen Proctor was a picture of calm as she came out of her front door, her eyes not glancing to left or right, her pipe clenched firmly to the corner of her mouth.

'You girls can go on. I'll see to it,' said Agnes's grandmother.

328

That solemn teatime on a typical English Sunday was the last time Lydia and Agnes saw each other before Lydia left for Flanders and Agnes filled her time before leaving for France. It was also the last time Ellen Proctor saw Edith Allen with a smile on her face. Her son was dead and her mind could not accept the fact.

Chapter Twenty-Nine

Agnes clenched her teeth at the thought of going to see Sylvester, the man who had thought that, as a domestic servant, she should be grateful he wished to seduce her. She really did not want to see him, let alone ask him for anything.

So what if she sent it by some other means than Siggy? Lydia had told her that she'd asked other people they knew if they could take the letter. Some had looked at her sadly; those who knew she was half German had regarded her with outright suspicion. But I'm totally English, Agnes thought to herself. Perhaps I might have more luck.

Time was not on her side seeing as she too was leaving for her wartime job. Running at times, she went to many places in an effort to get Lydia's letter received as quickly as possible. None was very hopeful.

'There is a war on. Things will only get worse before they get better,' said the postmaster, frowning at her as though she'd asked for a date with Lord Kitchener.

Dragging her feet, she contemplated her last resort, the person Lydia had requested she take it to in the first place: Major Dartmouth.

The very thought of the way his hands had groped her body still sickened her. Her thoughts naturally turned to Robert. What if she didn't deliver the letter? Without Lydia around, it wasn't beyond the bounds of possibility that Robert's affection might be transferred to her. Was she foolish in thinking it would? Was it possible he might stop treating her like a younger sister and instead make her his sweetheart?

So many what ifs. So many possibilities.

She stopped at a bright red pillar box, the letter suddenly seeming to burn a hole in her pocket. It would be so easy to post it into the yawning mouth. The fact that it wasn't stamped would probably be enough to get it discarded from the Royal Mail.

It didn't matter. Either way it would give her time to write to Robert and for her letter to go through explaining about Lydia leaving England. It would give her a chance with him.

Lydia is your friend.

The voice of conscience stayed her hand. Pushing the letter back into her pocket, she soldiered on, knowing what she had to do and certainly not looking forward to it. Lydia was her friend. She couldn't possibly let her down. Whatever it took, she would see this through. There was the possibility that Major Dartmouth might forget his previous attempts at seduction and simply remember her as the cook's daughter whom he used to play with when they were children. He just needed reminding of it.

She took a taxi through heavy traffic to army logistics in Whitehall. A young officer sitting behind the desk in the reception area looked up and, on seeing her, a smile lit up his face.

'Good afternoon, Miss.'

The young officer fixed his gaze on her face. He looked disappointed when she told him she wished to see Major Dartmouth. She'd heard via her mother's old friends at Heathlands that Siggy had been promoted.

'Lucky Major Dartmouth,' he said.

'It's not like that,' she advised him. 'I'm just an old childhood friend who needs his assistance with something.'

Hope brightened his face, his eyes opening wide and his dark moustache stretching with his smile.

'I'm so glad,' he said to her.

An orderly with hair as black as spilt oil went to inform Major Dartmouth that she was waiting.

The young officer behind the desk offered her a chair so she could sit down. 'No thank you,' she said with a gracious smile. 'I need to stretch my legs.'

The fact was, she was feeling nervous. Siggy Dartmouth was her least favourite person. He was unscrupulous, arrogant and selfish; that was besides being a gluttonous pig!

She paced up and down until the orderly re-appeared and asked her to follow him.

He led her along a passage lined with doors, their footsteps echoing over plainly painted walls and brown lino so polished it reflected the over-head lights.

They stopped at one of the many doors. Major Sylvester Travis Dartmouth said a label in yellow letters, recently painted by the look of it.

The orderly knocked on the door.

'Enter.'

'Miss Stacey, Sir.'

On seeing her, a tight smile twitched at his lips. His eyes devoured her like a man who hadn't eaten for a month.

She felt a cold draught as the door closed behind her. Her legs turned to water.

He half rose, waving a hand at the red leather chair facing his.

Agnes sat down, glad that the desk was between them.

'Well, well, well! If it isn't the cook's daughter. Agnes isn't it? If you're looking for a job, I can't help you. The army provides and all that! As far as cooking is concerned that is. Not women, for the use of...'

He laughed as though he had made a huge joke. He had, and at her expense. Her first inclination was to swear at him and make a sharp exit. She reminded herself that she was doing this for Lydia. Smiling wasn't easy, but she did it.

'I'm here on family business. It's regarding your cousin, Robert. I understand that you can get letters to the front line more quickly than anyone else.'

Resting his elbows on the desk, he regarded her over his entwined fingers. His knuckles were hairy. She couldn't remember noticing that before.

'And you have a letter for Robert?'

332

His eyes roved over her, pausing on those bits of her body he liked best. The urge to reach out and tip the open ink well over his head was immensely strong. She might have done so if it had not been for her continual fingering of the letter in her pocket. She had to brave this out for Lydia's sake. In addition, for Robert's. He was their only chance to get a message to him – wherever he was.

Gathering up her courage, she sat up straight and nodded. 'Yes, though it's not for me, it's on behalf of his fiancée, Lydia Miller. She's joined the Red Cross and has been sent to Flanders. There wasn't time for her to send it so she left the letter with me. I promised I would get it to Robert as quickly as I could. As you know, he's an aviator with the Royal Flying Corps. I understand it's not easy keeping up with the flying battalions. If you could get it to him, both she and I would be extremely grateful.'

She hated sounding so fawning, and squirmed at the predatory expression that came to his face.

'Ah yes. The flyboys precede the army, scouting out enemy positions. That's about all aeroplanes are good for, that and being lost or shot down.'

He stated all this as though in hope rather than warning. He hasn't changed a bit, thought Agnes, and bit back her bile at the thought of what was yet to come.

The Siggy Dartmouth she knew would want something in exchange from her and she could guess what it was likely to be.

'I can indeed pull a few strings – if I choose to.'

'I would be grateful. So would Lydia. You are aware that she and Robert are engaged.'

'There was a rumour, although... Unofficially of course.'

He reached for a silver cigarette case, took out a cigarette and lit it. 'Sorry. I forgot my manners, crass, hairy baboon that I am. Would you like one?'

He pushed the cigarette case towards her.

She shook her head. 'I prefer cheroots.'

'Doctor Miller's real name is Eric Muller. He's German, though I suppose you already know that.'

Agnes felt a fluttering of fear in her stomach, but held on to her air of confidence. She wondered if the news of Lady Julieta's opposition to the match had reached him. He gave no sign that it had.

'Yes. I know. He's lived in this country a long time. His wife, Lydia's mother, was English.'

Sylvester grunted and sneered all at the same time. 'Well, he's certainly shown where his true allegiance lies. I hear tell he's gone off to Germany with his tail between his legs. Another cowardly Hun! Well, the German army will be running all the way back to Germany with him once we've finished. The sooner we get started the quicker this whole sorry mess will be over.'

She didn't tell him that Lydia's father was still in London. Somehow, she thought it best he didn't know.

'By Christmas? Isn't that the consensus of opinion?' she said.

'Of course.' He frowned. 'You sound sceptical, my dear. Then, you are only a woman. What do women know about such matters? It's men that fight wars...'

'And women who keep the home front going and patch up their wounds. Nothing is ever certain is it? But still,' she said, laughing lightly, wishing she hadn't spoken her mind quite so strongly, 'as you say, what do I know, a weak and feeble woman?'

...but I have the heart and stomach of a King...

Those words spoken by Queen Elizabeth I at the advent of the Spanish Armada stayed in her head. It was doubtful Siggy would have known she'd led her army into battle anyway. He would probably envisage her safely sewing with her ladies in a fortified tower somewhere.

'I would hardly say you were weak and feeble,' he responded, the lascivious look in his eyes matching the smile that closely resembled a smirk. 'I like feisty women, as long as they don't overstep the mark, and you're most certainly that. I learned that last Christmas. Still, we can let bygones be bygones. We can start afresh. I suggest a night at the music hall. Tonight, shall we say?'

Agnes sucked in her bottom lip. Judging by the look on his face, he was daring her to refuse, in which case the letter to Robert wouldn't be going anywhere.

'Tonight is too short notice.'

Too arrogant to see that his interest had been rejected, he tried again.

'I'm free tomorrow night and Wednesday. Even Thursday at a push.'

'I'm not sure...'

'Aren't you?'

Her thoughts darted all over the place in pursuit of a suitable excuse. None would suffice if that letter were to get to Robert.

'I think Thursday would suit, though it would mean rearranging a few things.'

She smiled sweetly as she'd seen other, more easily impressed women do. She would not tell him that she too was going to war, whilst he sat here in his comfortable office in Whitehall; nothing would be gained by offending him.

Anything might happen by then. Siggy might get posted or even run over by a tram. Anything. However, she did her best to look pleased about the arrangement though she was feeling anything but.

'Good. Very good. I'll pick you up. I have a car. And my own driver.'

Pity him, she thought, knowing Siggy could be insufferably overbearing.

'Oh! Very good. I'd better give you the address. I live with my mother and grandmother in Myrtle Street.'

She gave him the full address and he wrote it down.

'Not a part of the city I know at all. I dare say my driver will know where it is.'

He got to his feet and made as if to come out from behind the desk.

'Now, how about a kiss to seal our promise to meet?'

She shook her head so that her mane of fiery hair floated around her head, her catlike eyes tilting upwards at the corners. 'Oh, I don't think so,' she said with a smile. 'My kisses are worth waiting for. Once I kiss you, you'll never want to kiss any other women. I guarantee it,' she said, her lips parted, the tip of her tongue sliding along her bottom lip.

She hated doing it, but he had to believe he had a chance with her. The letter had to get to France.

He seemed to think about it before jerking his chin in a curt, military style nod. 'Very well. I shall look forward to it.'

She placed the letter on the desktop, her long, slim fingers fanned over it.

'You will get it sent today?' she asked, her question teamed with a pleading smile.

His smile was terse, his eyes as hard as the brass buttons on his tunic. 'Of course I will. Without fail.'

'Thank you.'

Major Sylvester Dartmouth sank back into his chair, staring through blue smoke at the door Agnes Stacey had shut behind her. All pretence of being convivial had fallen from his features. His thoughts were dark and centred on himself and what he wanted, not what she wanted.

To think she had refused him at Heathlands and now had the temerity to present herself here, asking for favours.

The little tramp! He'd show her a thing or two. She needed bringing back into line, needed to know who was boss.

The letter lay where she'd left it. He eyed it thoughtfully before reaching across. The handwriting was handsome, his cousin's name beautifully formed by the feminine hand of Nurse Lydia Miller – Muller, he corrected himself.

337

She too had refused his advances. With gleeful aplomb, he leaned back in his chair, closed his eyes and thought of that time he had locked Lydia in the grotto on his uncle's estate. He'd thoroughly enjoyed doing that. He'd frightened her and he'd enjoyed frightening her. There was something immensely gratifying about frightening women. The professional women he hired put up with his violence, and why shouldn't they? He paid them well to have his way.

Lydia! She'd threatened to hit him with a large book. Agnes had actually done so. Who did they think they were? One was half German and the other was the illegitimate daughter of a lowly cook! They'd rejected him. Treated him with disdain and now they were asking favours. Hell would freeze over before he ever did anything for them.

Revenge, he'd read somewhere, was best served cold. Well, Lydia Miller and Agnes Stacey. You both refused my advances, now I will refuse to do you a favour.

As for his cousin Robert, well, he would have to marry elsewhere.

Gleefully, he ripped the letter in half once then in half again before consigning the remains to the wastepaper bin.

Chapter Thirty

Relieved that her mission had seemed to go quite well and that she'd left Major Dartmouth's office without him pouncing on her, Agnes whistled as she made her way home.

The smell of freshly baked bread and cakes wafted out from Pringles Bakery even before she got to it. The enticing aroma drew her in.

She bought cream slices for everybody, plus a fresh loaf.

Worried faces turned to her as she bounced into the kitchen and placed her purchases on the table.

She looked from her mother to her grand-mother. 'What is it? What's wrong?'

'They sent a messenger,' said her grandmother, her wrinkled hands clasped tightly together in her ample lap.

'You're to report for duty tomorrow morning. They brought your uniform. It looks a likely fit. And we've packed your bags. They didn't tell us where you were going; only that it was abroad driving an ambulance.'

Agnes eyed her mother's taut expression. She was trying to be brave, trying not to let the misti-ness in her eyes roll down her cheeks.

'Well, that's that then,' Agnes pronounced brightly. 'Time for a party. Cream slices all round!'

She knew there was no real party spirit in the

339

occasion, but this might be the last time she would see her family for a very long time.

Strangely enough, she felt no fear. She didn't even feel sad about leaving home. War was a terrible thing, but she viewed her part in it as an adventure, akin to her childish exploits of driving a car, and her desire to go up in Robert's aeroplane, and sailing a dinghy on the lake at Heathlands.

It would be dangerous, but on the plus side, she'd be beyond the reach of Sylvester Dartmouth, and that, she decided, was a definite plus!

If he kept to his promise, the letter to Robert was already winging its way across the English Channel. Soon she would be there too.

As for Lydia, Agnes sighed. She was envious that Lydia had already left for the continent and wondered how she was getting on.

Lydia retched but managed to keep her breakfast down. She felt guilty lying to Agnes, telling her that she was off to Flanders right away. Before she left, she had to deal with the small problem Robert had left her with; she was going to have a baby.

Under the circumstances, it was unfair to tell Robert. The war would take every ounce of concentration he could muster. Neither could she allow such a situation to prevent her from going to Flanders. The timing was all wrong! A war was far from being the best time to give birth.

She'd left a forwarding address with Agnes for when a letter came from Robert. Only, once he'd responded, she would know for sure that he still wanted her. In the meantime, she had to do something about the pregnancy. The Red Cross would not take her if they knew, and neither would anyone else for that matter. But she had to go to Flanders. She had to do something towards the war effort and the possibility of bringing everyone home by Christmas.

On leaving the house, Lydia took deep breaths of sweet morning air freshened by overnight rain. Her gaze swept over drops of dew spangling on spiders' webs.

The fresh air smell and the dew were favourite things that usually made her sigh with happiness, like lucky talismans to make her feel better. Today these things did not lift her heart.

She was now in the same predicament as Edith Allen had found herself in. Terminating a pregnancy was not an easy option; nobody could really understand what it took to do such a thing until they were in the same position themselves. It wasn't easy. Not easy at all.

If only Robert would get in touch; she was sure everything would be all right then. She still believed that despite the war they would marry. This was all so ridiculous; her father had been much respected before the war, and now he was finding his position difficult, though not all his patients had deserted him.

She sighed as she made her way to the hospital to collect a few things she'd left in her room.

A mob had gathered outside the hospital, ranged across the entrance. Her heart raced so fast she could almost believe she could hear her blood pumping through her veins.

One of those assembled, a man wearing a dark

felt hat that shaded his swarthy features, turned round and saw her. He said something she could not quite hear or understand. It sounded like Russian. The crowd parted, a dozen or more hollow, half-starved faces turning in her direction.

'Good morning. Nurse Miller, is it not?' The man now spoke in English.

Lydia recognised the man as the father of a small boy who had been brought in suffering from diphtheria. She recalled tending to the boy, which was why the man knew her name.

Her pulse slowed, though she was still puzzled. 'Has something happened?'

'We heard a rumour a mob was on its way to cause trouble. The hospital is important to us. We came to defend it.'

A huge surge of gratitude swept over her. The madness of war had not taken hold of everyone.

The few things she'd left at the hospital didn't take too long to pack, though the task seemed to tire her far more than it should. The small suitcase also seemed heavier and wearied her arms.

Sister Gerda, one of the German deaconesses in charge at the hospital, had remained in England, determined to carry on doing her duty despite everything. She took Lydia's hand in both of hers as they tearfully wished each other goodbye.

'Let us pray this madness will soon be over,' murmured Sister Gerda.

And I used to think she was so formidable, thought Lydia.

Once her hand was released, she brushed it across her forehead.

Sister Gerda frowned. 'Are you feeling all

right?' she asked.

Lydia nodded. 'Just a little tired I think. It must be all the excitement, and perhaps something I ate.'

That night she took some strong laxatives and had a bath, the water so hot it turned her skin lobster pink. If this didn't work she would have to seek a termination. But she would go to France first. She was determined she would. The next day she left for Flanders. She also bled. On the one hand, she was elated; her little problem had come to nothing without any intervention on her part. On the other hand, the one thing that had bound her to Robert was gone. A feeling of emptiness came with it.

Chapter Thirty-One

Lydia. Belgium, September, 1914

The air was still warm with summer heat and the crossing from England to the Hook of Holland had been calm.

The ferry was crowded with worried-looking people who had been strangely silent, either that or the throb of the ship's engine drowned out all other sounds. Lydia had reserved a cabin, but what with the rolling of the vessel and the green faces of fellow passengers, she stayed up on deck.

Her fellow passengers were grim faced, some because they'd left friends and family behind, some because they feared what would happen next. Some were merely seasick. Silence reigned, nobody wanting to express their fears for the future, their thoughts dark and forbidding.

She thought of her mother's journal, the one she'd found among the Christmas decorations. The world was at war and she was caught up in it. *Now is the time to note down what I can of my experiences.* There was no room to do that on the boat, and besides, the journal was buried deep in her suitcase.

But when I get there, that is when I shall begin.

The crowded train to Brussels was noisier, full of families racing home to France, Luxembourg or those towns in Belgium that had not yet fallen to the enemy.

Home, they're all trying to get home, she thought. Except me.

Her eyes filled with tears at the thought of the blood she'd shed, the first for six weeks or so. If it hadn't been for this war, she and Robert would have married and perhaps the child might have survived. All this worry, all this rushing around contributed to losing it. That's what she told herself, though in all honesty she couldn't know for sure.

All the same she couldn't help wondering what it might have looked like; whether it would have her grey eyes, his cleft chin, small hands or large, a determined wail in its demand for attention.

It.

Would *it* have been a boy or a girl?

She resolved not to continue torturing herself, but the other Lydia, the one who felt so much for

344

other people, decided she deserved it. Think of the future, she said to herself. Think of the good you will be doing, tending the injured brought up from the battlefields. Your duty is now to them.

Joining the Red Cross was a good idea, she told herself. The hospital was currently in an area still under Belgian control. Being a neutral concern it treated all nationalities, no matter which side they were fighting on.

They were to work and lodge in a splendid chateau especially bequeathed by wealthy patrons. It stood in its own grounds, surrounded by grass, gardens and plane trees with big leaves and widely spreading branches. It reminded her of Heathlands.

She was one of the first to arrive and look around the room she was to share with two other nurses. It was bright and airy and had once been a nursery. The walls were lemon and white. A handsome writing bureau stood near the window, a chair of blue brocade pushed up in front of it.

She looked at the bureau as she might an old friend; it was similar to her bureau at home. It occurred to her that it might have the same secret compartment, and if so...

She bit her lip. The photograph of her mother and the journal nestled amongst her clothes. The suitcase clasps snapped open, one after the other. Both the items she wanted were bound together inside a cotton nightdress. Before getting them out, she went to the bureau. The pattern inside was different, but familiarity with her own bureau made her feel carefully for one pattern standing a little prouder of the marquetry than the others.

A sharp 'click' and the secret drawer opened.

Seeing as there was nobody around to be upset at the sight of the photograph of her mother, she placed it on top of the bureau. It was possible that the writing desk would be used by her roommates, too, and she didn't want them reading the first few words that she'd written on the boat coming across from England. In the days that followed, she met Fleur, a Belgian nurse, and Esther, a tall blonde American. Both had brought photographs of their families and Lydia felt quite proud to show off the portrait of her mother; both girls commented on the likeness between Lydia and her mother.

Fleur had also brought a photograph of her fiancé, a French soldier who had donned the bright blue jacket of the Republican army and marched off to war.

All three girls agreed that they were lucky to have such a luxurious billet. Lydia commented to a fellow nurse that the chateau that filled her eyes looked far too grand to be a hospital.

'Imagine the balls they must once have had here, the ladies' dresses, the handsome men in tailcoats or military uniforms. And here we are about to turn it all upside down. What a great shame, I mean it isn't as though the soldiers will appreciate such a wonderful place.'

Her comment was overheard.

'A man in pain doesn't care where he is. He could be in a cow shed as long as there is someone there to ease his pain.' The speaker was a tall man with weary eyes and stooped shoulders, obviously a doctor.

'This way,' shouted the matron in charge, a tall woman with a kind face, a cottage bun hair style and the soft caring eyes of the nun she had once been.

The nurses trooped in after her, all amazed on seeing the beautiful interior of carved plaster-work, wall paintings and stained gaps where oil portraits used to hang.

'This is so lovely. Fancy turning it into a hospital,' said Fleur.

'Hopefully it won't be for long,' said Lydia. 'Hopefully the war will be over by Christmas.'

Fleur had soft brown eyes and full lips and looked as though she had plenty to say.

'I wish I could be sure. Pierre, my sweetheart, is serving somewhere between here and the coast.'

'We have to believe it will be over by Christmas. Nobody in their right mind would want this situation to go on for years,' declared Lydia.

The next week consisted of setting up beds in gracious rooms with walls of silken wallpapers and curtains scattered with peacocks in shades of turquoise, blue and dark green.

A smattering of injured men came in, a small trickle, the result of sorties rather than mass advances.

'The enemy are to our right and the Allies to our left,' explained a doctor with a balding pate and jet-black eyes. 'As long as they both go around us when they head for the town of Ypres, we should be all right.'

Loaded up with linen sheets, Lydia came across removal men carrying the last of the lovely furniture from the house. Its replacements were iron-framed beds, trolleys used for holding surgical instruments, and glass-fronted medicine cupboards fitted with stout locks.

She had heard from one of the cooks that the chateau belonged to an Italian count. Greta had worked for them and would now work for the Red Cross managing the hospital.

Lydia had commented that she was very brave to do that; after all, as a civilian, she could opt to get out, away from the front.

'Someone has to stand their ground,' Greta had declared, waving her arms around as though she were the last line of defence against the enemy.

Just three weeks after their arrival there was bad news. The British Expeditionary Force was desperate to seize and maintain a corridor through Flanders to the sea. The Germans were just as desperate to close it, thus cutting off the British supply line. Ypres was in the firing line.

The Red Cross post gained new neighbours, a precursor to a planned battle rumoured to take place around Ypres.

The Germans marched in, setting out their headquarters on the upper floors of the chateau. To their credit, they transferred a number of their army doctors to the hospital and agreed that they would come under the jurisdiction of the Red Cross superintendent.

Monsieur Dandier, the superintendent, assured everyone that as the Red Cross was a neutral organisation dedicated to saving lives no matter the nationality, there would be no interruption to their good works.

Most of the staff, with the exception of a few French and Belgians who found it impossible to maintain their neutrality, seeing as the Germans had marched through neutral Belgium, left. The Germans gave them safe conduct to the few areas still controlled by the Belgian army.

The noise from enemy guns still seemed a long way off, and although they were treating some injured soldiers, they had not been overwhelmed.

There was even time to relax. During a lull in her work, Lydia wandered through the extensive gardens, glad of the fresh air away from the smells of disinfectant and carbolic soap.

Like everyone else, she was becoming restless, dreading the sight of the injuries to come, but wanting to do something more worthwhile than winding bandages or checking and rechecking surgical tools and medicines.

The smell of summer roses filled the air. In those areas where tents had not been set up to take the overflow of casualties, vegetables grew and the boughs of fruit trees hung heavy with ripe apples, pears and cherries.

Lydia made for the orchard where the grass was long and made a comforting swishing sound against her skirts.

The chateau reminded her of Heathlands, and thinking of Heathlands reminded her of Robert. If it hadn't been for this war, they would have been married by now. The sad thought brought tears to her eyes, but she blinked them away. Robert must never know. If they ever did meet again, she would not mention the pregnancy. The pain to both of them would be too great.

Lost in thought, she did not hear the soft footfall in the loamy earth or hear the whispering of disturbed grass.

'It's started. Did you hear the guns? They are nearer now.'

The voice took her unawares. She jerked upright from the tree trunk she'd been leaning against. A few apples fell to the ground.

She recognised the doctor who'd commented on injured men not caring where they were treated. He was Franz Berger, a Red Cross doctor from Switzerland, who believed fervently in world peace and a permanent end to war.

Lydia brushed the leaves from her skirt. Just for once, she wasn't wearing uniform. Her dress was grey and her blouse a deep shade of purple. It felt good to be out of uniform. She was aware that such times would be rare. She had to make the most of it.

'No. I didn't hear it. I'm afraid I was deep in thought,' she said to him.

He bent down, picked a dark red poppy and handed it to her. 'I could see that.'

'This poppy isn't as bright as most of them around here,' she said to him as she stroked the petal from its outer edge down to the black stamen at its centre.

'Like blood,' he said to her.

She saw he was chewing something, his jaw moving from side to side. He spat out a cherry stone into the long grass.

'This is a lovely place, this orchard. It's unlikely to survive the carnage to come of course. Sad but true,' he added on seeing the disbelief on her face.

He turned his head as though expecting a shell or bullet to come shooting over his shoulder.

'Why do you think that? It's so quiet here.'

'This, my dear, is the calm before the storm. We must make the most of it. Explore while we can. Would you care to stroll with me down to the end of the drive? One last look at the outside world before we've no more time to do so?'

As they strolled towards the main gates, she thought she heard the sound of thunder.

She looked at Franz. His curt nod was enough to confirm she was wrong. It was not thunder. The guns had opened up on the Western Front – not far from where they were.

'We are between the guns and the town of Ypres,' he said to her. 'It's quite an ancient town. One might say of historical significance. Not for long, though. Not for long.'

They walked in silence, each closeted with their own thoughts, their footsteps raising dust from the dry gravel.

A sudden sound caused Lydia to raise her head. Franz did the same.

Wrought-iron gates set between pillars topped with mythical creatures bearing shields lay open at the end of the drive. She presumed the coat of arms was that of the family who owned the chateau.

A column of Belgian refugees was passing; everything they possessed in the world piled in unwieldy heaps on carts, some pulled by plodding farm horses with docked tails and bony rumps, some pushed by men and women with tired faces and the look of defeat in their eyes.

351

Children sat or slept on top of their meagre belongings along with a crate containing chickens, and even a goat or two. Dogs, their tongues hanging out, loped along between the wheels, glad of the shade and after many miles fleeing the onslaught to come, too tired to run yapping in and out of the long procession.

The people's faces, young and old alike, had strangely resigned looks, as though they were both grateful and surprised to find themselves alive and heading away from the fighting.

Lydia stood silently, watching them pass.

'So,' Franz said solemnly, 'it begins.'

'Line up, ladies! Straight if you please.'

The nurses dutifully shuffled their feet to achieve the required straightness.

'You've all done an excellent job. You may congratulate yourselves. Shake hands with your neighbours.'

The nurses smiled and did as requested. They'd worked hard. Everything was ready. Beds stood white, crisp and clean; glass, metal and wood sparkled. All they were waiting for were the patients.

'I can't wait to get started,' said Esther, Lydia's American roommate. 'I mean really started. Those poor boys. They're going to need all the help they get. So how do you feel?'

Lydia took a deep breath. 'I'm dreading it.'

That night she slept only fitfully. In her dream, she was at Heathlands, hand in hand with Robert, strolling around the lake. Somebody was

352

calling her away. She tried to shout back that she would not leave Robert's side. They were to be married and nothing...

'Lydie, Lydie! Wake up! Wake up! The first casualties have arrived.' Belgian-French Fleur was shaking her.

Lydia Miller jerked herself from sleep and, stupidly, her first thought was of altering her diary.

'Tomorrow; that's when they're expected. Tomorrow,' she said tiredly. 'It's still night.'

Lights flashed outside, skimming the darkness, and the sound of motor-driven ambulances barely overcame the frenzied shouting to open doors, assemble stretchers and turn the bloody lights on.

Her dream faded. Fleur was shaking her shoulder.

'They are here! They are here! Did you not hear them?'

There was no chance to answer. Lydia dressed quickly without washing.

'I must have gone deaf,' she muttered to herself. The noise from outside was deafening.

Men were shouting, horses neighing, engines rumbling and men, the injured men, screaming in pain and crying for their mothers.

Lifting their skirts above their ankles, the nurses ran down the stairs. The doctors, both the German military doctors and the neutral Red Cross, inspected men on stretchers and barked orders. The very air, which smelled of earth and blood, trembled with the screams of injured men.

Franz Berger was in the thick of it. He called for a nurse. Lydia, having just finished dressing a head wound, ran to help.

'Put your fingers on the carotid artery whilst I suture.'

Lydia pressed as hard as she could. Even so, blood pumping from the artery supplying the man's head spurted on to her starched white cuff.

'Press harder. It's not entirely severed. I can save him. I'm sure I can.'

He sounded anxious that he could be wrong, and angry that modern warfare could so easily sever arteries, rip out intestines and blow limbs from living flesh.

Lydia pressed as hard as she could, the tips of her fingers grazed by the needle and sutures. Thanks to both shock and ether, the man remained unconscious, his face smeared with sweat, blood and dirt.

'He was German,' said Franz. 'Now he is a dead German.'

There was no time to admit that she had not noticed his uniform. A broken man was a broken man, marred flesh torn to shreds in a war he most likely did not understand.

One after another they came, men wearing the uniform of the Kaiser's Germany, bleeding, unconscious or screaming with pain.

Doctor Berger made swift decisions: 'This one can be saved. This one might last until morning, this one ... fetch the padre.'

There was little time to look around, but Lydia's instinct alone told her that the chateau they had thought so big, was being overwhelmed. More and more injured men were arriving. There was soon a man lying in every bed. Soon, only floor space

354

remained and even that filled up quickly. Gone was any sign of white starched sheets; there was only blood, mud and the cries of men in distress.

There were shouts for more bandages, more medicine, more nurses, doctors and 'clear a little space there. Enough for a body.'

The injured men kept coming, one after another. Some of them stared at her, unsure whether she was merely a woman or they had finally arrived in heaven. Some, she realised, would welcome death, anything rather than the hell they had just been through.

They were all German. What did that mean, she asked herself? When she voiced her question aloud, the answer came swift and sure. The chateau was now behind enemy lines. Military law ordained that injured Allied prisoners would journey to a prisoner-of-war camp. The war for them would be over; Lydia wished it had never begun.

Endless injured men: endless running to get more bandages, more ether, and more morphine.

Darkness fused into day, day bled into twilight ... or was it merely that somebody had put out the lights then lit them again?

A firm hand landed on her shoulder. A firm voice sounded in her ear. 'Your turn to rest, Miller. And please do something about your cuffs. They're a disgrace.'

Lydia wanted to bark back at the matron that she'd had precious little time to attend to blood-spattered cuffs. Men were dying and in pain.

As it was, she couldn't find her voice. Her throat was too dry. Not a word would come out.

Just as well, she thought to herself as she went outside.

Disorientated from the hours she had spent on her feet, she tried to work out what the time could be. It was still dark, yet surely, it should be daylight by now?

Her legs, her eyes, her whole body ached, but the urge to get as far away as possible from the hospital overcame her weariness. The garden beckoned. The orchard with its autumn smells beckoned her most of all.

Stretcher-bearers wound their way between the olive-green tents, the latter filling up much more quickly than anticipated.

Lydia averted her eyes, glad of the full moon to light her way beyond the tents and the vegetable garden, to the walled orchard, where she might find peace for a while.

The orchard at night shone with silver amongst patches of velvet blackness. An owl hooted and a wild creature – possibly a fox – scurried through the grass.

The smell of fruit ripening was such a relief after the smell of blood and entrails, that Lydia found herself crying. It was so ordinary and yet so wonderful.

Suddenly she smelled tobacco. She saw the red cigarette tip shining amongst a patch of black velvet.

Franz moved into the light. He was in his mid-thirties, had a congenial face and a flippant, sometimes quite offensive way of speaking. After the hours of sewing up wounds and declaring which men could be saved and which could not, he seemed to have aged by another thirty years. Eyes reddened by extreme fatigue were sunken; his skin had acquired a greyish pallor as though all the blood had drained away, recoiling from the sights he had seen.

'There is no glory in war. Do you know that?' he said to her, his voice a despairing monotone.

'Did someone famous say it?' she asked, hoping he hadn't heard her crying.

'No. Just me. You'll cry a lot more tears before this war is over; such is the nature of war. I detest it.'

'If you detest it so much, why are you here?'

He made a sound that was somewhere between a laugh and a growl.

'It was expected of me.'

'Your family?'

'My wife's family are Prussians. They are proud of their military history. I think they were quite disappointed when Gerda married me. A humble Swiss doctor. They thought she could have done better.'

Lydia noticed the bitterness in his voice. 'My father is German, but lives in England.'

'I hope he is happy there.'

Lydia didn't confirm whether he was or was not. 'You have children?'

'Yes. Three girls. That too was a disappointment. The family insisted we produce at least one son to continue the family tradition. *Their* family tradition – certainly not mine.'

Lydia folded her arms and looked down at the ground. Her eyes stung. Tiredness was catching up with her.

She felt his eyes studying her. 'Your cuffs. They are bloodied.'

Lydia placed four fingers under her right cuff. 'I will have to soak them.' She looked up at the moon. 'I didn't notice the moon earlier when I went to bed.'

Franz laughed. It was the first time she had heard him laugh outright.

'My dear girl. A whole day has passed and another night. We have been on duty for forty-eight hours!'

Chapter Thirty-Two

Agnes. France, September, 1914

Agnes Stacey stood in front of the Right Honourable Hortense Corbett with an air that her superior could only interpret as insolence. Agnes kept her gaze fixed on the painting of the King and Queen on the wall behind and slightly above Hortense's head.

Hortense's brown eyes were round as buttons. Her jowls quivered. Her small mouth opened and closed like a goldfish drowning in fresh air. The officer in charge, Major Darius Emerson was sound asleep, worn out from over-long hours. Hortense was making the most of it, laying down the law to Agnes without him interfering.

'Regulation uniform is a skirt. Not trousers. Not jodhpurs. A skirt! I want to see you in a skirt like all the other ambulance drivers plus the regulation hat. Not that...' the Right Honourable Hortense paused, her large chest heaving as she took a deep breath before delivering the final facet of her criticism, '...that leather thing!'

'It's a flying hat. I take it you don't like the goggles either,' said Agnes tartly.

She watched gleefully as the woman's face reddened as though she were choking. She had grown up waited on by a houseful of servants. They had flitted around her, doing her will, never showing in their behaviour that they had opinions or were as human as she was.

Agnes had met plenty of her sort since arriving in France; from men of good family but not terribly bright leading other more worthy men into battle to young ladies who seemed to think that being a nurse meant looking saintly whilst soothing a fevered brow. Quite a few had been sick on peeling back dirty rags from septic wounds, picking out the maggots, cleansing the flesh of fleas and lice before applying new dressings.

Female ambulance drivers were less numerous than nurses, but the story was much the same. Dealing with the dirt, the stink of gangrene and the screams of men holding their own guts in place were either the making or the undoing of them. Those who recovered stayed; those that were sickened and traumatised went home to a gentler life. Not that they would ever forget what they'd endured; nobody could do that.

Hortense continued with her outburst, her accusations of unfeminine behaviour interspersed with declarations of her firm belief that the British

359

military was invincible.

Agnes said nothing. She'd learned quickly that her supervisor relished receiving an emotional response, preferably tears. Agnes gave no sign that the words pouring down on her head were having any effect. They were like so many pebbles thrown at a window. The glass might break or it might not.

Heaving herself to her feet, Hortense leaned on the desk with thick fists, her anger erupting into red roundels on each cheek.

'I can think of no reason why you wear such a ridiculous outfit!' she finally exclaimed.

'Goggles are far from useless. I used them when my windscreen exploded, hit by a piece of stray shrapnel. It was raining heavily. Without them, I wouldn't have been able to see. As for wearing trousers, they make sense. I can climb up and down into the back of the ambulance, and help to retrieve injured men from deep trenches. I'm doing the army's bidding, patching them up so they can fight again. One less casualty to upset the British public at their breakfast! We wouldn't want that now, would we?'

Agnes kept her gaze fixed on the face that had now turned as red as the poppies scattered amongst the corn back in August. Such a brief period of sunshine, summer sky and the passing fancy that the war was just a dream and they were merely here on holiday.

The small eyes regarding her narrowed, the thin lips pursed in a livid line.

'I have made notes. I will refer those notes to Major Emerson who, as you know, is the medical officer in charge of all of us. His decision will be final. Is that clear?'

'If you have to.'

Agnes was purposely casual in her response, as though she couldn't care less if they sent her back to England, her service record marked as unsuitable. Going back in fact would be anathema to her. Here was where she belonged. She had never felt more alive, more needed. She went out of her way to do all she could for these men. In her mind, every single one was Robert, and now he was out there, shot down, missing presumed dead.

Once outside, Agnes took herself into the shaded fruit garden to the rear of the property where the dark earth was barren around bare stalks.

The smell, the freshness reminded her of a similar garden, long before the war, when she was just a child, not sure of her place in the world, but loving those closest to her.

Leaning against a brick wall, she lit up a cheroot. She'd taken to smoking cheroots back in England in order to shock; cheroots formed part of her risqué, outrageous image, in the same way as did her leather helmet, goggles and jodhpurs. In the present circumstances, the pungent smoke falling into her lungs was especially pleasurable. She was tired. Tired and frightened. Shot down behind enemy lines, Robert was either dead, lost or already a prisoner.

Closing her eyes, she imagined herself back at Heathlands, the sound of clattering pans and her mother's voice coming from the kitchen, the smell of wood smoke mingling with that of the dark, loamy earth.

And Robert. There had always been Robert, Sir

Avis's nephew. She'd loved him from the first time she'd popped up in front of his pony. She'd loved him more on meeting him in the depths of a cold mid-winter when the ice on the lake at Heathlands froze over and the grass was thick with frost before being buried under six inches of snow. That was when she first became aware of him, though in truth they'd known each other since they were babies – not that she could remember very much about that!

The lake at Heathlands had attracted her, weak sunshine making it sparkle like a bluish-white mirror.

Sir Avis, her mother's very generous employer, had given her a pair of skates for Christmas. They were second hand and a bit too big for her, but her mother had said she would grow into them. Sir Avis had also bought her a new dress and chocolates, but the skates, with their promise of an adventurous outdoor pursuit, had captured her imagination. In January, the temperature outside plummeted and she picked up her skates.

Early in the morning, just before breakfast, she'd crept out of the house and made her way through the copse of tangled trees and down the path to the water's edge.

The rushes and tall reeds of summer were dried and shrouded in white. The lake was thick with ice. Her heart had soared. She would glide across the lake like a swan, though faster. Speed had always excited her.

After brushing snow from a handy rock, she'd sat down, unbuttoned and pulled off her boots. Bearing in mind that the skates were too big, she'd had the foresight to bring a spare pair of socks with her. She'd put these on quickly, totally absorbed in what she was doing; excited at the prospect of what she was about to do.

Wobbling at first, she'd made her way down the final few feet to the edge of the lake. She'd been just about to push forward, when a warning voice rang out.

'You can't skate on there. I say! You can't skate there.'

The boy shouting the warning was standing between her and the small copse of trees on the hill. Once he'd seen he had her attention, he broke into a run.

'Stop right there,' he'd shouted.

Agnes had looked at him, then back at the lake. She was close, so very close to fulfilling what she wanted to do. Nobody, she decided, including him, was going to stop her.

She'd pushed herself on to the ice, first one foot, and then the other. Without a single wobble, she sped forward, arms outstretched to either side, face glowing with excitement.

'I'm doing it! I'm doing it!'

She spun on her feet, amazed at her speed, enjoying the icy air on her face. She laughed and laughed.

'See? It's easy!'

The boy edged forward on to the ice at the side of the lake.

'Keep away from the middle! Come back!'

She heard his shout, but didn't obey it. This was living. This was wonderful.

'Keep away from the middle,' he shouted again.

She saw him edge further forward on to the ice as though he were placing his feet on stepping stones, one after the other.

'Can't catch me,' she shouted back.

Being only a child, she didn't fully comprehend the look of alarm on his face. It was a game, just a game; wasn't it?

Suddenly fine cracks spread over the ice that earlier had seemed so thick, so capable of taking her weight. She'd come to a stop and had watched, fascinated, as the cracks had spread out from where she stood.

Like cracks from a hard-boiled egg hit with a spoon.

Somehow, she could never remember how, she'd taken a flying leap from the breaking ice, back the way she'd come.

A sliver of a crack appeared where she'd landed; water began to spill upwards, flowing over the ice.

Pushing forward with all her might, she headed back, determined that she wouldn't end up in the cold water, sensible enough to know, even at that age, that it might be the end of her if she did.

He'd been waiting for her, halfway between her and the safety of the bank.

The ice was firm where he stood and she managed to skate all the way up to him.

She looked up into his face, saw the blue eyes, the wisps of hair curling out from beneath his hat.

She saw something else in those eyes then and heard the admiration in his voice.

'Hello,' she'd said, her tone far too confident for the average seven year old. 'Were you worried about me?'

The boy, who looked to be about four years older than her, had shaken his head in disbelief. 'You are the most amazingly brave girl I've ever met. I think I like you.'

Even now, looking back, she could feel how it was to bask in his admiration.

'My name's Agnes Stacey,' she'd told him. 'And you're Robert Ravening. I popped up in front of your pony. Do you remember?'

His smile had made her forget that the sky was grey and the air bitingly cold.

'Nobody could help but notice you.'

Smiling at the memory, she flicked the remains of her cheroot into the undergrowth. The smile did not last. Her face clouded. So much had changed. Robert had fallen in love with her friend Lydia. She'd survived the heartache, swallowing her pride and her pain.

A week ago, she'd received the news that the hospital where Lydia was stationed in Flanders had fallen into German hands. She'd assumed a Red Cross hospital would be spared occupation, but had found out otherwise.

She eyed the pale sun sinking behind pink clouds. What innocents we are, she thought.

It had felt as though she'd swallowed an iron bolt when she'd heard that Robert had been shot down. A navigator involved in the same skirmish had given her that piece of terrible news. So much for Siggy and his comments about flying machines being limited and not likely to get involved in real fighting, she thought grimly, and felt like crying and laughing all at the same time.

The injured navigator told her how he'd hid by

day and travelled by night, sneaking through the lines.

'Didn't do my leg much good, Miss, but at least I'm still alive. Next stop the Old Kent Road!'

She'd helped him down from the ambulance knowing by the rancid smell of his injured flesh and the bone sticking through his trouser leg that he would end up a cripple.

He'd escaped. He'd survived. There was a chance Robert might have survived too.

Two nurses helped him hop his way to the hospital. She watched until he disappeared from sight, though it wasn't really the navigator she was seeing. She was seeing Robert, injured, cold and alone.

He needed help. He might need an ambulance. She leaned against the bonnet of her own vehicle, feeling the heat of the engine suffusing through the metal. She had the vehicle and she had the will. She would do her best to find him.

Chapter Thirty-Three

Hortense Corbett, Agnes's superior, was true to her word. A great one for making lists and notes, she stood there in front of Major Darius Emerson with her completed notes on each one of the girls under her supervision.

Major Emerson had the patience of a saint, but even he failed to hide his exasperation, rubbing at his eyes and sitting back with a sigh. He was the son of a British officer of the Indian army and an Anglo-Indian mother, though nobody would guess that. He'd inherited the red hair of his father and a skin colour that was something close to Asian but lifted by the fact that his eyes were blue.

He had far more important things to do than study the copious lists this woman produced. The government had forbidden the likes of volunteer auxiliaries running hospital field units, but somehow this woman and her team got through. She obviously knew the right people, damn her!

He flicked through the papers without really reading anything. He just didn't have the time.

'Look, Hortense, I think you will appreciate it when I tell you that I'm snowed under with paper-work at present. Are there any pertinent points amongst your lists that need my attention right at this minute?'

'Oh,' she said, looking decidedly deflated. She so loved those lists, loved remarking on her 'girls'.

'Here,' she said, snatching the papers from him and stabbing at one particular sheet of paper, one particular name. 'Agnes Stacey is the most insolent young woman. She refuses to dress appropriately, insists in fact on wearing jodhpurs, a flying helmet and goggles.'

Darius Emerson jerked his chin as he read the particulars – just the first line. He'd met Agnes and liked her. Still, he had to play the part, appease this woman and get on with what was important.

'I think we have to ask ourselves if this mode of dress affects her performance as an ambulance driver. Reports already in my possession tell me they do not. In fact, I am given to understand that she is hard working, brave and willing to help anyone in need. Would you disagree with that?'

Hortense Corbett spluttered before collecting herself. If there was one thing bred into her, it was the art of collusion. If the major took the opposite view to hers, she had to appear to comply – even though she simmered with antagonism.

'If nobody objects to her outlandish outfit, then I cannot object. However, I do wonder how she was accepted with such an attitude. She is so unfeminine. Have you seen her driving that ambulance? Regardless of mud, stones or barrage fire, she drives it full pelt; most unseemly; most unfeminine.'

Major Darius Emerson, a doctor in peacetime, rubbed at his eyes in an effort to massage some life back into them. 'She does her job, Hortense. I'm happy with that.'

'That may be so, but...'

She went on to list a variety of reasons why they should perhaps review the situation. 'Perhaps at a later date?'

Darius pretended to be listening whilst considering other, more serious matters.

A pile of paperwork relating to the growing casualty lists destined for prominent posting in England and throughout the Empire was getting dangerously high. It was time to begin a new one.

Moderating his voice, he explained the situation quietly and confidently.

'It's quite simple, Hortense. Men are wounded

on the battlefield. Ambulance drivers are needed to collect them and bring them back here so I can put them back together again – as well as I can when they have bits missing and...' He stopped, the rest of what he had intended saying sticking in his throat. 'What I mean to say is,' he said, taking up a pencil and tapping it impatiently on his paperwork, 'that ambulance drivers are getting killed too. Agnes Stacey does her job well. She collects the wounded and brings them here. Added to that,' he said, a sarcastic note entering his voice, 'she is alive. We need her.'

Realising she had alienated the doctor instead of gaining his approval, Hortense made another effort to repair the damage.

Although it was hard to admit it – even to herself – she could see by Darius's expression – despite his weariness – that he was as susceptible to Agnes Stacey's looks as any man. Her face was a little too freckled to suit the accepted idea of beauty – that which is pale and protected from the sun by a lace-trimmed parasol – but all the same, she had seen the way men's eyes followed her. Albeit begrudgingly, she conceded that they were likely to be the best judge of female beauty after all.

Darius pulled his thoughts away from Agnes's vibrant good looks and tried his best to focus on the situation as he saw it.

'I think we have to tolerate Agnes's dress sense. I think we also have to fear for her in the present circumstances.'

Hortense frowned. 'Is there something I should know?'

He nodded wearily whilst pushing his hair back

369

from his face. 'It was reported a week ago that someone close to her, an aviator, is missing in action. One has to expect her behaviour to be erratic.'

'Erratic? She's very headstrong. Full of energy and high spirits,' Hortense said, as though that were something of a drawback.

Barely controlling some less than gentlemanly comments, Darius frowned at her. 'What a pity we couldn't bottle those high spirits and hand them out in big spoonfuls. Should do the injured no end of good and make our job a damn sight easier!'

Doctor Darius Emerson fingered the bottles of morphine, the ether and other painkillers, salves and ointments ranged on shelf after shelf of the medicine cabinet. He was tired, totally worn out with work – and the war, in his opinion, was hardly even started.

It was usual to keep such medicines under lock and key along with all the other lesser pain-relieving medicines he kept in the cupboard. How long would it last, he asked himself. Nothing could persuade him that this war would be over by Christmas. A great dread haunted both his waking hours and sleepless nights that the casualties would be overwhelming, that nothing would be decided in a few short months. If his instinct served him correctly, then the dressings and painkillers would quickly run out.

Anticipating opposition from senior officers, he had decided, off his own bat, to requisition greatly increased supplies from London. Hopefully, the supplies would come through before anyone noticed he hadn't gone through normal channels. If anyone did notice, he was for the high jump – unless his judgement proved correct, in which case his foresight would be rewarded.

A cold sweat broke out on his brow as he rubbed his eyes, then rested his head against the medicine cupboard, relishing the coldness of the glass doors against his temples. He headed outside.

'Major. Are you all right?'

His face turned towards her, the lightest point in the darkness, except for the blush of sky behind her, residual light and heat from the artillery barrage.

He recognised the lithe form, the confident way she approached him, the way the little light that there was made her hair look as though it were on fire.

'Agnes. What are you doing out here? Leave me alone. Get back inside.'

'I'm not in the army. I won't snap to attention.'

Agnes had had a bad day. She was burning with anger, sick and tired of seeing injured young men, their eyes glazed, their mouths open, crying for their mothers.

'This war is stupid,' she said angrily.

She stood close to him, her hand on his shoulder. She saw him look at it as though wondering what it was.

'Do you know what I think?' she said when he stayed silent. 'I think it is far better to make love, not war. Do you agree?'

It happened quickly, neither of them giving

371

themselves time to think again.

She didn't protest at his rough handling of her breasts or the speed with which he unbuttoned her trousers. On the contrary, she needed him to be doing this, to feel the heat of him, smell the mildewed dampness of his uniform. If this grunting, grinding, grabbing of flesh was sin, then it certainly didn't feel like sin, more like a need to prove physically that they were still alive. They were indulging in raw, physical, emotional sex, without frills or the pretence of committing to each other. Just simple lust to blank out all the horrors, they had seen and all the horrors to come.

Chapter Thirty-Four

November, 1914

Lydia had been apprehensive about writing in her mother's journal, but now it seemed the right thing to do. At least someone would know what her life was like if anything should happen to her. Someone would read it. Someone would know.

She had intended recording just incidents in the war, but the journal was filling up with memories, bits and pieces that came to her while bandaging wounds, assisting at an amputation, changing dressings smeared repugnantly with the yellow, greenish tinge of infection. Writing down memories of the past helped shield her against the horror-laden present.

Daylight hours passed in a blur of activity. Sleep was restless and came with dreams – nightmares – more grotesque than the days.

Like all the other Red Cross nurses, she was wearing more layers of clothes in order to keep warm. The fine summer had turned into a fair September, but it was now late November and the weather had turned bitterly cold.

The chateau might have retained more heat, but a few stray shells had left holes. The holes let in the cold despite the tarpaulin sheets fastened over them.

'I feel so fat in all these clothes,' Lydia said to Fleur, her Belgian roommate.

'We all are,' said Fleur. 'I'm wearing three petticoats and two dresses, I look twice as fat as I am, and I'm still cold.'

'One day all this will be over and we'll both be slim again,' Lydia said. 'The first thing I shall do is have a new dress made. Something extravagant and luxurious – and preferably made of silk!'

Fleur sighed. 'My family thought I was mad to become a nurse. I told them I was doing it so that the right side might win. Now I'm not sure whether that has anything at all to do with it. What's right? What's wrong?'

Lydia turned her face to a sudden commotion just outside the ward. Four soldiers were chasing a pig. The pig was screaming in alarm and heading directly for the nurses' refectory.

On seeing this, Fleur opened the door, the pig scuttled through and the door slammed shut.

Lydia stood beside Fleur, their backs against the door.

The four soldiers exchanged furtive glances.

'Can we have our pig back?' one of them said.

Folding her arms across her chest, Lydia glared at them defiantly.

'Is it really your pig?' she asked.

'We found it.'

'So it's not really yours,' said Fleur.

'It was requisitioned,' said one of the soldiers.

'It's for dinner on Christmas Day,' said another. 'For the men. Injured as well as uninjured. It has to be hung first. Meat is better after it has been hung.'

There was something wrong about letting them in to take their pig, but there was also something very right about it. The two nurses, Lydia and her friend Fleur, stepped to either side of the door.

'Poor pig,' said Fleur. 'It will soon be dead.'

Lydia nodded disconsolately. 'It will have plenty of company.'

The armies that had manoeuvred across France and Flanders during August and September, by the middle of October had become entrenched. Both sides had dug trenches, battened their walls with strips of wood, placed duckboards over the solid ground, the trenches growing in ever-lengthening tentacles.

Everyone prayed for respite between barrages, enough time to transport the injured from the lines to the hospital. Although damaged, the hospital had become a small oasis amidst the bloodiest warfare men had ever contrived. Ypres, the lovely old town just a few miles away, was at the heart of a horror to end all horrors.

Thousands of men on both sides had been killed or maimed, their crushed bodies hardly recognisable as men at all; like slabs of bloodied mud dug straight from the ground, the first task was to dig beneath their clothes, to wash and disinfect the flesh before wounds could be treated.

Days and nights went by when Lydia hardly had time to sit down let alone sleep, but Robert was always in her mind. She'd heard nothing from him. Had he read her letter? Did he know where she was? There was little time to dwell on what might have been or come to the worst conclusion possible, but it did happen. In her darkest moments, she believed he'd obeyed his family's wishes and would not be in contact ever again. Nobody had minded her father being German before the war. How quickly things change.

Letters from home were slow getting through, and stopped altogether once the chateau was surrounded by the enemy. Hopefully, the German hospital and those brave staff, including her father, who had remained despite the hostility of some, were safe. She sincerely hoped they were.

Most of all she hoped Robert was safe.

'Please God, he's safe,' she prayed whilst cleaning the eyes of a German soldier injured by shrapnel.

The soldier overheard her.

'You speak English?'

Reluctantly, because one could never judge the reaction, she told him her father was German, her mother English.

'I went to Oxford before the war.' Black fluid ran

from the corner of his mouth as he spoke, a mixture of blood and cordite coming from his lungs.

'Lay back. Rest,' said Lydia. 'Just rest.'

'I went to university in Oxford. My father bid me come home. I didn't want to. I wanted to stay. I had made many friends.' He paused, seemingly thinking it over. Finally, he said, 'Now my friends are my enemies.'

Lydia watched him die feeling both sorry for him and for herself. The war had only just started, yet had destroyed so much already. It had to stop. Somehow or another, it had to stop.

'Pray God it will,' she whispered.

One day, in a brief moment of catching a breath of fresh air away from the smell of dying men and gangrene, Lydia saw three aeroplanes flying overhead. The moment the German guns opened fire from the ground, she knew they were British and her blood turned cold.

The fragile flying machines banked in low in order to assess the enemy positions and did not return fire. She wasn't even sure they had guns and even if they did, the flying machines were tiny compared to the heavy artillery blasting shells up at them. Like bees flying through clouds of pollen, she thought, and her throat tightened.

Suddenly, she saw one burst into flames and fall to earth. It was hard to breathe. Her heart palpitated as she imagined the worst. She hoped the pilot got out safely, no matter whether he was British or German. Always she thought it might be Robert. If only there was news from the other side, but there was not.

Head bowed, she rushed back inside away from

the horror happening before her eyes and the fear in her mind. Keeping busy would help. Yes. Keeping busy would help.

She brushed past Esther, her hands shaking as she sorted out instruments in need of sterilising.

'Are you all right?' asked Esther.

Lydia wiped her hands and brushed her apron flat. 'Yes. Yes. Of course I am.'

There was no time for more conversation. When there was time to sit and talk, nobody did. They were too tired, too affected by the sights they had seen and the effort of trying to put right what the war had made so wrong.

In those quiet, precious moments, she closed her eyes, leaned her head on the chair back and thought of times past. It was close to midnight when she again ventured outside. The sky lit up with the firing of guns, the sound reverberating through the air like the mightiest thunderstorm that ever was. No lightning could ever be so bright or so frightening. Each flash meant the death of hundreds of men, perhaps thousands.

'Are you all right, Lydia?'

She knew it was Franz. His voice sounded tired as though he were dragging it along behind him. Without looking round she knew his face had altered, his expression sadder than ever. They all looked like that, the medical staff, all trying hard to do their job and already bone tired.

The one thing they held on to was their complete impartiality; an injured man's nationality counted for nothing. No matter that they were in German hands, they did what they could for everyone.

'The weather is turning colder,' he said to her. 'It will soon be Christmas.'

'It will.'

'The snow will already have fallen on the town where I used to live. It snows earlier in the Alps than in the valleys, usually around October. October is the beginning of winter.'

She saw his breath streaming into the air along with the smoke from his cigarette.

'Would you like one?' He held them out to her. She noticed they were Woodbines. British cigarettes.

'I got them from a dying Tommy. He gave them to me. Said he would have no use for them where he was going,' he continued.

Lydia regarded his features, turned angular by the small lantern hanging from a pole outside the tented extension of the hospital. He was staring into the distance, not focusing on anything more than the thoughts in his mind.

'How many men do you think have died so far?' she asked, surprising herself that she found the courage to ask. Not knowing helped her to cope and believe she had helped many survive.

'Too many.' He fell silent. She could feel his eyes on her and knew he cared for her more than he should.

'I have a bottle of brandy in my quarters. When we have the time, that is. It might do you good. It might do both of us good.' He sounded melancholy, overwhelmed by tiredness.

Lydia held her breath. Franz was a kind man and she respected him. It wasn't easy to decline his offer, but it was something she had to do.

Being alone with him would be dangerous.

Without saying another word or even looking at her, he flicked his unfinished cigarette to the ground, turned and went back inside the tent.

Lydia took one last look at the exploding sky before doing the same. By midday tomorrow, the hospital would once again be overwhelmed.

Chapter Thirty-Five

As expected, by ten in the morning, the hospital was overflowing with casualties. A call for help had gone out to the nearby village as more and more casualties poured in. The hospital was staffed by the Red Cross and did not differentiate between armies and because of this a larger number of civilians obliged in the hope of seeing their own soldiers, their own relatives.

Lydia had been on duty for five hours after refusing breakfast. She was ladling food into the mouth of a soldier with bandaged hands, his fingers almost burned to the bone.

The sight of his injuries and the smell of the food made her feel nauseous.

Somebody leaned into her line of vision.

'I have more bandages. I tore up my best linens to make bandages.'

The woman had an aristocratic bearing. One of the Belgian nurses told her that the woman was Countess Vianelle. 'She's very rich and knows just about everyone.'

Lydia grimaced. 'She's also a member of the class of person who started this war,' she muttered grimly. 'Over there,' Lydia barked at her without any deference to either her rank or her wealth. 'Take them over there to the dispensary.'

The woman continued to pester her, saying she had already tried there and been redirected here where bandages were sorely needed.

'Find somewhere,' Lydia snapped, feeling hot, flustered and more tired than usual. 'Anywhere there's a suitable space.'

The woman muttered to herself in English. 'No need to be so rude.'

Lydia being so busy was unguarded and answered in English. 'I'm not being rude. I'm just too busy to bother with you.'

Lydia turned cold. Since the arrival of the Germans, she had purposely avoided speaking in English, using German wherever she could.

'No point in igniting a fire under the enemy,' Esther had whispered.

Lydia agreed with Esther. Suspicion was aroused unnecessarily if certain German doctors or officers heard them talking to each other in English.

Esther Cohen's father had been a Jewish émigré into the USA. He'd fallen in love with a Swedish girl on the ship crammed with third-class passengers, all on their way to the New World.

Heartbeat increasing until it sounded like thunder in her ears, Lydia looked nervously into the face of the aristocratic woman.

'You speak English?' said the woman.

A little more composed, Lydia nodded. 'My

380

mother was English.'

The woman's eyes narrowed as though she were digesting the information.

'I see.'

'Over here, Nurse Miller!' Franz was shouting to her from further along the line of metal beds. She responded immediately. By the time she got back to the part of the ward she regarded as her station, the woman was gone.

After the early start, working without a break, by mid-afternoon Lydia was worn out.

Franz noticed this, his eyes heavy with disappointment.

'Go for a walk. Go anywhere, but get away from this charnel house, at least for a little while.' He paused as though about to ask if he could go with her. He couldn't of course. He was too busy, and besides she had already rejected an offer to drink brandy with him.

The late afternoon was melting into twilight and a crisp frost threatened. The cold air was welcome, like a cold compress against her throbbing forehead. Headaches had become a frequent occurrence, a result of too little sleep and the tension of concentrating on the job in hand for hours on end.

The buildings in the nearby hamlet, a small place on the very edge of Ypres, had a dusty look, the windows never sparkling, the frames trembling every so often in response to the artillery still battling it out over Ypres.

At present, the shelling was sporadic, almost as though the town was holding its breath, waiting for the final push when one side or the other would capture it.

There was laughter coming from the few bars and cafes that were open, comrades in arms staggering along the main street, arms around each other in brotherly affection.

They looked at her, acknowledging her as a pretty woman. One stopped and asked what she was doing there. Pulling her cloak around herself, she flashed him a sight of her uniform.

He touched two fingers to his helmet in acknowledgement and said, 'Thank you, Sister.'

She did not respond but fixed her gaze on the woman crossing the road behind him and disappearing into the church. She recognised her as the woman who had heard her speaking English.

It was on a whim that she decided to speak to her. Turning away from the street and the soldiers, she passed beneath a stone arch separating the medieval church from the street.

Shattered trees hung like wilted flowers at the far end of the churchyard. There was scaffolding around the ancient tower, which had suffered because of the intensive shelling of Ypres.

The carved door opened into the cool nave of St Pieters. Her footsteps echoed over the cool flagstones. The wooden pews, carved in the Flemish style, lent their ancient smell to the cold interior where even the dusty cobwebs shivered.

She'd expected to find the woman here, but there was nobody and no sound besides the scurrying of a mouse and the muffled sound of firing in the distance.

A thin veil of dust fell from the arched nave diffusing the light coming in through the windows.

It occurred to Lydia that she should go back

outside, but the carved statues looking down on her from their arched niches, the feeling of centuries of continuity, made her feel safe.

There was a door to one side of the altar, as intricately carved as the door at the entrance, but smaller, more intimate and hinting at the room where the priest prepared himself for the service.

As she approached the door, she heard what sounded like excitable whispers. A priest and a woman? Alone in that room?

She wasn't especially religious, but the possibility of the priest breaking his holy vows angered her. The church had felt so safe up until now.

The door creaked as she pushed it open.

The woman with the aristocratic features was there with the priest. She'd surprised them. She could tell that by the looks on their faces, but there was also something else. They looked frightened, their expressions strained as they considered what to do.

Lydia took in the scene. It was not what she'd been expecting. The priest was not breaking any vow. Between him and the woman, a countess if Lydia remembered rightly, lay an injured man. He was wearing the uniform of a French soldier.

The countess got to her feet. The look of fear was gone. She looked quite formidable, her head held high, her back straight, like somebody used to being in command.

'He's a French soldier and is injured. Will you help him?'

Lydia nodded.

Though their previous meeting had been brief, the countess obviously recognised her.

The man was sitting up, his back against the carved coffer where vestments were kept. His upper arm was badly damaged, shrapnel having sliced off a strip of flesh from it.

Lydia examined the wound, tentatively peeling a piece of shirtsleeve from out of the wound.

'Do you have bandages?' she asked.

She felt the man's eyes on her as she cleaned the wound, but also she was aware of the priest and the countess watching her too. She guessed what they were thinking. Enemy soldiers had to be handed to the local German military. The penalty for assisting in escape was death.

'Yes, I have bandages,' said the countess. She exchanged a look with the priest before opening a locked cupboard. Sliding a book to one side, she brought out a bundle of clean bandages.

'We are prepared for injured soldiers,' she said, though Lydia had not spoken.

'You will not betray us?' asked the countess in a faintly accented voice as she accompanied Lydia to the door.

'I'm a nurse. I cannot show favour to either side. I am obliged to treat everyone. The wound is clean. He can go home.'

Their eyes met in mute understanding. The man would indeed be going home and not into the hands of the Germans.

'We know the risks,' the countess said suddenly.

Lydia nodded. 'Of course you do.'

Lydia thought she would never see them again, but it turned out not to be so.

'You have an invitation,' somebody said to her

during a lull in the next round of fighting. 'Lucky you.'

She had to ask for time off and because of that, she showed the invitation to Franz. He studied the name at the top of the card. 'Countess Vianelle.'

'I quite understand if you can't spare me,' she said.

Franz fingered the card thoughtfully before handing it back to her.

'Just be careful.' His eyes locked with hers. 'Just be careful.'

Chapter Thirty-Six

It was the strangest sensation, sitting there drinking liquid chocolate with the Countess Vianelle and Father Anton with his button-black eyes, his angular features seeming almost demonic when added together with his slick black hair and long black garb. If it hadn't been for the fact that they were speaking French, Lydia could almost believe they were at a vicar's tea party in an English village. She had expected them to speak Flemish. The priest said Flemish was his native tongue, but the countess spoke Italian, English and French.

Today was a little warmer than of late. The smells of late autumn lent sweetness to the air: the scent of apples, pears and the tang of wood smoke from a gardener's bonfire further enhanced by brittle sunshine and a crisp blue sky.

Lydia was wearing a woollen suit of a dark

plum colour. Her favourite suit was navy blue, but the jacket had a peplum waist that stubbornly resisted fastening at present. This suit had a jacket that floated around her like a cape.

Both the countess and the parish priest frequently visited the injured men, bringing small things to make their stay more comfortable; soap, fruit from the orchard, as well as Father Anton's homemade wine.

Presented in bone china cups, the chocolate was delicious, though Lydia's pleasure was somewhat diminished by the fear that she might break one.

'Are you English by birth?' asked the countess in a slow, melodious voice.

'I am,' replied Lydia, carefully replacing the chocolate cup into its equally fragile saucer. 'As I mentioned when we last met, my mother was English.'

'Then we will speak in English. If that is all right with you?'

Though slim and small, with the most velvet brown eyes Lydia had ever seen, there was strength in that slight body; even sitting in her gold brocade sofa sipping chocolate, the woman sizzled with energy.

She wore an elegant flame-coloured dress with a cream lace bolero. Her small feet barely touched the ground. When she spoke, her voice was melodic yet strong.

They sat, the priest and the countess, on the brocade sofa, Lydia in a matching chair with a cream frame decorated in gold ormolu.

'I should not pry, but it seems strange that you are nursing so far from the Allied lines. There is a story behind that? Yes?'

Lydia became uncomfortably aware that the two pairs of eyes watching her did not blink once. She picked up her cup again, and nursed it.

The priest spoke. 'The fact is you helped the wounded man in our care and, so far as we know, have not betrayed us. The fact is we were afraid that you would...' He paused whilst exchanging a secretive look with the countess. 'But then the countess heard you speak English at the hospital. I understand the military distrust people who speak English. They are, as you might say, paranoid. Yet you go out and about as you please.'

'Yes. I suppose I do,' Lydia responded.

The countess cleared her throat whilst returning her cup to the tray. Lydia noticed the chocolate was barely touched.

Eyes as brown as the chocolate they had been drinking looked directly at hers. She noticed the thickness of the woman's lashes, the way they brushed her face, almost reaching her cheekbones.

The countess leaned forward, placing the silver spoon she had used to stir her chocolate into the saucer.

'The fact is, my dear, we need your help.'

'You help Allied soldiers escape; that's it, isn't it? That's what you do.'

The priest and the countess, who had had the good fortune to marry an Italian count, exchanged conspiratorial looks.

Father Anton nodded. 'We may as well confess that indeed we do help Allied prisoners escape.'

'You could get into very serious trouble,' stated Lydia, aware that she was gripping her teacup as though about to strangle it. 'You could get shot!'

There was a rasping sound as Father Anton rubbed his chin; he was one of those men for whom shaving once a day never really worked. His hair was dark, his chin a shade of blue and permanently needing a shave.

He nodded. 'Yes. You are right. We walk a tight-rope doing what we are doing, but we believe in our cause. Belgium, a neutral country, has been invaded. Yes, I am a man of peace, but I have to do something. The countess feels the same.'

The countess, as though applauding his sentiments, slapped her lap with both hands.

'Well, my dear, you have heard enough. You could betray us if you so wished, though I do not think you will. You have no real loyalty to the German cause. You ran away from a complicated love affair. That is what I think. You have no real allegiance to either side. Am I right?'

Lydia met the forthright look in the countess's eyes. Nobody had yet put her predicament so succinctly.

'If being patriotic means I have to choose between the good people I have met in both England and Germany, then I cannot do that. I am a nurse. All I can do is take care of those who are in pain and dying.'

'Would it be too much to ask for you to help us get wounded men home?'

Lydia sat very still. The two people sitting across from her looked tense as they waited for her response.

The war will be over and won by Christmas.

What a stupid prediction that was; Christmas

was only a few weeks away and the war was not over. Casualties were mounting; there were many who would never get home to see another Christmas.

The countess and the priest exchanged looks that seemed to say they had agreed a decision.

The soft brown eyes resettled on Lydia.

'Will you help us, Lydia? Will you help Englishmen and others to escape back to their lines?'

Lydia nodded vehemently. 'I think this will be a way of declaring my disgust with this war. So, yes, I will do it.'

The countess heaved her bosom in a deep sigh.

'You know the Cafe Dijon in the corner of the square in town?'

A vision of a small shop front peeking out from behind an orange and yellow awning sprang into her mind.

'Yes. I know it. I sometimes take morning coffee there with a friend.'

The countess stiffened as a fleeting look of alarm flashed in her eyes.

'Who is this friend?'

'Jan. I think he's the mayor's brother,' said Lydia.

She recalled their first meeting, the feeling that somebody on the other side of the cafe was looking at her. He'd had such a piercing look, such an amiable confidence. He had left his table and smiled down at her before purchasing a glass of wine for each of them.

She had tried to brush him off, but it hadn't worked. He'd been so amenable, like a lighthouse in a storm.

The two people who wished to recruit her smiled. 'Ah yes, of course. You are quite right. He is the mayor's brother and a very good friend of ours.'

It came to her in a flash that the reason Jan had sought her out was not entirely because he was attracted to her. She was, to all intents and purposes, a German nurse. As a citizen of a conquered country, he would consider it his patriotic duty to pay court to her in the hope of obtaining useful information, though what secrets were hidden in winding bandages and dealing with bedpans, she couldn't begin to guess.

'Soldiers sometimes betray details of their battalion movements to a sympathetic woman,' said the priest as if reading her mind.

A faint smile parted the countess's lips almost frivolously, as though she were contemplating kisses long forgotten. Lydia decided the thought of an illicit relationship amused her.

'You will continue taking coffee at the cafe three times per week,' she said, her voice naturally melodious, naturally seductive. 'We will get a message to you telling you when you are needed.'

Alarmed at the prospect of being asked for by name, Lydia sat bolt upright. 'Surely not? What if it is noticed?'

The countess smiled mischievously. 'Jan will continue to pay court to you. He will play the enamoured lover – though...' she paused, 'I do not think he is exactly acting the part.'

Lydia blushed. 'I have given him no encouragement.'

'He will pursue you hotly with gifts of chocolates, flowers and suchlike. On receipt of each item, you know you must present yourself at the cafe as soon as possible after receipt. Don't immediately drop everything; that will only arouse suspicion. Get away when you can, though casually, without fuss. Do you understand, my dear?'

Lydia nodded. She understood very well. An idea suddenly occurred to her.

'Is it possible that I can pass my letters for my family in England to one of the escapees perhaps?'

The countess shook her head emphatically, her lips pursed with disapproval.

'No. That is too dangerous. Capture can mean torture and the contents of your letters could put us all in danger. I'm sorry,' she said, on seeing the downturned corners of Lydia's mouth, 'I must ask you to promise me you will never do that. Never. Is that clear?'

Lydia voiced that promise, but in her mind, she contemplated what opportunities might come along. Your heart is ruling your head, she told herself and pushed the thought aside – at least for now.

A consignment of injured soldiers arrived from the front line in an assortment of vehicles; mostly horse drawn, the animals as bloody and mud spattered as the men lying groaning in the wagons.

A young man from Hamburg told her how much he liked horses and felt sorry for them. He died in her arms. Outside, almost as though saluting his passing, a series of gunshots rang out.

Knowing the truth, Lydia shuddered. Some of

the horses, their strength gone, their legs broken, were being put out of their misery.

The men brought in continued to suffer.

'What for?' asked a man blinded by shrapnel, unknowing that a surgeon was already sorting out a saw suitable for cutting off what remained of his right leg.

The surgeon winced. He had been barking out orders to the entourage of nurses around him. Now he was still, his expression drained and despairing. 'What for? You are questioning why we are fighting this war. I'm damned if I know,' he muttered.

The smell of men who hadn't washed for weeks was bad enough; added to that were the lice, the fleas, the boils and, for the most unfortunate, the foul stench of gangrenous flesh.

One amputation after another; the refilling of a gut torn open by shrapnel, the intestines pushed back in like so many pounds of sausages.

Sweat from her forehead dripped into her eyes, swiped off on the back of her hand.

Her arms ached. Her legs ached and her back ached. Hours went by until she was finally relieved.

'Rest, Nurse Lydia.'

Lydia looked at Franz's red-rimmed eyes, the tired paleness of his face.

'Go rest,' he said to her on reading her expression. 'Go rest. This will be a long war, Nurse Lydia. We have many miles to go until this is over. And anyway, you need your rest more than most of us.'

The effect of his words cooled her heated brain.

She shivered, nodded and handed over to another nurse. Time for rest, though not a proper rest. Her next job was to assist in the cleaning and bandaging of lesser injuries.

It was three o'clock in the morning before she finally left the ward, feeling she would suffocate if she didn't get outside, away from the smell of injured men, their moans, their screams and their shouting for their mothers.

Outside she threw her head back, closed her eyes and took great gulps of air. Not that it did much good. The sight of wounded and dying men seemed ingrained on her eyelids. On reopening them, she watched her breath rise frosted from her mouth to a star-filled sky. Her fingers closed over the note in her pocket. It was from Jan Janssens.

'I can't wait to see you. Meet me tomorrow I beg you. My love. My precious.'

Such romantic words amid all this carnage brought a smile to her lips though tears squeezed from the corners of her tired eyes.

'Take tomorrow off, Nurse. You have done enough for one day. More than enough.'

She had not heard Sister Drexel come up behind her and the sound of her voice made her jump.

'Thank you. But if you should need me...'

'I do not need overtired nurses. There will be a short lull in the fighting now. Everyone needs some rest, though God knows it is never enough. Go meet your lover. Live a little whilst you can. Escape from this carnage.'

My lover! Lydia almost laughed aloud; Jan looked the part of a lover, but so far had not played the part except in public when he took her hand or kissed her cheeks. Whatever would Sister Drexel say if she knew their relationship had more to do with escape than love? True escape, though not for her but for the soldiers trapped behind enemy lines. For three weeks this persisted, until the unforeseen occurred.

It was market day, so the cafe was crowded. There was something awe inspiring about the farmers and other country folk, setting out their wares despite the sound of the guns and rowdy soldiers, drinking themselves into oblivion so they might forget where they were.

Jan made the usual fuss of her, kissing her hands, then her cheeks whilst whispering sweet words into her ears – English words for the most part, plus some German.

Anyone overhearing would presume he was murmuring words of love. If they'd listened more closely they might ascertain that he was telling her how many men he was hiding and the schedule for getting them out.

She followed Jan out of the cafe on Vermeer Square to his house on Timmermann Street. She asked him where the street had got its name. He had murmured something about brotherly love. 'Like me and my brother,' he'd added.

The comment had made her laugh. The best way to describe the relationship between Jan and his brother the mayor were that they rubbed along.

Jan was the rebellious younger brother; Guido was more sedate and set in his ways. He did not exactly like the Germans but he made the best of the situation, hence the small cafe he owned on the left side of the square being full of disorderly soldiers and the more upmarket restaurant at the other end being full of equally disorderly officers.

Jan had explained. 'My brother caters for one and all – whatever suits his pocket.'

Jan's mother was fast asleep in a deep chair next to a roaring fire.

'I gave her a little something and made up the fire so she would give us no trouble. Here is her shawl. And her apron.'

Lydia did as ordered, tying the apron around her middle and covering her head with Madame Cecily's big black shawl.

Jan held his head to one side as he studied her appearance. 'Are you ready to confess your sins?' Wrinkles of amusement appeared at the corners of his eyes.

'As ready as I can be.'

The church was empty, though it was not always so. Those people who knew Jan's mother by sight came to mass or confession very early in the morning or just after lunch. Like her, they were of the older generation. Afternoons were the time for dozing and evenings were the time for supper before thinking about going to bed. The old are good at early mornings, thought Lydia.

The crypt where the men were hidden was down a steep set of stairs that wound ever downwards like a stone corkscrew.

Although they trod softly, their footsteps echoed against the cold stone of the ancient walls.

Three figures were huddled between two stone sarcophagi. Three heads jerked up when the heavy oak door separating the stairs from the tomb creaked open.

One figure seemed to unwind as though he'd been folded up like a deckchair. His head perked up higher than all the others did.

'Miss Lydia?'

Lydia held high the lantern with which she'd found her way. She instantly recognised the tousled red hair and pale face of the young lad who had been Robert's driver and tried to remember his name.

'Freddie?'

'It's me, Miss! Blimey ... excuse the language, Miss... But it's bloody ... sorry again, Miss. Lovely to see you, Miss. Really, lovely! Got lost, Miss. Got well and truly lost, I did.'

Lydia was genuinely pleased. There was a chance that Freddie might know Robert's whereabouts. First, she explained procedure as dictated to her by Jan.

'Freddie, it's wonderful to see you and we will do our best to get you to the coast and a fishing boat back to England. I would like to say we can get you home for Christmas, but this is a slow process. A few difficult events have held things up.'

'That will suit me, Miss.'

Her bright smile hid the sombre truth; a farm they regularly used had been destroyed, with the family and two escapees inside. Jan Janssens had impressed on her not to dwell on the setbacks but celebrate the successes.

They went through the usual routine of supplying the men with peasant-style clothing, though they did warn them that they were in danger of being shot as spies if they were caught.

Nothing they said could dampen the men's spirits. The thought of getting back to England in time for Christmas saw to that.

'We'll get sent back over again, but might get a bit of leave for our troubles, if nothing else,' said Freddie, his black button eyes alight with excitement before turning troubled. 'Sorry I can't tell you where the captain is, Miss. We came down together, but we scarpered in different directions when the bloody plane exploded. I saw a patrol and got me head down. When I popped back up he was nowhere in sight.' He shrugged. 'Sorry, Miss.'

Lydia bit her lip. 'What a shame you and he were up here and I didn't know. I thought he was serving in France not Flanders.'

'Flanders?' exclaimed Freddie. 'I thought that weren't a Frenchie accent I was hearing.'

'Yes. Not far from Ypres.'

'Ypres?' Freddie's eyebrows shot up so high, they seemed to be aiming at his hairline. 'Wipers!' he exclaimed, using the English version of the Belgian place name. 'Blimey. I didn't realise we'd strayed that far north. Still, the barrage was heavy.'

He glanced at her before turning swiftly away.

Lydia felt something move in her stomach; something like a bucket of cold water sloshing around inside. She knew he presumed that Robert was dead.

He saw her look and immediately tried to make amends. 'But 'e got out. I'm sure of it. He's one of the best in the Royal Flying Corps.'

It was small consolation, but helped. She had to believe that Robert was alive...

Despite the warnings, she had brought the letters she had written to Robert. Freddie will escape. He will get back to England and get the letters to Robert and to her father. If Robert got back that is. She hoped fervently that he had.

'This bottle is empty,' said Jan. He picked up a wine bottle. 'I will get more. And some bread and cheese. Father Anton has it prepared as though it is for him. The man eats too much.'

Whilst he was off fetching the food, and the three soldiers were enjoying what was left of the wine in another bottle, Lydia took Freddie to one side.

'Freddie, I'm going to ask you to do something very dangerous.'

'Can't be any more dangerous than fighting in this war, Miss Lydia,' he said, shaking his head, his merry eyes dancing.

Lydia fingered the bundle of paper in her pocket.

'I've written some letters to Robert. I would be very grateful if you took them back to England with you, though I must warn you how dangerous it is for both you and me.'

'You mean if I get caught?'

She nodded, took the letters out of her pocket and held them against her chest.

He shook his head. 'I'm not going to get caught, Miss. I'm going home and nobody, not even the Bosch, can outrun Freddie Fortune. Give 'em 'ere, Miss.'

Heart pounding against her ribs, she handed

398

him the letters.

'Don't let anyone know you have them,' she whispered.

Later she told herself that she'd been selfish to ask such a favour, but she hadn't been able to help herself. She had to let Robert know that even though she was effectively serving the German armed forces, she still loved him and intended to return to England.

'I have no allegiance to either side,' she'd written in one letter. 'I care only that injured men are treated as human beings.'

Chapter Thirty-Seven

December, 1914

The lovely sunset of two nights before was like a dream. Heavy rain lashed against the distorted glass of the windowpanes and clouds rolled like stormy waves across a sullen sky.

Days like this were good for taking her charges from one safe haven to another, from the safe house to one of the farms to the south. Tired fighting men looked much the same as tired farm labourers. The routine consisted of one man leading the horse, another sitting up beside a morose French farmer who cared little for the Germans and even less for good manners.

Today her confidence in wet dark weather was absent. Today was different. Through the pouring rain, she caught sight of a dark figure bent against the rain and wind. Jan was coming for her.

A blast of rain and wind entered with him.

Water dripped from the brim of his hat, his eyebrows and even his nose. Taking the hat off, he proceeded to beat it against the wall to dislodge what excess water he could.

'So,' he said, once he had decided that no more water could be dislodged. 'How is your love affair proceeding?'

Lydia knew he meant had she had any problems absenting herself from the hospital.

'I am the subject of much speculation. Some want to know if and when I am to marry my lover, but some...'

She laughed and shook her head.

Jan raised a querulous eyebrow. 'These others?'

She felt a mild blush warming her cheeks.

'Some nurses are curious to know what Belgian men are like in bed. They have heard rumours about Frenchmen being more passionate than any other men, so are wondering about Belgians.'

Jan tucked in his chin. 'I trust you told them that Frenchmen are boastful. Belgians are not. Besides I have my reputation to consider.'

Lydia laughed. 'I blushed demurely and suggested they find out for themselves.'

'Hmm,' muttered Jan whilst scrutinising the dank view beyond the window. 'I wish I could oblige, but alas I am already spoken for. Perhaps if I had sons they would oblige. But I have not.'

Lydia smiled to herself as she buttoned up her dark coat and slid a rough woollen shawl over her head. As before, today she would be Jan's mother and he would accompany her to confession. Jan was handsome and very sure of himself. At times, she thought he really was fond of her, but when she attempted to acknowledge or tease, he returned to his distant, sarcastic self.

Jan nodded at her. She nodded back. She was ready.

A wet wind blew briefly through the open door as they left. Anyone seeing them in this dull wet weather would assume it was just Jan escorting his mother to confession. No one was likely to enquire further, not with the rain running down their backs.

Candles fluttered in the draught as they entered the church. The interior smelled of beeswax and old things, ancient flags hanging ragged and moth eaten, candle grease and old wood mellowed with age.

A single lone figure sat just before the altar. Nobody was supposed to be here! Her heart rate quickened. She couldn't go back now. Everything was in place.

Lydia wasn't sure she recognised who it was but could not linger. She had no wish to have anyone questioning her identity.

She exchanged a quick look with Jan and knew he was thinking the same.

Tugging the shawl more closely around her face, she limped towards the confessional. Jan's mother had a bad hip. She was also a very pious woman who confessed at least five times a week and attended mass every day. Poor Jan was a busy man as far as his mother was concerned. It amazed Lydia he had time for anything else.

The confessional was dark, only the faintest light coming through the fretwork screen separating her from the priest. Jan had gone outside, to bring his cart of refuse to the side of the church. He would collect more from the priest's house. Beneath the refuse, a piece of tarpaulin stretched over a frame would cover the British service men hiding beneath it.

'Lydie?'

'Father Anton.'

The whole screen from ceiling to floor slid back without making a sound. Lydia followed the priest through another aperture at the rear of the confessional, turning sideways because the gap was narrow.

She closed the fretwork screen behind her using both hands. The screen slid quietly into place.

The aperture led into a passageway and a spiral staircase, so narrow that her shoulders brushed against the walls on each side. A draught of cold musty air came up to meet them. The stairs led down into the crypt, dominated by the tombs of Knights Templar and ancient crusaders.

The air smelled of old bones and rotten rags overladen now with the smell of living men, mud, sweat and weariness.

The three figures huddled like gargoyles between the tombs looked up at the sound of their approach. They no longer wore uniforms but the kind of poor-quality clothing afforded by farm labourers, disguises necessary for their escape.

Lydia held her breath. She saw only one man amongst the three, a face that stopped her in her tracks, that same strong face she'd dreamed of seeing so many times, feeling great elation, and then woken to find his presence had been nothing more than a dream.

The dancing blueness of his eyes, the strong face that looked so tired, though brightening when his eyes met hers.

He was here. Robert was here!

The tiredness accumulated by days of dodging the enemy fell from his face. Robert got to his feet.

'Lydia! I can't believe this! It's a miracle. A bloody, wonderful, marvellous miracle!' His voice crackled with disbelief. His eyes were moist. 'You're here!'

He reached out one arm then the other. She swayed, the gloomy surroundings swimming around her as she forced herself to take one careful step after another just in case – just in case – it really was only a dream.

'You're alive!'

He didn't smell good, but when she squeezed her eyes shut, savouring the taste of him, the sweetness of the moment, he might just as well have been smelling of roses.

Her eyes filled with tears when she looked up at him. He frowned as he regarded her. 'Something's changed about you. I cannot think what it is, but I will. I'm sure I will.'

The two of them moved into the shadows whilst Robert's colleagues were given food and drink. For the moment at least, he had no need of either.

Lydia shook her head. 'Never mind me. Did you get my letter?'

He shook his head. 'No. Mind you, anything – letters or parcels – takes an age getting through.'

'I knew that, so Agnes took it to Siggy. I – we thought it was the only chance of getting in touch.'

He shook his head. 'As you say, it's not easy, though...' He frowned. 'It should have come through eventually.'

Lydia grew angry when she realised the truth. 'He didn't send it! That pig of a cousin of yours didn't send it.'

He hugged her close and kissed her again. 'It doesn't matter. I'm here. You're here. Better than any letter. Did you get my letters?'

She shook her head. 'None.' She paused, thinking back and wondering. 'Being the daughter of a German was no problem before the war, but now...'

He placed a finger against her lips. 'It's still of no consequence to me. I would still have married you.'

'You could have been disinherited.'

'I could have stood that. I would still have had a pilot's pay.'

Despite their circumstances, she threw back her head and laughed. 'I wish...'

She stopped herself from saying how she wished she could turn the clock back, but this was no time for remorse. If she had been pregnant, it hadn't stayed inside her for long. Besides, she didn't want Robert to dwell on what might have been. The future was all that really mattered.

'You're leaving today.' She said it abruptly, at

the same time swallowing the lump in her throat. 'You're going home.'

Surprised by her tone, his expression changed.

'I can't leave you now that I've found you. I can't just go home as though there was nothing ever between us. Good God, Lydia, you're behind enemy lines. Do you know what the Germans will do to you if they find out you're helping prisoners escape?'

'I know very well. But it has to be done. And I'm in a position to do it. You'll be home for Christmas. Who knows? I might get back to England too before very long. The war can't go on forever.'

'No. You have to come with me.'

She shook her head vehemently. 'No. My absence would be noticed, and besides, you and your colleagues are to travel as farm labourers, men looking for work. Having a woman with you would be hard to explain and would put both the lives of your colleagues and those assisting you to escape in danger. No, Robert. You have to leave and I must stay.'

Though her heart was breaking, she forced herself to sound cheerful. She had to lie. She had to get him out of there.

She felt a shiver run down her when his fingers brushed her cheek.

'Promise me you will get home. Promise me we'll still get married.'

'Let's cross that bridge when we come to it. Who knows what the future might bring?' she said, still maintaining her cheerful facade.

'You're not fooling me,' he said softly. 'Our future is together. You still feel the same about

405

me. I know you do.'

'I'll be fine. Now just you take care of yourself and don't get caught. You're out of uniform. We don't want you shot as a spy.'

He managed a nervous laugh, wetness from the corners of his eyes lifting the dirt from his face.

'I understand. I'm a farm labourer. I look like a farm labourer. I shall sound like a farm labourer. Luckily my French isn't bad. Just wish I could have been a married farm labourer and we could have gone home together.'

'Good. We understand each other. And when you get back to England you can dine out on your little adventure... Just think of it... I still have work to do here,' she said bravely. 'And you too have work to do. As soon as you're back in England they'll have you up in a plane again.'

'I'll refuse.'

'No you won't. You love flying.'

'I love you too,' he said, his voice softening. 'I love you too, Lydia.'

She smiled through threatening tears. 'I know. And I love you. That's why I want you to go home. Go home and kiss those we love. Go home for Christmas and wish Agnes the greetings of the season for me. I presume she's still in England, or at least you can write to her. Will you do that? Promise?'

He nodded. 'Promise.'

'Now come along. We've no time for regrets or reminiscences.'

It was hard to read what he was thinking, but there was a hurt look in his eyes. She had no intention of revoking her sharp words. She had to be firm. He had to go. They had to say goodbye.

'I see. How far will you be going with us?'

'Only to the farm. Jan's mother often accompanies him to the farm. The refuse goes to feed the pigs.'

Robert forced a chuckle. 'Oh well. A second-class ride is better than a first-class walk.'

The sight of her remained before Robert's eyes as the cart carrying the pigswill bumped along the rutted surface of the country road. He'd definitely detected something different about her; she was still a sight for sore eyes, but more voluptuous, plumper than he remembered. Not that it mattered. She was still the woman whose presence tickled at his heart.

Chapter Thirty-Eight

Agnes. Christmas Eve, 1914

Agnes brushed at her eyes. The young man had broken bones too many to count and only half of his face was recognisable, the other half burned and hardly distinguishable as human flesh at all.

'Can you...?'

He gestured for her to light him a cigarette. She obliged of course, her hand trembling as she did so. She had recognised the insignia of the Royal Flying Corps and the fact that this young man was a navigator, the map-reader who sat behind the pilot. They had sustained damage over enemy lines, but the pilot had managed to land it.

'Major Ravening got out. I'm sure of that. But it's disorientating out there. We were separated. He might just be in enemy hands. I was found by a group of people helping downed fliers and others to escape. I was lucky. I came across a downed plane in a field complete with pilot. I helped him back into the air. Weight was critical so I had to leave a lot of my gear behind. Shame, but nothing important.'

'So Major Ravening got out? I know him you see.'

He flinched as she lunged forward, her expression intense. She couldn't help herself. She had to know.

He confirmed that he had and went on to describe what had happened in more detail, including the fact that the pilot and aeroplane he'd found in the field had limped back to the Allied lines, finally crashing just yards short of a safe landing where it had burst into flames.

Agnes sat there silently, frozen by fear but crazily thinking she would look for him, find him, and bring him out. To do so she would have to get close to the enemy lines.

Just over the border into Flanders, the navigator had said. Not far from Ypres.

They had moved up into that area in order to help with the carnage still raging in that sector.

The opportunity would arise to get close to the front line. She knew it would, and once it did, she would grab it with both hands.

From the very first, Agnes had acquired a reputation in the service for being outspoken and disobedient. Not only did she help carry the injured into the makeshift tents and shattered buildings that served as hospitals, she was also in the habit of checking on their progress – only those she particularly liked of course.

Tonight was Christmas Eve. Whilst waiting for a nurse she was scheduled to deliver to the forward field station, she had visited one of the injured men she'd brought back the day before. On the day she'd collected him from the front line hospital station, he'd been soaked in sweat and blood, but coherent. He'd told her that he was one of seven children from some town up north – she couldn't remember the name – only that the men in his family were miners who worked long hours in dreadful conditions and had precious little to show for it.

'Better I thought to sign up for this lark than go down the bloody pit,' he'd proclaimed, then apologised for swearing.

'So you got yourself into a bloody war instead of into a bloody mine. Now which do you prefer?' she asked chirpily.

He took a couple of puffs on the cheroot she'd given him and coughed a bit before rasping out a reply.

'Did two years in pit. Glad to come up. Didn't want to die down there now, did I? At least I've seen a bit of the world. Seen France anyway. And I crossed the sea on a boat to get here. Never been on a boat before. Met people from all over too. Blokes from India. Blokes from Australia. Blokes from Canada. Might go and settle in one of them places when this war is over. Me and Gertie. She's my intended...'

Hope had brightened his eyes as he'd rambled on and on about his life, his thoughts on the past and his plans for the future.

Agnes took a swipe at one moist cheek. Ex-miner Arthur Cox would not be going to Australia or Canada when the war was over. Neither would he be marrying his darling Gertie. The piece of shrapnel that had entered his body had shifted and cut an artery. The injury plus the infection that had set in had done for poor Arthur Cox. Aged nineteen, it said on his details. Major Darius Emerson, the senior doctor at the hospital, a rambling place housed in what had been a convent, thought otherwise.

'There's lots like him who have lied about their age. They came for adventure and ended up dead.'

She liked Darius. She found him easy to talk to because of their similar backgrounds in that she had broken through the class barrier to get there, and he had broken through the barrier of race. Neither mentioned that single night when they'd given in to what had been a mix of lust and despair, sex born of a need for mutual comfort. She knew he thought of that moment just as she did. Every so often, their eyes would meet, mutely acknowledging what had happened and what it had meant to each of them.

Between lulls in the fighting, they travelled together to a small cafe in the centre of the village. The bread was fresh, the cheese was strong and both made the wine they drank taste all the better

410

for it. She found Darius good company, and sometimes, just sometimes, she completely forgot about Robert. When she wasn't with Darius she re-assessed her relationship with Robert. It was hard to admit to herself that she didn't feel the same as she once had. Darius had taken his place.

They were sitting at a small table in a dark corner, both with their chins resting on their hands, looking at each other, drinking and eating, but not saying much at all.

'Can we meet after the war?'

'There,' she exclaimed. 'You've gone and spoiled it.'

He looked surprised, but also amused.

'Spoiled what?'

'We were enjoying the sound of silence. Silence between good friends is best of all. Nobody needs to speak. Silence is worth savouring. We have so little of it at present.'

He saw the dimple at one side of her mouth and wanted very much to touch it, to kiss it even. However, he had meant what he'd said about meeting after the war.

'More wine?' he asked her.

She nodded.

'As I was saying,' he said, raising the rather grubby glass and eyeing the blood-red contents, 'meeting after the war should be high on our list of things to do with our lives. At present we are savouring silence because it is so rare nowadays, but after the war it could well be a different matter. We will need to make our own noise because the guns will have fallen silent. You see my point? How can we possibly savour silence if we are no longer surrounded by noise?'

Her smile widened, her eyes tilting gently upwards at the corners. He loved the colour and shape of her eyes, the wildness of her hair, and her refreshing attitude to stuffiness and overblown officialdom. In the depths of sleep, day or night, he'd sometimes imagined how she might be to wake up in bed with...

Agnes was surprised at her own reaction to this charming man. He had blue eyes and a fresh complexion, in a funny way very much like her own. He was also a man of integrity and very brave, if standing up to the establishment was bravery. Probably the High Command might not interpret his actions that way. For instance, he purposely added more intense physical injuries to those with only light injuries, anything to give them a prolonged rest and save them from going back into battle too soon.

'Will you take me somewhere nice?' she asked him.

'Of course.'

'And you will pay the bill?'

'Of course,' he repeated, looking taken aback as though to do otherwise would be almost criminal.

Agnes raised her glass, screwing up her eyes as she studied the local wine.

'It's a deal – as long as there's nothing swimming around in the wine and the cheese isn't threatening to charge off around the room!'

The sky on Christmas Eve was clear and, so far, the guns were silent. She'd picked up the nurse, freshly arrived from England and full of patriotism and the fervour of a modern-day Florence Nightingale.

The nurse was presently hanging on to the door with one hand. Her other hand alternated between clinging to the seat and rescuing her starched cap from falling off.

'This ... road ... is ... very ... bumpy!' Her voice jarred on each word as they bumped along and her cheeks trembled.

'It's hardly Pall Mall,' returned Agnes and managed a tight smile. The poor girl sitting beside her didn't know what she was letting herself in for.

Speaking coherently was far from easy because the springs on the ambulance had gone rock hard on one side and were close to breaking point. They bounced along roads and tracks alike, more violently once they hit the shell-pitted terrain close to the front lines.

'Come on, Pretty Megan. Keep going. One last trip and I promise to get your springs fixed.'

Megan was the name she'd given the ambulance. She had named her after a maid at Heathlands, the one who'd once been in a relationship with the chauffeur.

They were travelling through an area where troops mustered around piles of mud and detritus spewed up from previous engagements. Every so often, the headlights would pick up the haggard faces of tired men sprawled around in groups, smoking, eating or reading a letter from home that they'd likely read many times before. An element of patriotic fervour still shone in the eyes of a few men, though how long that would last was any-

413

body's guess.

They were travelling to the most forward field hospital there was, one equipped for dealing with the less serious injuries and applying interim treatment before transfer. The nurse, a naive little thing in Agnes's estimation, was going there to 'save our brave boys'. Not long qualified, dear little Nurse May Wills had done a year on a ward at a hospital in Bristol but had jumped at the chance to join Queen Alexandra's Imperial Military Nursing Service and a posting close to the front line.

'All those poor men. The hospital got so crowded we had them laying outside the new King Edward the Seventh hospital on stretchers until we could make room for them.'

'That was a bit careless of them, not seeing this war coming. They could have made it bigger.' Agnes was purposely sarcastic, not that Nurse Wills noticed.

'Do you know any other members of Queen Alexandra's?' Nurse Wills had asked her.

'Yes. I do,' she replied, her smile hardened by experience. 'They march about as though they could do battle with anyone if they'd half a mind to.'

It was good to hear May laugh even if it was a little too light, a little nervous. Might as well laugh now, thought Agnes, before you see how things are; then you might never laugh again.

They finally came to a ramshackle barn with half a wall missing but its roof still in place. At one end of the building, a large tent added extra ward space. A piece of canvas plugged the other end, also acting as a makeshift door, lifting if the

414

wind was blowing in the right direction

Agnes brought the ambulance to a halt and pulled on the brake.

'Welcome to the Palace of Angels.'

'Palace of Angels! What a wonderful name!' Nurse May Wills sounded genuinely delighted.

Noting her companion had not heeded the irony in her tone, Agnes stared straight ahead. In these past months she had seen enough of field stations and hospitals. Her real names for them – she had more than one – were far less complimentary, but accurate: Castle of Casualties, Death Factory, Helpless Heroes; each name suited.

The newly trained nurse took in the field station's details with a blank stare; decrepit, half ruined and barely protected from the cold. The field station provided interim attention to the injured, enough to keep them alive until they reached the larger hospitals further back from the front lines

'Oh well. I suppose it's only to be expected. A bit smelly, though not really too bad.'

Agnes refrained from telling her that the smell would sometimes make her retch. Death had a smell all of its own, a mix of blood, gangrenous wounds and stomach contents. May could find that out for herself.

She lit and then breathed in the smoke from a freshly lit cheroot and watched as the smoke curled languidly upwards. She was smoking too much, but at least it smothered the smells; calmed the nerves too.

'Do you want me to help you with your things?' she asked, not wanting to but feeling obliged.

The girl's attention remained fixed on the place Agnes had brought her to. She shook her head.

'I'm sure I can manage. After all I'm going to have to put up with a lot more than carrying my own luggage, am I not?'

'Very true.'

Although she admired the girl's saintly enthusiasm, Agnes knew from experience that it would be short lived. However, being positive would help her cope – at least for a while.

'Why do you call your ambulance Pretty Megan?' asked Nurse Wills, her eyes fixed on what she'd let herself in for.

'The boys like it. When they're lying in pain I find it helps to distract their minds to tell them they are being carried away from the slaughter by Pretty Megan.'

'With an ambulance name? How does that work? How very droll,' said the nurse, turning now to face her.

Agnes blew a cloud of smoke upwards and watched as it swirled and whirled and tried to escape from the ambulance cab.

'I tell them it was my sister's stage name and that she was famous for doing a naughty fan dance dressed in nothing but parrot feathers.'

The nurse looked at her round-eyed and gasped. 'Did your sister really do that?'

'No. I have no sister. I lied. As I said, telling stories and lies helps take their minds off their pain.'

The pale face of Nurse May Wills, a girl from a sheltered background who had answered her country's call, shone with admiration.

'Oh my. Oh my. You are so clever. And so brave. So very, very brave!'

'It's not me that's brave,' Agnes said softly.

A male nurse came out and took Nurse Wills's bag. Agnes waited until the man held the canvas door back exposing a triangle of light from within the ward.

Once they were out of sight, she checked the passenger door was shut, put the ambulance into forward gear and turned the wheel.

The few lights of the field station fell back behind her. She wondered how poor little Nurse Wills would settle in. A field station was bleak compared with a proper hospital. A great many men arrived close to death. The medical officer in charge had the job of choosing who was likely to live and who to die. He did this even before they were offloaded.

Within minutes of leaving the field station, she was en route for the front line. For some reason the evening seemed unnaturally quiet. The sound of guns firing could be heard, but softly, way off in the distance.

Agnes sang the first two lines of 'Silent Night'. She fell to silence, not willing to believe that the guns had fallen silent simply because of the season.

The silence was as strange as the darkness. The ambulance bumped along over the uneven ground. Such silence following months of fighting.

She'd heard the line of trenches stretched all the way from the Atlantic to the Swiss border.

Men had battled over inches of mud since Mons but ended up entrenched at Ypres. The first battle

417

at Ypres had claimed nearly eight thousand casualties. Tonight, at least in this sector, was different. Christmas Eve and for once – just for once – the guns had fallen silent.

There were tracks at all angles through the mud, fanning out and criss-crossing each other like a giant crossword, all roads leading to the trenches.

Darius had told her that he used to come on holiday to this area, and being a keen rambler had walked these lanes and fields where men now fought and poppies and corn used to grow.

'I recall a high spot about here,' he'd said, referring to a tattered map hanging from the wall in the cubby hole he called an office. 'From here you can see everything. There's a copse here where I used to have a picnic. Just the world and myself. What a lovely time it was, before the world became bloody...'

'Point it out on the map,' she'd said to him. 'Tell me where you were so happy on that long ago holiday.'

He'd done so willingly, not noticing that she was memorising everything he said and every detail he pointed to. He trusted her completely and she trusted him. He wasn't to know that the information would be retained and put to good use at a later date. Agnes forgot nothing.

She had left him to his reminiscences, a faraway look in his eyes as though he were trying to recapture what was past and lost.

Agnes had always had a good memory and Darius did not seem to care that he had divulged delicate information.

The position, the slight rise, the copse of trees; she'd worked out where it was and what she might see from such a vantage point.

Pretty Megan trundled on, her springs groaning in protest as her tyres kept rolling over the rough terrain. There was darkness all around except where the headlights picked out the shapes of sleeping men. Curled up like foetuses, the lower part of their faces protected from the frost by coat collars or mufflers wound around like bandages, tin hats pulled down over their eyes.

Few heard the rumbling of Megan's engine and her creaking springs. Agnes reckoned that even if they did question an ambulance being so close to the line, they would put its closeness down to the unofficial Christmas truce; men had made up their own minds; miracles happened at Christmas.

The headlights bounced around in time with the bouncing springs of the vehicle. All was uninterrupted darkness until something moved, a figure leaping in front of the vehicle. Blinded by the lights, the figure, almost as black as the night itself shouted and fired a shot. Agnes heard it ping on to the cab roof.

Hauling the wheel left to avoid the man, the front wheel hit a rock. There was a loud crack as the worn spring broke.

Thinking she'd fired back at him, the sentry let off a second shot. This time it shattered the windscreen. Agnes felt something hit her head before everything went black.

Chapter Thirty-Nine

''Ere. Give 'er a drop of this.'

Agnes tasted brandy on her tongue followed by a pleasant burning in her throat.

She coughed and spluttered a bit.

'Steady on. Don't drown the poor woman.'

'Sorry, Sir.'

Agnes's eyes flickered open. She found herself looking up at an officer to one side of her, a corporal on the other.

She whispered the prepared lie. 'I think I lost my way.'

The officer smiled. He had a kind face and eyes that might have been bluish black – she couldn't tell too well in the dark. The corporal had a sandy moustache. A third man, a private by the looks of him, was holding a stub of candle.

'Where were you heading?' asked the officer.

'To the RFC field up here, somewhere along the front line. I was told to pick up a wounded observer.'

She could have said a pilot, but refrained from doing so. The Royal Flying Corps would find an aircraft to get a pilot to hospital rather than wait for an ambulance.

The officer shook his head. 'I'm afraid you're too late.'

Agnes's heart skipped a beat. 'Is something wrong?'

She couldn't bear it if Robert had been injured. Please God, she prayed, don't let it be so.

'They pulled out weeks ago. Somebody in the High Command believes it's the job of the infantry to win this war and that using flying machines is just a fleeting fancy.' His face turned sombre. 'The Germans don't see things that way. Their flying machines are lethal. Still,' he said with improvised brightness, 'that's of no interest to you. I'm getting my man to mend your ambulance. He's pinched a spring from my staff car. We'll get you back to base in no time.'

Agnes raised herself on to her elbow and began to protest. 'Please. I don't want to be any trouble to either you or your poor man.'

The thudding in her temple made her wince.

The officer smiled. 'I think you need to get back. It's just a graze, but it'll hurt like hell in the morning – as though you've been drinking too much cheap wine. And don't worry about Hopkins working on your ambulance all night. It was him taking the pot shots at you; seems only fair that he should be the one putting you to rights. Come on. Let's get you on your feet.'

Agnes's thoughts were in turmoil. For one terrible moment when he'd said she couldn't go to the RFC, she'd thought it had been destroyed. She couldn't bring herself to contemplate life without Robert. You've loved Robert since you were children together. Nothing is ever going to change, except ... her feelings for Darius were growing.

The officer misunderstood the sigh of relief and the more relaxed expression that came to her face.

'Ah! I can see the prospect of getting back to base has restored your spirits. Well, I can make things even better than that. I can loan you my driver; Hopkins again I'm afraid. You'll be sick and tired of the man before very long. The blighter deserves to make full amends. I've half a mind to court-martial him...'

'No! Please don't do that.'

The ensuing grin on the flat round face told her that he hadn't been serious.

'Do not worry, my dear. I think he's learned to be more cautious. Now listen. How about you dine with me tonight? Not much of a dinner, I'm afraid. My dear mama sent me some tinned steak and a Christmas cake. My man is cooking it up right this minute. It shouldn't be too bad. Not, I should point out, because my man is a good cook, but purely by virtue of washing it all down with a bottle of whisky and a bottle of burgundy. What do you say?'

There seemed little choice. Although she was hardly dressed in a ladylike manner, he treated her courteously, cupping her elbow as he helped her down a stout wooden ladder and over duckboards to his cramped but cosy command centre.

'I call it Buck House,' he said to her. 'Though the carpet's a little threadbare and the chandelier battles bravely to lift the gloom.' He pointed to the single light bulb as he said it, the grin on his face failing to lift the gloom from his eyes.

'I call my ambulance Pretty Megan.'

He laughed. 'Very droll. Well, it all helps keep spirits up, don't you think?'

Agnes looked around the small square of space

dug out from the very earth. Planks of wood held in place by pit props kept the earth at bay. Miners from South Wales and Durham had been responsible for building much of the network of trenches creeping across France and Flanders.

The single electric light bulb hung above a table on which were charts, a pair of field glasses, a set of dividers and a small brass compass. The only other pieces of furniture were an armchair, its horsehair innards touching the floor, and two dining chairs, most likely requisitioned from a house abandoned by its owners.

The officer introduced himself as Major John Saunders.

'Agnes Stacey,' she said.

'And this is Cook,' said the major as a red-cheeked man carrying a pot came in. 'Cook by name, cook by nature. Isn't that right, Cook?'

A man of about twenty with bushy brows and the nose of a boxer grinned at her. He was wearing what looked like a bed sheet tied around him to serve as an apron.

'Indeed, Sir. Indeed. And right pleased I am to be of that calling.'

With a few vegetables added, the stewed steak turned out to be extremely satisfying, as did the Christmas cake.

Major John Saunders chatted amiably in a general manner, only lightly touching on war. Most of his conversation was about home, family and the wonderful time he'd had in the summer.

Agnes found that she was very hungry and hardly spoke at all at first. She also sensed that the major was desperate to talk to somebody other than his colleagues or subordinates, especially to a woman.

'That was delicious,' she said to him as he poured the wine. 'It's been a long time since I was invited to dinner and, as you can see, I'm hardly dressed for the occasion.'

He laughed at that.

'At first I thought you were a man. It was the trousers. I've only ever seen female ambulance drivers wearing skirts.'

'I prefer trousers,' she said between mouthfuls of yet another slice of Christmas cake. 'More practical.'

'How do your superiors view that?'

'I don't care. I'm the best ambulance driver they've got.'

Major Saunders leaned back in his chair, his eyes fixed firmly on the delightful creature seated across from him. 'I don't doubt it,' he murmured, and then added, 'Do you mind if I smoke?'

'Do you mind if I do?'

His eyebrows went skywards when Agnes took out a cheroot, though not in condemnation. He liked strong-minded women and this one, with her dark blonde hair and those enticing eyes, reminded him of his mother.

'Cheroots. I am even more surprised.'

They had only just lit up when Private Cook came to take the dishes away.

'Just so you know, Sir. It's a clear night. You can see all the way to the enemy trenches. Something's going on there. I can hear singing and see lights.'

John Saunders thanked him then turned to

Agnes. 'Would you like to see the enemy trenches?'

She searched his expression. Was he being serious?

'Is it possible?'

He nodded. 'Come on. Let's take advantage of the peace and quiet.'

To her surprise, he took her up one of the scaling ladders used by the infantry to scale the trench wall. They were immediately facing the enemy trenches.

Agnes swore beneath her breath. 'Are we safe doing this?'

'I think we are.'

Taking hold of her hand, he dragged her with him to a hidden spot and firm ground between some bushes.

'Now look over there.' He pointed carefully towards where the Kaiser's army were entrenched.

She looked to where he was pointing. Small pinpoints of light shone from triangular shapes all along the leading edge of the enemy lines.

Agnes narrowed her eyes in an effort to see through the darkness.

Major Saunders had brought his field glasses. 'Look through these.'

Bracing her legs to make sure she had a firm foothold, she raised the heavy binoculars and gasped at the sight that met her eyes.

'I can see candles. And trees! Christmas trees! Decorated Christmas trees! They're all the way along the trench! And they're singing.'

Just as the cook had declared, the strains of a carol sung in German, 'Silent Night, Holy Night', came drifting through the darkness.

She lowered the binoculars, her face a picture of amazement.

The major nodded. 'Yes. It appears they're human after all.'

The melancholia in the major's voice made her look at him. His eyes were moist.

'Still. Must not read too much into it, must we! Christmas won't last forever.'

'It's amazing. And lovely. I hope that...'

A choking sensation came to her throat.

The major read her mind. 'You have a sweetheart in the trenches?'

She swallowed the dryness that had enveloped her mouth and stilled her tongue.

'A friend. And not in the trenches. He's a pilot with the Royal Flying Corps. An aviator. We've heard nothing from him for over four days. They say he came down behind enemy lines... I hope he survived. I hope he can get back...'

She felt a strong hand kneading her shoulder. 'I wish all the best for you. What's your chap's name?'

'Robert. Robert Ravening. We're lifelong friends.'

'We're attempting to send a radio message to your people back at base. Is there anyone in particular you'd like us to inform?'

'Yes,' she said. She nodded just the once; it hurt to do more than that. 'Doctor Darius Emerson.'

Chapter Forty

December 26th, 1914

The guns resumed their tumultuous barrage immediately after Christmas.

Wave after wave of injured men were brought into the hospital, some crying, some screaming, some oddly silent and staring with unseeing eyes.

Lydia worked until the world swam before her eyes. She looked down at her blood-covered fingertips, unsure whether the blood was hers or from one of the injured soldiers.

During a lull, Franz ordered her outside. 'You need a little rest.'

'So do you.'

'I'm ordering you.'

'I won't go unless you come too.'

The poor man was almost at breaking point and had been for some time. Goodness knows what's keeping him going, she thought to herself.

He caved in to her demands, his tired eyelids falling heavily, his face almost as pale as that of a man close to death.

There was no time to seek out the orchard, to smoke a little whilst they breathed in the smell of the frosty ground.

He sucked in the tobacco smoke two or three times before speaking.

'How will history regard this war, I wonder?'

Lydia shook her head. 'I suppose it depends how long it goes on and how bloody it gets.'

She felt his eyes on her. No matter how tired he got, there was always something in those hazel eyes, a look as incisive as the cut of his scalpel.

'I've asked permission to carry out blood transfusions. It's been done before, earlier this year and in this country. Belgium. Who would have thought it?'

Lydia looked at him in amazement. 'My father mentioned something about that.'

She recalled his comment that Belgium had carried out the world's very first blood transfusion. They had been sitting in the comfort of the house in Kensington. She saw again the soft furnishings, dust motes dancing in the sunlight that poured through the windows, the vase of early spring flowers. She could still smell the perfume of the bright yellow daffodils and more delicately hued narcissi. She could see her father, sitting there glowing with amazement and itching to know more.

It seemed such a long time ago, and yet it was only a few months.

She couldn't help smiling. 'Hmm. I feel as though I've lived two different lives, the one before war was declared, and the one I'm living now.'

'I won't ask you which you prefer. It is not good to be alone in such difficult circumstances.'

There was something insinuating about Franz's comment, yet surely all he'd commented on was the fact she was alone on a battlefield?

'I'm hardly the only woman nursing in difficult circumstances. There are hundreds, thousands of nurses doing the same thing, I shouldn't wonder.'

'That was not what I meant. Your circumstances, your personal, physical circumstances...'

She met the look in his eyes and knew he was alluding to something she had been denying for months.

'I think I have a ... problem,' she said finally.

He eyed her pensively, one hooded lid drooping slightly. 'Would you like me to examine you?'

She looked away, shocked and still unable to face the absolute truth. Her belly was bigger. She'd heard of things like this happening before; a pregnancy, a miscarriage, but a foetus, one of twins, remaining.

'I'll be fine. Fine,' she repeated softly. For now at least she had no wish to face the truth.

She felt him eyeing her intensely, but did not meet his searching gaze. She needed time to think this through. What to do next? That was the question.

They sighed at the sound of vehicles approaching. More ambulances. More casualties.

'Back to work by the sound of it,' said Franz.

They both threw their half-smoked cigarettes to the ground, grinding them underfoot.

A staff car pulled into the area in front of them and two officers got out. The vehicle immediately behind the car carried a team of armed soldiers.

'Fraulein Muller?'

The senior officer clicked his heels and saluted.

Lydia looked from one officer to the other, a feeling of dread lying like a lump of iron in her stomach.

She nodded and responded softly. One soft yes because all the strength had gone from her voice and her body. She knew immediately what had happened.

Franz stepped in. 'Is there some problem?'

The officer jerked his chin in acknowledgement. 'Fraulein Muller is under arrest.'

Again, he used the German version of her name.

Franz stepped forward, his tiredness absent and a new hardness to his tall, lithe body.

'There must be some mistake.' His voice was loudly defensive.

Lydia touched his arm. 'Franz, it is all right.'

'No it is not. I cannot see one of my nurses marched off on some stupid pretence. Tell me what she has done,' he demanded.

The officer was polite but firm.

'She is accused of helping Allied soldiers escape back to their lines. We already have her accomplices under arrest.'

Franz held his ground. 'If they say she was in with them, they must be liars.'

Even before the officer fetched the bundle of letters out from his pocket, Lydia knew that the worst had happened.

Lydia fainted.

Chapter Forty-One

Her cell was a small room in the west wing of a chateau to the south of Ypres in northern France and far from the sea. The room was comfortable, having a table and chair, a bed and a writing desk set before the window. The window looked out over acres of rolling parkland and starkly naked trees. The war was a long way from this place.

She had been allowed to bring all her personal effects with her; her clothes, her books and her journal, a lovely item that she'd had very little time to write her name in until she'd been incarcerated.

A number of people were kind to her. The pastor provided to attend to her spiritual needs, and Brigid, wife of an officer who brought her food and did her laundry.

'I am being paid for this,' Brigid explained in an accent Lydia found difficult to follow. 'I would not do it otherwise. You are a traitor to Germany.'

'I'm only half German,' Lydia explained. 'My mother was English.'

'That is no excuse for helping the enemy escape,' said Brigid.

'Yes it is. Neither the English nor the Germans are my enemies. They would all prefer to be with their families. Do you have children?'

'Three. They are with my mother back in Cologne.'

'Wouldn't you prefer you and your husband

were home with them?'

Lydia could see that Brigid was not that bright a girl. There was something innocent in the look of her, like a spaniel trained to do only the most basic of tricks for her master.

There was to be no formal trial. The information was imparted by the colonel in charge, a brusque, heavy man by the name of Blucher.

She'd stood in front of him, her hands behind her back, her eyes looking above his shaved head to a picture of the Kaiser. He had presented his evidence and asked her for any comment she would like to make before he passed sentence.

'I only ask for clemency,' she said. 'I wanted the war to end. I thought helping soldiers to escape might help me achieve that end.'

'Pah! This is what happens when women are allowed so close to the front line,' he said to one of the other officers present. 'If women ruled the world there would be no wars. Do you know that, Ender? What would men do then?'

The young officer, Ender, a fair-haired man with uncommonly pale eyes, looked at her then at his superior.

'We would be forced to stay at home.'

'We would indeed,' proclaimed the colonel, clasping his meaty fingers together before him. 'It is in a man's nature to make war. It is not in a man's nature to cook or wash dishes. That is women's work. It always has been and always will be!'

Lydia smiled. Whatever would Agnes think of that? Sir Avis Ravening had told Agnes that she could be whatever she liked in the world of the future. It all depended on intelligence and diligence.

The colonel saw her smile.

'The fraulein thinks this is funny?'

Lydia calmly met the gaze of the middle-aged man with his tight-fitting collar and starkly shorn head.

'I was just thinking that the world can surprise us at times. Who knows what the future will bring?'

There followed a meeting of three shorn heads, the colonel and the other officers charged with the task of passing sentence.

The moment she saw the grave expressions, the unrelenting coldness in their eyes, she knew what her sentence would be. Death by firing squad.

'Might I have writing paper?' she asked. 'I would like to write to my family and friends.'

The head of the panel that had condemned her, eyed her as though she had asked for the crown jewels or a troupe of acrobats; nothing so mundane as paper.

'You may write to your parents.'

'My mother is dead.'

'You may write to your father. One sheet of writing paper,' he said to his clerk. 'Enough for bequests. That is all.'

They brought her things from her room. Putting her clothes away gave her something to do. Hidden amongst her underwear she found the picture of her mother and, to her great joy, her mother's journal.

Once she was alone, she placed the portrait on the small pine table, the journal next to it.

She eyed each in turn. Even though the photograph was sepia coloured and not terribly clear, her mother's look seemed so forthright, as though she were trying to tell her she was close by, that she had never left her.

She stroked each item in turn and wondered at the strange calm that had come over her.

Before picking up her pen, she read again in the journal the few words her mother had written; such sad words, and yet she felt as though her mother was telling her something. Write about how you feel. Write in a direct manner to those you love and to those who love you.

Tingling with inner warmth and the feeling that there is no such thing as an ending to life, she picked up her pen and opened the journal. The unblemished paper glared at her, as though inviting her to open up her heart and say whatever she had need to say. *Almost as if my mother knew I would have need of this... First, the date...*

26th December 1914
My dearest Robert,
I can hear a choir of wounded soldiers singing carols close by. I would like to think that you too are listening to carol singing where you are, safe back home for Christmas.

It was my 23rd birthday two days ago and was probably the last birthday I shall ever have and these are the last Christmas carols I shall ever hear.

I am writing these words in my mother's journal, something I have avoided doing up until now; it seemed such a sacrilege.

You know I wish you well, and that I would love to

be with you. Things have not turned out that way and it is almost certain that I will never see you or Agnes ever again. I love you both. Do take care of each other, and if you should marry and have children, please do me the honour of naming one after me. I will soon hear the guns for the very last time. In the meantime I reside in a small room which is comfortably furnished. I am allowed books. I am also allowed a Bible and have been provided with one in English even though they know I speak fluent German. It is as if they are attempting to diminish my German side by their bigotry, refusing to accept me as one of their own because of what I did. The irony makes me smile; in England I was regarded with suspicion because of my German inheritance; in Germany the situation is reversed. Neither saw me as patriotic and could not understand that all I care about is treating injured men no matter what side they fight on.

The pastor has informed me that a firing squad is being selected. It will not be long now, though I am told a physician will first examine me to ensure I am healthy enough to stand in front of a firing squad! Funny, if it wasn't so tragic.

I regret my life will soon be over, but please do not weep for me. Carry on living. Carry on loving, and if Agnes can fill the void I may have left in your life, then please marry her and be happy.

27th December 1914, 11 a.m.
Dear Robert,
I cannot possibly sleep at present, so yet again I write another note for you in my journal. I think the glorious summer of 1914 will be remembered as the last vestige of the old order, the class system, the wide

gap between rich and poor before our world ended.

Up until the call to arms, life in England carried on as if it and the sunshine would go on forever. Remember you coming down to the cottage in the middle of the night. Never forget it. I certainly will not.

In those last Sundays of peace in that wonderful summer, people still went to church in the morning and walked off the excesses of a large lunch in the park or the countryside. God was in his heaven and everyone knew their place.

It was June in that heady period before the assassination of the Austrian archduke and his wife; that terrible event which set Europe alight. But something much more dramatic happened between us. I hope you will always remember it.

Lydia put down her pen and closed the journal. The pastor had promised to get it sent to Robert via friends who were travelling to Switzerland.

'Have you said all you wish to say?' the pastor asked her.

She nodded, her arm held protectively across her stomach. She and the life growing within her would die together. She could not let Robert know about the child. He had to go on living. Receiving news about her death would be bad enough. She couldn't bear for him to grieve for years and years as her father had done for her mother.

He would have been devastated to know there had also been a child so the secret would die with her.

Chapter Forty-Two

October, 1918

Sitting across from Doctor Eric Miller at his Kensington house, Robert Ravening was struck how war and the loss of his daughter had aged him. His face was more drawn, his hair no longer abundant as it had once been, and there was sadness in his eyes.

Doctor Miller was staring blindly into the fireplace where smoke wreathed sluggishly from dusty-looking coal. The fire was in need of a poker being plunged into its depths even if it only resulted in a small flame. At least it would cheer things up a little. Robert leaned forward, picked up the brass-handled poker and stirred a tongue of flame from the heart of the fire.

'I'm so sorry,' he said once the poker was resting next to the coal scuttle. He looked down at his clenched fingers. Relating the details of how he had come to receive the journal had been strangely soothing, as though it would somehow soften the blow. It did not of course. He'd also made the mistake of not noticing that the first few words were written by Lydia's mother. This was bad enough in itself, though nothing compared to his mistake with regard to the portrait that had arrived with it. He'd thought it was Lydia; it certainly looked like her. Doctor Miller had only glanced at the portrait before telling him otherwise.

'My wife. Emily. She died when Lydia was born.'

'And now you've lost your daughter.' Even to his own ears, Robert thought the comment clumsy and inconsequential. But what else was there to say. 'Look. Would you like me to leave the journal with you?'

'She wrote the journal for you, not for me. You must keep it. You may keep the portrait too. It's all in the past and I feel that as one gets older, the past becomes another country. All things fade away.'

To Robert's ears, it sounded as though Eric Miller had turned to stone. On reflection he realised that Doctor Miller was keeping everything bottled up. He wanted to reach across and tell him to air his grief. He knew from wartime experience that keeping it bottled up inside was not good. But still, one couldn't blame him, he thought to himself. He's lost so much.

Kate Mallory, who was sitting next to the doctor, seemed to read Robert's thoughts. She reached out and placed a hand on her husband's shoulder.

'My poor dear.'

They had been married in February. The journal had not arrived until late July having travelled first to Switzerland in a diplomatic bag thanks to kind friends. Even though Switzerland was neutral, it too was affected by the wartime postal service.

'Will you be going back soon?' asked Doctor Miller, still looking into the grate.

'Yes. I was lucky not to be injured when we crashed. I was also lucky that I met Lydia's friends. They helped me escape.' He chewed on

438

his bottom lip as he mulled over their present circumstances; were the people who helped him escape still alive? There was no way of knowing.

Kate Mallory, who was now of course Mrs Kate Miller, sighed heavily. 'When will this terrible war end?'

Robert spread his hands. He was as nonplussed as everyone else. No one knew.

'Let's hope it will be over by next Christmas,' Kate added, though she didn't sound convinced.

Robert left the house feeling greatly saddened. The war kept old friends apart, though it certainly threw enemies together. But at least it's drawing to a close, he told himself.

There had been a lifting of spirits ever since the Americans had entered the war, not that things had changed right away. The war had dragged on, but the fresh troops and fresh ideas gradually made a difference. He could feel in his bones that it would soon all be over.

He hadn't just come to London with regard to the journal and visiting Doctor Miller. He also had legal business to attend to.

Lady Julieta's health had been deteriorating for some time, but the old saying about a creaking gate lasting forever seemed to have been ringing true – until a wet winter and the onset of pneumonia. Robert had inherited everything.

The offices of Grafton, Cheeseman and Sachs were situated in a rambling old Regency building in the west end of London.

The day was warm and reminiscent of that brilliant summer of 1914 before the world had tipped into the abyss.

The house in Belgravia had passed to him along with everything else his uncle had left in trust.

He spent the night there, though restlessly, Lydia on his mind.

By day he went about his business in London, liaising with solicitors and accountants, dealing with his parents' estate and the vast sheep station in Australia. His parents had both died in a typhus epidemic out there. Perhaps that is where I shall go, he thought to himself. Plenty of open space, fresh air and no reminders of that bloody war.

Reminders of war were everywhere in London. Things looked run down and shabby, men selling newspapers standing with the aid of one leg and a crutch, blinded men using white sticks, men rattling tin cups under his nose for a bit of loose change... There were also a lot of widows and orphans.

He dug in his pocket for yet more coins to aid a man who could not get work because of his injuries.

'So where were you?' he asked one injured man after another.

'Ypres.'

'The Somme.'

'Cambrai.'

The last response came as a complete surprise.

'First I was in the Somme, and then I ended up in the German hospital. You'd never believe it would you? I was in the German hospital right here in London.'

Robert smiled sadly. He already knew about this from Doctor Miller. 'They're good people.'

After tossing the man another florin, Robert hailed a taxi. He still had to make that appointment with Mr Cheeseman at his solicitors.

The taxi wound its way through milk carts, brewery drays, coal carts and the hansom cabs that were still horse drawn and still in business.

Compared to the years before the war, horse-drawn traffic had diminished, replaced by vehicles powered by petrol engines.

'It's gettin' worse every year,' grumbled the taxi driver. 'More and more doin' away with horses. Bound to 'appen of course, what with the war and all that.'

'I suppose so,' said Robert, resigned to the fact that the taxi driver was going to enlighten him.

Eventually, after a long drawn-out lecture on why there were so many more petrol-driven vehicles, which was apparently down to the army selling off its stock, they arrived at his destination.

Mr Cheeseman was dwarfed by the size of the desk he sat behind. His large nose and prominent chin seemed to jut forward of the rest of his face. Dark wisps of hair tickled the edge of his collar, but it was almost entirely absent from the top of his head.

He managed to reach across the desk to shake Robert's hand, and offered him a drink, which Robert declined.

Robert made himself comfortable. 'I thought everything with regard to Lady Julieta's will had been finalised. I take it everything is in order?'

'Indeed,' said Mr Cheeseman, holding his head to one side as he nodded. 'However, a more personal matter has come to light regarding your parents' will. A personal note in amongst the papers that I...' His bright black eyes scrutinised his client as though weighing up his suitability to hear this personal news.

Robert fidgeted in his chair. Besides the death of his aunt, this year had also seen the passing of his mother. His father had preceded her by only a few months. He'd thought everything was finalised, mostly by the lawyers in Australia, the papers finally coming to England for final ratification and probate.

'So what was overlooked?' Robert asked.

Mr Cheeseman's smile was conciliatory. 'Nothing was overlooked by the firm of Grafton, Cheeseman and Sachs, I can assure you,' he replied indignantly. He followed his remark by tossing his head in the same odd sideways motion as when he'd nodded.

Perhaps he has an impediment of some kind, thought Robert. Not that it mattered much to him. On the whole Cheeseman did a good job, but he wanted it over with. He wanted to get on with his life, such as it would be without the woman he loved.

'Your mother left this letter to be passed to you after her death. It was written some time ago and deposited here at this office.'

'Not in Australia?' Robert was taken by surprise. It wasn't often that either of his parents came to London. They'd abandoned England a long time ago after making arrangements for his education. He'd rarely seen them since.

Mr Cheeseman made a big issue of clearing his throat. 'Your mother wrote the letter a short time after you were born. She told me it was to be by way of a deathbed confession – just in case...' He paused again, his lips and jaw moving as though chewing over what he had to say – and what had to be said.

'I think you'd better read it yourself.'

Robert took the letter that was handed to him, unfolded the letter and began to read.

My dear Robert,

I have given instructions that this letter is to be read after my death, which I hope will not be for a very long time yet. I trust also by that time the inheritance I foresee coming to you will have happened. Sir Avis is, I think, a man of his word even though his morals can be somewhat lax on occasion.

The truth is that the child I longed for never came to be. Your father, that is the man whose name appears on your birth certificate, could not give me the child I longed for. I grew impatient and, distraught, I fell into the arms of my brother-in-law, Avis. The man you regarded as your father was unaware of this so when you came to be, he was overjoyed and I was glad. He never knew the truth and I never told him. However, I did not want you displaced by any child born of Sir Avis's marriage to that dreadful American woman. I wrote this letter as proof that you are the undisputed heir and that Heathlands and everything else would come to you. Do forgive me for shocking you and also for leaving you in England whilst I supported my husband in Australia. I felt it was the least I could do just in case he should look at you and see his brother. All my love.

Robert refolded the letter, aware that Cheeseman was seeking some sign of distress or even of anger in his face. He felt neither of these emotions. In an odd way he'd always suspected there was a reason why he was left throughout most of his childhood in England whilst his parents – those whose names appeared on his birth certificate – stayed on the other side of the world. They'd been like strangers to him and in a way, he could understand why. Perhaps in an effort to come to terms with what she'd done, his mother had never left his father's side, and his father had never left Australia.

Tucking the letter away in an inside pocket, he rose to his feet. 'I trust our discourse is at an end?'

Cheeseman got to his feet too, extending his hand. 'We are indeed. I do apologise for dragging you across London, but the letter was of a somewhat personal nature. Your mother was a lovely lady. She confided in me,' he said in answer to the questioning look on Robert's face. 'I take it you'll be off to the front again shortly once you've finalised your affairs in London.'

'I will, but first I have a wedding to attend. A dear friend of mine is getting married.' He glanced at his watch. 'I should make it in time.'

'Well, I dare say they'll forgive you if you are a little late,' Cheeseman said cheerfully.

'I doubt that. I'm the best man.'

Agnes was a picture in a cream satin gown with a thick lace peplum and matching trimming on the shoulders. A circlet of silk flowers and pale green leaves served to heighten the colour of her hair. Her complexion glowed, a blush the size of a rosebud on each cheek.

Major Darius Emerson was wearing full dress uniform.

The two of them exchanged smiles at the altar before the vicar intoned the old familiar words: 'Dearly beloved...'

The wedding reception was being held at a hotel only a few yards from the church. Robert stopped for a smoke outside the church, watching as the guests made their way chattering and laughing to where the food awaited them.

He was just imagining what his own wedding might have been like, when he saw Sir Avis's old butler, Quartermaster, leaning carefully on his stick to place a bunch of flowers on a grave.

After putting out his cigarette, Robert shoved his hands in his pockets and wandered over.

'Sir!' Quartermaster exclaimed, his old face more wrinkled now than ever, but still brightening with the warmth of his smile. 'So nice to see you again.'

They shook hands. In doing so, Robert glanced down at the grave.

'A relative of yours I takc it,' he said amiably.

Quartermaster shook his head. 'No. Just old Mrs Stacey. She was the cook before Sarah came. It was a Stacey before that of course. As you know, Sir, it's traditional for staff in certain positions to pass their names on to their successor.'

Robert controlled his expression. Inside it felt as though something had exploded. 'So Sarah inherited the name?'

Quartermaster nodded. 'That's right, Sir.'

He took his pocket watch out and looked at it. 'Better be getting along, Sir, or there'll be no food left. Are you coming, Sir?'

'Yes.' Robert took only one step. The suspicion that had suddenly exploded in his brain needed addressing by somebody who might know the truth. Quartermaster was that person.

'Reg,' he said, using Quartermaster's real name as he gently clutched at the butler's sleeve. 'Are you saying that there never was a Tom Stacey? That Sarah never had a husband?'

A look of dismay froze the old butler's features. His nod of agreement was barely perceptible; because there's more, thought Robert. There's a lot more.

'Tell me,' said Robert, not relinquishing his grip on the old man's sleeve.

The old man was unbowed. He took a deep breath and straightened. 'No adverse gossip will escape my lips. You must draw your own conclusions.'

'Sir Avis was Agnes's father?'

Quartermaster eyed Robert's arm. 'If I could ask you to unhand me, Sir...'

The steady look in the butler's eyes said it all. He hadn't answered Robert's question with words. One look, that was all it took to tell Robert that Agnes and he shared the same father. It explained why Sir Avis had been so fond of Agnes, willing to discuss anything she'd expressed interest in.

In November the war finally ended. Robert never returned to combat.

Chapter Forty-Three

Two weeks before Christmas – 1918

Agnes walked in a circle around the thick rug covering only a small portion of the wide oak floorboards. She paused to give herself time to imagine a gathering of Puritans sitting around the refectory table at one end of the room. Surely she'd seen the same grouping in a painting somewhere?

'Heathlands hasn't changed much,' she said, tilting her head back to take in the ceiling's ornate plasterwork; globules of stalactites ending in a Tudor rose. 'There isn't much time to get it ready for Christmas, but if you insist, I dare say we'll do our best and all pull together. Domestic servants to tackle a house this size are thin on the ground nowadays. The war changed all that.'

She glanced at the handsome man standing in the middle of the hall, his features framed by the light flooding through the window behind him. The window was big and square, the casements' lead-paned triangles that had survived the centuries without replacement.

Robert Ravening was older and had a more rugged aspect to his features. In all other aspects, he seemed unchanged.

'I want it to be the way it used to be,' he said wistfully. 'Aunt Julieta didn't go in for big gatherings at Christmas or any other time for that matter. I want to organise a real Christmas just as it used to be before the war when Uncle Avis was alive. Who knows, it could very well be the last of such Christmases, thanks to the war.'

Agnes attempted to reassure him. 'As I've already said, servants are not going to be too easy to get.'

He shrugged. 'Who can blame them? The factories pay better. Domestic service will never be the way it was. The war changed everything. Everything,' he added, though softer, more thoughtfully.

Agnes heard the pain in his voice and knew immediately to what – or rather to whom – he was referring.

'At least she sent you the journal.'

Robert shook his head. 'I wish I hadn't left her there. I blame myself.'

Agnes turned away so he wouldn't see the tears in her eyes. There was no doubt that he'd loved Lydia dearly and so had she.

She sighed. 'We owe it to her to continue. It's all we can do.'

He nodded. 'I suppose so.'

'I appreciate what you're doing, Robert. My family are grateful, certainly my mother.'

'I prefer the familiar,' he said. 'We can't recreate what Heathlands was, but we can go some way to making it a home again.'

Agnes smiled warmly. All of Agnes's family would be employed by Robert in the house in London and on the Ravening estate.

'I'm used to you all,' Robert had said when Ellen

448

Proctor had chewed over the prospect of moving from the East End.

'Family matters,' she'd stated at last.

They took it she meant she'd agreed to the plan and, to their relief, found out she had.

Robert looked out through the window at the expanse of parkland surrounding the house. He rubbed at the condensation currently misting the panes. Not that it did much. A wintry mist was hanging like sad veils over the trees.

His thoughts were his own. He would hold Lydia in his memory, not on his shoulder, but in his heart where she had always belonged.

He voiced his hope that she was at rest, though somewhere in his heart of hearts he dared hope for a miracle. Unfortunately, the Germans had not been in the habit of forgiving anyone, not before the execution of Edith Cavell when they realised what a colossal propaganda mistake they'd made.

Like Lydia, Nurse Edith Cavell had served in the war, tending to both friend and foe alike. Eventually, when her hospital had fallen behind enemy lines, she had become involved in a network helping Allied personnel escape. The Germans had found out and shot her for it in 1915. The American newspapers had gone wild with the story.

Agnes saw his sad look, and went to his side, gripping his arm tightly. 'Come on. Let's see what my mother is up to, shall we? She is so excited at the prospect of a Christmas here like it used to be.'

They made their way to the kitchen and the butler's pantry arm in arm.

Armed with lists and a pencil, Agnes's mother

was opening cupboard doors and scrutinising shelves.

On seeing them enter, she shook her head at Robert.

'Your aunt's cook didn't keep much in the larder and what there is isn't fit for much except pigswill.'

'Aunt Julieta didn't entertain much.'

Agnes's mother grunted an unintelligible response. They all knew that Lady Julieta had become an invalid and a recluse in her final years. Eaten up by bitterness and disappointment, she'd taken to her bed where food was brought on a tray and visitors discouraged. Robert had finally come into his inheritance on her death though he hadn't seen his aunt for a long time before, mainly on account of the war, though partially because of her reclusiveness.

Although the house was in good enough repair, the few servants who had not gone off to war had taken advantage of their mistress's lethargy and neglected to keep the place clean. The smell of dust and the greasy windows were evidence of that.

'I shall need to do a total restock,' proclaimed Sarah Stacey, her old efficiency fully restored. 'I noticed on the drive through the village that George Davis is still in business. He always was a very good butcher. So is Mr Barker, the green-grocer.'

'I believe it's being run by Mrs Barker. Her husband died a year after receiving the news of their son's death. He was an only son.'

The silence that followed Robert's comment was

short lived, but it was full of unspoken sadness. Too many men had died. Too many women were widows or in mourning for beloved sons. Britain alone had suffered three-quarters of a million dead and husbands would be in short supply for some years to come.

'I'll drive you into the village,' said Agnes to her mother. She turned to Robert. 'You did say you had some paperwork to deal with?' she added, her fine fingers gently stroking Robert's arm.

He grimaced. 'Too much paperwork. Worse than being in the army.'

Agnes smiled. 'I doubt that.'

The weather was crisp and cold, the fields they passed bare and brown, asleep and waiting for spring.

Both the butcher and greengrocer were pleased to see Agnes and her mother.

'The old place just ain't been the same without you in charge,' they said to Sarah.

There was no hint of condemnation regarding the rumoured relationship between Sarah and Sir Avis. Their businesses had prospered before Lady Julieta had moved in and had gone downhill from then on.

Agnes watched as her mother ticked each item off her lengthy list. A portion of produce was loaded into the car for immediate use and weekly orders placed.

'Just like the old days,' proclaimed Mr Davis.

'Well!' said Agnes's mother with an air of finality. 'I think we will have a reasonable Christmas now. We'd better get back or your husband will think we've got lost.'

Agnes laughed. 'He's used to my wild ways. Anyway, I think he'll probably be perusing the cellar. Luckily, for us, Lady Julieta spurned the demon drink. There should be plenty of wine and spirits left down there.'

'And wasn't it lucky that your grandmother and I thought to make Christmas puddings weeks ago?'

'Amazing that you got all the ingredients needed.'

'Ask no questions, tell no lies,' said her mother and winked. 'It was our way of celebrating the end of the war. The eleventh hour of the eleventh day of the eleventh month; when the guns finally fell silent. Other people went out and danced in the street. Your grandmother and I looked to the future and made Christmas puddings.'

Agnes drew the car to a halt in front of the door leading directly into the kitchen.

The sudden tapping of a walking stick sounded along the red tiles that formed the path at the back of the house followed by an enquiry as to whether they needed help to unload.

Placing her hands on her hips, Agnes smiled then laughed at the sight of her husband.

Head and shoulders dusty with cobwebs, Doctor Darius Emerson appeared, followed by the equally dusty butler, Quartermaster, who was now more bent with age than ever. The stick was his.

'I take it you've carried out a full inventory of the Christmas drinks situation?' laughed Agnes as Darius swung her around in his arms.

'We won't go dry,' he replied. 'Will we, Quartermaster?'

'Certainly not, Sir.'

The thing was, she and Darius had seen so much and shared so much. He understood her. He'd admired her pluckiness, her determination to get through everything. He'd also seen how she'd been affected by the injured and dying, writing letters home for them, using humour and every feminine wile to keep their spirits up, to help them fight to survive their terrible injuries.

After helping take the supplies through to the kitchen, they walked for a while in the kitchen garden. There was little growing, just a few sorry cabbage stalks and onions that had long gone to seed. The three gardeners the estate used to employ had gone to war and never come back. One had died, one seriously injured and the other had decided he could make more money in a factory.

Darius hugged her arm close to his side. 'So how is he?'

She knew he was referring to Robert. She sighed.

'I don't think he'll ever get over it. It's not just the fact that she was condemned to death. He feels guilty because it happened shortly after she helped him escape. He keeps thinking he should have insisted she got out with him. I think perhaps she thought he might be better off without her. Things are going to be difficult for some time to come. Forgiveness after such an horrific war might take a long time. There's a lot of bigotry about. I suppose there will be for some time.'

Agnes continued. 'That's how people are. Lady Julieta was adamant that Lydia's loyalty would lie

453

with Germany and informed Robert's parents to that effect. I don't know how they responded or whether they agreed or not, but what I do know for sure is that it wasn't true. Her first allegiance was to injured men no matter what side they were on. You know her father married an actress named Kate Mallory?'

'The poor man. It's easy to say that it should help with the loss of his daughter, but it must be hard for him.'

'He's thrown himself into his work. He still practises as a doctor from his house and at the hospital. I suppose it's all he can do. The German hospital stayed open all the way through the war and he stuck with it. They all survived surprisingly well. People were grateful for free medicine no matter the nationality of those dispensing it.'

It began to snow a week before Christmas. The gravel drive leading from the main gate up to the house was indistinguishable from the parkland to either side. The hills in the distance looked as though someone had sprinkled them with icing sugar.

Robert hired a man from the village to do odd jobs around the old place. A war veteran, Godfrey Williams was missing half a leg and keen to get any job he could. His first task was to chop up and haul in logs for the fireplace in the great hall. Green boughs of holly, fir and mistletoe, bound with scarlet ribbon just as they used to be, decorated the high mantelpiece and hung above ancestral pictures. Pride of place went to a fifteen-foot-high Christmas tree. They dusted off the painted box containing the tree decorations.

Agnes was ecstatic. 'Look! There are even a few candles. Some haven't been used at all.'

Amongst them were the ones they had made as children; the silver star Robert had made, the snowman made by Agnes from white cardboard, the round blob Sylvester insisted was a robin but didn't look like anything. All the same, they had hung it up in memory of Sylvester who had died of the Spanish Infection which had been rife, although it had died down in the summer, but was likely to reappear this winter...

Darius stood on a stepladder whilst Agnes handed him the decorations.

'What about the top of the tree? Do we have a star?'

Receiving no response, he looked down at Agnes. She was dangling the star from her finger-tips, watching as the light caught it and sparkled. 'Are you going to hand me that star, or do you want me to place both you and it on the top of the tree?'

She looked up at him. 'We put it up the Christmas Lydia stayed here.'

He winced because she'd sounded so abrupt, but it couldn't be helped. It was all she could do to stop from sobbing.

He came down from the stepladder and took her in his arms.

'Cry, why don't you? It's about time you did.'

'I've never been a cry baby.'

'Well, now is a good time to start. You've got a lot to cry about.'

Big, wet tears slid down her cheeks. 'I wouldn't

455

want Robert to see the star,' she sobbed. 'He'd remember.'

'It is good to remember,' whispered Darius before burying his face in her hair, closing his eyes as he breathed in its fresh scent.

Robert, who had been listening unseen just outside the open door, turned away.

Beyond the great oriole window looking out over the front of the house, the night was drawing in. All was darkness though a new moon was shining shyly from behind a curtain of cloud.

He'd heard somewhere that a new moon meant a new beginning.

On hearing Quartermaster shuffling up behind him, he turned and asked him if it were true.

'Is it a new beginning then, old chap?'

'I suppose it has to be, Sir. The war is over. It has to be a new beginning. Peace at last.'

Quartermaster half turned then, as a thought struck him, he turned back again.

'It's also said that one can make a wish on a new moon. That's what I've heard, Sir.'

Robert heard him leave. He'd wished on that moon so often, mostly wishing for the war to be over. So what did he wish for now? That he didn't feel so guilty at being alive, when others were dead? Yes, that and Lydia laying down her life so he might live – even if her last request that he married Agnes was quite impossible, though of course, Lydia hadn't known that and neither had he mentioned anything to Sarah. He just looked at her now and again, seeing the beauty she had been and understanding why Sir Avis had looked after his cook and the child of their union.

The only thing they had talked about was the money he'd left her in an ancillary will he'd stipulated not to be declared until after the death of his wife, Lady Julieta. It struck him then just how kind the old man had been. He'd had many affairs with many women, but not only had he loved Sarah, he had also purposely avoided hurting his widow. Although they had not lived together for years, he had respected her position as his wife. There was something good in that no matter whatever else he was.

It occurred to him to pay another visit to Lydia's father; he'd appeared pretty desolate on his last visit. It was still early days, but perhaps they might support each other in their sadness.

Decision made, the next morning he rang the bell to summon Quartermaster. The old man had officially retired, but there was a scarcity of men wishing to return to domestic service. Quartermaster was slow and getting slower, but he knew his job and, anyway, Robert quite liked having him around.

'I'm going to London this afternoon.'

'So close to Christmas? Beg your pardon, Sir. I didn't mean to imply that you shouldn't go...'

'No need, Quartermaster. I just feel I need to visit a few old haunts. I'll be back by Christmas Eve. Agnes would never forgive me if I wasn't.'

Chapter Forty-Four

Christmas Eve, 1918

'Will Santa Claus know I've moved to England?'

The small girl's comments drew smiles and warm looks from fellow travellers on the train heading for Ravening Halt. Her upturned face glowed as she awaited her mother's response.

Her mother stroked the child's face. 'Of course he will. Santa Claus visits good children all over the world, except that here they more commonly call him Father Christmas.'

Steam clouded the window of the carriage just before the train entered a tunnel. The lights came on though their glow was only feeble.

Lydia smiled as she patted her daughter's pink cheeks. 'Soon be there,' she said softly.

The little girl, who seemed to be no more than four years old, snuggled against her mother's side. She closed her eyes for just a moment before they snapped open and she asked another question.

'Will we see the old man again?' she asked.

'You mean Grandfather?'

The little girl nodded.

'Yes, Olivia. I dare say we will.'

Her father had wanted her to stay and they had stayed, just long enough to see his eyes come alive with pleasure at the sight of his daughter, whom he'd thought was dead, and Olivia, a granddaughter he hadn't known he had.

On arrival at Ravening Halt, a distinguished gentleman wearing a bowler hat and an officer wearing the uniform of a naval captain vied to help her with her valise.

'It's only small,' she said, smiling sweetly. 'I'm only here for the day. I have a return ticket.'

Her father had suggested they telephone Heathlands to make sure somebody was at home. He tried and had been trying for hours, but had finally given up. They'd already tried telephoning the house in Belgravia, but nobody answered.

'Agnes said that Sir Avis and the whole household went to Heathlands every Christmas. I presume Robert is carrying on the tradition.'

Her father had conceded that the telephone wasn't working properly. 'Nothing seems to be working properly just yet,' he said.

He'd clung to her before she left, not letting go until she had promised to return. She'd said that she would.

Full of apprehension, she thanked the two gentlemen who had been so polite to her and felt their eyes following her all the way to the exit.

The stationmaster doffed his cap. The only other woman waiting at the station glanced at the woman wearing the dove-grey coat and hat, a small child in a red checked coat and hat dancing along at her side.

'I need to get to Heathlands,' she said to the stationmaster. 'I don't suppose there is a taxi.'

He shook his head. 'Mind you, it ain't far to walk.'

'I remember it not being too far, but it's my

little girl you see. Her legs are getting tired. Isn't that right, my little sugar plum?'

Olivia stopped dancing. 'If I walk slowly I'll be all right. It's just that my feet keep dancing even when my legs don't want them to.'

Robert had made the decision not to hire a chauffeur unless he really needed one, though Agnes insisted she could do the job far better than any man could. He'd had to remind her that she was now a married woman and her husband might not wish her to drive. Besides that, she was expecting their first child, and anyway, he quite liked driving himself.

The journey from Heathlands was short and the snow had melted thanks to the watery rays of a midday sun. The train from London had just pulled in. This same train would be turned around, the locomotive unfastening from its carriages, puffing its way down to the turntable, a vast circular plate on which it would stand whilst being turned to face the opposite direction.

Robert had always been fascinated by locomotives, big brutish things made of iron and steel, snorting steam like some latter-day dragon. The locomotive was in the process of being reconnected, enveloped in clouds of steam as it eased itself into position.

Wonderful stuff, he thought to himself, and grinned; that was before the iron beast gave a creaking roar before seeming to settle into itself, hissing like a snake.

Lydia came out of the lavatories clutching her

daughter's hand, and made her way outside. At last Olivia's dancing feet had agreed with her dancing legs. She was flagging badly, asking to be picked up when in all honesty she was too big to be picked up.

'Darling, you're a big girl now. I'm sorry, but you'll have to walk, unless we can get a lift... Oh my!'

She said it softly, but Olivia heard.

'Is it Santa Claus?' Olivia piped up.

Lydia couldn't speak. Her mouth was dry.

Or it could be that her father had managed to get through on the telephone. She had told him she didn't want anyone upset, but ultimately he would do what he thought was best for her whether she wanted it or not. What am I doing here, she said to herself. Her father had thought it a good idea. She'd thought it too, but now she was here, now she was looking at the car she knew the chauffeur used to drive, her courage melted. The car was here to collect someone or had dropped somebody off. The chauffeur was probably back there on the platform waiting for somebody to arrive. Yes, it had to be somebody arriving, perhaps not on this train. Perhaps on the one from Oxford. That had to be it. If he'd been dropping Robert or somebody else off, the car would already have left, the chauffeur driving off by himself. But it wasn't. It was parked here.

Her courage failed her. 'Let's go back on the train,' she said to Olivia.

Olivia began to cry. 'What about Santa Claus? You said he lived in a big house and we were going to see the big house.'

461

'Not today, Olivia. I don't think he's home.' Her voice faltered. Her courage was failing her. Her father had assured her that Robert still cared for her, but it had been so long ... four long years...

Lydia marched quickly back on to the platform, almost dragging Olivia behind her, she was protesting that much.

Finally exasperated that her daughter was making so much noise, Lydia bent down, turned the little girl to face her and attempted to make her understand.

'Olivia, darling. We have had a lovely train ride, and now it's time to go home.'

'No!' The little girl had the same adamant jut to her chin as Lydia had once had. Her mother recognised it as such and knew immediately that she wasn't going to win this argument, not without a great deal of fuss and tears.

She glanced through the arched entrance to the platform.

'All right,' she said softly, stroking her daughter's face and wondering at her wilfulness. 'We'll walk and I'll show you the lake. Would you like that?'

Yes, of course her daughter would like that. And all you've got to do is find your way there, she reminded herself. You got lost there once before. Remember?

The fireman on the 2.15 back to Paddington shook his head as he wiped his dirty hands with a cloth that was almost as dirty.

'No chance. The firebox is busted. Somebody let the fire go out, stupid sod! Then heaped in the coal and got it red hot quick as you like instead of taking it slow. There's a crack a mile wide in the firebox. That's it and all about it.'

The driver swiped at his greasy black brow, muttered a curse and tilted his hat further back on his head. Swinging himself down from the cab, he stood at the side of his engine waiting for the stationmaster.

The stationmaster was far from pleased. 'Good job there's not too many passengers, but everyone is going to 'ave to be informed. Who's the bloody idiot who broke the bloody firebox?'

'Bad language won't get you anywhere fast,' said the driver, whose own bad language could be pretty colourful at times. Turning his back on the stationmaster, he swung himself back up into his cab.

The stationmaster had been contemplating making a cup of tea then sitting down with his newspaper and a packet of Rich Tea biscuits. Seemed that part of his afternoon was to be put on hold. The only passenger waiting to board had been hanging around at the end of the platform, studying with interest the mighty steam engine and the turntable at the far end of the rails.

He heaved a big sigh. The tea, biscuits and newspaper would have to wait. First things first, inform the solitary passenger, the only one he could see hanging about on the platform, that the train wasn't going anywhere. He'd have to wait for the next one. He looked for the young woman with the little girl, but couldn't see them. They'd obviously walked to where they wanted to go.

'Excuse me, Sir.'

The tall man whom he'd noticed had walked with a limp when he'd bought his ticket, turned round. If this man hadn't been an officer during the war, then I'll eat my hat he thought to himself. His face looked vaguely familiar, but then he'd seen so many faces passing through these latter years.

'Sorry, Sir, but the service to London is delayed. A technical problem you might say.'

Robert nodded. He'd been totally absorbed in watching the locomotive going through its paces, slowing and then finally stopping before it had properly linked up with its carriages. It was also then, just towards the end of that manoeuvre, that he'd felt something – something of a premonition as though somebody had tapped him on the shoulder, urging him to turn round.

The feeling was fleeting and when he actually did turn round, he wasn't surprised to find himself alone. He was getting used to being alone, but also of hoping and dreaming that the past had never happened and Lydia was still alive.

'That's it for today, then?' he asked, pulling the brim of his hat forward.

'Until 3.15, Sir. That's if we can get this locomotive out of the way.'

Robert grunted. 'Is it likely to take long?'

The stationmaster shook his head. 'I couldn't say, Sir. But if you would like to wait... I could supply you with a cup of tea and a biscuit.'

His eyebrows rose questioningly, his eyes wide and glassy. It wasn't often he invited anyone in to take tea in his comfy little office, but now and again he felt a need for good company. This

464

gentleman looked a likely contender.

The atmosphere in the stationmaster's officer was congenial and warm by virtue of a glowing coal fire. A copper kettle of indeterminate age and myriad dents sounded as though it were chortling with mirth as the water boiled.

'I'll let it mash,' said the stationmaster as he poured on water then stirred the contents of a big brown pot.

They talked generally whilst waiting for the tea, the subject always coming back to the war and what each of them had done in it.

'I was reserved occupation of course,' said the stationmaster. 'Had to keep the trains running, didn't we?'

'Of course you did.'

'In the trenches were you?'

'No. Flying through the air.'

The stationmaster adopted the look of utter amazement that Robert had become used to. Some people could still not quite believe that a man could fly through the sky like a bird – or an angel.

'It's wonderful times we live in,' remarked the stationmaster, shaking his head in amazement. 'Can't say I fancy the idea meself. A bit too dangerous for me. Hats off to you though. Can't 'ave been easy.'

'It wasn't. I was shot down a couple of times. I won't ever be able to run a race, but I can still walk. I'm grateful for that.'

The sun suddenly came out, filling the room with light and extra warmth. Robert eyed the view from the window. The station was small and surrounded by rolling fields and bare trees. Although not looking their best at this time of year, he thought how beautiful their bare branches seemed. Here and there the snow had buried into crevices in the trees' trunks.

'It is nice around here,' he said softly to himself.

'It is that, Sir. Never found a better place,' echoed the stationmaster.

Robert fell to silence. The steam engine was silent. There was no sound from the driver and his fireman, the latter whose job it was to feed the fire with shovelfuls of Welsh steam coal.

'You can almost hear a pin drop,' said the old stationmaster.

He wasn't to know it, but his comment was in tune with what Robert had been thinking. It was so peaceful here and what exactly was there in London? Nothing. All he would do in London was visit old haunts and those friends that were still alive. He would also have visited Doctor Miller and together they would have discussed Lydia – but that, he realised, was like opening up an old wound. He could now understand why Lydia's father never mentioned her mother, had no memento of her in the house, and had avoided celebrating his daughter's birthday, which was also the day his dear wife had died. It was best to forget, to live with the memory but not wear it on one's shoulder.

'I think I'll forgo that trip to London.' He rose to his feet. 'I think there's snow in the air.'

After thanking the stationmaster for the tea, he went outside and looked around him, taking big lungsful of air as he did so.

The truth hit him that he belonged here in this tranquil place where the grass was still green and muddy fields were only that way when they were under the plough, not churned up by shell fire or the tracks of that other new weapon of war, the tank.

The muffled bell of a telephone in the station-master's office suddenly disturbed the calm.

He heard somebody call out.

'Sir! There's a telephone call for you.'

He turned to see the stationmaster waving at him.

He didn't bother to ask who it was for. He could guess. There were few telephones in the area. The stationmaster had one, so did the local doctor. Heathlands had the other. He wondered who it was and what they might want. He should have been on the train by now, so how did they know they could reach him?

He took the telephone from the stationmaster.

'Sir!' Quartermaster always sounded out of breath even though his duties were far lighter than in the past. He'd specifically left his sister's and re-tirement because he was bored. However, it hadn't occurred to him that he wasn't so fit as he was. Quartermaster was an old dog who wouldn't lie down.

'What is it?' Robert asked.

'Miss Lydia, Sir. Doctor Miller rang to say she caught the train and should be there with you now. Doctor Miller's telephone has been out of order for a while. He's been trying all day to get in touch with you.'

Robert felt as though a clapper from a mon-

467

strous bell was banging around in his head. Had he really heard what he thought he'd heard? Was he going mad? Surely Quartermaster was wrong. He couldn't really mean Lydia – could he?

'Sir? Are you still there?'

The telephone with its speaking device was fixed to the wall. The earpiece hung limply in Robert's hand.

A voice in his head told him to pull himself together. He asked Quartermaster to repeat what he had said.

'You say she's here? She's alive? Is she alone?'

It wouldn't have surprised him if she wasn't alone, perhaps with a new man in her life. It had been so long.

'With a child, Sir. A little girl. I believe her name is Olivia and she is just coming up to four years old.'

Robert let the speaking device fall, clutching it to his chest as he attempted to collect himself.

He addressed the stationmaster. 'Did you see a young woman with a small child alighting from the London train?'

The stationmaster reached under his cap and scratched his head. 'Yes, I did. She asked about a taxi and I told her there weren't none. Don't know where she went though. Set off in that direction she did. Walking I should think.'

Robert dashed to his car. Perhaps he might meet her on the road, or perhaps she might make it to Heathlands by the time he got back.

His thoughts reeling, he turned the nose of the car towards home. 'Please don't let this be a dream,' he said to himself. 'Let it be real. Let

468

Lydia be alive.'

And the child? Olivia, Quartermaster had said. Her name was Olivia.

The sun was shining bravely through the trees and although most of the snow had melted, it still clung in dirty heaps to the edge of the drive.

Lydia had planned to walk up the long drive to the front door, knock lustily and beam broadly at the sight of a host of surprised faces. It was the only plan she could think of, in fact not really a plan at all. She was too apprehensive for a proper plan; too much emotion was involved.

As it turned out, the feeble plan came to nothing thanks to Olivia who had skipped in and out of the trees bordering the drive. A squirrel, out to top up his winter food, descended from his home high up in a beech tree and ran towards the lake.

Olivia ran after it, calling loudly to it.

'Olivia! Come back!'

Lydia ran after her. At one point she slipped and stumbled on the icy grass. By the time she'd righted herself, Olivia was out of sight.

Through a sudden gap in the trees, she saw a flash of sunlight on water. Water was a magnet for all children. Lydia only hoped her strong-minded daughter wouldn't come across a patch of frozen water and presume she could walk on it.

It began snowing, small flakes swiftly growing into big ones.

'Olivia! Come back. Don't go any further. I'm warning you, don't go any further!' Her voice soared, but there was no response and no sound of a breathless child, oblivious to danger and the wishes of her mother. The child was high spirited and curious, always asking questions, always wanting to explore the unknown.

Smooth cobbles formed the path running down through the trees to the lake. Even the crepe soles of her brown suede boots slipped on the worn surfaces. She had to get to Olivia. Where was she?

The grotto! Even after all these years, the thought of the grotto chilled her to the bone. Olivia would be as attracted to a cave as she was to water.

The entrance to the grotto loomed like a black toothless mouth on the other side of the water. Just as when she had been here before, rushes, their leaves dried from cold, rustled in the wind. She heard the sound of something – possibly a rat – sliding into the water.

The closer she got to the grotto, the faster her heart beat. The shadows of late afternoon were lengthening and if they didn't get back to the station soon, they would miss the train.

It might have been her imagination, but something moved in the dark chasm of the grotto.

Pan.

There was no Pan of course, but anything could happen in that dank, dark place.

'Olivia!'

She heard the sound of footsteps. Olivia stepped out of the grotto, her hand in that of a man, a man Lydia instantly recognised.

'Robert!'

She noticed one of his shoulders was held slightly higher than the other, a direct result of an injury to his leg. There was a more drawn look to his face, but then, she thought, most men who had fought in the war had that look.

'I parked the car in the drive. I saw the red coat flashing through the trees. I know how children are with water – I followed her...'

He stood there, shaking his head, his eyes filling with tears – speechless. 'She is mine, isn't she?'

Lydia nodded. 'Yes.'

Olivia looked up at him and there was no fear in her face.

'Are you Santa Claus?' she asked.

'Better than that,' Lydia managed to say. 'He's your father.'

Tears poured down Robert's face. Lydia fell against his chest. His arm wrapped around her, crushing her against him, his cheek resting on her head. Their tears mingled.

'There's so much I want to know,' he said to her.

'And so much I want to tell you.'

'Can I have a cuddle too?' asked Olivia. Her round little cheeks had turned pink with cold, but her eyes were bright with interest.

Her parents reacted automatically, both of them reaching down to bring their child into their hug.

Robert whispered into Lydia's ear.

'I can't believe you managed to escape the firing squad. The circumstances must have been exceptional.'

Lydia tilted her head back and looked up at him.

'You remember the men on either side were singing carols and lighting candles in the trenches that Christmas?'

471

'I did hear of it.'

'Well, I had something of my own Christmas truce. I had to be examined by a doctor before being shot – odd, but true. One must be healthy to be executed. It's thanks to Olivia that I'm here. It appears I was expecting twins. I lost one but the other hung on. It happens sometimes.'

'When I was sent your journal I was told you were most likely dead.'

'The hospital was shelled. We were lucky to get out alive, but had to run for it. I didn't have much choice but to go where I was told to go. Forgive me for letting you think I was dead, but I thought you would have settled down yourself. I thought you and Agnes...'

Smiling sadly, he shook his head. 'We're too closely related I'm afraid. Sir Avis has a lot to answer for.'

'I didn't know that at the time. News was slow incoming, but now...'

Lydia looked up at him, noticing lines where none had been before, the small flick of grey hair above a red mark on his temple. He'd been injured more than once. 'You survived, Robert. I am so glad! Does your leg hurt?'

He shook his head impatiently. He didn't want to talk about himself. He wanted to know what had happened, why she was alive when he'd been led to believe she was dead.

'Tell me what happened, Lydia. For God's sake, tell me what happened.'

She nodded. 'Yes. There was a law forbidding the execution of a pregnant woman because the child was innocent. It had a right to be born. Therefore,

I was acquitted, though only on the understanding that I would reside in Germany under the supervision of the Krupp medical facility, until the war was over. It was a long war, Robert. Four years I waited. Four long years. I was taken to Essen. That's where the Krupp factory is. I gave birth to Olivia there. After that, I nursed in the company's hospital. Once the armistice was declared, I made arrangements to come back here.'

'My darling.' He kissed her forehead. 'You should have written to say you were coming.'

'I wasn't sure I would be welcomed. I thought if I wasn't around, you'd marry Agnes.'

'That could never be,' he said, more vehemently than he should have done. 'There was an impediment...'

His voice trailed away.

Lydia cocked her head to one side. 'An impediment?'

He looked away. It wasn't easy to drag family skeletons out of the cupboard. Normally he would have kept the door firmly shut on the lot of it, but this was Lydia he was speaking to, the woman with whom he wished to spend the rest of his life.

'There was never a Tom Stacey. Did you know that?'

Lydia smiled and shook her head. 'I am not a fool, Robert. Sir Avis's fondness for Agnes was far more than a master for his servant – or the daughter of his cook. There was also a likeness. I never mentioned this before, because ... well ... it didn't really matter. I don't care about background. If I like someone, I like them. That is all that counts. But what difference would that have

473

made to you marrying her? Sir Avis was only your uncle...'

She saw him shake his head and saw the look in his eyes. This was what it meant, she thought, to love a man this much. She didn't need him to speak. The look in his eyes said it all. Sir Avis was more, much more than an uncle and judging by Robert's expression, he had been his father both figuratively and literally. Such things happen in wealthy families, so she'd heard.

He smiled, his eyes filling with tears. 'I can barely...'

She touched his lips with her fingers as though attempting to catch the sob she knew was coming.

'Agnes and her mother are up at the house, with Agnes's husband. We're going to have a Christmas like the ones we used to have.'

'Will it be like a birthday party?' asked the young child he now knew was his daughter.

Robert smiled down at her and then at her mother, all the time stroking Olivia's forehead. 'Oh yes. A birthday party on Christmas Eve and then it's Christmas Day.'

Epilogue

There was another party on Christmas Day, though not until the evening. First there was the wedding of Robert Ravening and Lydia Miller, their daughter as bridesmaid. The local vicar having been moved by their tale of lovers reunited

– and also the fact that the groom was the new lord of the manor – had agreed to marry the couple, unusually on the twenty-fifth December, hardly an unknown occurrence but one arranged at short notice. Thus, the wedding was attended by their friends at the house, plus people from the village and what family they had. Lydia's father and Kate came up from London. Her father had recovered from the strain of his war years and his grief for the daughter he'd thought he'd lost, but the experience had taken its toll. He was not the man he had been, but his wife had given up her career and stood by him.

The bride's bouquet consisted of white Christmas roses and variegated ivy.

'Just like the ivy clings to the wall, so you'll always cling together,' Agnes had said to her with a smile.

The two friends had cried on seeing each other again. In the short time since Lydia's return from the dead, they had swapped brief versions of what had happened to them since they'd last met.

'There's so much to tell,' Agnes had said. 'So much we've been through but we've plenty of time to catch up now.'

The smell of the evergreens decorating the church permeated the air, and although it was a cold day outside, the warmth of their companionship overcame that.

Lydia had met Agnes's new husband Darius, had seen the loving looks he exchanged with Agnes, and knew her friend was happy.

It had also emerged that Sir Avis had left Agnes and her mother a small inheritance and a cottage on the estate. That was where Sarah now lived with her own mother, Ellen Proctor.

Having been reunited with the love of her life, Lydia thought her happiness was complete but then her father had wished her a happy birthday on the eve of her wedding – Christmas Eve. He'd tried to explain how he'd felt at the news that she'd been executed.

'I thought of all those birthdays never celebrated and the fact that you would be having no more birthdays. I was devastated. I so wanted to put the clock back, and now suddenly I've been given another chance. Happy birthday, Lydia my dear.'

Lydia felt full up with so many heartfelt emotions. They had all been through so much, and so much had changed. Not just the world at large, but people had changed and that included her father.

The grief he'd once carried as a chip on his shoulder now only existed in his heart, and that, she concluded, could only be a good thing. The world was changing but with Robert at her side, good friends and family in their lives, the future seemed infinitely brighter.

Historical Note

Nurse Lydia Miller is a character of fiction, a figure caught between two opposing factions.

Nurse Edith Cavell was real, shot by the Germans on 12 October 1915. For a time she attended boarding school at 1 Eldon Road, Clevedon, near Bristol. The house is now a bed and breakfast.

Her most famous words on which I based Lydia's story were:

'Patriotism is not enough. I must have no hatred or bitterness towards anyone.'

There are a number of ceremonies planned for 2015 to commemorate her death:
http://www.revdc.net/cavell/page35.html

This Large Print Book for the partially sighted, who cannot read normal print, is published under the auspices of

THE ULVERSCROFT FOUNDATION